Before Goodbye

MIMI CROSS

Before Goodbye

SKYSCAPE

SKYSCAPE

Text copyright © 2016 Mimi Cross

Published by Skyscape, New York

www.apub.com

Amazon, the Amazon logo, and Skyscape are trademarks of Amazon.com, Inc., or its affiliates.

ISBN-13: 9781503949720 (paperback)
ISBN-10: 1503949729 (paperback)
ISBN-13: 9781503951280 (hardcover)
ISBN-10: 1503951286 (hardcover)

Book design by Shasti O'Leary Soudant

Printed in the United States of America

To Brian
(Because I said I would.)

"I'll meet you there when
the evening writhes
I will know the location
by the look in your eyes

The void and the vista
the fugitives gone
I'll see you there
at the Hotel Vast Horizon . . ."

—Chris Whitley, "Hotel Vast Horizon"

PART I: SUMMER

MOTIF

CATE

Toe taps and tongue clicks.

"Tika tika tika tika."

Nods. And hand gestures.

"Tika-ti. Tika-ti."

I watch, transfixed, as classical guitarist Gabriel Tomas Garcia has Cal play the same twelve measures again, and again. Each time, the music is the same. Each time, it is different.

Over and over the master teacher articulates the running sixteenth notes, their incessant motion broken only by the occasional eighth note, until finally, at the end of the section, Cal hits the final note, a whole note with a fermata hovering above it like a watchful eye.

The fermata tells the player to hold the note beyond its standard value, relying on his discretion as to duration. In other words, you hold the note as long as you want.

This is a surprisingly subjective idea for composed music.

Cal holds the note— and the rest of us hold, too, the dozen or so students who sit on the folding chairs that ring the classroom, all willing victims to the music's power. We hold our bodies still, and we each hold our breath, as if the music has encircled our very throats like an impossibly beautiful noose.

The main theme of a Bach fugue—that's what Cal's working so hard on. The subject. The seed. Garcia is attempting to show Cal that if he doesn't catch this germ, doesn't suffer the sickness—as well as find the cure—he will fail in his musical endeavor.

So says the master in so many words.

Only in this case, *so many words* means no words at all.

"He didn't *say* anything," I point out to Cal now. "Not for the last thirty minutes."

Our class has just ended and we're up in Cal's dorm room, sitting on the unclaimed twin bed across from his. It's the second day of the Manhattan School of Music's Summer Guitar Intensive and Cal's assigned roommate hasn't shown up yet. Cal's guess is car trouble, my money's on stage fright. Programs like this, although they're open to high school students like us, like Cal's no-show roommate, are geared toward professional players. They're basically pressure cookers.

It's cooking in here, too, the steamy New York City summer seeping somehow into the supposedly air-conditioned dorm. But despite the heat, as we continue to dissect Garcia's pedagogical methods, I shiver. "Seriously, he didn't say one word in the entire last half hour of the master class."

"He didn't need to."

"I know. That's what's so amazing. It's . . . supernatural, really, when you think about it."

"You're saying Garcia's supernatural—because he didn't say anything?"

I laugh. "Not Garcia. *Music.* It's . . . ghostly. All that work learning a piece, woodshedding with guys like Garcia—it doesn't change the fact that we pull it from the ether. We play the music, then it's gone. Gone until the next time we summon it, call it up from nothing but a piece of paper covered with little black circles of ink."

"Like raising the dead."

"Exactly!"

"Or adding water to sea monkeys and watching them squirm to life."

I punch Cal in the arm. I can do this because he's one of my best friends. I can also ignore his response to the blow, his mock indignation—which I do, and continue.

"Music's haunting, you know? Just think about the way a melody gets stuck in your head."

"An earworm."

"That's a really gross image. Besides, I was thinking more like, maybe we can't let a melody go, because we need it. It's a primitive need, I think, because music itself is primitive. It's . . . instinctual. We respond to music on some animal level."

"Maybe you do." Cal laughs. "For me it's more like a really hard math problem."

This whole time Cal's arms have been wrapped around his guitar, and now he plunges into the piece he's played so many times today, drops into the racing waves of sixteenth notes like he's an Olympic swimmer, and maybe his attention's been on the water all along.

Instantly captivated, I listen, and this time it's the music that makes me shiver, goosebumps rising on my skin.

A muffled ringtone comes from Cal's backpack, and although he ignores the call, the sound has obviously interrupted his train of thought, because he stops playing.

I start to protest, when I notice he's staring at my bare arms.

"What?" I say.

He reaches out and brushes an index finger across the fine hairs standing at attention along one of my forearms. I think I may feel them stand a little straighter now.

The moment hangs, making me think of that gorgeous final note, of the way Cal used the fermata to make it sing. At the end of class, we'd applauded both teacher and student and they bowed their heads, Cal's shining black hair swinging forward. The afternoon sun had blinded me for a moment, so I couldn't see. Then he'd straightened, blocking the bright light once more, but not completely. It still shone on the gleaming wood of his guitar, transforming it to gold.

I'd daydreamed in that instant that the gold was real. That it was payment for playing the entire piece for us at the start of the master class—for taking us on a journey, then delivering us back to the starting point, possibly forever changed.

I feel like this could change me, too, whatever's happening now, between us.

But . . . what exactly is happening? Cal smiles at me, then laughs a little. The bed jiggles slightly. And just like earlier, when, after holding that note beneath the bull's-eye for exactly the right amount of time, he'd released it simply by lifting his fingers soundlessly from the nylon strings, he somehow releases me, in this moment, or his laugh does, and I begin to breathe again.

But what was that? It's confusing, the way we were bound together for a heartbeat just now.

It was only his finger, only my arm. It was nothing.

Suddenly, his fingers are flying over the strings again, playing that motif for the millionth time, and I think once more that it's true: Words are like second-class citizens here. We're learning the language of music, a language where silence counts as much as sound. The spaces between the notes—we talk about them, too. The places to breathe, and to rest, to just . . . exist.

We are, of course, already quite fluent in this language. You have to be, just to get into this program, and to stay in for ten days. You've got to work your ass off. Or at least I do.

For another minute or so, I watch the way Cal gets lost in the music, his dark hair swaying around his shoulders as he plays. Then I stand up.

He stops playing. "Where are you going?"

"I've got to go practice," I say. "Some of us need to, you know." Teasing him further, I tell him I'll be holed up in my room for the next ten days and that he should send food and water. "But don't worry, I'll live. I live to practice. That's what I'm here for."

I turn to leave and, to my surprise, I feel Cal's fingertips on the back of my hand—the same light touch as before.

"Not me," he says softly.

"Oh yeah?" I look down at him, musing. "And what are you here for?"

Outside a cloud passes before the sun. Or maybe it's later than I think and the sun has disappeared for the day behind one of the soaring skyscrapers I used to love so much when my family lived in Manhattan. Either way, I'm momentarily distracted as the room darkens.

Cal's fingers loop my wrist.

"I'm here for you, Cate. Always."

A beat later it begins to rain, and Cal starts playing again, an improvised melody, a counterpoint to the raindrops that hit harder now, sharply striking the dorm room windows as real weather moves in.

And so the moment to speak passes—or maybe I'm more like Gabriel Tomas Garcia than I thought.

By the time I go, Cal's playing sounds like it's part of the storm.

WILDERNESS

DAVID

Lifting the canoe off my shoulders, I use a rolling motion to bring it down the side of my body and onto the tops of my thighs. From there, I ease the boat into the muddy shallows at the edge of the opaque green lake.

Almost immediately, a thin trickle of water seeps into the bottom. This is not good.

There are still two days left till the end of the trip. Two days until we reach base camp, a laughable description for the cluster of flimsy wooden lean-tos poised precariously on the granite ledge of a pine-shadowed island in the middle of nowhere. Still, the island's where the floatplane picks us up. Then we van it to the airport. But with one less canoe . . .

Rubbing a hand over the back of my neck, I watch as water pools in the boat's silvery bottom. Someone's been careless on the other end of the portage, probably putting the aluminum canoe down on a rock. At least one of the rivets along the seam has popped.

Besides lining up the canoe alongside five others and tying the excuse of a bowline to a low limb on a nearby pine, there's nothing I can do right now. I pull off my flannel. The T-shirt underneath is soaked with sweat. It stinks. Week four, and we've been pushing across the chain of lakes for five days straight. But tomorrow's a rest day. Washing some clothes might be a good idea. If I don't fall for the siren song of my sleeping bag, which may or may not have a girl in it.

Six guys. Six girls. Two guides who treat the term lightly. Add a complete lack of civilization, and even with the daunting distance we've trekked, there's been plenty of time to—

The water winks. I do a double take. Under the ubiquitous spotlight of the late July sun, another canoe spins slowly at the center of the lake. An escapee. The silver shimmer of the empty belly of the boat flashes again now, a slightly curved grin, taunting me.

It's as if the vessel knows I can't resist playing hero. Never have been able to.

Really, the lake isn't so wide. Anyone in the group could swim to the other side in twenty minutes, which means I can do it in less. It feeds the falls, but that doesn't matter. If we lose the boat, we're screwed. I peel off the T-shirt, yank off my hiking boots, slosh into the water.

A second later, my feet lift off the bottom. Deeper than I'd thought. No worries. A few strokes and the canoe's an arm's length away. I grab the raveled bit of rope dangling off the bow and turn back, surprised to feel the current tugging around my legs.

A movement just beyond the shoreline at the barely visible trailhead catches my eye. Dan, Dan, the Portage Man—one of our fearless leaders—is emerging from the woods. He stops when he sees me. Goes still. Then he folds his arms, an unreadable expression on his face.

My foot strikes a rock. It's big enough to balance on, which I do, grinning at Dan, though I'm pretty sure he won't even crack a smile. He doesn't like me. Whatever. This trip's not going to change me or how I act. I just need to get through it. More proof for Dad that I can be like Jack.

Jack. My brother. He came here, too. Hiked these same trails. Maybe swam in this lake.

An image forms before I can stop it: Jack, in the water. Not here on the surface with me, but beneath.

Some bug—a greenfly or mosquito—dives toward my eyes. I swat at it. The picture disintegrates.

Lifting the bowline to show I've got the canoe, I begin pulling the boat toward shore.

It pulls back.

My feet slip on the muck-covered rock. I yank the thin line—

The rope snaps.

The canoe turns in slow motion, heading for the falls. For the first time, I hear the rush of them. Still, I dive after the boat, catching Dan's words just before I go under, his voice echoing over the water, louder for a moment than the roar of the falls, than the cocky voice of my ego.

"David! Don't be an asshole!"

The water grabs me—

Pulls me under.

Then somehow the sky sucks me up—

Drops me—

Over

The falls.

The roar of the water fills my ears as I manage to lift my head out of the churning white froth and snatch a breath that's nothing but

Water—

Takes me down.

Thud. My shoulder. On a rock or—the bottom. I can't breathe.

Reaching out I grasp—

Nothing.

My face slams stone. A thunderstorm rages inside my head. Water rages around my body.

Lightning shoots through me as

Sharp scrapes my stomach, gouges the skin along the side of my pelvis—

A knife?

Pain—

CEDAR

CATE

The water holds me . . . and I float. Eyes closed, face up. Summer-warmed. Water-cooled.

Laurel and I both float. Drifting, on the still surface of our secret cedar pond.

A mountain of white clouds passes over the Pine Barrens. The russet waters of the pond darken to carnelian. A merganser's buzzy call sounds from the nearby Winding River.

"What is this," she asks, "our fourth summer?"

"Mm-hmm." But I know she's not really counting. She's thinking. Thinking it's the first time we've ever been here without her older sister. The first time that Laurel has driven us.

"You have your *license*," I say.

"Yep." I can hear her grin. "I'm going to drive us around the world. This is it."

"The start of everything," I respond.

"The start of everything," she agrees.

With a slow roll, I turn my face into the tannin-rich water and dive under.

I'm an otter, a seal. A mermaid . . .

Coming up for air at the far edge of the pond, I examine the sprawling roots of a huge cedar hanging over the water. The tree must have been felled by a recent storm, a bad one, apparently, if it took this giant down. I reach up— run a finger along one of the slick, dark roots that have been ripped from the earth. My finger comes away muddy.

Laurel continues floating on her back, eyes closed, smile wide, her long white-blonde hair fanning around her face, painted pale orange by the cedar water.

My lips stretch into a smile just from watching hers. "Lovecats?" I ask.

"Lovecats," she answers, smile growing to grin, grin bursting into laugh.

This is another one of my favorite things about Laurel, how easy it is to make her laugh. I laugh too now. *Lovecats* is a kind of code for us, used to cement an agreement or solidify a plan, so named because of "The Love Cats," a song by the Cure that we used to dance around to when we were tiny, and my mom had grand—or, probably more like *weird*—plans for us. Laurel and I can still sing the song at what we figure is record-smashing speed, though thankfully, we forgot the dance steps years ago, or so we both claim.

Today, *Lovecats* is an affirmation, a celebration of our best-friendness on this perfect July afternoon, in the summer before our sophomore year. Definitely, this is the beginning.

I slide my hands through the reddish water. The color reminds me of Cal's guitar . . .

With a small splash I slip beneath the surface, then come up, next to Laurel. "It was so amazing, having him at the intensive this year."

"You mean your Guitar Guy, and the oh-my-god-I-can't-believe-you-spent-ten-days-in-New-York-City-without-me intensive?"

"That's the one. He lived a staircase away from me in the residence hall."

"Ooh, that sounds convenient."

"*Pff*. It wasn't like that."

"Too bad. So what was it like? But wait—isn't he always there?"

"No, you're thinking of Classical Kids."

"Oh yeah. God, you went to that forever. I swear you cut your baby teeth on guitar strings. We were still in Huggies when you first started going."

"Ha. Not quite. I was four."

"Four. Right. I can still see it: you and your itty-bitty guitar. Did Cal have a tiny guitar, too?" Laurel laughs.

"He did, but there's nothing tiny about him now—it's been three years since either of us has been in Classical Kids, you're way behind, L. Well, actually I'm way behind—way behind him. I can't believe he spent the last two summers studying in Spain while I—"

"Hey, don't be talking trash about my Lovecat. You're awesome, Cate."

"Not as awesome as him, nowhere near as awesome as him. Do you know what he's working on? His teacher gave him—"

"Don't know, don't care. I'm a Cate Reese fan. And besides, he didn't go to Europe *this* summer, he went to the same thing you did— that workshop, intensive, whatever—which means you guys are on the same level, so you can stop worshipping him. Now, get back to the dirt."

"Hmm, okay. Well, first of all, we were inseparable."

"*We're* inseparable."

"Well, yeah, but he's a guy. It's a different kind of inseparable. L, I really like him."

"*Like him*, like him?" Laurel smiles her contagious smile, looking like some kind of aquatic Cheshire cat. "But you guys are BFFs, aren't you? I mean, not like us, but as much as a guy can be. You have that music thing, and you're more like brother and sister, if you ask me."

"Which is why I'm not asking you, I'm telling you—things are different now, between us. I don't know about other music schools, but Manhattan School of Music has practice rooms that are open 24-7, and one night—"

"Please! No sordid details."

"Hey, you're the one who asked for dirt. Besides, I told you, it really wasn't like that . . ."

"But? I sense a but."

"But it could be. If I could just . . . I don't know. His playing is just so flawless, it's—"

"Perfect, yes, I know. You've always lusted after his guitar chops, but what about his body? Are you lusting after that now, too? Isn't that what you're saying?"

"Laurel! I don't know. Maybe. But nothing happened. I mean, everything happened. We went to all the afternoon classes together—master classes led by some of the best classical guitarists in the world—and all the evening performances. Afterward we'd sit in one of the lounges, write up the required critiques, compare notes . . ."

"Sounds like work."

"Sure, but it was incredible. We basically lived and breathed music."

"Glad you didn't suffocate. So he's obviously still cute?"

"Shut up. Of course he's still cute. I mean, definitely, he's cute, but when he plays, he's just—beautiful. So intensely focused, so—"

"Busy. He's like you, right? Practices a million hours a day? Wants to go to a conservatory, wants to—"

"So?"

"So you guys don't have *time* to go out. He plays. You play. You both have school, boarding school for him. Sutton Prep, right? North Moore? That's a haul. I mean, he may live close by, but he's always away. Just saying, Lovecat—well, my gut's saying—you're too much alike, and no relationship can survive on emails and music camps—intensives, whatever."

"Your gut. Right." I pinch her waist. "What gut? And don't forget phone calls and actually seeing each other. We do see each other once in a while. He's helped *so* much when it comes to my playing—I would have quit a million times without him. Still, remind me never to tell you anything ever again."

"You don't have to tell me. I'm your best friend." Laurel grins. "I can read your mind."

"Can you? What am I thinking?" But before she can answer, I dunk her. And when she comes up spluttering, I tell her that Cal's playing a concert in the city and I'm going.

"Groupie girl! Why aren't *you* playing?"

"I am, just not the same night. We're both playing, as part of Strings with Wings, but my set is during the post-festival wrap-up, in early autumn, and his set's at one of the pre-festival gala events. Also, FYI? I don't think classical musicians have groupies."

"Well they should. Everyone should. And what the heck is Strings with Wings?"

"It's a festival slash fundraiser, for various charities. Venues all over the city participate, and the shows are spread out over weeks, from the Bitter End to Lincoln Center, every kind of show, every kind of player. The only parameters are (one) you must play a stringed instrument, and (two) you must have mega talent. Unless you're a student, then you're in the Pupils with Promise part of the program and you can skate on your potential."

"As I recall, you've never liked skating." She skims one palm along the water's surface. "But I remember now, you told me about Strings with Wings. It's like, a pre-audition audition."

"Right. All the schools in the Northeast send scouts."

"Jeez, you really have to have your shit together to play that gig, huh."

"Yes. And I'll need a new dress, so you have to go shopping with me. In fact I may need two dresses. Because after Cal's performance? We're going out—yes, *out, out*. On a real date."

"*Now* you tell me! Cool, Cate Cat. But today—the only place you're going is under!"

And this time, she dunks me.

MORPHINE

DAVID

I struggle up from the depths of a watery nightmare—

Jack.

My pulse is racing. I will it to slow. It won't. I can't control it, can't control—anything.

Jack. I haven't dreamed of him in so long. I close my eyes.

He hadn't died like that. But. He is gone.

Gone, yet everywhere.

After my older brother Jack died, my father tried to replace him. With me.

Over the years, I worked hard at being Jack.

I became The Fastest. The Smartest. The Most Popular. *The Best.*

Then all was well in the spinning world of our family, because my father was happy. He had his Golden Boy, his replica of himself. His Plan to Achieve Immortality was back on track.

Until now.

Fingers plucking at crisp hospital sheets, I stare at the acoustic ceiling tiles. The tiny dots that pierce them make random patterns, a universe of pinpricks, of nothing.

Voices from the nurses' station carry down the hall. My father's is among them. Booming. Authoritative. Demanding attention. Demanding *respect*.

I don't really need it for my leg, but I push the button on the morphine drip anyway. Pump it once, twice.

QUARTET

CATE

Because neither of us has a car and we're coming from two totally different places, Cal and I take separate trains to separate stations and meet on Seventh Avenue, where we fall into an embrace made clumsy by his guitar case and my indecision. I can't decide whether to kiss him on the lips or the cheek. The swervy little smack ends up at the corner of his mouth.

And then there is this big blank moment where things feel, well, awkward.

Cal and I practically grew up together, at least musically, and we've had some of the same teachers. We've played concerts together, talked about music for hours, and have nearly identical tastes in music—composed music, that is. That's all we listen to. Plus we've exchanged a million emails (well, I write most of those), so there's no reason to feel uncomfortable. But I do, and I think he might, too. I'm sure my maladroit kiss didn't help, but what the problem really is—I think—is the slow crawl of attraction that seems to have started at the intensive.

It's like we want to fly from the nest of our childhood friendship, only we don't have the wings yet. We're still all eggshells and something too slippery to name.

So we walk the remaining half a block not talking about music, or anything else. Cal, at least, has an excuse. He's busy navigating the packed sidewalks with his guitar. Me, I'm busy feeling strangely stiff.

"You look nice," Cal says with a nod toward my dress.

"Thanks." Nearly every piece of clothing I own is as black as this dress, since musicians, especially classical performers, should be heard and not seen. With its flared calf-length skirt and sweetheart neckline, I consider this one of my dressy dresses. I've worn it for several performances—recitals, really. "You look nice, too."

Cal glances down and runs a hand over the lapel of his dark suit. "Thanks, but . . . I don't know. Looks like I'm dressed for a funeral, not a gig."

"A gig, ha. Like Carnegie Hall is just a gig."

"Yeah, well." He looks down again, not at the suit but at a point near the ground. This looking-down thing gives the impression that Cal's shy, but he's not. He's modest. He's also the most talented guitarist I've ever known. Maybe he's not as talented as some of the teachers we had this summer, but Cal's only seventeen and still a student, like me. He's also my inspiration. He's the person I play for, when I'm practicing alone in my room. *How would Cal play this passage?*

Now he lifts his slightly almond-shaped eyes. They're dark, nearly as black as his hair, but sparkling somehow. Dad has told me more than once that my eyes are the same shade as the winter sea, so I can't imagine they're as interesting to look at as Cal's lively eyes, but he holds my gaze as if he thinks they are. This is new, this kind of eye contact—part of that slow-moving attraction that's bringing us closer yet at the same time, somehow, separating us. It's confusing.

Before I know it we're at Carnegie Hall heading into the Stern Auditorium slash Perelman Stage, an elegant space that holds over two thousand people, where I've seen my teacher, Marion, perform more than once.

Feeling relieved, I start to say, "I love this place—" But then someone's shaking Cal's hand, ushering him through a door I hadn't noticed. He presses a ticket into my palm.

"Sorry. Come find me after, okay?"

"Okay." I watch him slip through the doorway. Seeing him from behind, I notice the swing of his hair and the way his dark suit shows the line of his shoulders. He carries himself with confidence and poise. Other people, women mostly, are watching him as well.

I imagine what Laurel would say if she were here, how her eyebrows would lift.

Guitar Guy's looking good. I get it, Cate Cat.

When I get to my seat, I text her. The text is record breaking in length because it's not enough to tell her that Cal looks hot in a suit. I describe the way his hair hangs down his back, how sophisticated he seems, not at all worried about his performance like I'd be. Now that we're actually on a date—well, a sort of date—I tell her how his eyes go bright when he smiles.

Wow. She texts back. Tks for the book. Does this mean ur going to apply to Manhattan School of Music? That's where he's going to go rt?

No, I tap quickly with my thumbs. It means—

The lights dim. I quickly power down the phone without sending.

Onstage, Cal becomes beautiful. The stage lights shine on his hair, on his guitar, as he plays the tried-and-true Albéniz piece, "Mallorca." I've never played the piece, and depending on the transcription, it can be incredibly difficult. The audience seems to understand this, and when Cal finishes, the applause is thunderous.

He follows the Albéniz with Bach's Cello Suite no. 2 in D Minor, which has of course been arranged for guitar. All six movements of the piece are so familiar, I can feel them in my fingers. *Prelude, Allemande,*

Courante, Sarabande, Menuets, Gigue—I know them all, but I've never played them as well as Cal. For twenty minutes, the audience is nearly as still as he is. I'm on the edge of my seat for him, but he plays every note perfectly and, finally, I start to relax. This is his gig, not mine. He begins Walton's Five Bagatelles, and I allow myself to get swept away.

Cal finishes the Walton and leaves the stage, but before the sound of applause has died, he reappears followed by a trio of string players. I've never seen this combination of instruments before—it's basically a string quartet, featuring classical guitar in the place of one of the violins.

When Cal, the single violinist, the viola player, and the cellist tear into their instruments and wrest out a version of "Paradise" by Coldplay, the hair along my arms rises to stiff attention. "Paradise" is string-heavy, anyway, so the cover makes sense, but when the musicians add eerie vocal parts and start tapping the sides of their instruments, I'm blown away.

Finally the piece winds down, but the audience is wound up. The concert hall vibrates with the sound of clapping and calls of "Bravo!"

Covered in goosebumps, I'm vibrating, too, with emotion. Before the musicians have even left the stage, I'm turning on my phone, completing the text I'd started earlier.

It means—I'm in love.

STITCHES

DAVID

Being still is the hardest part.

Not that I'm hyper or anything. I know guys like that, and I've never been one of them.

What I have been—among other things—is a jock. I'm used to being in motion.

Right now, I'm a patient, one who's misbehaved and disregarded doctors' orders to take it easy. I've overdone it, ripping open the long, neat row of stitches that snakes up over my hip bone.

When it happened the first time, I was appalled to discover that the fiery pain along the split in my skin was strangely satisfying.

When it happened again, I skipped straight to satisfaction.

The pain is like a sea of white noise I can slip into. At the same time, it slips into me, filling me up, so I can't think. Can't think about what happened, or about what I'm learning from sitting still. What I'm learning about myself, about the other things that I've been besides some kid who plays sports really well.

I have to embrace the pain anyway, because I won't take anything for it. When I was in the hospital, the morphine gave me nightmares, so I won't take the prescribed pills. I don't need my reality twisted. What's happened is nightmare enough.

Books by my bed, movies on my laptop, porn on the Internet—there's a whole world at my fingertips, full of things I've enjoyed in the past, but now, no. Just like the texts, emails, and phone calls from friends: these things don't interest me.

It's because of what happened in Canada—obviously—but also because of the stillness, what it's showing me. Things that are more painful and ugly than a gash that takes eighty-four stitches to close. More painful and ugly than broken bones jutting out of bloody skin and a smashed skull—

Jesus. I can't stop seeing that day. Can't stop seeing Dan.

Because, of course, it was not Jack, long dead, who was with me in the water that day.

If only, if only, if only. If only he hadn't come after me.

I understand now why sitting still is something so many people avoid.

Shifting on the bed, I pull the damp T-shirt away from my chest. The humidity's crushing, pressing down on me like a weight. I feel almost dizzy as I reach over to the bookshelf next to the bed, grab my headphones.

Because there is one thing that helps.

Music. Listening to music.

Letting it wash over me.

BLOOM

CATE

Riding my bike along Chapel Hill Road, I inhale the scents of summer. There are a couple of precious weeks left before school starts and everything is green, green, green . . . The well-kept world of Middleburn is overgrown and wild.

This is the secret side of New Jersey, a voluptuous, verdant side that tourists, their eyes on the state's white coastal beaches, rarely see, let alone explore, that New York City transplants caught up in their rush to return to the hive on their daily commute often take years to discover.

The horse fences running alongside the road become a blur of white as I spin past the endless fields. Shadows fall across the road where the woods begin.

At the edge of the woods, the prevailing scent is of sunbaked pine needles. A little farther in, it's the moist, warm odor of earth—at least that's how it is in back of the barn behind our house. The woods are thick with low bushes and tangled vines, mountain laurels, and spike-leafed hollies.

The red barn is almost as old as the invisible British campsites along Chapel Hill Road. The historical marker at the bottom of our street where it Ts into Chapel says the soldiers left in 1778. After we moved here for real in June and this place morphed from weekend hideaway to home, I started wondering about the soldiers, who they'd been, if they'd made it home, or if they'd died here. The barn, with its dark horse stalls filled with Dad's paintings, started to creep me out. The way the ceiling of the rickety building disappears into shadow high above the tilting floor of the hayloft, making me think of some kind of primitive cathedral, decaying.

It's ridiculous, because before we actually lived here, I'd always thought the barn was cool. When Mom and Dad first started leaving me alone, it was out here, not in our Manhattan apartment. I remember exploring the barn by myself, daydreaming all kinds of stories.

That was around the same time I started babysitting Kimmy Bennet, so I must have been twelve. Funny how, at twelve, the barn had seemed mysterious, exciting, but at sixteen . . .

The wheels of my bike leave the ground for an instant as the road dips down. The temperature drops slightly now. The smell here in the hollow is different, more complicated: green things growing atop previous autumns, a whiff of horses from a nearby farm, although "farm" isn't the right word for the massive estates set back in the woods or beyond the fields.

None of the estates are visible from here, but like everyone in Middleburn, I know they're there. Their owners are rock stars, politicians, and wealthy New York techsters: Northeast royalty, old money and new.

The woods, though . . . they are royalty of another sort. Mighty maples. Ancient oaks. In many places along Chapel Hill Road nothing borders the backs of these towering trees but more woods. Even at my house on Lenape, just off Chapel, out behind the red barn, it's like there's no rest of the world beyond their stretching sovereignty.

When I get to the Bennets' I remember: David is home, and he's *been* home, for over a month. I just haven't seen him. That's because he's basically been living in his bedroom. Not that we ever hang out, but I usually see him a lot when I'm at the Bennets'. By the pool, in the kitchen, watching TV. He's always coming or going, with friends, or without. There's always a phone in his hand.

"He's bummed about his leg," Kimmy told me a couple of weeks ago. "I signed my name on his cast with hearts *and* flowers, but it didn't cheer him up."

David had been hurt on a canoe trip, but it still didn't make sense. A broken leg, crutches—it didn't seem like enough to stop David I-Can-Do-Anything Bennet.

"Or *anyone*," Laurel snickered when I told her about David's self-imposed exile from society. After that, I hadn't thought too much about it. About him.

The rest of the Bennets are at their beach house in Montauk. They always spend the last two weeks of August out there, and it seems weird that David didn't go, but I guess it makes sense. How do you have fun at the beach when your leg's in a cast?

Kimmy's cat Midnight strolls into the kitchen. I feed her, then organize the mail. After that I check the garden. The bluestone-bordered squares are lush with blowsy roses and fat tomatoes. I pick the ones about to burst.

There's no question in my mind why David isn't taking care of these things. Not only is he laid up, but these jobs are mine. Mrs. Bennet has paid me to do them for the last three summers, as well as on random weekends when the family's away.

About to leave, I picture David up in his room. He's let three calls go to voicemail since I've been here, and suddenly the idea of him spending the last days of summer alone makes me feel bad.

So instead of heading out, I go upstairs, where a long hallway runs the length of the house. At the end of the hall, I climb a short flight of steps and knock on his bedroom door.

He doesn't answer, but I hear music.

Slowly, I push the door open—

Then stop short, staring at the boy on the bed.

The sense of entitlement that previously issued from David Bennet like a fragrance is gone. On his face—a face so good-looking you have to remind yourself that staring isn't polite—is an expression of uncertainty. His mouth works, his smile a flickering flame that won't catch.

"Go away," he says flatly, turning his face to one side.

Quickly, I shut the door. My hand freezes on the knob, heart beating hard.

Kimmy's older brother has turned from gold to shadow.

Briefly, I consider calling Montauk. *Has David been like this ever since he got back from his trip? What happened to him?*

I don't call his parents, but the next day, I knock on his door again.

When he doesn't answer, I ask—through the door—if he needs anything.

"No," he says. "Nothing."

After feeding Midnight, I leave. The following day, though, I can't help myself. *He seems so different, his transformation so total. He can't be okay.*

This time when I ask if he needs anything—again through the door—he assures me in a clipped voice that he is *fine*. But then he says, "Wait."

I wait.

He says, "Yes. I need . . . something. Company. Come in. Please."

I open the door.

"I'm sick of TV, sick of computer games. Sick," he says under his breath, "of myself."

Then his smile slips into place, and although he's thinner and pale, he looks more like the boy I've always known. Although I am beginning to suspect I don't know him at all. That, perhaps, no one does.

Even on crutches David stands tall, with the erect posture of an athlete. In combination with his slightly patrician features, this bearing makes him look strangely formal.

The cast and crutches barely slow him on the stairs, and once he's settled on the couch in the den, I perch on a nearby chair and wonder, as we talk about music and movies—me, haltingly; him, fluidly—if David Bennet even knows himself. Because as we speak, I become convinced that this well-mannered hospitable boy is not who he pretends to be.

I'm not sure what, exactly, convinces me of this. It may be that sliding smile. The way it disappears, then reappears, a quick series of sunsets and sunrises, when before it held at midday.

Or maybe it's the way he's sitting so still now. He's usually a whirl of motion.

I'm surprised when he asks me to come back the next day, but I do, laden with movies. It's rainy and gray, perfect weather for watching. I've brought a bag of salty-sweet kettle corn.

"You said this one's your favorite?" He holds up *Waking Life*, an older Linklater film.

I nod, but all at once feel uncomfortable; my choice suddenly seems way too weird. And also because—David Bennet? *Why am I even here?*

"Why do you like it so much?" he asks.

"Um . . ." I can't seem to think.

"Okay," he says slowly.

My cheeks heat.

He asks me to pop in the disc.

After the movie we watch another. *Say Anything* from the late 1980s.

As the credits roll, David and I both agree. Diane would have gone to the window.

"The movie could have ended there," David says. "With him blasting the Peter Gabriel song. Those lyrics . . ."

I picture John Cusack holding the boom box but can't really remember the words.

"You look like her," David says suddenly. "Like that actress, the one who plays Diane. Her eyes look like yours, and that—tremulous thing. You've both got that going on."

There's no way I'm going to ask him to define "that tremulous thing." And then I don't have to, anyway, because now he continues, saying, "It's not like you're nervous. It's more like . . . underneath—" He breaks off, shaking his head. "Forget it. I don't know what I'm saying."

"Um. Okay." And now I *am* nervous, for no real reason, and everything feels kind of awkward. So I just say, "If she'd gone to the window, you're right. The movie could've ended there."

But David shakes his head again now. "Actually, no. Not everything is . . . resolved." Then he looks away and mumbles something. I think he says, "The dad."

The next day things have shifted for him. When I get there he's low. The shadow boy's back, and I feel the pinch of his sadness. He's prone on the couch with a magazine. He says hi but won't meet my gaze.

So I go out to the garden and pick a flower, an insanely perfumey rose. It's blown out and bright red, the biggest one of the bunch. Inside, I hold it under his nose.

He raises an eyebrow but swings his way to the porch, where he looks over the wall to the garden. He makes a small sound that becomes a true laugh. He turns and looks at me then.

His smile is back, and it's . . . beautiful.

"Thank you," he says quietly.

But oddly, the more we hang out, the more stilted our conversations become.

It's not surprising that *I* have trouble talking. Finding the right words is like a quest for me. But that *he* has so little to say is different. Very.

Over the years, I've seen David a million times at the Bennets'. Usually on his way to some game, or a party—or a date. I've seen him with at least a dozen girls, and he's never been at a loss for words. I've seen him whisper in their ears before vanishing upstairs with them.

Once he got his license, he'd drive off with those same girls—or different ones. It was almost as if it didn't matter who they were, as if all the girls were . . . interchangeable.

I scowl at the memory. No, finding the right words is my problem, not his.

And yet, even though I struggle to find the right things to say, after a few afternoons of sitting on that porch, or hanging in the den, each of us with a book, or listening to music, I discover that just being around David makes me feel good. Happy. As if I haven't been before.

Or maybe it's just the music. We listen to so much of it. New bands I've never heard of, some older bands as well—and songwriters, lots of songwriters.

One day David puts on a song by a singer-songwriter named Suzanne Vega. The guitar part isn't classical, but there's precision to it—a steady, pulsing repetitiveness that instantly takes me to the same still place practicing does. Only this isn't a series of scales or a challenging étude, or like any piece I might play. It's a woman singing about being like a marble, or an eye, a woman singing about scattering like light.

"What's this song called?"

"Small Blue Thing."

"Can we hear it again?"

We listen to the song six times in a row. It's delicate without being fragile. The guitar is a steel string and it sounds like an ominous fairy tale. David thinks it sounds like "silver clockwork." We both agree that the singer's voice is preternaturally calm.

I'm fascinated by the way she sings the word *fingers*, by the rhythm of it, by the way the word seems to begin in one place and end someplace totally different. It's like a single-word haiku. The music moves in a somewhat circular manner, and then, the word leaves her lips— a subtle meteorite that doesn't speed across the heavens but, rather, *glides* across a dark expanse of sky until it lands somewhere else—another spread of stars, maybe another universe.

And yet there's not even a breath between that word and the next. *How does she do it?*

David is mesmerized as well, but at some point I realize he's watching me intently.

Yet I can't care, this song is like a . . . portal. It's leading me into another way of listening. Yes, I've listened to guitar pieces in this way, but never to a *song*, never to words.

Glancing again at David, I get the distinct impression that he *has* listened to lyrics in this way. The thought gives me chills.

"I didn't realize a song could be so full. Full of something other than what the lyrics mean. So full of—"

"Invisible things?"

I'm so surprised I don't reply, but suddenly I feel certain. This is the real David Bennet.

DEAD END

CATE

Almost two weeks of afternoons slip away like this, where it's just the two of us.

Some days go by so fast I stay for the evening, staying later and later each time.

Finally, as the last days of summer sidle by, David seems to settle somehow, becoming someone between the busy, popular guy I've watched coming and going for years and the shadow boy I caught a glimpse of that day when I'd knocked on his bedroom door.

But I think about that shadowy boy, and it makes me want to ask David what happened in Canada. Then I catch him studying my face or watching me walk into the den with whatever CD he's asked me to get from his room, and . . . I don't know. I just want to stay like this, immersed in music with him, in the lyrics he listens to so intently. The music I consider to be his.

Then suddenly, it seems, his family is back and I have no reason to go over.

At first, I think it's no biggie. That the only reason I even *want* to go over to the Bennets' is to see Kimmy, get back to babysitting so I can support my own music habit. I'm still practicing nearly every day, but I've fallen behind in listening. I need to keep up on the latest classical recordings, need to listen to the way a performer like David Russell births a melodic line into existence note by note, as if he's carefully pulling a fine gold chain from the magician's hat of his guitar, link by smoothly forged link.

The night before school starts, Laurel asks where I've been.

When I tell her, she immediately accuses me of crushing on David.

"You've got a *thang* for him, Cate, simple as that. Bye-bye, Guitar Guy."

But it doesn't feel simple. And she must be wrong. Because having a thing for David Bennet would be a total dead end.

Besides . . . I'm in love with Cal.

VASCULAR

DAVID

I imagine my father's blood, coming to a rolling boil. Hot as this end-of-summer weather.

"How will you be ready for the fall season?"

"I won't."

"Excuse me?" A vein stands out along my father's temple. He grips the steering wheel of the Porsche, one of several luxury cars he owns.

Like many of his possessions—and most family members—my father treats the cars as extensions of himself. Now we careen dangerously around the corner of White Oak Ridge Road.

We're on the way home from seeing my orthopedist. The fact that my father found the time to take me to the appointment shows just how concerned he is, although not necessarily about me personally. More like about me as an investment. He'd drilled the doctor about recovery time, physical therapy. Drugs.

"We've got to get him on the football field," my father said, his tone intense. "There must be something you can do. Practice is starting, and if my son's not ready . . ."

Dr. Grant addressed my father's concerns but in a way that was, let's say, open to interpretation. Then he smiled broadly at me as we were leaving, practically winked. We didn't need to exchange a word—we both knew what he was doing. Taking the ball out of my father's hands. Putting it in mine. Even though I'm certain he intuited that I was going to drop it.

Dr. Grant is a cool old guy. I appreciate how he has enabled me to do what I need to do.

My father, however, does not.

As we get closer to home I can practically hear his pulse pounding. His face reddens as he voices his vehement disagreement with the good doctor's open-ended diagnosis.

"It doesn't matter," I interrupt as we pull into the driveway.

"What could you possibly mean by that combination of words?"

Slam! The driver's side door.

"I mean, it doesn't matter if I'm ready or not. I'm not playing this year."

Micromanaging each movement now, each breath, willing myself to remain calm, I shut the passenger door as quietly as possible.

"What the *hell* do you mean, you're not playing 'this year'?" he explodes. "*This year* is it! The culmination of everything we've worked for! The college we've chosen . . ."

But I've stopped listening. "The college *you've chosen*," I want to shout. "Your alma mater."

All they want is a carbon copy of Jack Bennet. A golden goose to lay a winning game, which is exactly how I've been sold, as someone who can take a collegiate institution to the top of the sports publicity pinnacle.

As I stumble back into what becomes a one-sided conversation ("I'll study—I just won't study the playing field"), it pisses me off that my offerings, though they're admittedly drenched in anger, are not accepted. My father would rather be furious, would rather fight.

He'd rather declare later that Scotch-soaked evening, as he aims his bleached smile at me like a loaded gun: "Employment, then, if you're not going to be a part of the athletic program for your senior year."

"What, school isn't enough of a—"

"It is not. You will work. You will replace every hour that you would have been on the playing field, the ice rink—*the goddamn away-game buses*—with an hour of gainful employment."

He drains his glass. But he's only finished with his drink, not with me.

"Now," he says softly, and the hair rises on the back of my neck. The change in volume is not an indication that he's less upset, but that he is more so. "How about student council? And what about"—his voice drops to a whisper, "the debate club?"

"I'll—I'll keep doing those."

"Well. That's a relief."

"I'm sure it is," I'm tempted to say. "The ability to talk people in and out of things is what you prize most. Manipulation, coercion, persuasion—your 'work,' work that takes you away from home constantly, depends on those skills. And the physical feats that gave you your 'leg up in life'? You insisted I master those, too. Thanks. The coaches have been great stand-in dads."

But I'm not a complete idiot. Those words remain unspoken.

"So, then, do you have a job lined up?"

"How could I?"

"You will by the time school starts."

"Fine."

"No, it's not *fine*." He runs a hand back through his hair, straightens the knot of his tie even though it doesn't need it. "But it will have to do."

Translation: "*You* will have to do, because your brother Jack is gone."

He allows a small smile to twist his lips when he sees that I've understood this. Then he spins on his heel and strides away. As he passes the row of mirrors lining the front hall, he checks his reflection. He has a few pounds on me, but anyone can see: we look just alike.

It makes me want to smash every mirror in the house.

SPACE

CATE

"We need," Mom says, "to nudge the Arts Council." (Or something to that effect.)

Dad sighs. Or shakes his head. Or mutters a response.

Mom briefly replies. Or applies mascara. Or blots her lipstick.

Their eyes meet in the mirror above the table in the hall.

This is the daily ritual.

Dad asks why she can't catch the last ferry, why she has to stay over in New York. Mom lists the reasons. The list shall not exceed the amount of time it takes to finish applying her makeup. After that, no matter what Dad's saying, she's out the door.

Often, there will be a last-minute skirmish, with bags or a coat, gloves or an umbrella. There will most likely be keys involved. House keys. Car keys. Today it is the latter.

"Shit!" The daily ritual is by no means silent. "Cate? Do you have my car keys?"

"Why would I have your car keys? I don't even have my license yet, remember?"

"Damn. We have to deal with that."

"Yeah we do, we're not in Manhattan anymore. Or at least, I'm not."

Mom blinks a few times, fast. "Catherine. You and your father had all summer—" She cuts herself off. Cuts us all off, whenever she can.

Dad clears his throat, but he doesn't stand a chance. He hasn't had his coffee yet. Mom's had a pot. And even if he matched her cup for cup, Dad's nocturnal. He paints all night.

Dad's in a hurl-paint-at-the-canvas phase. He's like Jackson Pollock, maybe with bigger issues. Sometimes when I go into the barn, he's standing in front of the giant easel he's rigged up and doesn't even know I'm there. Sometimes he does, and we have a sort of conversation.

"Are you coming in for dinner?"

Daub, daub, brushstroke.

"I'm buying."

"Hmm. Maybe." Splat.

Other times he'll turn away from the canvas and actually look at me. Although it's more like he's looking through me. That's him in work mode.

At that point, I might repeat the question, but more likely, I'll give up and leave.

Occasionally, when I'm at the door, he'll have one last thing to say. Like,

"Ah." Swish.

I'll turn at the sound— and find the canvas transformed. Something light made dark by lines of black. Something pleasing turned terrifying by a dripping arc of red, as if the painting has suddenly begun to bleed.

Dad's paintings are beautiful and frightening. They sell for a lot, which is good and bad. Mom says that while his work is selling so well he'll never slow down. But Dad will never slow down, period. Painting's what keeps him alive. I'm not sure how I know this.

If I want to stay clear of Dad, I stay out of the barn. Avoiding Mom during the mayhem of her morning routine? Is trickier, but necessary.

Talking to my mother at this time, even to tell her the whereabouts of the item she's seeking, is to risk getting caught in the cross fire of clicking heels and verbal abuse. It's basically volunteering to be a target for her double-barreled gun of criticism and blame.

Dad's moods can be equally turbulent, but he mitigates his mercurial personality with art. Colors it with oils and acrylics. On the days he doesn't paint, it just depends. Is he excited about a new idea? Did he get the grant he applied for? The gallery exhibit he wanted?

Dad has works in the permanent collections of MoMA, the Whitney, and the Guggenheim. But that isn't enough, will never be enough. There is no "enough" when it comes to art, apparently, which is why it scares me. That and it's messy.

I love Dad's paintings though, and I love Dad. He loves me. But his veins are filled with paint instead of blood, and if I asked him what he loves about me? What he loves about Mom? He wouldn't be able to tell me. He'd have to paint a picture.

He might make a sketch first. Or scribble a list, the way I do, to get my thoughts lined up.

Dad's love list would be a visceral thing:

Heart. Soul. Love pump. Playground.

Scarlet. Vermilion. Crimson. Red.

Apples. Temptation. Strawberries. Rhubarb.

Cherries. Compassion. Garnets. Bed.

Rubies. Pearls. *Pearls.*

Don't cast your pearls before swine, Cate.

Splat.

Now I watch him and my mother for a minute longer, wondering how Dad would even know if I were casting my pearls.

The answer is, unless my pearl casting was connected in some way to one of his pieces, he wouldn't. And neither would Mom.

It's not surprising that they have no idea today is the first day of school.

BRICKS

CATE

Laurel drums her fingers on my open notebook. "What are you writing?"

"Probably a bad poem."

"Is it a love poem for Guitar Guy? And can you stop? I haven't seen you all day." But even as Laurel says this, she peers past me to the other side of the cafeteria. "Definitely," she says.

Laying down my pen, I close the notebook. "Definitely?"

"He's looking at you."

"Cal doesn't go to Middleburn High, so how, exactly, could he be looking at me?"

"Cal? Who's Cal?"

"Ha-ha."

"Glad you're laughing, because seriously, how can you even think about that guy, even if he is a guitar god, when, you know—" She nods at something over my shoulder, her blonde brows arched so high in exaggerated anticipation, they look as if they might take flight.

I can't help laughing, but I don't turn around. I'm pissed at her. Not really pissed; it's just, she's in love now, and we've barely spent any time together since the cedar pond. If I can do anything to annoy her, I'm going for it. I let another beat go by.

"Cate, I'm telling you! Don't you feel his *soulful stare* burning into your back?"

She widens her eyes— her idea of a soulful stare, I guess. "You look like an owl," I tell her.

But knowing she'll probably start pointing if I don't look behind me, I finally do.

Suffused in September sunlight, David Bennet stands by the open fire door. He's not looking at my back or any part of me. He's gazing into the distance like he's . . . looking for yesterday. He's leaning forward just slightly, favoring his right leg like he does now, appearing as if, at any moment, he might slip away.

Imagining where he'd go, I get only as far as outside, someplace outside. Nearby maybe, one of the gently rolling fields broken by white wooden horse fences and edged with tall oaks. He's got one hand on the doorframe, a foot on the threshold, as if he's on his way. Now he looks up at the impossibly blue sky. Then he turns his head and swings his gaze toward— me?

Rod Whitaker appears out of nowhere and *pounds* David's arm with his fist.

Rod Whitaker. Shit. I'd almost forgotten he'd be here, that I'd have to actually see him at school. Suddenly I feel a little sick.

Hiding a grimace under a surprisingly savage grin, David turns swiftly and grabs Rod in a headlock. In less than a second, even though Rod is the bigger of the two boys, he calls for mercy. It all happens so fast, but I'm pretty sure David's eyes met mine, just for a heartbeat.

"I think you should go rescue David," Laurel suggests with a grin that implies something very different than a rescue mission.

But David's fine, despite the fact that Rod's jeering in his face. I'm the one who's not okay.

Rod Whitaker.

"You should go over there," Laurel persists. "You might save a life."

"I'm David's sister's babysitter, not his."

"That's not what you told me last niiight," she singsongs. "But okay, let him perish, I mean I can see why you would. Rod the god. He is a bit of an obstacle. A hot one, but unfortunately as we all know, also a dick. Now, if he could just learn to keep his mouth shut—oh, and not act like such a dick—he might be okay. For someone. Although I can't think who. Actually, it looked like he was bothering *you* at the party last weekend. What was that about?"

"Hebotherseverybody." I answer so quickly that the words run together.

Laurel tilts her head to one side. "What is it, Cate Cat?"

"Nothing. It's just . . ." My hands are shaking. I slip them beneath the orange cafeteria table and squeeze them until they stop. "Tell me how that works, L. How can you think Rod's hot when he's a total jerk?" I'm concerned, really, that she's able to hold these two opposing views at the same time.

"Hot factor eclipses jerk factor, that's what Dee says. Also, I don't *really* know just how much of a dick Rod truly is, I mean . . ." She shrugs. "I've heard stories. Like, that he has a serious drinking problem, and that he's spent time in juvie. Did you know he ended up in the hospital last year with alcohol poisoning?"

But I think if Rod Whitaker was poisoned by anything, it was probably his own blood. Something innate. Now I imagine him bleeding, his poisonous blood dripping blackly.

"Look!" Laurel suddenly commands, slapping her hand down on mine.

"Ow!"

"Rod's leaving. Go."

"No thanks."

"Why not? You're in *high school*. Staying faithful to Guitar Guy is—wait. You're not worried about that rumor, are you? David probably hasn't even heard it. And come on, he knows you're not gay."

As if on cue, Dee Carson slides onto the bench and slings an arm around Laurel's neck.

"But don't you wish you were?" She kisses Laurel, who looks slightly helpless in the presence of Dee's blinding smile and bright-blonde corkscrew curls.

But I barely notice Dee. *That rumor. That rumor* must be spreading, because I never mentioned it to Laurel.

The bell rings. There's no time to reply to what Laurel—or Dee—has just said. No time to tell Laurel that I think Rod Whitaker started *that rumor*. No time to say, "Cal and I don't have anything going on that requires faithfulness." Not really. Not yet.

Although Dee has just sat down, at the sound of the bell she springs back up and grabs Laurel's hands, yanking her to her feet. Her fingertips rain on my head.

"Cate? Deal. If you *like* quarterback boy—David?—just let him know. That's what I did with Laurel. Pretty much as soon as I saw her." She looks at Laurel expectantly.

"Um, yeah, she did. Let me know, that is. But you don't have to, you know, go outside your comfort zone or anything. I was just goofing around, Cate, just teasing. You know that."

"Wait a minute," Dee objects. "Didn't you say Cate should just sleep with him? Get it over with? He's the one, right, the one she's been hanging out with for the last . . ."

But the rest of her words are drowned out by the noise in my ears. A rush of blood.

Time wavers. Then Laurel and I are in this little freeze-frame of a moment, our best-friendness bouncing back and forth between us like a rubber ball. As we look into each other's eyes, a dozen things are being said, or maybe unsaid.

Dee flutters at the edge of the frame. Tucking a strand of Laurel's pale hair behind her ear, brushing a piece of nothing off her sleeve.

"Th-that's not exactly what I said," Laurel stammers. "Cate, I didn't really tell Dee anything. It's just, you're going to see David practically every day now that you actually live here and we made it to high school. We had our doubts," she says laughingly to Dee, who's scowling darkly at her now.

Laurel's just trying to lighten the moment, but it feels like another betrayal.

"No doubts about Cate Cat here," she continues, nodding at me. "With her perfect grades and notebook collection—but me, I failed algebra, like, a thousand times."

But watching my beautiful friend wrap an arm around Dee's willowy waist, it's hard to imagine her failing anything, except, at this moment, maybe our friendship. To her credit, she tries again, to make up for the sellout.

"Dee, you have to hear Cate play guitar. She's got mad skills."

"Oh yeah?" Dee does her best to look bored, but Laurel's gotten her attention. "I play guitar. Took lessons for a whole summer—"

"Yeah, no," Laurel interrupts. "I mean Cate's *amazing*. She plays classical guitar and—"

"Time to go," I say brightly. But my comment doesn't seem to register with either of them. Dee's too busy pinning Laurel with a needle-sharp glare. Laurel, well, she's on the receiving end of said glare.

"Ooh," says Dee, continuing her attempt to impale Laurel with her eyes. "*Amazing*, huh?" Now she turns to me with a saccharine smile. "So when do I get to hear you play?"

"Hmm." I pretend to consider her request. "How about never."

"Oh, Cate," Laurel says. She turns to Dee. "Cate's not really into playing in front of people, but she—"

"I said I'm not into playing in front of people *at this point*, Laurel. I'm a student. I mean, obviously I play in front of people at my recitals, I play in front of people in master classes—"

"Just not in front of the muggles."

"Laurel—"

"So she's played for you?" And even though Dee's the one who asked the question, she pulls almost imperceptibly on Laurel, as if she doesn't care about the answer, just wants to go.

At that, Laurel gives me an apologetic look, and for a second, I think things are going to be okay, think she's going to say something like, "Well duh, of course Cate's played for me—we're best friends."

But instead she just nods. "Yep, she's played for me, and she could play for you, too. Cate, you don't have to treat performing like some kind of sacred act. It's not life or death. You could just *play*, in front of Dee, in front of anyone. Same with David, you could just go talk to him. You could do more! It wouldn't kill you."

Now the space between Laurel and me expands. The ball of best-friendness bouncing outside our box, going wide, till it bounces out of sight, till there is no box, no frame that holds just us.

She makes it sound easy. Playing in front of people, playing at all. Talking to a guy like David Bennet, in the middle of the cafeteria. She makes it sound like she doesn't know, like I hadn't told her *just last night*, what my problem with David is. How I can't seem to act *normal* in front of him anymore. How my tongue ties itself in knots half the time I'm around him. How the worst part is, I never know when it's going to happen.

Or maybe the worst part is that I confided in Laurel, and she turned around and told Dee. Sounds like they discussed things in detail. David Bennet, and me—she knows I'm with Cal! Well, sort of with him. She definitely knows I'm in love.

The sights and sounds of the cafeteria flood back in, and though I don't really mean to, I glance over at David, who's turning his back on

Rod. The gesture reminds me that while David and Rod are—*were*—on tons of teams together over the years, they've never been good friends. Maybe never really friends at all. And definitely not since Rafe Hall's party.

I've seen Rod taunt David, like he did a few minutes ago, but I think that's about the extent of their relationship at this point. David's obviously pissed at him. Even now, before he turned away, David looked at Rod with murder in his eyes.

This, of course, makes me like David even more than I already do, which annoys me, because it means Laurel's right—only she isn't. Cal's the person I want to be with. He's perfect.

I start, as Dee waggles her fingers in farewell—in my face—yanking on Laurel's hand for real now, and I think that maybe playing on some team with a guy you don't like is a little like this. Like me having to get along with Dee. Because isn't that what I'm going to have to do if I want to be on Team Laurel? Although after what just happened, my stomach twists with Laurel's betrayal.

But then she and Dee stop short, and I follow Laurel's gaze to a pack of boys on the other side of the room. Suddenly, my feelings don't matter so much.

Half the football team is clustered on either side of the double doors like Cerberus squared guarding the gates of hell. They're eyeing Laurel and Dee with a sort of fiendish delight.

As Rod Whitaker joins them, his gaze wanders up and down Laurel's legs. One of the other boys lets out a low whistle in coarse appreciation, or possibly in warning.

In response, Laurel glowers and appears to grow slightly taller.

Dee, on the other hand, seems to get smaller, not because of the many pairs of eyes on her, already watching to see what she and Laurel will do, but because she's leaning into Laurel, saying something in her ear. And even though the gesture's intimate, the words are loud enough that I have to wonder if she wants me to hear, because I do.

"Why does she even like him? Isn't David Bennet the senior boy toy?" She snickers. "But I guess *hot* factor eclipses man-slut factor, right?"

"Dee, remind me why you're still thinking about him, why it even matters to you. Do you not see it's feeding time at the zoo?" Under her breath Laurel mutters, "Did I say a minute ago that I didn't know just how much of a dick Rod truly was?"

"Ugh," Dee grumbles, possibly in answer to what Laurel has just said, but more likely at the realization that the bundle of boys is now blocking the cafeteria doors.

My cheeks are still warm from the thought of Laurel talking to Dee about me, but a second later I suck in a breath as the dogs by the door begin to howl.

Quickly I hop up from my seat at the table—

Rod Whitaker's gaze shifts just as fast.

If he hadn't noticed me before, he definitely does now. It's the last thing I want.

He shoots me his ferocious white sickle of a smile.

In my peripheral vision I see a group of girls slouching against the wall by the radio station, eyes narrowing with envy as they watch Rod separate himself from the wolf pack and head toward me.

But those girls don't know.

Laurel breathes my name. "Cate?"

There's no time to answer her unasked question. I don't want Rod Whitaker coming one step closer to me—to any of us.

Linking arms with Laurel and Dee, I spin them around—

And tug them out the back door.

HEAT

DAVID

Out through the nearest set of swinging cafeteria doors.

Out through the main entrance of the school.

Outside.

I take a deep breath. Take another. Swear I won't kill Rod Whitaker today.

I decide to walk home, even though my leg is screaming. It feels good to be moving, to be sweating, but the *desire* to move pisses me off.

Walk it out, Son. Run it out.

Those words. They've been my father's solution to everything. And I've listened.

Now I'm done listening. But my body . . . still craves what it craves.

Sweat beads on my brow. Soaks the back of my shirt.

It's interesting that anger is associated with a temperature, but happiness isn't.

Dick went hot with anger.

Fear is also assigned a temperature.

Jane went cold with fear.

On top of everything that's happened, on top of the earthquake in me—it's too much. And yet, if I could keep it to that, to temperature, it would be simple.

Dick is so, so angry. Easy. Dick is hot. Go in the pool, Dick.

Jane goes cold at the thought of—

Fine. Jane's cold. Put on a sweater, Jane.

But nothing's simple. Not anymore.

At night I wake up in a cold sweat. I'm hot. Cold. Both. A cold sweat makes no sense.

Just like it makes no sense that something awful can happen when something awful has *just* happened. Horror stacking up on top of horror.

Sometimes, when I wake up from The Dream, I'm drenched in that cold sweat. Sometimes I find that my fingers are still dreaming. Clawing at the sheets.

At the start of The Dream, I'm in the canoe. In the stern. Which means I'm supposed to be steering.

Dan is in the bow. Which means he's supposed to be watching. Watching out.

The bow of the boat goes over the falls first.

But somehow, the part with the roaring falls isn't the worst part of The Dream. Not anymore. No. The worst part of The Dream is the new part.

When my sister Bryn shows up in the canoe.

She's in the middle. Sitting in the bottom of the boat.

A sitting duck.

Last night, for the first time, there was another girl in The Dream as well, a girl with dark hair, gray eyes. She stood across the water from me, on the shoreline of a long blue lake. The water was calm, the surface smooth as glass, and the girl waved me over—

But the lake turned to tangled sheets and I couldn't swim across.

DUET

CATE

A day and a night, Cal texts. But he doesn't mean he's sleeping over. He means he'll be here at noon on Saturday, then drive back to school late Saturday night.

Laurel's right, North Moore's a haul—almost three hours—so I've got everything planned. We'll go out to lunch at Caffeine Scene, then to the Dey Estate. After that I'll play him my set. The Strings with Wings post-festival shows are coming up, and I can use all the help I can get. Since we don't live in the city anymore, I only see Marion every three weeks.

I text back, I'll make you dinner.

Or I'll take you out, he replies. But it'll have to b an early night.

We have a guest room you know, I text. Then, biting my lower lip a little, I add:

Tho my parents probably wouldnt notice if u didnt sleep in it.

A minute ticks by.

Afraid that if I don't stop chewing my lip I'll draw blood, I move on to a thumbnail.

Finally, Cal answers, but it takes a second before I think to turn the phone sideways. When I do, the combination of symbols transforms into a wide-eyed face. I'm still laughing when he texts again, saying he's got a gig playing Sunday brunch at a restaurant near his school.

But we'll have a whole day and dinner and DESSERT. The wide-eyed face appears again.

Ok, I tap, still grinning. I'll just have to be satisfied with that.

A breath later he texts, I'll make sure you are.

WISH
CATE

The Bennets' car pulls in front of the school and I shut my notebook. Bryn and I climb in.

Mrs. Bennet immediately begins talking nonstop at Bryn.

Bryn sighs heavily, her way of talking back.

"I mean it, Bryn, I do *not* like the way that boy was looking at you, and I *heard* what he said. Can't you tell a teacher?"

"Mom, 'that boy' is Rod Whitaker. You *know* him. He's been to our house. And no, I'm not going to go whining to some teacher who's not going to do anything anyway."

"That boy has never been to our house," Mrs. Bennet says. "I would remember."

"If you were ever home—"

Her mother starts speaking again, as if Bryn isn't. "I do *not* want him in our house."

"Neither do I," Bryn mutters.

As if Bryn hasn't just agreed with her, Mrs. Bennet keeps up her assault. "Did you see the way he looked at your—" She glances in the rearview mirror at Kimmy, whom she'd picked up first at Middleburn Elementary, and drops her voice to a whisper. "At your *backside*?"

"He looks at everyone's ass that way, Mom, he's a player. He's worse. He'd fu—"

Kimmy's head snaps up at the same time Mrs. Bennet shrieks Bryn's name. Quickly I ask Kimmy a question about the book with the yellow cover she's been reading.

She holds it up—a Nancy Drew—but her gaze ping-pongs back between the two headrests of the front seats. Mrs. Bennet's voice is so loud I can almost see it.

"I loved those books," I say. "I read them all. Can't remember how many there were—"

"Fifty-six, the original books by Carolyn Keene—not a real name, by the way."

Kimmy doesn't have the blonde hair and blue eyes that her mother, father, and sister have, the blonde hair Bryn recently dyed inky black. Instead, her serious little face is framed with chestnut hair, like David's. Her eyes are brown with flecks of gold, David's eyes.

For a second she's five again and it's the weekend. I'm twelve and out from the city, staying with my parents in the old farmhouse they bought before I was born.

Laurel's father, a lawyer and Dad's best friend since first grade, is the one who told Dad that buying something in horse country was the opportunity of a lifetime. The Ridgeways moved to Middleburn when they had Laurel, and that's when they became friends with the Bennets. Mr. Bennet is also a lawyer, at the same firm as Laurel's dad. Laurel ribbed me on the phone the other night, saying that I owe her big-time. That if it weren't for her, I wouldn't even know David. I told her that would be fine. Her scoff-snort was so loud, I asked if she was choking.

"The original fifty-six books are the best." Kimmy's thin voice pulls me back into the car. "The newer stories are lame, less about mysteries and clues, more about boys." She peers up toward the front seat, a turtle poking its head out of its shell, as her mother and sister argue heatedly about this very topic.

"Sounds like you've read them all," I say.

"Sounds like you know them all," Mrs. Bennet snaps at Bryn, who's just recited a long list of David's friends, including Rod.

Kimmy nods, but her attention rivets again on the front seat as Bryn launches the word *sex* through the air and it explodes like a bomb.

"I don't want to hear about that!"

For a second I imagine Mrs. Bennet letting go of the wheel, covering her ears.

"Come on, Mom. I'm seventeen. Let's not pretend I'm a virgin, but do you really think I'd sleep with that *hulk*? Seriously, is that what you think of me?" Bryn's voice is shaking a little.

"I don't know what to think of you lately. And, honestly, this is not the time or place to be discussing it." Our eyes meet in the rearview mirror, and Mrs. Bennet shoots me a questioning look, as if I might possibly know what to think of Bryn.

We pull into the Bennets' driveway, and Bryn is out of the car before the engine's off, mumbling something about not knowing why she's actually trying to talk to her mother, that she has *friends* to talk to, before slamming the door and wheeling away from the vehicle.

And she does have friends, lots of them. But Bryn is her own spinning planet. When I picture her friends, I see a group of guys and girls standing around her, wistful moons orbiting an untouchable Earth.

I go round to help Kimmy, but of course she doesn't need help: she's not five anymore, she's nine. Still, I focus on her, trying to let Bryn's dark matter disperse.

Kimmy starts toward the side of the house, probably headed straight for the pool. But when the front door swings open, she changes direction, cutting me off so I stumble over my feet. Taking the front steps two at a time, she leaps at David— who swings her up in his arms.

And I have the weirdest wish then: that he'd do the same with me.

"Hey, Babysitter, what are we doing today?"

If Bryn is the earth, David's the sun. He smiles and light moves through his eyes.

He seems to actually be waiting for my answer, which is . . . odd. His family is back, school has started, and life is morphing into its normal summer-is-over shape. Part of that normal is I'm Kimmy's babysitter. Another bit of that normal? David is Kimmy's older brother, who has never shown any interest in me. I'd assumed that those couple of weeks, coming as they did after the preceding month, where David had mostly stayed in his room recovering from some kind of accident he'd had on a canoe trip, were a fluke. Still, when Mrs. Bennet called me to babysit, I leapt at the opportunity, hoping the little hollow in my gut might go away, hoping to prove Laurel wrong, because if this swooping feeling in my stomach has to do with David—

David, who is still waiting for my answer.

Okay. It's not last week, or the week before, it's *now*, but I'm so busy wondering if David is actually implying he wants to hang out that any possible answer I might give him remains a mystery. Before I can solve it, Kimmy is prattling to David about her day and he's laughing, then frowning as the voices of Bryn and Mrs. Bennet—who have disappeared into the house—bounce sharply off the granite countertops in the kitchen, stabbing the air around us.

Then David is impossibly balancing Kimmy on his hip, one arm around her, his other outstretched, holding the door for me—

And I'm ducking under his arm—

Which he lets fall, his fingertips landing on the small of my back.

In an instant, that one single point—a spot just between the hem of my shirt and the top of my jeans where David's fingertips are warm on my skin—becomes the focus of my entire being.

He has *never* touched me before. The feeling it gives me is amazing. His touch lights up my body and muddles my brain. *What is he doing?*

Dropping my gaze to the floor, I try to walk normally, taking a few steps across the foyer.

Then the sensation is gone, and I look up to see David flipping Kimmy upside down— before setting her gently on her feet.

WATER

DAVID

I swim, but it's not enough. Not enough to drown the buzzing energy. Not enough to dissolve me.

I lift. I run, even though it hurts. But I don't talk anymore. That's what it feels like. Instead, I *watch*. I look. And just . . . keep everything in. Hold it in. Feels like I'm walking around with a fire inside. Maybe it will burn me up.

At night I dream about fire and water, but at school . . . no one knows. Sometimes little bits of the fire seep out, a harsh word here, an incomplete assignment there, and I pull back. Because even though I'm slowly figuring out how stupid everything up until now has been, I don't want to hurt anyone. I'm the only one who deserves to be destroyed, though I wouldn't mind taking Dad down.

The other day Trish said I was lame 'cause I wouldn't stroke her ego. Tammy just wants me to stroke her thighs. Those two. Went out with one and then the other. Trish, then Tammy. Then Tammy, then Trish. Still not sure which girl I miss. Boyfriend and girlfriend, then something less . . . a hookup, a ride home; each girl's a hot mess. They both blame me. They should, I guess. But it's over for real this time. Like with the others . . . I'm just done.

Keep your eye on the ball, Son. Keep your eyes on the prize.

But my eyes have been on the wrong things. The prizes . . . are not what I want.

And maybe it's because I hang back now, watching, that I see her. If I were still a blur of motion: football, track, grades, girls—*girls, girls, girls*—I would've missed her.

She's like . . . a still point.

All around her, the world twists and turns, but she is still. Like the horizon.

GLITTER

CATE

Stopping midstride, I stand in the doorway of Bryn's bedroom and listen.

"Northern Ontario, some kind of wilderness camp. Not Outward Bound, but intense like that. What? Two days. Friggin' trip was almost over. They helicoptered him out.

"The two shrinks Mom and Dad sent him to disagree on everything, of course. I told them not to bother with Dr. Finn, do you think they listened?" Bryn cups her hand over the phone and glares at me. "What?"

"Nothing, I—nothing." For a second, I continue to stare at Bryn. She's sitting on her canopy bed, the frame of which has been spray-painted silver and drenched in glitter. More sparkly stuff shines from the midnight-blue walls and ceiling, where she's painted her own take on the universe. She pushes back the abyss of inky hair from her face and narrows her eyes.

Turning quickly, I step into the bathroom across from her room and shut the door—not all the way. My heart is pounding.

"No one, just Kimmy's babysitter. Yeah, he was banged up pretty good, but not compared to the other guy."

My stomach tightens.

Bryn laughs, but the sound twists in her throat, morphing into one flat word. "Dead."

Then she's silent for a long moment. "The break itself wasn't too bad. His leg healed well, superfast, the doctors said. He just got his cast off. Yeah, as soon as he did, my dad was all like, 'Oh, David's fine now.' I'm like, yeah, if you don't count the fact that he's totally depressed and won't do anything or hang out with anyone. What? Survivor guilt? Huh. Don't know.

"*No* sports. Dad is *pissed*. There goes the scholarship, not to mention Dad's whole weirdo-clone thing. Then there's Mom. I mean, 'Dahling, what ever will we chat about at the Club?'

"He signed himself out of school twice already. Must be nice. Yeah, he turned eighteen in August. He doesn't go anywhere except the backyard. Swims a million laps a day, like he's possessed or something. Obsessed. You'd think, after nearly drowning, the pool would be the last place he'd want to be."

I can't breathe for a second. *David nearly drowned?*

"He's a Leo—dude, enough! Are you hot for my brother or what? Duh, of course you are. Ha. You expect me to believe that? Fine, then you're the *only* one who hasn't slept with him."

"Cate?" It's Kimmy. Trotting down the hall, I find her in the middle of her bright-yellow bedroom. She's already changed into a pink polka-dotted bathing suit, and now she slides her feet on the green shag carpet, striking a pose. "Wanna dance?"

Before I can answer, my eyes follow a glimmer of dappled light dancing on the ceiling. I walk over to the window. Down below in the yard, sunlight bounces off the pool—

And David Bennet executes a smooth dive, disappearing beneath the sparkling surface.

GOLD
CATE

Sitting on the concrete pavers at the edge of the Bennets' aquamarine pool, I dangle my legs in the water. Just the cool feel of it washes the first week of school away.

Kimmy inhaled her snack, and now she's bouncing up and down on the low diving board.

"Why aren't you in your suit?" *Boing, boing*— the stiff board barely moves beneath her.

"Forgot it."

"But you *have* to come in with me!" She flips into the water.

The sun-warmed concrete feels good against the backs of my thighs. I bunch my skirt higher. Mom says long skirts make me look *dowdy*, but I like that no one else wears them. Not that I want to stick out as the new girl; although, I'm not really new, not like Dee.

Dee's family moved here from Manhattan, like mine did, but she doesn't know too many people yet. No one knows her. Maybe that's why she's so irritatingly possessive of Laurel.

A lot of people in Middleburn know me. They know me from the public pool, from the country club the Ridgeways and the Bennets belong to—the same club where Laurel met Dee. They know me from the parties Laurel and her older sister, Grace, have taken me to over the years. The kids around here know me, and I know them. Then again, we don't really *know* each other. Still, they've seen me around Red Bank for years and vice versa, mostly at Listen Up!

I've been going to Listen Up! for as long as I can remember. Not often, but always. Even when we lived in the city, whenever we came out to the old farmhouse, Laurel and I would get together and go. It was our Saturday-night ritual.

We'd browse the used books and CDs, leave for pizza, come back, wander through the vinyl section. Sometimes we went through the glass doors toward the rear of the shop so I could check out the guitars.

We also liked to check out the guys who worked there—or, we used to. Most of them rotated through, but the guy with the blue hair and the shaved-head guy have been at the store forever, along with a girl named Delsey.

Laurel sort of knows shaved-head guy—everyone calls him Bird. He graduated with her sister and is a monster guitar player. He didn't always have a shaved head, but he's always been fun to watch, talking about music or demoing guitars.

"He must have started working here when he was, like, six." Laurel said once about two years ago, as we watched him from behind the *W*s in the vinyl section.

"Weren't we about that age when we started hanging out here?" I'd asked.

"Uh-huh," she'd said, not taking her eyes off the boy. "Your dad brought us, remember?"

"Kind of." I watched her watch the boy. "He's gotten kind of hot, right?"

"I guess."

"You guess? Since when do you *guess* a guy's hot?"

Laurel gave me an appraising look.

"L, what's with the stink eye?"

"Well . . . here's the thing."

I waited, but she just stood there, looking at me.

"Hello? The *thing*?"

She took a deep breath then, and slowly blew it out before she said, "Cate, I'm gay."

I opened my mouth. The word "Oh" popped out. And then there was a big old silence.

It wasn't that I had a problem with what she'd said. It was the fact that she hadn't told me *as soon as she knew* that got me, that jabbed me in the stomach like a finger. I was pretty sure she hadn't just figured out she was gay while we stood behind the *W*'s in the vinyl section.

"So you decided this, when?" I asked. "Yesterday?"

"A while ago." Laurel looked around the store at that point, so I did, too. But it was just the two of us and Bird, the guy whose hotness was possibly in question. "And it's not something I decided," she continued. "It's something I am. It's not a decision," she emphasized, echoing what she had just said. "It's something you know. Unless . . . you hide it from yourself."

Neither one of us mentioned the time she'd made a pass at me.

Not that it had made me uncomfortable, it's just that I'd thought she was joking, or had heatstroke, or had been in her parents' liquor cabinet. Because none of those things were uncommon, plus Laurel tried on a lot of hats over the years while I'd been, well—solidly, and possibly boringly—me. Not that this was a hat, not at all.

"Okay, you're gay," I'd said. "Fine. But the last time we went to the beach, and every time before that, come to think of it, *you* always picked out the good-looking lifeguards—not that there's a trick to that—which means that even though you're into girls, your ability to appreciate beauty hasn't diminished. So, what about Bird—hot or not?"

She'd shoved me into a display of Bruce Springsteen CDs then, and I'd shoved her back.

And that had been it. It wasn't even a blip on my radar, although for her, telling me had been a big deal. Did she really think our friendship would be affected by whom she went out with?

Then again, she's in love, really in love now, with Dee—who I don't like, and who hates me. And *this* is the confusing part. Not the fact that Laurel's a lesbian, but that she'd fall for such an asshole. L probably goes to Listen Up! with Dee now. We haven't been since July.

Turning my face to the sun, I close my eyes, trying not to think about it anymore . . .

Sensing Kimmy walk over, I murmur, "So this is where summer disappeared to."

"Yep. We hold it hostage back here for as long as we can."

My eyes snap open—

David's the one standing over me, not Kimmy. My stomach leaps— which annoys me.

"We keep the pool open until Thanksgiving," he continues.

"Thanksgiving." The single word seems to be the only one available.

"That's right. We heat it, of course."

I bet you do.

David Bennet has never seemed to take up so much physical space before. He's wearing shorts and standing so close to me I can see the curling hair on his legs—one of them paler than the other—the way the sunlight turns it coppery gold. His eyes are golden, too, his hair edged with light. He brings a hand to his brow, shading his eyes, causing them to darken.

Then he starts to undo his shorts. Two points against me—or maybe *for* me, depending who you ask—I don't look away. He's wearing bright-orange swim trunks beneath them.

"Guess you're ready to go swimming." *Duh.* I'd like to disintegrate now, please.

He laughs—at me, I'm sure. "Yeah, I was home for lunch. The water was great, but I didn't have time to change. Paid for that." He scowls a little.

"What do you mean? Were you late?"

"No, but my trunks were still wet, so by the time I got to science . . ."

I grin.

He starts toward the deep end. "Go ahead, yuk it up. At least tomorrow when you hear the rumor that I wet my pants, you'll know it's not true."

Rumor. The word makes me go still. Has he heard the rumors about me?

The diving board shudders.

"Cannonball!" Kimmy yells from over by the pool house.

And I'm soaked.

"Who's laughing now?" David says as he comes up by my feet. He hadn't bothered to take off his shirt and it sticks wetly to his chest, his arms. His hands close around my ankles now, thumbs fitting perfectly in the hollows just below my anklebones.

"Cate!" Kimmy calls from over by the pool house. "C'mere!"

Cupping my hands, I scoop as much water as I can hold— and dump it on David's head.

Blinking water from his eyes, he grins, tugging on my ankles. "That the best you've got?"

Kimmy calls for me again.

"Look!" I point across the pool, and David's head swivels. Quickly I pull my legs up out of the water, my feet slipping through his fingers.

"Hey!" he shouts in surprise.

Laughing, I jump up and follow Kimmy into the pool house. The sink is set into a surface of smooth river rocks instead of tiles. A mirror hangs above it. Shining eyes peer out at me. My skin is flushed, my dark hair beaded with water droplets.

"Change." Kimmy presses a suit into my hands and pushes me into one of two booths with swinging saloon-style doors.

"Kimmy!" I wave the two tiny pieces of bright-red cloth above the doors. "I can't wear this! Bryn will kill me." *And I'll basically be naked.*

"Sorry, you can't come out till you change!" She giggles, holding the doors closed.

Muttering, I strip down and slip into the microscopic bikini. David's the only one who's worse than I am at saying no to Kimmy. Looking in the mirror, I suck in a breath— I actually fill out the top, and then some, but the bottom? It hangs on my hips. The suit is not sexy like it would be on Bryn—it's slutty. I groan.

Kimmy yanks the door open. "When did you grow boobies?"

Heat spreads up my neck. "I've always had . . . breasts." Pushing past her, I grab a towel from a stack next to the sink. When I turn around, she's staring at me, at my face.

"David's right." A little grin creeps across her freckled face. "You *are* the pretty one."

"Um, thanks." I wrap the towel securely around my waist. *Had she been there?* In my memory, it's always just the two of us, David and me.

One Saturday last winter, before we'd moved here full-time, Laurel dragged me to Saks to go shopping. She needed a dress for her older sister's party, which was going to be a big deal, because Grace was graduating early, leaving high school and heading off to Cornell University.

We ran into Bryn and her friends Stephie and Niffer, who were planning for the party as well. Kimmy floundered in their wake under an armload of outfits.

Feeling sorry for Kimmy, I took half the load, which is how I wound up playing minion, fetching dresses for the girls while their mothers chatted over the nearby jewelry counter.

Out of nowhere David had appeared in the ladies' lounge, a dark suit thrown over his arm. He'd flung himself onto one of the pink padded benches.

"Are you going to the Ridgeways' party?" he asked as I hurried by.

For some reason, the way David sat there in the women's dress department—looking way more comfortable than I felt—got to me. Plus I was pissed to be taxiing dresses around. Giving Kimmy the seriously garish gown that Stephie had asked for in a smaller size, I sat down.

"Of course I'm going," I said. In retrospect, I sounded pretty snotty.

"So how come you're not part of the parade?" David waved a hand, indicating the other girls. And as Niffer made a show of adjusting her cleavage, he grinned in appreciation.

"I've already got a dress." *Why do you care? And why do you have to leer at Niffer like that?*

"Cool." He pulled an iPod out of his pocket, started scrolling. "Bet it looks good on you."

I stared at him. "What?" The *t* at the end of the single word sounded sharp enough to skewer something.

"Oh c'mon." He scowled slightly, glancing at Bryn's friends preening in front of the mirrors. "Don't pretend you don't know it. Games like that." He shook his head.

"What are you talking about?"

"You. I'm talking about you."

He sat back then, like he wanted to see me from a different angle, and made a vague gesture that began at the other girls but ended at me. "You're the pretty one."

Time slowed just a little as I looked at him, and he held my gaze. That's when I noticed the perfume. Freesia. Or grapefruit. Something fresh, and just the tiniest bit peppery. Then he leaned toward me, and I smelled *him*. Soap and sunshine and chlorine from the pool—

I stood up abruptly.

His eyebrows lifted in surprise.

Then, I walked away. I hadn't believed him, not for one second. What if I had?

Kimmy and I head back outside now to the winking turquoise pool.

The water rocks with movement. David must have just left.

I'm relieved. And disappointed.

NYLON

DAVID

Cate, in Bryn's suit, does not look like Kimmy's babysitter. Does not look like a still point. She's all flowing movement and blowing hair, and yet—

"Hang on." Bryn comes up behind me. Her eyes flick from the window up to my face, then back again. "You're being all pervy over Cate, what the fuck?"

"No, I—I'm not. I wasn't. I just—I couldn't do laps with Kimmy in the pool, so—"

"So, what? You're *visualizing* them?" She narrows her eyes. "David. Cate's, like, twelve."

"Actually, she's sixteen."

"How do you—wait, why do you care? She's like, our sister." Bryn stalks outside, letting the screen door snap behind her. Her voice is only slightly muffled through the glass. "Hey, that's my suit! What the fuck, you guys, just help yourself to my stuff." Bryn points at Cate, insisting she change, then starts giving Kimmy a hard time. But her eyes dart from the two girls to where I stand behind the glass.

My lips twist. I want to call out, "Our sister? Really? Like you and Kimmy are sisters?" Lately, Bryn hasn't given Kimmy the time of day. It pisses me off. But I don't say anything; instead, I wonder if this is how Bryn really sees me, a lowlife who wants to boff the babysitter.

Then I feel this new thing. Embarrassment. All the girls I've been with . . .

Not that I was ever like Rod. I never took advantage, always got a resounding *yes*. It's just, there were so many.

Now, all of a sudden, I'm wondering why. *Why so many?*

Because it makes you different than Jack.

Not good enough. Not anymore.

Because it feels good, idiot. Because you can. And because you're good at it.

Definitely not good enough. Not good enough for Cate.

She's still in the pool. Bryn has relented and let her keep the suit on. It doesn't really fit her, and the way it slips around her hips makes it easy to imagine tugging it down—

I run my hands over my face. Then I look at *her* face. She's laughing with Kimmy, water dripping off the tip of her nose.

My stomach feels weird. Like I'm driving Dad's Porsche too fast over Blue Meadow Bridge. The idea of Cate, with me, makes me horny. And sick at the same time.

Like I'd be lucky to have sex with her, but she'd just be . . . screwed. Like all the others.

I'm not going to touch her. I'm just—not.

ICE

DAVID

Oblivious to the golden autumn afternoon, Sunday skaters pack the old armory.

Kimmy's here somewhere, gliding—and tumbling too, I'm sure— around the professional-size ice rink, with her friend Sam. I'm to taxi the two of them up to the house, along with Cate Reese, who's been watching them.

I scan the ice, looking for Kimmy's pink jacket.

In the hall I'd passed a group of guys I know, suited up, ready for hockey. Which means free skate is just about over. I keep looking as I step into my skates.

I don't miss hockey, but I miss skating, so I'd purposely arrived a few minutes early. Now I step out onto the ice, part of me wanting to fly, to blow by these Sunday-afternoon drivers. But there is another part of me that is wary. Worried my leg will betray me.

I see Cate now, standing on the rubbery floor by the gate, watching the skaters through the tempered glass above the boards—watching me, I think. I skate over to her.

"Oh, hey," she says. Her tone is casual, her gaze flickering past me now. Maybe she wasn't checking me out, but I smile anyway. Can't seem to help myself despite the fact I've decided not to flirt with her.

"Why aren't you out on the ice?" I ask. But before she can answer, Kimmy slams into me, like she still hasn't learned how to stop.

"Omigod, Davey. Sunday free skate has the most obnoxious kids! You should have come earlier! Hi, Cate!"

"Hey, Nanook." Cate ruffles Kimmy's hair. Kimmy's friend, Sam, comes to a stumbling stop next to her. The two look up at Cate with adoring eyes and I get the weirdest news flash.

Cate would make a great mom. I swallow.

As if I've said something, Cate's eyes lift to mine. I grin, can't help it. But so does she.

Kimmy glances back and forth between the two of us.

"Um, you guys?"

"Ah—time," I say. "Time's almost up. We'll be back in a couple of minutes, okay, Cate?"

She nods and I set off with the kids for another turn around the rink, which is how we wind up being the last ones on the ice.

We're about to exit through the narrow gate when a knot of hockey players starts through.

The goalie is a padded giant. The rest of the team looks slightly robotic, I think, for the first time—all big black skates and dark uniforms. The wire cages set in ebony helmets give the players a menacing look—hard to believe any of these guys are in high school—and they all resemble Darth Vader. This, I think, is what it looks like from the other side. Or maybe I just know these guys too well. There isn't a Luke Skywalker among them.

A few of the guys slap my palm in greeting.

"You screwed us, Bennet," says another. He taps the ice with his stick.

Finally, Kimmy and Sam are heading through the gate, stepping out onto the rubbery floor. Behind Cate, the last hockey player decides she is in the way. He pushes past her. It's Rod.

Only, he doesn't really make it past her, doesn't go through the gate. Instead, he kind of stumbles—

His hands land on Cate.

She jumps back.

He laughs, then he steps onto the ice—

Where I block him.

"Whitaker. Say sorry." My gaze flicks to Cate, who gives a little gasp. It's hard to believe she hadn't recognized Rod until I said his name, but I can tell by her reaction that it's true. It's like she's blocked him, too, from her mind.

"You can't be serious." The bulk that is Rod Whitaker moves surprisingly fast now, ducking under my arm, slicing circles around me.

Then he lets his skates scrape sharply on the ice, coming to a quick stop.

"No way," he says.

I press my lips together. Don't want to say anything in front of the kids.

Cate says, "Kimmy, Sam, meet me in the warm room."

Rod swings his stick, hitting an imaginary puck in her direction. Then he smiles at me broadly, and says, "If you're planning on doing that girl, you might want to get her away from the ice. She's already one frigid bitch. Gave her a try at Hall's party." He skates halfway across the rink, shouts over his shoulder, "You know, the one where I got cozy with your sister?"

I shoot after him.

Out in the middle of the rink I catch up to him, but before I can say anything, he shoves me, hard. Then he throws one hand up. A signal.

"David!" Cate screams.

I spin around. Another black-clad boy is skating fast in my direction.

Fiery pain burns through my leg as I crouch, then slide, not away but toward the boy. When he's close enough, I grab his stick, and with a quick movement, jerk it up—

His weight shifts into his heels, his breath escaping with a grunt as he lands hard on his back— goes skidding across the ice.

Somewhere a whistle blows. Players swarm the rink. The boy who'd gone down so hard gets up— cheeks reddened with more than just cold. Rod yells a string of obscenities at him, skates away.

"That was messed up," Cate mutters to me as we pass the crowded benches in the hallway leading to the warm room.

"Whitaker's a lot more than messed up," I say in return, the ice of the place in my voice.

Kimmy and Sam are standing at the window that overlooks the rink. Kimmy is wide-eyed, but she doesn't say anything, just sinks onto the bench.

Sam flops down next to her, says to me, "You're like, a hockey ninja. That was cool."

"Yeah, not really. Don't ever date a hockey player, Kimmy." I sit, too. Take off my skates. "Actually, don't ever date, period."

I grab my sneakers, glancing up at Cate. "I played ice hockey for twelve years," I tell her, slipping into my sneakers. I'm not sure why I share this bit of information.

She has no idea, either. I can tell by her single raised eyebrow.

"Too long," I say, standing up.

I look away from her and across the room, though I'm not looking at anything in particular. Or maybe I'm looking at everything—that's suddenly what it feels like. Like I'm seeing everything for the first time. It's a weird feeling. I try to shake it off.

"You guys ready to go?" I ask.

Kimmy yells, "Yes!" Then shouts for me to carry her stuff before she tears out of the room with Sam, racing down the long rubber-floored corridors toward the exit.

I pick up Kimmy's pink coat and the duffel embroidered with her name. The coat looks so small. I run my fingers over the stitching on the bag.

When I look up, Cate is watching me, her expression curious. I can almost hear a question formulating in her mind.

But she only says, "Thanks for asking Rod to apologize. But don't next time, okay? Don't go after him again. At least, not for me."

I don't say anything, but I want to. Want to tell her, "I have to go after him. I have to make him pay. I'm just not sure yet how much."

I want to tell her other things as well. That something is shifting, inside of me. That everything is changing, although I'm not sure what "everything" is yet.

More than anything, I want to tell her what happened in Canada.

But there's a tight feeling in my chest, because it's like, behind every *thing* I want to tell her, there's something else. So I don't say a word.

SUGAR

CATE

"The cookie dough that ate New York," David says, checking out the large bowl of batter on the Bennets' kitchen counter as he roughly towels his hair. He's got another towel draped around his neck, and water drips down his arms. He's obviously been in the pool.

I was in earlier, with Kimmy, had been glad to go in, to wash the icy air of the armory from my skin and the image of Rod Whitaker, in his bulky black uniform, from my mind. I think David may feel the same way.

He grins now. "Why are you making so many?"

"Kimmy's taking them to school. Plus—"

"Plus I'll eat at least a dozen."

"They're nowhere near ready to eat."

We both stare down at the dough sitting in the mixing bowl on the counter.

"I've heard you actually have to bake them before you can eat them."

I shoot him a withering look. "Aren't you supposed to be somewhere?"

"Yes. At the table, with a plate of cookies."

"You're funny. The dough has to sit for few more minutes—" I break off as he moves closer, peering pointedly into the bowl. I roll my eyes. "Fine. I suppose the batter's ready enough."

David's eyes skim over me. His lips part just a little, like he's about to say something, but then he looks away. It's weird, but that quick glance—even though I've changed back into my clothes—makes me feel like I'm still wearing my suit, which, this time, I'd remembered to bring.

Feeling self-conscious, I push back a few damp strands of hair that have fallen around my face. I scoop a tablespoon of batter onto the baking sheet, then another. I'd had my hair trimmed recently and the front is just a little too short. It falls forward again. This time, when I shove back the stray strands, I inadvertently smear cookie dough across my cheek. *Great.*

David laughs. I glare up at him, then feel my expression falter as he leans in, brings a gentle finger to my face, and wipes my cheek.

Kimmy bounces into the kitchen just in time to see me with dough on my face.

"Kimmy," I warn.

But she's already swiped a finger full of batter. *Flick.* She whips it at David.

It's on.

I grab the bowl, but David reaches round me. My stomach *swoops.* He doesn't seem to notice we've momentarily collided, just grabs a gob of dough, catches Kimmy, and smudges it across her nose. Kimmy wiggles away, dips both index fingers into the mixture—

"Pow, pow!" she shouts, launching dough at David and—I don't know why I'm surprised—shoves some in my face.

"Hey!" Whirling, I grab at the dough with both hands as David bumps me from behind, reaching for more ammunition. Kimmy's shouting as I spin, fingers full, only to find myself pinned, squashed between the counter and David. I have no choice. In a preemptive strike, I reach up— and smear cookie dough across his face. His mouth opens in surprise, and I stick in a batter-covered finger. His lips close over it and we both go still, eyes riveted on each other.

When he sucks, I feel the pull down below my naval. There's nothing but him.

It's only a few seconds, but everything changes. Then someone turns the world back on.

Giggling hysterically, Kimmy goes for the bowl. Springing into action, I shout and whirl, lifting it over my head. For a minute, David and I play a dangerous game of Keep Away.

"This may not end well," I say breathlessly, stretching on tiptoe to pass the ceramic mixing bowl once more over his leaping sister.

"Then maybe it shouldn't end." He's really got the most beautiful smile in the world, but his eyes are serious. My breath hitches— there's not enough of it.

"Every beginning has an ending," I say.

He scoffs. "Bad song lyrics. And who's to say anything ends. Forever is now."

Kimmy jostles me, and I nearly drop the bowl. David's words are jumping in my head like Kimmy hopping around the kitchen. Taking advantage of my momentary confusion, David snatches the bowl away from me. Once it's in his hands, he spins it like a basketball—

Kimmy and I shriek—

But David does nothing more than deliver it to the kitchen table. Then he heads out of the room, saying, "Call me before they cool down, okay? I like the chips melty."

Melty. I sink into a chair, not sure what exactly I'm feeling, then startle as David pokes his head around the doorframe.

"Oh, Kimmy," he calls. "You've got batter on your face."

She lunges toward him and they race outside.

A second later, Kimmy's high-pitched squeals echo through the yard—

Splash!

UNDERTOW

DAVID

Scooping her up from the kitchen chair is so easy, I almost feel sorry. Her hair smells deliciously of cookies.

"You're soaking me! Stop! Let me at least change back into my suit!"

But that would defeat the purpose and we both know it.

There's something about seeing Cate riled that's so satisfying. Like I'm not the only one off my mark. I let my wet hair drip onto her face. She struggles to get away.

Kimmy is still in the pool with all her clothes on. I toss Cate in, then jump after her.

She flounders up out of the water and grabs my shoulders, as if she's strong enough to push me down. I play along and let her sink me, pulling her under in the process. The water's cold from last night's rain.

Our eyes are open. Cate's are bright, nearly the same color as the turquoise walls of the pool. Her cheeks puff out, and my mouth opens in a laugh. Hers does too. The air bubbles rise together.

Bending my knees, I pull her onto my watery lap. She doesn't resist. Her back is against my chest. Her wet, jean-clad hips nestled against mine. Her neck is within kissing distance.

Kimmy cannonballs in.

Cate wriggles out of my arms.

We meet on the surface, both of us breathless.

GUITARS
CATE

Cal pulls up in a white Volvo and gets his guitar out of the backseat.

"You made it," I say, smiling.

"I did." He hands me a sheaf of sheet music and I shuffle through it. It's all duets. A dozen pieces arranged for two guitars. Some of the pieces are familiar, but some are not.

That's because they're by Cal.

"Wait, you composed these? When? When did you start writing?"

He looks down in that way that he has. But then he looks back up and meets my gaze. His eyes go bright, and for the millionth time I wonder how such dark eyes can even *be* bright. It's like he has a laugh trapped inside of him. Then he kisses me quickly on the lips.

"Let's go inside," he says.

My heart gives an extra thump as I lead him up to my room. Along the way I offer him coffee, tea, water. He just shakes his head, his dark hair swinging.

I walk into my room in front of him, then turn back to see him standing just inside the doorway, looking around. In his jeans and white T-shirt he looks so . . . normal.

But I know he's not. He's brilliant. By the looks of those pieces, maybe even a genius.

He lays his guitar case down and, for a minute, we just look at each other. I swallow.

"Let's play," he says, then crouches and unclasps the latches on his guitar case.

My cheeks grow hot. Ducking out of the room, I grab another straight-backed chair from down the hall, thinking inexplicably of Chapel Hill Road, picturing how one side is fenced-in fields while the other is untouched tenebrous woods. I'm filled with a strange energy, like I've had too much coffee.

But then we start playing, and any attraction, any sense of our new awkwardness, anything at all, and everything disappears.

We skip lunch at Caffeine Scene. Skip the Dey Estate.

"I'm resisting the urge to kneel at your feet," I say after we play through the duets.

Cal just looks down, possibly at his feet, and shakes his head. But then he looks at me, a slight scowl on his forehead, a small smile on his lips, as if he's trying to figure something out.

He says, "I can think of better places for you to be."

I don't know what to say. So I run my set for him. He gives me some new ideas, and I run it again. This time he stops me when he has a suggestion to make.

There are moments, as I try to articulate his ideas, when I feel nervous. Moments when I feel put out, by the way he tells me to finger something or use a different inversion of a chord I'm already comfortable with. Sometimes he plays a line or two, to show me what he means.

Sometime around sunset, he tells me he's starving. Reluctantly, I nod. I want to keep going, want to master the new, minute changes that are making all the difference. My ideas weren't *wrong*, but his are better.

He senses my frustration. "Sometimes you have to think outside the box, break a few rules." He pulls me out of my chair. "That's the only way to find your voice."

But until he says this, I hadn't realized my voice was what I was looking for.

STARS

CATE

"So where'd you get the new wheels?" I ask as we drive through the fading daylight to a seafood restaurant in the Highlands.

"Why, you still need driving lessons?"

"Well . . ."

Cal laughs. "It's fine with me, but you'll have to ask my uncle, seeing as it's his car."

"He'd probably be cool with it."

"He probably would be. The next time I'm home, we'll give it a go."

We ride in silence for a few minutes, and I think about how Cal lives with his uncle but doesn't, since he's always away at school. Not for the first time, I wonder about his mother.

But then Cal flicks on the radio, and we're talking about music, and it's all that matters.

Out on the wooden deck of the restaurant, tables thump against each other as the wind rises. In the summer, tourists tie their boats up at the dock and sit outside, but off-season, it's just locals in a half-filled dining room. The walls are hung with fishing nets, and the corner where we sit is strung with tiny white lights. The tablecloth is covered with paper. I ask for crayons.

Cal's eyes actually sparkle now, like some boy from a book. We try to outdraw each other, and as I color, I feel able to speak more freely than I usually do. I talk about my family.

As he has before, Cal wonders how my parents can be so wildly successful yet so unhappy. I tell him I don't know. But the way he's phrased it tonight, *wildly successful yet so unhappy*, reminds me suddenly not of my parents, but of Mr. and Mrs. Bennet.

I draw the row of oaks that runs along Chapel Hill Road, and Cal, who's been talking excitedly about a Julian Bream recording, falls silent, frowning at the long line of trees.

"It was an accident," I confess into the quiet that has come between us for the first time since the car ride over. "Me, I mean. My parents never wanted kids. Did I ever tell you that?"

"No. But they're happy they had you, I bet. They must love you."

"Sure. My mom never says it, though. Which is fine. I don't think it would mean much coming from her at this point. We hardly spend any time together—she doesn't know me anymore. Maybe she never did. Besides, it doesn't mean anything, to just *say* 'I love you.'"

Cal looks at me quizzically.

"It's what you *do*, right? And how can you do anything to show someone you love them if you haven't taken the time to actually know them? I remember one Christmas she gave me a diary. I'd never expressed any interest in writing, so later I asked her why she'd given it to me.

"She said, 'You're always so still, so contemplative.' What she meant was, 'You sit around doing a whole lot of nothing, Cate Reese.'" I laugh.

"But she was right," Cal says. "About the writing. She does know you. You've always carried a notebook around, ever since I can remember. You had one with you at the intensive, always. You have that whole shelf full of them in your room."

"But that's the extent of my writing. Incomplete journal entries, band reviews for blogs I never submit. Bad poems. More and more often I'm jotting down music. A melodic line, a chord progression. I think it's because, more and more often, I feel like words don't work."

"That's because you're a musician. And unless you learn to read minds—"

"Words are inadequate. They're flat, you know? It's not what someone says, it's what's *behind* what they say. Or in addition to what they say. Or, like I said before, what they *do*."

"I don't know . . . I like words. I use them quite frequently." Cal smiles, and I jump in.

"See? *That* is what I'm talking about—a smile is the perfect example. A smile can mean—or imply—even more than a bunch of words, more than what someone is actually saying. Or a smile can mean something in *addition* to what someone says. Or it can mean the opposite."

"Your thing with words," Cal's saying now, "did you ever think that's why you turned to music?"

"Maybe. I just wish I could . . . master words. I want them to *fit* what I actually mean. Want everyone's words to fit what they mean."

"Sounds like you're talking about honesty, or the lack of it. Or authenticity. Maybe I'll start writing stuff down, like you do. That pile of notebooks in your room—"

"Will be great bonfire fuel someday."

"That's not what I was going to say!" Cal laughingly objects. His hair swings forward as he leans toward me. He tucks it back behind his ears. "I was going to say, you probably have a million great song lyrics there." He taps on the back of my right hand. I'm holding a red crayon.

"*Pff.* I doubt that. But—" I look down at his hand next to mine and draw a heart. "You never know."

When we get in the car, Cal tells me he's glad I like the duets so much and that he's got the perfect gig for us. He pulls out his phone.

"You're just going to call? Don't you have to send something? A press kit? CD?"

"Not for this." He looks down, and the smooth curtain of his hair slides forward, dark as the sky outside the car windows. Again, he hooks it back behind his ears. "Only because I've played Fusion before."

"I've never been there, where is it?"

"Brooklyn," he says, searching his contacts.

"Isn't it kind of late to call?"

"Club owners, musicians, we're all part of a strange breed. We never sleep, you must know that." He taps the screen. "You'll really like this place. It's a music mash-up. Jazz, singer-songwriters, bands, classical players like us—everyone plays there."

He doesn't put the call on speaker, instead he tips the phone toward me and I lean in. His head brushes mine, and we smile at each other as the woman on the other end of the line tells Cal she remembers him. She says sure, she has a slot for him and a friend, *for us*. She tells him he can have as many friends as he wants sit in, but more importantly, he needs to fill the room.

Cal frowns when she says this, looks serious, which reminds me of how he looked the last time I saw him onstage. A little thrill goes through me as I picture the way he plays, with such control. Now I look at his hand holding the phone, his slender fingers. I imagine what they might feel like, touching me. I picture him touching my cheek, maybe, and looking at me the way he did when I was playing earlier. *He speaks my language. Speaks it better than me.*

After setting a date and time, Cal hits "End," and just like I'd imagined, he touches me.

Well, my hair. He tucks a strand of it behind my ear, the same way he does with his own.

Then he starts talking about music again.

I've never known someone like Cal—someone like *me*—who spends hours a day practicing, someone who's basically built a life around music. Sure, I've known Marion's other students, and everyone *likes* music. Some people even love it, but that's not the same.

The image of David Bennet scrolling through his iPod pops into my head—but I dismiss it. Dismiss him. He could never get me the way Cal does. He's not a musician.

Cal smiles now and his eyes do that bright thing. "So we're set," he says.

But I'm not really thinking we're set for the gig. I'm thinking, we're *a* set, like a pair. I'm thinking he's perfect, and that we're perfect together, and that the slow crawl of attraction is speeding up.

But suddenly I realize how late it is. And although it's a Saturday night and my curfew is rarely enforced, in some strange realignment of the planets, my parents are both home tonight.

"Crap."

"What is it?" Cal asks.

"Your car's about to turn into a pumpkin."

"Oh yeah? What about your gown?"

"Shredded rags."

"Shredded rags?" We're pulling onto Route 36, but despite that, Cal looks over at me. "Sounds okay."

Then he puts a hand on my knee.

He's perfect. We're perfect together, but even though I've imagined him touching me, now that he is, I—

"You've got really bright eyes," I blurt.

"Bright?"

"Bright. Like stars."

"Wow, thanks, you mean, *star* stars?"

My cheeks heat, yet still I start to say yes— but the word gets snatched away by the night as Cal rolls down his window, tilting his head to the side now, so he can see out and up to the sky.

"Any stars up there?" he calls over the wind and the road noise.

Then he stops looking for stars and glances at me. The rushing air whips his hair around.

"You said your mom never tells you she loves you, that she doesn't know you."

"That's right."

"Do you think it would mean something if someone else said it?"

"Said what?" The wind gusts around my ears. Cal's driving too fast.

"I love you." He glances over at me again with those dark-yet-somehow-bright eyes, his words hanging between us, swaying in the wind.

I think of this afternoon, how I'm so much more prepared for my concert now, because of him. I think of the warm palm, cool fingertip feel of his hand as he pulled me from my chair, and how at dinner, he cared enough to listen to me talk about my mom. And all of a sudden I want to tell him, want to say, "Yes, the stars are out tonight. They're in your eyes. And—I love you, too."

But I can't *say* that. It would be weird. We've never even really kissed—I can't just say "I love you," the way he did. Plus, he doesn't mean it—he's only asking me a question.

Still, for a second, I know I've cheated him, cheated us. I'm playing by the rules, but sometimes, like Cal said, you've got to break the rules. We're musicians. Artists. Should we live by the same rules as everyone else? We're *alive*, shouldn't we be able to make our own rules?

"Cate!" Cal shouts above the wind. "Did you see that? Did you see that shooting star?"

We're on Chapel now, with its white fences running along one side of the road. The car dips down into the hollow and my stomach drops. And I so wish I'd said it—at least the part about the stars being in his eyes. But I don't have the courage. I can't even bring myself to tell him to close the window, even though I'm cold, because it seems really . . . unadventurous. I should tell him, though, that he's driving way too fast.

"Damn." Cal jerks the wheel of the Volvo and adrenaline shoots through me. The upturned tail of a deer is a white blur, vanishing into

the miles of woods that run along the opposite side of the road. "Sorry about that."

"It's okay," I say.

But it's not, because now another deer *leaps* out of the woods, onto the road—

"Another one," Cal shouts. "Another shooting star—"

"Cal!" Somehow my voice is both a whisper and a scream.

Then we're sliding— fast and slow at the same time.

Wide as a wall, a massive oak tree looms up in front of us.

This can't happen. I'm just getting it.

My whole life is trapped in my throat.

Cal yanks the wheel—

GLASS
CATE

Gravity
fails
Sound detonates
Smashed
stars (Stars!)!
all over me
All
over.

PART II: FALL

NIGHT

DAVID

The invasive spotlight at the back of the house hasn't registered my presence. Standing in the dark, I look up at the starred sky.

So bright tonight, the stars seem close enough to touch. Then I blink, and they're back where they belong—distant and definitely out of reach.

The pool lights are on. The water glows green. Its surface is both inviting and alien.

Just as I'm considering stripping off my clothes and slipping in, my father appears in silhouette at the back door. As he steps outside, the sensor kicks on. Light shoots across the yard like a flash flood, spotlighting him as he strides in my direction.

If this were a race, fast as the light is, it would lose.

The sharp and startling sound of the screen door snapping shut seems to be lagging behind as well. I only hear it as my father stops short at my side, creating the illusion that his arrival is accompanied by the sound of a slap. Also, he doesn't stop quite short enough. The same height as me, the same width—he is in my personal space. He means to be.

Inwardly, I berate myself for not telling him, for taking the coward's way.

He squints in the glare of the artificial light that has extinguished the stars in the space of a breath and, all at once, seems bright enough to supply a road crew with enough illumination to build a highway at midnight. The light is as intrusive as the blinding bulb of an inquisitorial lamp, and my father seems to realize this, because now he shifts suddenly so that the white glare pierces my eyes instead of his.

"I spoke with Dean Thomas today." His voice comes from behind his teeth.

Even though I knew what this was going to be about, my supper turns to stone in my stomach. Despite that, for a fleeting moment I have the urge to ask if Dean Thomas is still in Gryffindor, or if he's gone over to Hufflepuff, where I'd always believed he belonged. But my father wouldn't get the joke, and in this case, Dean isn't a first name.

My father's talking about the head of St. Lawrence, where I was to go on a full scholarship next fall. St. Lawrence, the college of his choice. St. Lawrence, his alma mater. The same institution of higher learning I recently phoned to say I would not be arriving at next September as planned. No, not because of the injuries I sustained on the trip, but because—

I'm sorry, it's just not a fit for me.

I'm not a fit for me.

This last thought is an epiphany, flares in my brain now, like the sudden burst of sensor light that blew the night apart. A projectile pyrotechnic I can feel in my body, this urgent revelation is a fuse flashing color, flashing warning red behind my eyes.

"Did you *hear* what I *said*, David? I spoke with Dean Thomas today!"

Stunned as I am, I'm well trained, so other than saying, "Yes, sir, I heard you," I hold my tongue.

He, however, does not. His abusive words fall like lashes.

"Are you really that much of an *idiot*? Can you possibly be so *stupid*?"

Without answering his questions, I take a step back. I need to think.

But there's no time. It happens fast.

Out of the darkness, his fist hits me hard in the face.

Like that, I'm on the ground. I feel with my fingers. My lower lip is split, near the corner. The bruises I can hide, but this—as a child he bullied me, and in the last year or so he's shaken me, shoved me. He's punched me in the arm, the stomach, the kidneys.

But he has never made me bleed.

Now he yanks me to my feet—*one blow, two*—and takes me down again.

Standing over me, he runs a hand back through his hair, as though knocking me to the ground is simply a form of exercise for him. I want to shout up at him, "Right! Way to keep yourself in shape. The shape of the bastard you are."

But I can't. My brain has shut off. And even if I could, I wouldn't. I'm shaking. This is a new low—or maybe just a different variety of low. Whatever it is, it's confusing. Scary.

So instead of saying anything, I climb to my feet, one hand on the back of my head, feeling the lump already rising from where I hit the ground. I'm breathing hard.

So is my father. The white light behind him renders him a dark form, eyes glinting with a challenge.

For a brief moment I'm tempted to rise to it, to take a swing at him. But this is just one of a million thoughts tumbling through my head, part of a landslide, an avalanche. He's changed the rules of engagement. I need to get my balance on this shifting ground.

My sense of humor recovers first. I consider offering him a Gatorade. Next I consider asking if he could wait a while before he uses me as a punching bag again because I'm still healing. Finally, I consider stealing one of his precious cars. But I'm not sure what I'd do once I was behind the wheel, and that scares me more than he does.

My father's neck muscles stand out, taut cords above a white collar, red tie. He narrows his eyes—always a sign. *There's more where that came from, boy.* So again, I remain silent while he studies me with a critical eye, the way he does after he's pushed me around, making sure he hasn't roughed me up to the point where someone will notice.

His eyes widen slightly when his gaze falls on my lip—

Then he laughs, buddy-punches me in the arm. "Better put some ice on that, then go to your room. Wouldn't want your sisters to know what a clumsy young man you are, would we?"

As familiar as everything is—the yard, the glow-stick green of the pool—it's all strange and surreal.

This time, my silence is a problem.

My father's chest seems to expand as he takes a step toward me. "Would we?" he repeats softly. He is an animal, coiled.

Head throbbing, lower lip numb. I swallow. Taste blood.

"No, sir." My heart is kicking in my chest. *No.*

ANTISEPTIC

CATE

"I need to get *out*," I scream, feet kicking toward the doors at the back of the ambulance.

Next to me, a young man wearing a white jacket gets a needle ready.

"I don't think so," an older man on the other side of me says to him. His hair is gray, his skin papery. He's also wearing a white jacket. Now he adds, "Not yet."

"But she's hysterical," protests the one with the needle.

He can't be much older than me. He's just a boy, a boy with a sharp-looking needle.

"Keep that away from me! I'm fine. Where's Cal? Where's the boy who was driving?"

"You don't want that in her if she goes into shock."

"I'm not going to go into shock," I shout. "He's bleeding, the driver, you left him!"

"Did someone call her folks?" the older one asks. I may as well not exist.

"They called the number on her cell that said 'Home,'" Needle Boy says. "No answer."

"Turn *around*!" My voice twines with the sound of the siren. "You've got the *wrong person*!" I tug at the straps holding me securely to the gurney. "Listen to me. The driver. The boy who was in the car, where you found me?" Only, I don't remember them finding me, don't remember what happened, except—

Cal. His face. Blood.

Who are these guys?

I must have said it out loud, because the old man replies, "Emergency medical technicians."

"Volunteers," says the kid.

"I know *that*," I snarl. I'm very close to freaking out. It's a new feeling. A scary feeling. Twisting this way and that, I whimper, "These straps are too tight."

"Miss, you need to try and relax. We're almost at the hospital."

My stomach spins sickeningly.

Cal is in another ambulance. That's what it is. He's safe; he'll be fine.

The ambulance finally stops. When Needle Boy opens the door, I smell the ocean, salty and feral. We're at Monmouth Medical by the beach.

As soon as the older EMT unstraps me, I jump out of the back of the ambulance.

"Hey!" the younger guy shouts. "Hold on. You need to be checked—"

But I run toward the red letters that read "EMERGENCY" and hit a button beside the doors. Nothing happens. The EMTs' voices carry over to me as I jab the button, again and again. I no longer smell the sea. I smell my own sweat. The odor is unfamiliar, strangely bitter. The smell of fear.

"Let her go. You did your job. She's here."

"But that car was totaled." The young guy's voice is tight with anxiety. "She might—"

"None of the blood on that girl belongs to her," the older man says. "Trust me, you can't help her. No one in there's gonna make a difference, either. I've been doing this a long time. She *knows* what happened. Just can't face it. And when she does . . . nobody'll be able to take away that hurt. No medicine for it. Not on this earth."

The goddamn doors finally slide open. My nostrils fill with the scent of antiseptic and air-conditioning, with citrus and alcohol—

I shake myself awake.

OAK
CATE

The rhythmic words form themselves.

The trio of girls circles the tree that brushes the sky that buckles my knees.

Buckles them so badly I can scarcely stand. I lean on my bike.

It took only a few minutes to ride here, because the tree—this massive oak with so many objects already pinned and nailed to it that it appears positively festive—is not far from my house. In fact, it is horribly close, less than a half mile away.

Finally, I've come, but now, I'm stuck. Stranded on the other side of Chapel, unable to make it across the street to where the tree stands firmly rooted, unmoving and majestic.

I stare at the ring of half-burned candles round the foot of the tree, stare at the girls, and stare at the tree itself. The tree that stands in front of me, yet also lies across my heart where it fell with the sound of ripping metal.

This is the tree that totaled the car that killed the boy that Cate loved. That Cate was too stupid to tell that she loved, too scared and too worried to say that she loved.

"The House That Jack Built," that's the nursery rhyme, the singsong cadence eerily skipping through my head.

The three girls step slowly round the tree. They wear identical navy blazers with crests on the pockets and short plaid skirts. They must be friends of Cal's. Good friends or school friends, I'll never know. I'll never know if Cal studied with them, or kissed them, or took them on unexpected musical journeys in search of their voices—but they're searching now, or at least it looks that way. And I want to tell them they will not find Cal Woods here. I want to tell them their pilgrimage is misguided.

Cal is dead. Not gone. Not missing. Dead. I need to face it. But I can't.

I'm sorry. We're closing storybook land early today. The house that Jack built has been obliterated. We will reopen never. Have a happy ever after!

Mother Goose. Motherfucker. This tree is alive, and Cal is dead.

The girls crane long, graceful necks. Bend at their hips to read the letters and cards that cover the tree like wrapping paper. Daisy chains twine round the rough bark, potted mums sit among the tree's twisty roots. One of the girls gives me a little wave. My stomach lurches, and I want to scream, "It's too late—he's gone. You won't find him. You won't see him or hear him play ever again. He was beside me and then he was just blood, just gone."

He'd looked at me. He'd looked at me and said, "Another one! Another shooting star—"

Then the world exploded.

Now he's dead because of me, because I wouldn't open my mouth and say "Slow down."

Two simple words.

Cal Woods. *Cal.*

I want to rip the bark from the tree. Wear it like a shroud.

The Killing Tree. Cars drive by it, not knowing, one after the other. Each car preceded by the sound of an engine, followed by a shush. There is no scream. No tearing metal. No crash, even though all the cars seem to be going too fast.

It seems wrong, to just ride right up to the towering oak, so finally, I throw my bike down on somebody's lawn. The back wheel is still spinning when I cross over and stand in the tree's shadow.

I hadn't realized just how much stuff is nailed to it—I swing my gaze away. It catches on the long white wooden horse fence running parallel to the road.

"Rest in Paradise. We will love you forever."

My fingers fly to my mouth. Words cover the flat white boards of the fence.

"We will never forget you."

"Cal, I wish I hadn't been so angry with you. If you were here, I'd take those words back."

"Watch over us, Cal, we won't forget you, man. You were my best friend."

"Cal, this isn't fair. You were the best boy with the prettiest eyes ever, xxoo, Lisa."

"Man this sucks. We miss you! MC."

"Cal, you were my best friend. I wish we could go back to the beach and talk for hours the way we used to. Love you forever, friend. Stevo."

"Cal, I didn't know you, but my son did. I hope you two are playing guitar in heaven. Mr. Z."

A lump forms in my throat, a flimsy dam that bursts as the last message blurs before my eyes:

"Stay Lifted Up."

Sobbing, I turn away— but there is the tree itself.

It's covered with photographs the weather is already ruining and cut flowers—wrapped in cellophane, tied with ribbon—that are dying.

A plastic rosary that looks like it might glow in the dark hangs from a nail. There's a hammer near the base of the tree, along with a whole bag of rusty nails, left for anyone else who wants to hang something on the already crowded memorial.

Circling the tree, I find more photos safely tucked into clear plastic bags. My legs quiver.

A pair of sneakers, a hoodie from Sutton Prep, empty cigarette packs—two of them. Did Cal smoke? I'd never seen him smoking, never smelled cigarettes on him, but . . . my eyes flicker back to the fence. How can there be so many things about Cal I didn't know?

Now my gaze travels down to the place where the bark has been ripped away from the trunk of the tree, and there, written on the smooth inner layer of the wood, are more words.

"Luv U 4-Ever. Don't leave us. Leah."

I keep waiting to wake up from this nightmare, but it's not happening.

"You are gone from this place but never from my heart. Christina."

There's more, but I have to stop. Have to stop reading. Stop thinking.

A black backpack hangs from the branches of the tree, one of those cloth ones that shops give away at grand openings. It makes me think of a bat, or a black ghost, the way it's stretched out between branches, and I ponder its significance. Up high near the backpack, a package of guitar strings is attached to the tree with a screw. Below that is an 8x10 of Cal.

The picture is in one of those glass frames without any kind of edge or border. It is pristine. The early autumn winds and rain have not touched it. In the photo, Cal is wearing a white button-down and a tie. It's a school picture—recent—Cal's last school picture ever. I gaze into Cal's nearly black, but somehow bright, eyes. He looks like he's about to laugh or say something.

"Tell me," I whisper.

But I was the one who should have told him something, who should have said, "The stars are in your eyes—I love you."

Would he have pulled over? Would I have touched him, run my fingers through his hair? What if we'd stopped and spent a minute looking in each other's eyes? Would that have been the same minute that tore Cal from this world?

Next to the pots of flowers that rest among the twisted tree roots is a plastic container. The faded words on the lid read: "You have suffered a great loss. Please feel free to take some of these. We hope it will help you."

Already, hope fills me as I crouch down—

But as I'm about to pull the lid off the bucket, I realize it's full of literature from a religious organization. Words from the fence flash through my brain—

"Rest in Paradise." Does anyone really believe that's where Cal is?

Sinking back on my heels, I picture my dad, scowling and grousing about the Catholic Church, how they're all about money, how they take away people's freedom, their choices.

But there'd been that moment of hope, when I'd read the words on top of the container, and I *want* that hope, I cling to the feeling now, even as it fades.

And then, just like that, the hope is gone. Cal is *gone*, and I wish, wish, *wish* that when he'd put his hand on my knee I'd said, "Pull over. Pull over and kiss me."

A dangling cross spins slowly on a brass chain, glinting in the golden light. Next to it, someone has tied a bundle of Magic Markers. But I don't reach for the markers, or the cross.

Tear after tear rolls down my face, and I feel like I might never come out of this crouch, might never get back up. I want to curl into a ball, stay under this tree. Dissolve into the dirt.

I don't know how to get through something like this, but the answer isn't in a plastic bucket. It's not at the tip of a marker.

I feel my face contorting, sobs jerking through me. *I want to go home.*

But—I *am* home. My house is just down the road. *So what is this feeling?*

I just . . . I thought we had time. How can this be real?

"Help me," I mouth to no one.

DRAFT
DAVID

From: David Bennet <dbstealshome@gmail
.com>
To: Cate Reese <lovecatcate@gmail.com>
Date: Oct 1, 2013, at 7:14 PM
Subject:

Hey Cate, I heard you were in a car accident.
I also heard that you're okay, but it must have
been

SAVE THIS MESSAGE AS A DRAFT?
THIS MESSAGE HAS NOT BEEN SENT AND CONTAINS UNSAVED CHANGES.
YOU CAN SAVE IT AS A DRAFT TO WORK ON LATER.

DON'T SAVE—CANCEL—SAVE

From: David Bennet <dbstealshome@gmail.com>
To: Cate Reese <lovecatcate@gmail.com>
Date: Oct 2, 2013, at 11:43 PM
Subject: Hope you're feeling all right.

Hi Cate,

Haven't seen you around school since you were in that accident. Not even in the cafeteria. Guess our schedules are totally opposite. Or maybe you're a vampire and don't eat.

Maybe you're taking some time off, I don't know, but I haven't seen you in a few days and apparently you haven't returned my mother's calls, so, just wanted to make sure you're okay. Don't know when you're coming over to babysit. Maybe you're not up for that, but Kimmy misses you. I miss you.

Call, will you? Or answer this. Or text. Send a howler. Something. Anything. xx, DB

SAVE THIS MESSAGE AS A DRAFT?
THIS MESSAGE HAS NOT BEEN SENT AND CONTAINS UNSAVED CHANGES.
YOU CAN SAVE IT AS A DRAFT TO WORK ON LATER.

DON'T SAVE—CANCEL—SAVE

PINE
CATE

"The second thing to remember is that our relationship with our dead Christian loved ones isn't dissolved by death—we pray for our dead in case they are in purgatory for a time, and ask them to pray for us."

"*'In case they're in purgatory for a time'*? What the *hell*?" Laurel whispers. "Is that supposed to make anyone feel better?"

We're sitting so close I can smell her perfume. Closing my eyes, I breathe it in, trying to block out the sickeningly sweet scent of lilies that fills the church. Resisting the urge to bury my face in her shoulder, I hold her hand so tightly the ring on my middle finger presses painfully into my skin.

"And the first thing?" Her angry whisper hisses in my ears. "Were we supposed to catch that?"

I find her ferocity strangely soothing. My parents, my friends in the city—the one or two I've told—their feather-soft sympathy only makes me feel worse.

"No idea," I say, stealing a glance around the church. I've never been to a Catholic Mass. Everyone is sitting impossibly still. But stillness is gone from me forever. I cross my legs. Uncross them. Recross them. It feels like my blood itches. Smoke rises from a swinging censer. Everyone seems to know when to sit and when to stand. All I know is I want to run.

Afterward, at Cal's uncle's, a plate of food I can't possibly eat is pressed into my hands by someone I don't know, and I'm backed into a corner. I try not to stare at Cal's mother, whom—unbelievably—I've never met, and who, I'm pretty sure, was not at the church. She wears no makeup and her feet are bare. Her long black hair is loose and the same shiny black as Cal's. I just know that, if I were to touch it, it would feel like silk. Feel like his. She's beautiful.

Cal's mother has the precise movements of a classically trained musician, which she is, and which is why Cal lives—

Lived.

Which is why Cal *lived* with his uncle. Cal's father left when he was small, and that, Cal had told me, was the reason for his mother's relentless touring. She never got over it.

As she circulates through the room, Mrs. Woods does not cry, and although I don't catch everything she's saying, I hear a few words here and there. Her slight Chinese accent makes me think of birdsong. Just watching her makes me feel better.

But I am in a corner. Murmuring voices, the sound of clinking forks and knives, people passing glasses—I need to get outside.

Cal usually came to my house whenever we managed to get together, so I'm not that familiar with his uncle's place, but then I remember the den. Making my way through the throngs, I slip into the empty room and jerk open the French doors— but there are dogs everywhere it seems, on the patio, in the yard. I don't know who they belong to, but they bar my way with snarls and thin dog lips pulled back over sharp-looking dog teeth.

Someone grabs my sleeve, yanks me back inside, slams the doors shut.

"Watch it, Cate Cat, those things ain't show dogs." Laurel crouches down, pushes her nose against the glass. She bares her teeth in imitation of the beasts and they bark. One dog begins to howl. Laurel howls back.

This strikes me as weirdly hilarious.

"Come on!" Laurel growls at the dogs. "Tell me how you *really* feel."

The dogs go crazy, jumping at the glass. I know she's being cruel, but the chorus of dogs is just so funny that I finally let out a little howl of my own. "'Angelheaded hipsters burning for the ancient heavenly connection to the starry dynamo in the machinery of night.'"

Laurel stands up. "Finished that drink I gave you earlier, huh?"

"Yeppers. What was in it?"

"You don't want to know. But you feel better, right? You must if you're quoting your dad."

"Not my dad. Allen Ginsberg. 'Howl.'"

"Yeah, well, I knew it had something to do with your dad. It's one of those whack recordings he listens to while he paints, right? How about you, make any masterpieces lately?"

She's referring to the time we sampled a dozen bottles from my parents' liquor cabinet, then went into the barn and helped ourselves to Dad's paints and blank canvases. We swore we were making great art. It was the only time in my life Dad got really mad at me, less about the booze, I think, and more about the art, or rather, lack thereof.

Hoping he wouldn't realize just how many canvases we'd ruined, Laurel had gotten Grace to drive over, and we'd loaded up the back of the Ridgeways' SUV, then driven to the 7-Eleven on the outskirts of Red Bank. There we dumped our artistic efforts and Grace made us drink massive amounts of coffee.

Thinking about it now makes me laugh. I try to stifle the sound, but it hiccups out.

"Yeah, you know what I'm talking about." Laurel gives me a conspiratorial look, and suddenly it's just the two of us. I can tell her now. I swallow my laughter.

"Laurel, I need to tell you something."

"Anything," she says, her smile fading.

"I think . . . I was in love with him. I mean, I know I told you, texted you that night, but . . ." I pause as the priest's words whisper in my head: *For he created all things that they might be.*

With difficulty, I continue. "I know it now. In a different way. I was—I *am* in love with him."

"Aw, Cate." Laurel slings her arm around my shoulders, and I sag against her.

Even though she's my age, I've always seen Laurel as the older sister I never had. But right now I feel older. Ancient.

Holding on to each other, we take a few shuffling steps over to a small velvet love seat and plop down. Her face is so full of sympathy—I start crying again.

"I was going to tell him to slow down," I say tearfully. "You know me, 'safety first.'"

"Yeah, that is you," she admits quietly. "But it wasn't your fault—"

"It is! I should have said something. I *knew* we were going too fast, but I didn't want him to think I was—I don't know. Boring. He was so *amazing*, just the way he thought, about music. Laurel, I've known him since I was *four years old*, what am I going to do? How can I—" I take a shuddering breath. "The intensive, that's when everything started to change. Oh, Laurel."

Laurel nods slowly, pursing her lips like she's trying to make sense of something. "You guys really did click. You obviously liked him a lot . . . you were friends for a long time."

"My whole life!" Fresh sobs rack my body, and I have a horrible weightless feeling, like I'm a kite and someone's cut the line and I'm sickeningly free in a too-big sky. Like the time Laurel and I took kayaks into the ocean and I got dizzy because we were out so far and the water went on forever and there was nothing but deep blue beneath me—I wasn't attached to anything.

Also, I feel drunk. Drunk, yet different than drunk, from whatever Laurel put in my drink. But that blurry feeling works—it's the spinning off into a too-big space feeling I can't deal with. So I stuff it down now, bury it with everything else I can't handle, with that night, in the car.

Laurel strokes my hair. Time ticks by, I don't know how much—I hate time now. Time is a horrible, misleading thing. You don't know when it will come apart, when it will be up.

Finally she says, "Everything's going to be okay, Cate, and . . . I think you should feel better just knowing . . . Cal loved you."

"But *why*? He was so talented, so brilliant! And I'm just—"

"You're not *just* anything," Laurel says fiercely. "Not just *anyone*. God, Cate, why is it so hard for you to believe that people are into you? You're *you*. And that's why Cal liked you. Because of who you are. I know you guys had the music thing, but he was into *you*."

But I can't help feeling she's wrong. The wrongness jostles for a place inside me next to the pain—pain that simultaneously makes me feel like I'm hungry, and like I can't eat.

All those years—*he made me want to play*. I'd never be as good as him, we both knew it, but I tried, and he encouraged me, because we were friends, but mostly, *because of the music*.

"I'm canceling it," I say now to Laurel. "Canceling the gig."

"Your concert in the city? The Strings with Wings thing?"

"No, I—I have to play that show." *Do I, though? How can I?* Right now I can't even imagine picking up a guitar. But I don't say those things. I just tell Laurel about the gig Cal booked in Brooklyn. "But there's no way—"

"Cate," Laurel interrupts. "You don't have to think about that right now."

But I do need to think about it, and I need to cancel, because I'm not going to play that date. Because why? All these years, I was trying to keep up with Cal. Yes, I played because I wanted to; I played for me. But even more, maybe, *I played for him*. He—was my muse.

KETAMINE
CATE

Sitting on the bed, I stare down at the little packet in my palm. One bump. I don't even need to take it all, just mix some into a glass of juice, like Laurel did at Cal's uncle's house.

Thanks, Laurel. You're a Lovecat.

Something moves outside the window. A tree branch. It's so dark out tonight.

Dark inside, too. Inside my head.

I run a finger over the packet. The way the paper is folded makes it look like a miniature envelope. Laurel gave me a whole pile of them.

Where'd you get it? I'd asked.

Does it matter? Feel better, Cate Cat.

I picture now, inside the envelope, instead of white powder, there's a tiny letter, embossed with minuscule script. "You're invited," I imagine it says in a formal font, "to get the hell out of your life. RSVP—"

But there'd be no phone number, no date. Instead, it would simply say, "before you lose it."

Fine. I'll RSVP. Yanking open the bedside table drawer—where a dozen other tiny envelopes smile up at me—I grab a pen, and with a hard little laugh, write my name on the envelope in the fanciest writing I can manage.

Cate Reese

And for my date? My plus one?
Carefully now, I add:

No one.

CHARM

DAVID

I've been sitting in the cafeteria for less than a minute. Already, I'm surrounded.

Trish and Tammy strut by—separately—on their way out, glaring at each other, scowling at two freshman girls who've sat down on either side of me. Next to the girls are more girls, friends of the two who are bookending me I think, but I don't know. I don't know too many freshman girls. They all seem to know me.

The guys at the table are no mystery. Former teammates of mine, they're probably on the fence about whether they should be hanging out with me at this point.

Two of the guys look at the girls on either side of me, exchange knowing glances. They nod approvingly, as if they agree with something I've done, or am going to do.

I'm about to leave when the girl on my right, who is very pretty, puts a hand on my arm. Thinking she's about to ask me something, I remain seated.

But she doesn't ask a question, doesn't say anything at all. Just presses her thigh against mine under the table, while the girl on my left talks to her about an upcoming party.

Girls. Girls are the one thing that I do better than Jack. Than Jack did.

That's what Rod Whitaker calls it. "Doing girls."

"Hey, Bennet, wanna do girls today?"

The thing is, I've never needed Rod for this game, never even saw it as a game, really. I take girls very seriously. I'm indebted to them. They are the only things that remind me:

I'm not Jack.

Girls are the only things that make me, *me*. Or they were. I thought they were.

I just referred to girls as "things," twice. That is fucked up.

I'm fucked up. But that doesn't make me unique.

Jack was fucked up, too. Obviously. Or he wouldn't have killed himself.

Jack was everything, then suddenly nothing. Nowhere. Or somewhere. Depending on whom you ask. What you believe.

As far as Jack and girls, though, maybe it comes down to this: Jack was not . . . *sensitive*. Simply translated this means: he was not fluent in the language of girls. And I am. Or I can be. Apparently. Thus: girls.

My father, at least, painted Jack this way. "A strong, unbending boy," he'd say. For many years things went on this way, my father telling and retelling the legends of Jack.

But the diaries say something different.

I was thirteen when I found the stack . . . a veritable treasure trove of Jack.

I'd gone down to the basement, looking for a part, for the water rower, I think. Things had been moved around that day, as if someone else was searching, too.

The diaries were full of lyrics, none by Jack, but carefully copied. A collection of sorts, I guess—his favorites, all the songs he liked.

The lyrics alternated with other entries, pages written in Jack's neat hand. There were detailed accounts of track meets. Tennis matches. Even marching band. There were mathematical equations written down as well, movie reviews, and camping tips.

He wrote in bursts about these things, but the lyrics were the steady pulse, running through, between events and boring student council notes. A steady pulse at first, that is, that then became erratic. He was desperate, I think, toward the end. Wrote, "My head feels full of static."

Awkward dates, strained conversations, a girl who turned him down for prom. These were the last things he wrote about, these girls, and one line to our mom:

"I'm sorry, but it hurts too much. I love you."

I glance at the two girls beside me, one then the other. They jostle me gently now and again as they talk across me, ocean waves at low tide, eddying around a jetty. Their eyes flick up to my face, then away—scurrying sandpipers, like their smiles. They imagine I'm listening.

Girls like my manners, they like that I read. That I'm *sensitive*—that's what girls call it. When they call it anything. When they need an excuse for why they want to have sex with me.

I think girls want sex as much as guys do. But girls, for some reason, have to keep this a secret. It's an unspoken thing I can't fathom, but there it is. Any girl who lets that secret out? Gets branded by enemies, sometimes by friends. *Slut.* But no one calls me a name, except in jest.

Some girls think it's cool that I play—played—sports. Others like that I'm an AP student. A few girls I've dated are into money and know that my family's got big bucks. But mostly I think they just want to touch the muscles along my arms, my chest. Touch the ridges of my abdomen, look at my face—they talk a lot about my face. Then they say, "I love you." It makes them feel better.

"Our boy has charm," my father said one night, looking canny.

"What he's got, darling, are your good looks." My mother ran her fingers through my father's too-long-for-a-dad hair as she said this. She used to do that a lot. Touch him. But not in the same way girls touch me. More like clinging.

Later, when we were alone and my father had downed another drink, he said, "She didn't used to be so helpless, but after Jack . . . well. She's right about your looks, though, Son. They working for you yet? Mine always did."

He'd sized me up then, his eyes glinting in a way that made me feel uncomfortable. I smiled uncertainly. He laughed, swirling the drink in his hand. Then he poured himself another. Clink went the ice cubes. I was about fourteen at the time.

Not too long after, I found out what he meant. Found out I could be someone Jack hadn't been. That I could forget about Jack for a while. Forget about everything but skin on skin.

This belonged to me, this gift with girls, something I didn't have to work so hard at, like all the Being Jack stuff. Like with my entire imitation Jack life.

Here, finally, was something I was good at.

The pretty girl on my right reaches across me now. Takes a phone the other girl's offering. They both giggle as they lean into me. The girl on my right is offering more than a phone, and she wants me to know it. When the girl on my left sits back, the girl on my right does not.

She's wearing a scent that doesn't suit her. A woman's musky perfume. Still, her top is cut low, and when I look down, I see the shadowy promise between her breasts.

She looks up at me before I have a chance to look away. Now I feel her hand on my leg—noncommittal at first, then firmer when I don't object, and close, closer to my crotch.

My body responds—I hate myself. Adjusting my jeans, I stand— Her hand topples away.

Still she asks me, "Do you want to do something later?"
I scan the cafeteria for Cate Reese.

SWEAT

CATE

David Bennet's walking toward me, but he's not *here*, that's the only way to put it. He's not in this gym, not in this world. (And certainly not in this detention, because why? In what universe does David Bennet get a PE detention?) His head is down, and for some reason, I imagine he sees earth beneath his feet rather than the supershiny floor. Imagine he sees rocks, and dirt, and pine needles. That he sees Canada.

I'm not sure what gives me this idea, except . . . David makes me think of the outdoors, of woods and fields and . . . air.

His chest hitches up and down like he's been running, or trying to. Spots of color top his cheekbones. I might not have noticed except that the bones of his face are so prominent these days. I notice the faint shadow along his jawline as well now, and the smudges beneath his eyes. I notice his long lashes—

And the fact that we're staring at each other.

"What are *you* doing here?" He's clearly surprised, and for some reason, that gets me.

"Me? What about you? Aren't you supposed to be on a playing field somewhere scoring points for some Middleburn team?" My voice is too high. It sounds wrong. I'm overreacting. It's just—I feel strangely put out that he's here. I'd been thinking about Cal and trying to write—I don't know—something. I know he can't know that, but still I feel . . . naked.

"I quit the teams," he says softly. "I thought . . . you knew that."

And then, David Bennet blushes. I'm stupefied.

"Oh. Right. I did know." Of course I knew.

"No, I mean, why would you know?"

"Because I'm at your house practically every day?" *And because . . .* The afternoon light slants through windows set high on the walls, hitting his eyes. *Because of that, the golden spill of honey in your eyes. God, what's wrong with me?*

"You are," he says, "at my house a lot." His brow furrows, as if he's attempting to solve an unusually difficult problem, something I imagine is a rare thing for David Bennet, for whom everything seems to come easily. "But not lately."

"No, not lately." Lately is not something I want to think about. And maybe that's why the past rises unbidden, memories suddenly tumbling through me: *David lounging on the couch, or laughing on the phone. Playing football in the yard, the stretch of green beyond the pool. David in the kitchen, making Kimmy pancakes—handing me a plate, a CD, the remote. And those sunlit end-of-summer days . . .*

"Extra credit," he says suddenly, like he's just found the answer. "That's why I'm here."

"You need extra credit? You can't take it with you, you know."

David's smile fades.

"I mean, when you graduate," I say hastily. I don't want to talk to him about this, about Cal, about how all I can think of is dying. How it can just happen. But even my throwaway comments are laced with dark thoughts and death, like I can't keep it in.

"True," David says. "You can't." He's still looking down at me, only, it's like he's looking *into* me now. Like he's . . . searching. I fidget and see him take in my discomfort.

He smiles one of his David Bennet smiles. "Okay," he says. "That's not why I'm here. Although I figured if I clocked a few miles on the track Close and Henderson might let me off easy."

"Close *and* Henderson? Both of them gave you a detention?"

"Several."

"For what? You're their rock star."

"*Was* their rock star."

When he lifts his hands to push his hair back from his face, I notice his shirt is soaked with sweat. Close and Henderson may or may not let him off easy for whatever he's done, but David's obviously gone for a punishing run, and I want to ask why—why he insists on running when his leg can't possibly be up for it yet. Why he pushes himself to the point of pain.

"Okay . . . so, what did you do?" *Besides quit the team, all the teams, all the clubs.*

"Nothing. Just—got involved in a scuffle."

"A scuffle."

"A fight. Nothing major, although . . . I may have broken Rod Whitaker's nose." He wrinkles his own nose as he says it, as if the idea is distasteful.

"Oh." *Oh.*

David drags a thumb across his lower lip, looks away. Slowly his eyes sweep the enormous gymnasium. It's a gaping, hollow place now that the October late-day gold has slipped from the windows. We're both thinking about Rafe Hall's party, I'm sure of it.

"Close, Henderson, they're probably pretty pissed," I say quietly. "Senior year. Star quarterback. And . . . you're not sorry you hit Rod, are you? You did hit him, right? Is that how you 'may' have broken his nose?"

"Yes. I should have done it that day on the ice. Should have done it sooner than that. And no, I'm not sorry, but . . . I am kind of mad that I let him get to me. That I lost my temper."

"I'm actually kind of proud of losing mine." The words spill out.

"Calm, cool, and collected Cate Reese blowing up at someone? I can't see it."

Calm, cool, and collected? "Trust me, you don't want to see it."

"Oh . . . I don't know about that." He sits down on the bleachers next to me. "I wouldn't mind seeing you lose it." His grin is wicked— then suddenly gone. Checked, between folded lips.

"I—I could never get mad at you." My cheeks grow warm.

"You might." He looks down at his hands. Then he asks, "So who are you mad at?"

But I don't want to tell him how I yelled at Dee in PE and then felt out of control. How I'd kind of *liked* the feeling of giving over to anger, of letting go for once. How I'd liked the buzz of adrenaline that raced through me, the way it made me forget about everything, just for a minute, like getting high does.

Thank God Laurel made me that to-go bag after the funeral. Ketamine . . . in some ways it's like music, it mirrors the *feeling* music gives me. I get the good feeling, but without the work.

For when you're really sad, L had said as she put the package in my purse.

As if David knows what I'm thinking of, he says, "I heard about the accident you were in, with that guy." His voice is soft. It makes me think of how he is with Kimmy.

That guy. So he doesn't know. Of course he doesn't know, how could he? Why would he?

Then again, how could he not know, how can anyone not know?

Yes, stupidly, like everyone else, I'm attracted to David, but I loved Cal—how can anyone not see the gaping hole in my chest where my heart's been ripped out?

The answer is, they can. I see the look in their eyes. Hear their pity-ing voices, echoing all over school.

Isn't she the one who—

Shh! Yes. She's the one. That Lucky Girl.

Love. It's a totally different thing than a crush. And losing love, that touches everything. Or maybe it's just me, losing Cal, but I swear, I can't pull out of this. Can't pull the music out of *me*, the way I did before. Every note I play . . . sounds different now. I can't find that sweet spot on the strings, can't get those full tones that come once the warmth of my body, the warmth of my hands, has opened up the wood grain of the guitar.

Maybe it's because there is no warmth in me, no *music*. The music was in Cal.

"I'm sorry," David says in that same feather-soft voice.

I just shrug, swallowing around the lump in my throat. I can't share this with him. Why would I? Shoving my laptop into my backpack, I pull out a notebook. He gets out a tablet.

After a while we shift in our seats, move to the floor. David lies on his stomach, propped on his elbows. Rain patters the windows high up on the walls.

I draw a staff, some bar lines, a handful of notes. Beneath the notes I add a few words.

Summer. Fall. Every dream I dream.

I stare down at the page in confusion. Then strike a line through all of it. *I need to get home and practice.* The final Strings with Wings concert is coming up—my concert. I'm not ready.

It's weird to even think about it: I'll be on a different stage, in a different venue, but I'll be part of the same series of concerts that Cal was part of. It seems horribly unfair, that the concert dates should even continue, with the players playing, the audience attending, the notes ringing out.

But the other show—the one that Cal booked in Brooklyn—that's not going to happen. I need to call and cancel—can't believe I haven't. But every time I think about calling, about saying that Cal can't play, saying why, my brain just . . . shuts down.

After a few minutes, David asks if I want to see some pictures. To see the screen I move closer, lie next to him. Which feels kind of weird, and kind of good. And because it feels good, I get this idea that being even closer to him would feel even better. So in the next several agonizing minutes, I inch my leg over, till it's nearly touching his leg.

I point to the screen and my forearm brushes his. When we touch, everything else falls away. Accidentally on purpose I knock my ankle against his calf.

As we look at photos, we barely speak. Each time I anticipate the tiniest touch between us—all of them accidental on his part, I'm sure—my stomach dips, and I wish so many things.

I wish David would go back to being Kimmy's semi-anonymous older brother who was too busy to pay attention to me. Wish the charged air that hangs between us these days would disperse, and at the same time wish I had the courage to breathe it in.

Mr. Close doesn't show, but we stay for the entire hour anyway. All the while I revel in the energy buzzing through my body. It's mercifully distracting, despite my silent mantra:

David Bennet has slept with a million girls. I am an idiot, idiot, idiot.

LICHEN

DAVID

"Fungus?" Cate asks incredulously.

"Hard to believe, isn't it?" I hadn't meant to show her the pictures from the trip, but lying on the gym floor with a thin layer of energy pulsing between us, connecting us almost, I'm not so afraid. Of course there are lots of photos I won't show her—can't look at myself without shaking, breaking down: the last campsite, the falls. I stay clear of those.

Sharing the miniature worlds of the lichen I'd captured through the lens of my Nikon, this feels dangerous in a different way. But I want to do it. Want to show her.

"Some of them look like coral, or . . . sea anemones." She reaches toward the screen, as if forgetting we aren't looking at an actual photograph, or the thing itself. I get a chill. Her arm brushes mine and I get another, goosebumps rising beneath my shirt.

"This one looks like a flower, like Queen Anne's Lace."

I'd edited a lot of the lichen photos. Altered the exposure of some, so they look almost like X-rays. Others pulse with color. A few are black-and-white, the contrast stark. Striking.

"Lichens aren't actually fungus," I tell her. "They're composite organisms, consisting of a fungus and a photosynthetic partner growing together in a symbiotic relationship.

"Did you know lichens occur in some of the most extreme environments on earth? Arctic tundra, hot deserts, rocky coasts. They're also abundant in rain forests, wooded areas, on bare rock, including walls, gravestones—"

We both kind of freeze.

"You must think I'm nuts," I finally mutter.

"No, I'm just . . . surprised."

I want to tell her, about the watching, the new kind of seeing. But I don't think I can explain it. Explain how I'd sat there for weeks, struggling with the stillness. Struggling with the fact that someone was dead because of me. I don't know how to describe how I'd started looking at things differently, looking at all—

But I took the lichen pictures before.

I feel almost dizzy. *I'd already been looking—it had nothing to do with Dan.*

I'd been looking before—for something that wasn't my father, wasn't my brother.

My brother. Who'd been so alive one minute, but not the next.

Dan had been the same. There, then—gone.

The two deaths tangle in my mind.

"What are you looking at?" Cate asks me.

Her eyes. I'm looking at her eyes now. They're opening onto a world, like the photos, like the pool when I swim and swim.

I swing my gaze back to the screen. "Lichens have also been used in dyes, perfumes—medicine, too. Sorry. Didn't mean to stare."

"It's okay."

We go quiet. I open a music application. We listen.
Once in a while Cate shifts. Now her ankle bumps my calf.
I think of the girls at lunch.
Move my leg away.

BOULDER

CATE

David tells me his father hadn't let him use any of the Bennets' cars today. He laughs a little after he says this, the sound short and dry. The late bus is long gone, so we walk up the twisty back streets leading from school to Chapel Hill Road. We come out on the part that's just been repaved. It smells like tar. Our houses are in opposite directions.

We're close to the end of the driveway that belongs to Circle Stables. David eases himself up onto the largest of the peanut stone boulders that sit below the swinging horseshoe-shaped sign and holds out a hand. Taking it, I hoist myself up onto the reddish rock. It's only a little bit damp. The sky's overcast, promising more rain.

David keeps hold of my hand for an extra second—*does he?* When he lets go, his hands turn to fists. He presses them against his thighs.

"Cate. That party . . . the weekend before school."

My throat tightens. "What about it?"

"You know how you—needed a ride?"

I nod. *Can we please not talk about this?*

"I didn't go back. After Rafe and I dropped you off, he dropped me off. At home."

"Okay."

He shakes his head. "My sister. Rod . . . gave her some trouble."

I stop breathing. Was it the same kind of trouble he'd given me? I can't imagine it, not Bryn. "It's—my fault," I say haltingly. "If I hadn't needed a ride—"

"How is it your fault? I'm the one that left her at the party."

"But if it wasn't for me, you would have been there for her, would have gotten Rafe—"

"Maybe. But it wasn't your fault, okay? Just forget that idea."

I nod.

"Bryn, she feels alone in this. I thought maybe if . . . look, I wanted to know—*want* to know—what did Rod say to you? What was he saying, before I—*damn*—" David looks down. Running a hand back through his hair, he takes a deep breath. Blows it out.

Before you shoved him off me? You mean, how did it get to that point? How did Rod Whitaker's hands wind up on me?

Suddenly I start to shout. "Why does he even care so much about Laurel and me? It's bad enough Laurel's dating a jerk, bad enough that I see her less than before. This isn't how we planned it! I moved here, and we didn't even see each other for half the summer!" Words gush out of me like blood from a wound. "And now Rod, and his—his idiot posse. They're making it worse, with their stupid comments, in the cafeteria, the halls. As if I could *make* someone a lesbian. Where does he get his stupid ideas? Like, I must have 'turned her,' because 'No gay girl looks like Laurel.'" I bring my fingertips to my mouth. "Too much information," I murmur.

"No, not at all." David gives me a perspicacious look, although his next words don't match it. "But I'm confused."

A long minute goes by. Then I whisper, "Rod said he'd straighten me out." My voice is so quiet that for a second I think maybe I didn't say anything. "That's what he was telling me, when you—when you knocked him off me."

"He said he'd 'straighten you out'? By mauling you at a party? By—" David's eyes turn dark. "That's idiotic."

"I know."

"And you're not even gay!"

"I know!"

"You're not, right?"

"Would it matter if I were?"

"No! I mean, yes. I mean, it shouldn't matter to anyone. The only reason it matters to me is because—" David watches a stream of cars streak by. In a moment the road is empty again.

"Because?"

He continues to watch the empty road. Then he says my name.

"Cate."

The way he says it gives it weight somehow. My name, coming from his mouth, sounds important, and it feels, for a second, like he's talking about someone else, someone beautiful. The weirdest wish fills me, to be the person whose name he's saying.

"Cate," he says again, as if he hears something special, too, or he's saying a word that's new to him, a word he wants to remember. "I like . . . being around you."

He turns to me now, his eyes finding mine. A kind of space opens inside me.

But he can't mean this. So I slide off the rock and start walking. His short laugh follows me. It's different from earlier. More . . . hollow, like the shadow of a laugh. Then he's walking next to me, and I want to remind him that his house is the other way, but of course he knows.

At the bottom of my street we say goodbye. Halfway up, I turn around. Down on Chapel, David stands with his thumb out. I imagine what Laurel would say, how her voice would whisper-hiss like it does when she's sharing a secret.

"No one in their right mind would leave him *by the side of the road, manwhore or not. "*

But I don't need to be played by David Bennet, especially not now.

REACH

DAVID

I would've kissed her, but all of a sudden Cate was standing, gone from her seat on the rock, gone from the moment, that second where I thought maybe she, maybe we—that maybe I was good enough for her.

I'm glad she stood up, put herself out of my reach.

It takes the entire walk home to convince myself of this.

ALCOHOL
DAVID

Clink. Ice cubes submerged in liquid, knocking against the side of a glass. The sound greets me as soon as I open the front door. My father is only a few feet away, in his study.

Clink. The sound is a part of him, coming again now, reaching me where I sit on the stairs, taking off my shoes. I can almost see him behind the closed study door, the heavy crystal tumbler in his hand, a perpetually present prop.

Not wanting to *actually* see him, I head up to my room.

The sound of the ice in his glass, the glint in his eyes, I remember both from that day, The Charm Day. Or maybe I remember it from every day. Scotch and water, twist of lemon.

When I was tiny, Dad used to ask me to mix his drink with my pinky. Then he'd sip, and I'd lick my finger. Medicine. Something worse. Maybe the memory of that taste is why I don't like to drink, except for a beer now and then. Or maybe I don't like to drink because he and my mother do. Either way, I don't like it, so I don't do it.

But Rod does.

Rod drinks the same way he plays sports. It's an all-or-nothing proposition. Extreme.

One day after school, Rod and some other guys from the football team organized a kegger at the Dey Estate. A lot of people got trashed, including a slightly familiar spindly freshman Ron started making moves on late in the day. Most of the other kids had drifted away by then, headed for home or wherever kids go on a June afternoon two weeks before the end of the school year.

"Giving out your quarterback smile like candy," Rod slurred. "So where's yours?"

I laughed. "My what?"

Rod gestured vaguely toward the girl.

I shook my head. Said I was out of there.

"Yeah?" He reached out, snagging the girl's hand, reeling her in until she collided with his chest. I watched her bob unsteadily against him. Found myself thinking of a balloon, on a string. "How about we go to your house?"

I hesitated. It wasn't like I wanted to take some drunk girl home with me, but leaving her there didn't seem like the best idea, either. Coffee, then a ride, that's what she needed.

The girl was bird-boned and leggy. We held her up between us. She did okay on the walk.

When we got to the house, we took her up to my room. Then I went back downstairs for some food. I figured a sandwich would be good for Rod's friend.

The smell of coffee filled the kitchen. I opened the refrigerator, searching for cold cuts, condiments.

But after a minute, I realized I wasn't really looking for anything, just staring into the bulb at the back of the fridge.

Rod Whitaker doesn't have any friends.

Rod had teammates, not friends. He had a gang of guys.

Almost automatically, I reached for the bread. Cheese. Pickles.

Meat.

Rod also didn't have a girlfriend. He had one-night stands, or fiery, truncated relationships. At parties he sought dark corners, backyards, parked cars—*drunk girls.*

My father passed me, heading for the coffeemaker. "Smells good."

I nodded, looking down at the half-made sandwich. Bread spread with mayo.

Hair rose on the back of my neck.

I raced upstairs—

The two of them were on my bed—Rod kneeling over the girl.

"Rod, that's not cool, man!" She was on her back with her shirt rucked up, cutoffs around her ankles.

"You do it all the time," he mumbled, pushing down his pants.

"Not like that, you've got to stop—she's out cold!"

At the sound of my father answering the front door, we both froze.

A woman's voice made its way up from downstairs. "Her friends said she was with David and another boy, that the three of them left the Dey Estate together."

Sandy. All at once I remembered the girl's name, knew why she looked vaguely familiar. She lived a couple blocks away.

I hurled myself at Rod.

"The fuck, Bennet?" he hissed, rocking sideways before regaining his balance.

"Honestly, Jane, I haven't seen her."

And now it was me whose balance was in question, as my father's words ricocheted—*I haven't seen her.*

The sound of the doorbell ringing had been lost in the halls of the house, yet I could almost hear the ice cubes—clink—the swirling liquor in my father's glass. Could almost see him shrug, his blue eyes earnest without even working at it. *Honestly, Jane.*

His voice came again, pinning me in place.

"I've no idea where David's gotten off to, don't think he knows your daughter. I'll ask Betsey when she gets home, but she's up at the Short Hills mall with Bryn and Kimmy, so . . ."

So I can stand here and lie to you.

And he was. He was totally lying. He'd *just* seen me in the kitchen. But that wasn't the most awful part. No.

The most awful part was that he'd seen *us* when we'd first arrived.

"Mr. B," Rod had exclaimed, laughing as he stumbled to a stop on the stairs that led up from the foyer to the second floor. The girl had been cradled against his chest at that point. But my father had given her nothing more than a cursory glance, had just greeted Rod with a conspiratorial smile, a shake of the head.

"You boys behave yourselves, hear?" Steps unsteady, he'd disappeared into the study.

A moment later, the theme from the evening news blared from behind the closed door.

Rod had swayed on the stairs for a second, then asked, "He doesn't mind?" Without waiting for me to answer, he continued up the steps, staggering more from all he'd had to drink than from the weight of the girl in his arms. "Your dad's cool, dude."

Honestly, Jane. *I haven't seen her.*

The front door shutting with a bang echoed through the house—

Rod echoed too, repeating his words from earlier. "Your dad's *way* cool."

Then he climbed on top of Sandy.

Whatever insidious ice had frozen me in place thawed in an instant. "Whitaker!" I grabbed hold of his shoulders—

He shook me off like a dog shedding water.

Leaping on him, I locked one arm around his neck—

He flung his head back, smashing my nose, knocking me to the floor, where my head hit the desk. By the time I got to my feet—

He was done.

"You ought to go for it," he said, zipping up.

"I ought to call the fucking cops!"

That made him pause. Then he said softly, "But you won't." And headed for the door.

In the doorway he turned around, smiled, his mouth curling tightly, at the corners.

The smile he reserved for opposing teams, for his enemies.

"Because that daddy of yours wouldn't want his cocktail hour interrupted by the po-lice. Hey, speaking of David Senior—David the first? Are you a second, Bennet?" He laughed. "Seriously, speaking of your dad—and seconds—think he might like a go?" He nodded toward the bed.

My hands turned to fists. "Get the hell out."

"Yeah, think I'll be on my way. But really." Again, he inclined his head toward the bed. "You ought to take a turn. Nothing like a girl who doesn't talk back, you know?"

CONNECTION

CATE

The sheet music perches on the black metal stand, a stack of white flags begging for surrender. But I will not. The music itself looks like a war zone: Pencil strikes are everywhere, the pages filled with casualties—discarded fingerings, interpretive markings. Added, then savagely crossed out. I am trying desperately to get the changes right, Cal's changes.

The upcoming concert is my inspiration to get up in the morning. Making these changes is my homage to Cal, my connection to him.

But the Brooklyn gig . . . that show was for *us*. I need to cancel, yet can't make the call.

There are so many people I can't seem to call, my friends in the city—some who knew Cal. A few have called me, but I'm not sure that it matters. They all seem a lifetime away.

Besides the addition and blackened subtraction of musical direction, there are comments written in my music: maybe I'm just a crazy person with this boy in my head.

Cal Woods is not the only guy on my mind.

When Mr. Close finally showed today, he acted like he didn't know why David and I were there. He probably just didn't want to punish David for something everyone wanted to do, and he didn't want to punish me because he doesn't even know who I am. Half the time in PE I'm like a ghost. Or maybe Close knew I didn't deserve a detention. Yes, I served a volleyball at the back of Dee's head, but it couldn't have hit her that hard, I can't spike for shit. Of course the volleyball incident was right after I went off on her for telling me not to call Laurel. That *was* a big deal—to me, but not to her. So neither of these things should have sent her crying to Close. I think she was just pissed at me because of that guy she was talking to earlier.

I haven't been able to go into the cafeteria for lunch since the accident—too many people, too many eyes on me. Hardly anyone at school knew Cal, but the fact that I was in the car with someone who died in an accident on Chapel Hill Road means that now everybody knows me.

So I've been going to the library with my lunch, when I remember to bring it, but I didn't quite make it today. I couldn't. Couldn't stop crying.

Laurel heard I was having a meltdown in the girls' room and came looking for me. We'd just taken seats outside on the stone wall surrounding the patio when Dee appeared at the far end.

"Dee." Her name was a small noise escaping my lips, a sound not at all like Laurel's secret sharing whisper-hiss, but more like choking. Dee was the last person I needed to see.

Laurel waved a hand dismissively. "Don't worry about her. You're all pale. I'm going to get you some food."

I nodded, then glanced back at Dee. But she'd already turned away, calling to a tall boy with dark hair standing at the edge of the woods that border the closest playing field.

Even with everything I was feeling, as the boy approached the patio, I was struck by his looks—he had that kind of face. Plus, he seemed familiar for some reason. But it wasn't his face or the odd feeling of familiarity that got my attention. He was carrying a guitar case.

I watched him, watched Dee bum a cigarette. But when she started using it to gesticulate, jabbing it angrily in his direction as she spoke, he appeared to stop listening. His eyes flitted from face to face—

Till they landed on mine.

One summer the Ridgeways took me to Montana, to a dude ranch called Triangle X where we rode horses all day. Out West the sky is somehow higher and wider, bluer.

Even from where I sat on the wall, I could see the boy's blue eyes. They reminded me so much of that sky . . . I couldn't look away.

Dee followed his gaze and shot me a cyanide smile, then tugged on his arm. But even as they were walking away, the dark-haired boy's eyes held mine, his head swiveling to keep the connection. There was a slow-motion feel to everything as my head turned, too—

But then Laurel returned, plopping down on the wall, and time snapped back to its normal tempo. A minute later, I'd forgotten all about the boy. But maybe Dee hadn't. She's with Laurel now, but who knows. Maybe she had a thing with this guy.

I picture her jabbing her cigarette in his direction. Obviously, she knows him well.

So, right, I bet that's what it is. Not the volleyball, the boy.

Then again, Dee would find a way to hate me no matter what.

No one has ever really hated me before, except . . . That night, the night David insisted on talking about. Wasn't what happened just another kind of hate?

My left hand travels automatically up and down the fretboard, fingertips splayed like spider legs, running scales again and again. The fingers of my right hand dutifully hop from string to string— but these exercises don't absorb me, not fully, not now.

Closing my eyes, I concentrate harder. Hammer-ons, pull-offs, *be stiller than still*. Classical musicians must not move, must not let our bodies express. The *music* expresses. We are merely the vehicles for the composers. For Saint Cecilia, for the Muses. Maybe, even, for God.

I do not play an instrument; I am the instrument. I serve.

My fingers move up and down the fretboard, skip, skip, skip across the strings . . .

Silently, a window in my attention span slides open.

At first I notice nothing, too busy playing . . .

But then a dark intruder—a recent memory—slips over the sill like vapor.

SILVER

CATE

"Damn. We should have come sooner."

"Told you, man, last party of the summer."

"Forget summer, last party on the *planet* is more like it. Come on!"

The running commentary comes from the knot of boys walking in front of me. They break into a trot now, cutting across several meticulously mowed lawns as they head for the rambling Tudor on the corner of White Oak Ridge Road and Long Hill Drive.

The front door of the Tudor is wide open, as are the windows. The house is lit up like a Christmas tree.

Fireworks scream overhead, and a cheer erupts from a crowd gathered at the top of a grassy slope alongside the house, as a shower of stars spill from the sky. The slightly sulfurous smell of gunpowder and the lemony scent of citronella mingle and hang in the hot, humid air.

Another round of fireworks explodes as I start up the front walk, the bright light of each bursting rocket gleaming in the eyes of the appreciative onlookers. Paradoxically, at the bottom of the slope, the shining surface of a long, rectangular reflecting pool shows nothing but night.

I've never been to one of the Halls' infamous open-house parties. Sammy Trumpet—a pink-cheeked, white-haired retired cop known for his bowler hats and bad puns—directs traffic at one end of the long curving driveway. The party must have a parental seal of approval, if not an actual parent somewhere on the premises, although that's hard to believe.

I'm supposed to meet Laurel here but wonder how I'll find her.

"Remind me again why we can't go together?" I'd asked her that afternoon.

"Dee wants a date night."

"Really. Biggest party of the summer and she calls a date night?"

"Just meet us there, okay? *Please?*"

In lieu of an answer, I'd growled into the telephone.

Laurel had purred in response. "Lovecats?"

"Lovecats," I grumbled. Then, because I thought maybe I'd been too hard on her, I added, "Far be it from me to stand in the way of true love."

"And true love it is. And truly, *you* are a love. Cat. Thanks."

In the end it didn't matter, because I got caught up in practicing. The party started at seven, now it's after eleven. I text Laurel to tell her I'm here.

Climbing the wide stone steps to reach the front porch is like swimming upstream. Then a group of girls, the current I'm struggling against, inexplicably changes direction. Suddenly, we're all heading the same way—till the girls come up against a wall of boys who were apparently trailing behind them and who have stopped short now in confusion. So the girls stop too—

Just as Bryn Bennet emerges from the house.

The boys and girls turn as one— flowers toward the sun, an instant audience for Bryn.

A few call out her name. She answers and says something about the music inside. She's laughing, her long blonde hair shining in the glow of the porch lights. In fact, she's perfectly positioned so that it appears she's standing in a spotlight.

But after a second it becomes clear: The porch lights aren't creating this effect. It's Bryn herself, radiating beauty and entitlement, the twin stars she was born under.

She doesn't hear me when I say hi as I slip by.

Inside are more people I know—I wave—and people I don't know. People I'd like to know—I smile—and those I wouldn't. Rod Whitaker falls into this last category.

And yet when I see him, towering over the crowd, tall and so good-looking, for a second I'm flattered by the way he stares intently at me, just before he introduces himself.

I laugh a little. "We've already met."

"No, I would remember *you*. You're new. Going to be a freshman? What's your name?"

"A sophomore. Cate Reese. And I'm not exactly new. I've been coming to Middleburn my whole life."

"You're new to me." He smiles. It's a suggestive, expensive smile, the kind that probably paid some orthodontist's mortgage for a year: all big white teeth that, in conjunction with his full lips, give him the appearance of satisfied carnality. Now he fires off a round of questions, like he *has* to get to know me as quickly as possible. Like I fascinate him. The transparency of it all kind of amazes me. I'd have expected more subtlety from a senior.

After a brief back-and-forth he says, "Maybe I do know you. From another life." He runs a finger down my bare arm. "*Feels* like I know you. You believe in destiny? Fate?"

I roll my eyes. Apparently, he's never noticed me at the Bennets', but he's been hard to miss the dozen or so times I've seen him with David's crowd over the years.

"No. I believe in free will."

A hip-hop track blares from another room. Good groove, great melody. Misogynistic lyrics. I wonder where Laurel is. It's definitely time to go look for her. I start to turn away.

"So how about it?" Rod says.

This confuses me. It's like I've missed the first part of whatever he's said. "Excuse me?"

He laughs and kind of paws my shoulder. Only it turns into a little push, then another.

"Hey!" Somehow as we've been talking, we've drifted down to a part of the house that's apparently undesirable. There's no beer. No food. No bedrooms. We're in a sort of formal living room, probably the only spot in the house that's missing at least one of these things. It's also missing people.

He shoves me again, harder, yet in a way that might look playful to anyone watching. But there is no one watching.

"What are you doing?" I start to move past him. I can just see the crowd through the doorway at the other end of the room—it's steadily thinning as people head toward the kitchen, or the backyard, or wherever the smell of barbecue is suddenly coming from.

He blocks me. Laughs. I try to dart around him. He grabs my hand. Brings it to his lips.

"What's your rush?" And this time he doesn't push me, just comes so close I have to back up or his body will be against mine. I yank my hand from his, but in my hurry to move I trip, almost falling down a pair of steps descending into a den. Shelves full of trophies glint in the low light. He's not even a second behind me.

He reaches out, makes a fist around my ponytail. "I like your hair."

My back bumps a bookcase lined with gleaming gold cups. "Stop. *Stop it!*"

"Want some?" He takes a swig from a silver flask that's appeared in his free hand. Then he brings the flask to my mouth, pulls my ponytail so hard that my head snaps back. "Here, wrap your lips around this—I'll give you something bigger in a minute, if you're a good girl."

The liquid—vodka?—spills over my mouth.

"The better to kiss you," he whispers. His lips are wet, the bitter taste of orange juice filling my mouth, along with his tongue. I push, push, *push*— hard against his chest.

But the only thing that moves is his hand, the one holding the flask. It presses into my back now as one of his massive arms wraps around me, and the front of his body makes its way up against the front of mine. I whimper.

When he finally breaks the kiss, he shoves the flask at me again. Says, *"Bite it."*

And I do. I clamp my teeth down on the cold, ridged metal, holding it in my mouth, praying someone will walk in on us before he has a chance to kiss me again.

The sour citrus flavor of *him* mixes with the metallic taste of the flask and the sharp scent of alcohol. I gag— but even though he must feel my body lurch, he continues pressing against me, tonguing my ear, spewing terrible, twisted words into it.

Now he pulls the flask, hard and fast— my teeth rattle over the metal. His mouth hits my mouth with bruising force.

Then he jerks back— his mouth, his body, mercifully falling away—

And he goes over sideways with a shout.

Something—*a crutch*—has sent him sprawling. I see another crutch now, and a tall boy supported between the two. David Bennet.

In a daze, I look up at him.

His smile is lopsided.

Rod climbs to his feet howling, "Bennet, you fuck—" Then he slips, crashing to the floor.

Someone flicks on the lights. "What's going on?"

Laurel. Suddenly, I'm barely holding back tears. I grab her arm. "Let's go, can we go?"

Dee appears next to Laurel, scowling furiously at her. More people press in from behind them, separating us.

David stands between the growing crowd and me. "Are you all right?"

And I try. So. Hard. To hold myself together. But I'm breaking apart. Bits and pieces of me chip off. Hover overhead. Look down at the scene.

"Fight!" someone shouts.

"Whitaker's on his ass!"

"No way!"

David's voice is soft. Steady. "I'm here, Cate. What do you need?"

His words are the ground. Solid. They bring the earth back beneath my feet and I nearly collapse into him with relief. But I don't, because— of everything. And there are too many people. I don't want them to know—know anything. David's on crutches, I might topple him—

My swirling thoughts are interrupted by a shout. The room is terribly crowded now. Rod Whitaker is wrestling with some boy on the floor and there's laughter and talk of who's going to come out on top, but then the fight turns ugly. Fists fly. I want to run. Voices twine around me. Laurel's is somewhere low in the mix. Responding to Dee, then saying, "But she's okay, right?"

I see the top of her blonde head now—she's being pushed from the room by a group of senior girls spilling in through another door. She calls out, "David? Is Cate with you?" David gives Laurel a high sign, says something about *home*. "Okay!" she shouts over the crowd. "See ya, Cate! I mean I can't *see* you, but I'll see you soon!"

And she doesn't see. She didn't see. She doesn't know.

But David does. I'm humiliated. Embarrassed. I take a step back—

Right into the mass of jostling bodies. *Mistake.* All the bodies are Rod Whitaker's body, crushing against me. Stuck in the crowd, feeling sick to my stomach, I go stiff.

Someone shouts, "Hall, man, you've got the tiger by the tail!"

"Watch it, Rafe!"

Through the sea of people I can just see Rafe Hall looking unconcerned as he deftly maneuvers Rod away from the boy he's been fighting. The boy, looking relieved, slips away. With a flash of insight, I relate to him. He hadn't wanted a fight anymore than I had. *Victim.* The word springs to mind, but I shove it away just as quickly, focusing on Rafe. It's astounding how swiftly he's taken control of the situation.

He's a head shorter than Rod Whitaker and very slim, and I realize now I've seen Rafe Hall with David many times over the years. With his calm demeanor and neat white lacrosse shirt, it's hard to believe he's the host of such a rowdy party, but maybe his older brothers are the wild ones, or maybe it's just the guests who are wild. Animalistic.

"Hall, you black-belt demon! Nice work."

"Little sloppy there, huh, Whitaker?"

"Yo, that's what happens when you drain a keg."

"Shit, Whitaker drains a keg every day."

"Bet he pays Bennet back big-time."

"What for? Steckler was the one who practically had him pinned."

A snort of laughter. "Steckler's lucky he escaped with his life. Bennet's the one who took Whitaker down—with a friggin' crutch! Rod's not gonna let that slide, not once he sobers up."

"Yeah, lucky for Bennet, that's not gonna be anytime soon."

"Anytime *ever*." More laughter.

But David doesn't appear to be listening to this conversation, or any other. He's making his way over to where I stand, squashed in the middle of the crowd, a good part of which has started gyrating and grinding—the music's blaring now, someone's obviously cranked the volume. I'm not thrilled to be in the middle of the dancers, but I'm happy to be invisible. Nobody knows I had anything to do with what just happened. Nobody except David.

When he reaches me, he lifts a hand, like he's going to touch my shoulder, or my face. The crutches make the gesture awkward, and then he seems to think better of it anyway and draws his hand back. Someone asks if he saw the fight.

He shrugs. Doesn't take his eyes from mine. "Was there a fight? I must have missed it." Then he lowers his voice. "I'll find us a ride, okay?"

I can't answer.

There's a fist in my belly. Another clenching my throat. Squeezing my words.

BLUE

DAVID

I haven't seen Cate since I walked her home two days ago. Well, nearly home.

I'm not sure what happened between us that afternoon, but it was—something. Even though she walked away like it wasn't, even though I let her.

And even though I've convinced myself that she's too good for me, too . . . innocent, I can't forget the way her hand felt in mine when I pulled her up onto the red rocks that mark the entrance to Circle Stables. The way our hands *fit*.

No, that's not right; it wasn't our hands. It was . . . us. It was the way I felt inside when I held her hand in mine. That's where the fit was. Inside.

Now one of the double doors to the band room slaps open and Cate stalks out, looking like she doesn't fit anywhere. She walks head down in my direction and I can't see her face, but I can tell by that walk, by the hunch of her shoulders, that she's upset, maybe—crying?

"That's her," some girl says as she closes a locker.

"Who is she?" her friend asks, looking up from a cell phone.

"Someone who doesn't need you talking shit about her," I snap at the two girls, who go wide-eyed before scurrying off. Cate glances up— cuts suddenly across the hall, disappearing into the girls' room. I lean against the wall near the door, planning on waiting for her to come out. But after standing there a while, I realize she's not coming out. Not anytime soon.

Reluctantly, I leave my post. But that afternoon, weirdly, it seems like every conversation I overhear is about her.

"She was driving."

"She was hitching."

"She was the passenger—she almost *died*."

"Did you see his picture online? He was so cute."

"*So* cute."

"Were they—"

"I don't know."

Were they? I have no idea. Just like I have no idea when I became someone who listens to other people's conversations instead of having my own.

It's difficult to picture Cate, hiding in the girls' bathroom, surrounded by pink tiles, white sinks. *Had* she been crying in there? Getting sick? Washing her hands over and over like Bryn did for days after Rafe Hall's "open house"?

I'm glad Cate's friend didn't go to Middleburn. I'd hate to see another locker shrine spring up like last year, when Kenny Miller died. Hate to see Cate have to deal with that.

They made a shrine for Dan. Not at his locker—he was in college— but at Ship to Shore, the store in Portland where he worked part-time. One of the girls from the trip sent a photo of it, tucked into a get-well card filled with sexually explicit wishes for a speedy recovery.

It made me feel bad, but it also reminded me. I really didn't know Dan, hardly at all.

And yet, I knew that his toothbrush was blue.

I knew this because Dan was always doing "just one more thing" before he turned in. Most nights he'd do all those last-minute things with his toothbrush hanging out of his mouth.

I also know that, for some dark reason, Dan hated his father. I never found out why, though, or how he handled his feelings, because—he died. Because of me.

I guess what I know *about* Dan spans a wide range. Does that count as knowing him? When do you cross the line between not knowing and knowing someone? *How* do you cross it?

For a month I lived closely with thirteen other people, surrounded by a wilderness of water. One of us died. The rest of us survived, but only by helping each other.

You'd think that'd be a surefire way of bonding, of knowing each other. But it's not.

If the girl who sent the photo of Dan's locker shrine *knew* me, she wouldn't have sent it at all.

Because she would have known it would remind me of Jack.

REFLECTION

CATE

Heart skidding in my chest, I jerk upright in bed—

Another bolt of lightning splits the afternoon. The wind is wild, the branches of the huge maple growing just outside the bedroom windows are slapping hard against the house. It's an old house. The gutters need to be replaced. The rain pours down the glass. Tears pour down my face.

I'd been dreaming about Cal. Looking for him in a hospital emergency room.

There'd been an enormous aquarium—red-orange fish swimming languidly. Like oversized drops of blood, drifting.

For a second I'd felt like I was on the wrong side of the glass and couldn't breathe. The automatic doors of the emergency room kept sliding open with a whisper: *shh.* Then closing with a sigh. There was no one there but me, yet the doors kept opening and closing— open, close, open, close. I realized I was standing on the mat that triggers the doors. I stepped off.

"Cal," I'd tried to say, "slow down." But my throat closed, like the shushing glass doors.

Now the radiator across the room knock-knocks and I start— then scowl at the ancient coil of metal crouching in the corner like an ill-formed dragon.

I must have fallen asleep. Ketamine . . . it can be kind of tricky like that. One minute you're totally high, the next you're out. I only took a little after school, but then I laid down.

Now I slip off the bed and go over to the windows. Forehead against cool glass, I look out at the backyard. If I squint, the leaves of the maples that edge the yard become a ring of misty fire. Leaping through would land me in the woods, where it's already dark. Deciding I'm in the same time zone as the forest—that sleeping really is the best escape—I get ready for bed.

But it nags me, how much I really need to practice. So I get out of bed and sit straight-backed and still, feeling the smooth wood of the guitar through my cotton nightgown . . .

I'm dismayed once again at how different the music sounds without Cal in this world. The deep end of the ocean, metamorphosed into a salt flat.

Still I practice for four hours, until finally, swaying with hunger and the need for sleep, I put the guitar away, wondering suddenly as I do, what it would feel like to never take it out again. To close the case forever, like a coffin.

After brushing my teeth, I climb into bed, reaching over to the nightstand for my phone. Opening the voice memos, I hit "Play," then close my eyes.

And there he is. There I am. Running notes fill my ears . . .

The Bach sounds the best. Of all the pieces, the Bach showcases our perfection.

But this glorious indulgence is cut with yearning, with the *wish* for Cal to exist.

And suddenly I realize it's *this*—this *wanting* that I'm listening to. I'm listening to our playing, plus my emotions, the ones I feel *now*. If I set them aside . . .

Tick, tock, clockwork. Our duets are dry—how did I not hear it before? It's the same flat expanse I'd experienced while practicing tonight.

There's another voice memo. It's us goofing around. I'd forgotten I'd recorded us laughing and improvising and sucking (mostly me) and flying (mostly him). These efforts have something the composed pieces don't, a kind of passion. An *aliveness*.

The recording ends now and I listen to it again, then play the first one over. The Bach especially, the one I'd thought was the best, is a desert. A boneyard.

Abruptly I stop the playback. Then skip to a third voice memo.

The recording begins with a burst of laughter, and then Cal is playing like a monster. I come in, my notes tentative as I try to follow his lead. And then—

Songs?

Sitting up, I lean over the phone. Okay, they're not really songs, but they're definitely the beginnings of songs.

I can see that day perfectly. Hear myself humming while I restring my guitar. Not aware that I'm creating melodies on top of Cal's improvised chord progressions. Or maybe he's fitting progressions to my melodies. It doesn't matter. It's good. The music is good. The songs, they only need . . . words.

Now I listen to one song idea after another, quietly captured by my phone because I'd forgotten to hit "Done."

Because I wasn't Done. We weren't Done—we were just getting started.

I squeeze my eyes shut. How can Cal be gone while I'm here, when we're both connected to the same immensity, to music? Covering my face, I rock back and forth.

Finally, decades later, I open my eyes—

And see movement in the mirror.

The remnants of this afternoon's ketamine high? Or—

Something shifting—there it is again. A play of shadows and light. Fish through water.

Goosebumps rise on my arms as I stare into the oval mirror that hangs innocuously over the dresser across the room. Feeling like an idiot, I wave both hands. My reflection waves back. I make a horrible face now, and surprise—*not*—I see me, making a face.

Another movement, at the window—

Just a flurry of yellow leaves, the wind picking up.

But somewhere during the time it takes for my gaze to shift—

He arrives.

A breeze that's not a breeze but more like a touch lifts a few strands of my hair and—

Cal's reflection stares at me from the mirror, his face so close to mine that if I turn—

But then I do turn, and of course he's not beside me.

Heart beating hard, I turn back to the mirror—

And there he is. The mirror shows him clearly, walking away. Black hair swinging as he heads out the door.

I whip my head around. The door is closed, just like I left it.

Leaping off the bed, I race to the door and yank it open—

But there's only me, in the hall. A girl with a cell phone clutched in her hand, like she's holding on for dear life.

WORK

DAVID

It doesn't feel like work. Based on this alone, my father would disapprove of my new job.

But that's not why I haven't told him I'm working at Listen Up!

I don't want him coming in here. I don't want to see him sneer at the rows and rows of records, the dusty shelves of sheet music. Don't want him in the back of the shop, where there's a room filled with guitars, their curving bodies and unlikely colors as fascinating to me as their unique sounds.

Amps, instruments—I'm learning a lot from the kids who've worked here for years. Guys who—despite their blue hair or tattoos, their piercings and posing—are really no different from the guys I grew up with. They're just obsessed with music instead of sports, though my father wouldn't see it that way.

So I've told him I'm tutoring, which is true—I'm doing that, too. He doesn't like it, but he hasn't challenged my choice. At least not yet.

But this store . . . I've been coming here forever—Bryn, too. It feels like home, but better.

Delsey, a girl who's worked here as long as I can remember, has taught me the most. Bonus: She talks to me like I'm a person, not a body, or a face, or a potential trophy winner. She's as obsessed as the guys, has no time for anything but music. We're all about music—the bands, the songs.

At first, Rod's arrival doesn't set off alarm bells, just tinkling chimes on the door.

And come on, a Saturday night, two minutes to ten? We're ready to lock up. The end.

But then with a "Hey" and an "Aw" and a "Just take a sec," Rod wheedles his way inside.

My hatred rises up like a specter. *I should have broken more than his nose.*

Phones buzzing, thumbs tapping, drenched in cologne—a half a dozen wet-haired, whiskey-breathed boys trail Rod into the store. Wolverines without football uniforms but wearing uniforms nonetheless: not-warm-enough-for-the-weather T-shirts stretched tight over pumped biceps, snug jeans revealing bulges. Their overbuilt bodies take up the space of twelve instead of six. Game over, they're ready to play.

"Make it quick," Bird says. "We're closing." The overhead lights glint off his head.

Rod stumbles to a stop at this announcement or, maybe, because he finally sees me.

"Bennet! The fuck? You work here with the freaks now?" Then he turns, gesturing to his profile, to his nose. "Looking good, huh? You've probably been worried about me, yeah? But as you can see, you didn't do much *damage*." He leans toward me as he says this last word, and there is no mistaking his intention. But the door chimes ring again before he can press his point.

Half the senior cheer squad flounces in, damp autumn air clinging to their hair, their clothes. The scent of decay mingling with the smells of strawberry lip gloss. Shampoo. The boys at the rear of Rod's posse become distracted. I'm grateful. I can't take on all of them, just one. I step forward.

At the same time, Trish pushes through the crowd—

Now I'm the one distracted.

In my defense, anyone would be. She's got some guy's jacket tied around her waist, only not around her waist exactly. More like her rib cage. As a result, her breasts ride high in a shirt cut low, her exposed milky skin making me think of Rafe Hall's sister, all that Ren Fair stuff she's into. Talking ravens, Tarot cards. Push-up bra cinched so tight—when she swung herself on top of me that one night we were together, her breasts rolled in my face.

Glitter-lashed, candy-mouthed—Trish falls against me, hugging me tight, whispering something slurry in my ear. She smells of peppermint schnapps and that perfume she wears.

Before I can disentangle her, Blaise Mitchell grunts in protest. Lunges forward—

The girls ooh but hurriedly pry Trish's arms from around me.

Two guys—Studer and White—hold the protester back but look to Rod for direction.

His eyes glint with malice as he considers the situation.

Bird says they all need to leave.

Objecting noisily—"WTF?" "Free country, man." "Faggot!" "Your head looks like my cock!"—they go, their harmless insults muffled now by the plate-glass windows that front the store.

Gesturing obscenely, grabbing the girls from behind, my old teammates bump and grind their way into the night. Blaise Mitchell's gripping Trish's hair. Rod flips me off with both hands, then grabs one of Trish's arms. She laughs as the three of them trip through a giant sidewalk puddle. Rod laughs, too, but his eyes are hooded. I hate to think what might happen to her. Hate myself for not trying to keep it from happening.

Bird looks at me. Shakes his head.

I shrug, say, "Yeah, I don't get it." But I do get it. I just don't want it. And I was never that . . . low.

Was I?

No. I would have never, ever, held tight like that to Trish's hair. I would have carried her over that puddle like it was a threshold, like she was a bride.

In the end, what we had wasn't a big deal, but I'm not a jerk. I knew I'd see her around.

Knew I'd have to live with myself.

I shudder. That scene? I don't want it. Not anymore.

All I want now—is to destroy Rod Whitaker.

Instead, I take a stack of advance copy CDs and head out.

GUEST LIST

CATE

"I've only heard one song off their CD," Laurel says while we're waiting in line. "But it was amazing."

"Glad to hear it." *Since you dragged me here.*

We inch forward and I catch a glimpse of the inside of the Winery. It's definitely a step up from the clubs where Laurel and I usually go to hear music, and easier to get to—we took the boat to Wall Street and walked up from there. We were supposed to grab something to eat, but dinner morphed into cheap drinks. Now I'm glad we had them because it doesn't look like we'll be able to afford anything at this place.

A knot of groomed men in suits huddle at a polished bar to our right, talking to a striking woman in a low-cut blouse. Waiters and waitresses race around with glasses and trays, their work clothes hipper than my best ones—none of which I'm wearing. Not that I care. Okay, I care a little, but really, I'm not up for this, for having "fun."

But L had insisted, "You need a girls' night." Which only reminds me of all of my friends here, girls from my old school, that I should call to come out. Friends I haven't seen since I moved from Manhattan. Not that that *they've* been great about keeping in touch.

Musicians hustle back and forth between the front door and another door next to the stage, carrying guitar cases and amps, mic stands and lumpy duffel bags. The long rows of tables are already packed, mostly with girls and women, their black-linered eyes shining with anticipation.

Seems like I'm the only person in the room who'd rather be home in bed.

Finally, the guy at the door is squinting at our fake IDs. We try to look bored.

After a minute he says, "Twenty-five each. Show starts at eight. Seven-thirty rolls around and you're not in your seat? We sell it. Label showcase tonight. The boys want a full house."

"We're on the list," Dee says, pushing in between Laurel and me.

Oh well. I'd hoped she'd gotten lost in the ladies' room. Laurel elbows me. I sigh.

The bouncer cocks his head. He's waiting for us to pay. Or leave. Although when Dee launches into a tirade—"The singer is my cousin. He said he'd put us on the list! Check again. Dee Carson plus one"—I think maybe he'll just toss us out. Laurel looks embarrassed. I look past the crowd at the wide stage littered with cables and effects boxes.

There's a guy standing onstage with his eyes closed, whispering into a mic. He's wearing a black-leather jacket, black jeans, black boots. His dark, slightly curling hair has fallen forward, partially obscuring his face. Now he makes a low sound in his throat. A shiver goes through me. He says, "One—one two." Then steps back. Suddenly his eyes snap open—

And look directly into mine. *Blue sky.* The déjà vu hits a heartbeat later.

Dee waves and the boy's dark brows lift. Leaning once more into the mic, he says, "You made it." But he's still looking at me.

He jumps off the stage and joins us by the door. The bouncer says something to him about the guest list, about numbers. I remember what Dee said: "Dee Carson plus one."

The boy looks at Dee, at her arm around Laurel's waist. He looks at me. Then the bouncer.

"No can do," the bouncer says, holding up a hand. "Gotta stick to the count tonight. Lot of VIPs, couple pricey seat fillers. I've got this girl's name." He nods at Dee. "Plus one."

Thanks, Dee. But I don't really care. I'm happy to go home and start to say so.

The boy interrupts. "Cool." The word has a slight Southern bend to it. "So my cousin and her girlfriend can take a seat at the band table. I'll take care of Angel here." He puts his arms around me and draws me up against him. My stomach drops down around my knees.

"Sorry," the bouncer begins. "But—"

"But nothing," the boy says. "Gotta have my girl with me." I try to back out of the circle of his arms, but he tightens them around me, brings his lips to my ear. *"Play along,"* he whispers.

At the same time he shifts his weight—or does something, moves somehow—so that he appears taller, even than the bouncer, who's actually taller than him. The light nearest us slants across his eyes now, eyes that are currently fixed on the bouncer with laser intensity.

The intensity is in direct juxtaposition to the boy's voice, to the Southern lean of it. His voice is a rocking chair, tilting back. *Come up on the porch, sit for a bit.* His eyes are an endless sky. *Look too long—you'll lose yourself.*

I like the way the edges of his words are rounded, any sharp corners smoothed off by the South. I'm not so sure about the intensity.

Apparently the bouncer likes his voice too, or maybe he's just helpless against the battery of understated threat and Southern charm. He waves a hand and we walk in, weaving between tables, heading toward the soundboard. One of the boy's arms is still around me, looser now, his grip matching the lazy smile he's giving me. He points in the direction of an empty table for two.

Laurel says, "Cate Cat, are you good with this?" But she's grinning, eyes darting between me and the boy.

What choice do I have? I nod.

She waggles an eyebrow. I pretend not to notice, and Dee whisks her away.

The boy's arm drops from my shoulder. "Is this cool? Sorry I can't seat you with Dee."

"Please. You're doing me a favor."

"What's that?" Southern sway.

"Nothing. Don't worry about it. I don't mind standing."

His smile is quick now. White lightning. "Enjoy the show." He starts to turn away, then stops. "Hey, you're about to see me bare my soul—how about you tell me your little secret."

"My secret?" Reflexively, I scan the room.

He spreads his hands out. "What's your name, Angel?"

He's right—there'd been no time for introductions. But before I have a chance to say anything, someone shouts from the stage. A thin girl with an electric guitar, a muscle-bound drummer, and two horn players are already in place. Now they begin to play.

"Oh *man*," the boy breathes. He bounds over to the stage and hops up, grabbing an upright bass off a stand. Then he steps up to the mic.

The drummer plays a languid, suggestive groove on an earthy-sounding snare, and a simple guitar line unwinds like the start of a story, possibly a bedtime story, but definitely not one for children. A keyboard player near the rear of the stage who I hadn't noticed before plays a few sparse figures, his tone reminiscent of an organ. Finally, the bass slides in. My hips start to move.

When the bass takes the melody from the guitar and drags it down low, I can feel the thud of it in my chest. And when the dark-haired boy arcs his body over the upright and starts singing—stage lights washing out his sky eyes, glinting off his dark hair—something deep in my belly melts a little. If the timbre of a person's voice coincided with a time of day, the sound of his voice would be dusk. I love it.

The girl behind the soundboard frowns in concentration, one eye on the band, the other on the board, her fingers constantly adjusting the levels. I don't know if it's what she's doing or if it's the acoustics in here, but the sound is amazing—I can practically hear the pads of my new friend's fingers sliding on the strings, little whispery cries adding another dimension to the notes.

Now one of the horn players takes several measured steps in time with the kick drum, approaching the dark-haired boy. He leans in— and their mouths nearly meet on the mic.

When I hear their two voices together, an ache settles in my chest. I might just die of pleasure. The bass line pops against my sternum. I close my eyes.

When I look next, God-I-can't-believe-I-don't-know-his-name is wrapped around the gleaming upright, and the band is drifting into another song, something about fortune-tellers, escaping, and a leap of faith.

Staring at the boy, at the way he's curled around the bass, I find myself wondering how it would feel to take its place . . .

Then I wonder how it would feel to take *his*.

AFTER PARTY
CATE

The band's energy is still buzzing through me as I make my way toward Laurel and Dee.

"So is it love?" It's the singer. He and the drummer are working the room, handing out promo postcards, passing around a mailing list.

"Sorry, what did you say?"

He laughs, the music still in his voice. "What'd you think of the show?"

"Actually—you guys are amazing." I watch the drummer dealing with a bunch of fangirls. Lots of kisses. Wandering hands. He's wearing a smug expression, but hey, who cares? He's got awesome chops. "I'll probably have a pretty bad case of post-concert depression," I add.

The singer laughs again, and I kind of startle. Except for Laurel, I can't think of the last time I made anyone laugh. *I* am definitely not laughing; I'm thinking of this guy's voice, of the music. Of the band's last song, which is still humming through my head—

"Medicine is on its way down . . ."

It feels like that song—all their songs—is the first thing I've really *heard* in a long time.

I look up at the singer, but he's looking down at his cell phone, his hair falling around his eyes—

Like Cal's hair. My lower lip finds its way between my teeth.

The boy glances at me. "That's cute," he murmurs. "The way you bite your lip like that." He looks back down at his phone, then slips it into a pocket. "Dee's new school, that's where we met and yet didn't meet, right? Another brick-in-the-wall place out in Middleburn, where all the horsey folk live. Politicians. Hot moms. Springsteen land. I've spent a lot of time there, but I remember that day. You were checking me out."

"*Pff.* Right." But I'm a beat late. He grins, running his eyes down to my toes and back up.

And it's that—the I-can-see-through-your-clothes once-over—that jogs my memory. Suddenly, I know why his face is so familiar. His face is famous. Not from movies or TV, but close. It's a face made famous by marketing, by an ad campaign that ran about two years ago, I just can't think—

"Cologne," he says, looking away now. "Don't strain your brain. No one remembers the name." He drops his voice a little—he knows the musician's secret to being heard over a crowd: speak softly, don't shout—and I notice the way it resonates in his chest. "Hey, at least it got me into video. Started at NYU after that gig. Film major. But, yeah, I told them, people aren't going to remember a string of Italian words, even if those words imply that whoever buys this shit's gonna get laid every night. They're going to remember my face."

And his face is memorable. Sky eyes set in shadow. *He's* memorable, with his sometimes lazy, sometimes lightning grin, his dark curling hair. Beneath his leather motorcycle jacket he's got on a black T-shirt, and I can't help noticing now how it clings across his chest.

He catches me looking and kind of smirks. "So you're coming to the next show, right? You and your girlfriends?" He hands me a postcard—

Deep Dark Love
deepdarklove.com

—and says, "Maybe we can get you up onstage for a song or two."

"What makes you think I play?"

"By the way you listen, by the look on your face tonight. By these." He reaches for my left hand, lifts it so I can see his fingers running over the tips of mine. "Calluses."

"You're pretty observant."

"Yeah, you know what I'm observing right now?"

"What?"

"That you still haven't told me your name." He runs a finger down the center of my palm.

"Cate Reese." I slip my hand out of his. "And yours?"

He gestures with one hand, half imaginary-hat tip, half two-fingered salute. "Dale Waters, at your service. So, are you going to come?"

I turn over the postcard. On the flip side there's a list of venues. Manhattan, Brooklyn, Connecticut. I glance up at him. Have a hard time visualizing him in Connecticut. "Maybe."

But he doesn't hear me. Some girl has just thrown her arms around him, and now he's lifting her off her feet.

Laurel and Dee appear at my elbow. "We have to go or we'll miss the ferry," Laurel says.

Dale Waters releases his latest victim and turns to Dee, who crushes him in a bear hug, presumably saying goodbye. A second later she spins and grabs Laurel, who grabs me. We race across the club.

At the door I glance back. The singer is standing onstage, coiling a cable, slow smiling in that lazy way of his while a group of girls cluster around him and the next band sets up.

The drummer bears down on the girls now, with a pile of postcards and a clipboard. I wonder how many email addresses they walk away with after a show like this.

We're outside, deciding which corner is our best bet for catching a cab, when Dale Waters appears in the doorway of the Winery.

"Hey, where you girls going?"

"We've got to grab a taxi," Dee hollers as she follows Laurel across the street.

"C'mon, Cate!" Laurel calls. "If we don't catch a cab in the next two minutes, we're not going to make it."

"Great show," I say to the singer. "Thanks for the comp. See you." I start across the street. *No cabs in sight.* Laurel and Dee are halfway down the block looking for a better spot.

I'm surprised when the boy follows. More surprised when he says, "Where?"

"Where what?"

"Where are you going to see me?"

I laugh. "I don't know."

"You're not so great at saying what you mean, are you?"

A little flame of anger ignites somewhere inside me. "How can you—"

"You said you'd see me. So, come on. Where? I want to see you again."

"Oh, right. You're just looking for bodies, to pack your next gig."

"Whoa, that is a loaded remark, Miss Cate Katydid. Cynical, too, if I may say so."

"You 'may say' whatever. It doesn't mean I'll listen."

"Fickle girl. You sure were listening earlier, but that's how it is, right? People only love you when you're playing."

I glance sharply at him. But he's grinning. That was just a throwaway comment, a slightly misquoted song lyric. He can't possibly know that I feel like it's the truth, that I felt just that way, about Cal. Maybe about everyone. If I didn't play guitar, and play it really well . . .

"I—I was listening tonight, yeah. Your band's really great. But—" We're walking fast now, trying to catch up with Laurel and Dee who, I'm guessing, are headed for Broadway. "But I really have to go." And now I smile back at him, because even though I figure he just wants to make a new fan, I actually kind of like him, and I love his music.

He glances at my mouth. Then he lowers his head slightly in a defeated, deferential nod.

And I can't help laughing again, because this humble expression only makes him more attractive, and I'm pretty sure he knows that.

"O-kay," he says, drawing out the second syllable of the word. "Since you're so sure. But since you can't hang out, how about you let me call you?"

"Cate!" Laurel and Dee are on the next corner, a yellow cab idling in front of them.

"Sure, fine." He hands me his cell, and I quickly thumb in my number.

His lips twist— it's a knowing look, although I'm not sure what it is he thinks he knows.

Then he gives the slightest bow and that two-fingered hat tip salute, before he takes a step backward, and another—his slow smile simmering—then finally turns, jogging off toward the club.

I run in the opposite direction and hop into the waiting cab.

Before I can even catch my breath, I'm being subjected to Laurel's laughing interrogation.

Dee's eyes make me think of those narrow slots in castle walls, the ones for shooting arrows.

I'd give her the same go-to-hell look, but I'm laughing too hard.

EMBER

CATE

The next evening I'm sitting on the front steps, melodies tangling in my head. I can't seem to bring myself to go inside. The house feels . . . too empty.

At the same time, it feels too crowded.

Maybe because Mom's home.

I miss my mom, but it's been so long since she's *acted* like a mom that I'm kind of used to the feeling. Used to her not being around, although she's around more than Mrs. Bennet.

Between my fingers, I pinch the stem of a dried leaf, twirling it idly, before bringing it to my nose. After I inhale the wasted scent, I crush it against the step, brown into blue, rolling the fragile leaf body on the cool stone till it's dust. I blow on it— but it doesn't disperse. Instead, it catches on a cobweb hanging in a corner below the edge of one of the steps.

Mom's hardly been home since we moved here. It's like she put in a month or two, decided the suburbs weren't for her, then slipped away to the city. I'd overheard my parents talking about her disappearing act one night. Dad had been surprisingly supportive.

"You're an artist, Jan. You might say you're not, but you are. You're a shadow artist. Your *art* is supporting other artists. For that you need the city, the stimulation, the clients.

"It was one thing when this was our getaway, a place of splendid isolation . . . But let's face it. The suburbs, even suburbs as rural as Middleburn, aren't for you. The PTA? Not an artists' colony. And Cate can take care of herself."

Cate can take care of herself. Huh.

Then Mom asked Dad, "So how is it the whole setup is working for you?"

Standing outside the barn, flat-out eavesdropping by that point, I'd pictured Dad adding a daub of color to his canvas. "I can paint anywhere."

He can, too. As for Mom . . . fundraisers, bake sales, playground politics . . . it doesn't sound fun to me, either. I do fine in school, despite the fact that I have no "parental presence," so what does it matter? Let my mother live her life. It's either that or slow death by depression.

My mother's depression. That's how I learned to cook. It started with breakfast. One day she didn't get up to make it. I was ten.

Maybe *I'm* depressed. Maybe that's why my playing sounds like crap. For the millionth time, I picture Cal's face next to mine in the mirror.

The door opens behind me. "Oh! Cate," Mom says, bringing a hand to her chest. "You startled me."

I raise an eyebrow. *I'm sitting here like a church mouse, you whip open the door, but I startled you?* But I know what she means. I'm forever startling her with my mere presence. Apparently, she's never gotten used to having me around.

"Ah—I'm going out. But I thought you and your father might like to have some stir-fry."

"You made stir-fry?" Hope and disbelief jockey with sarcasm in a struggle for dominant vocal tone.

"No!" She sounds shocked. "I mean, no. But the ingredients are, well, in the kitchen, and your father would love to join you for dinner." Translation: I should make dinner and fix a plate for Dad, because he's already started working, and if I don't take food out to the studio, he'll paint all night with nothing in his stomach but caffeine.

"I've got to run and catch the ferry." She pulls on a pair of fitted gloves. I nod, and she blows me a kiss, then clicks away on heeled boots, headed for the garage.

I'm just standing up when a movement at the side of the yard catches my eye. Across the leaf-littered lawn—red-and-gold distractions—someone ducks into the trees.

No. Not someone—no one and nothing. Just a gust of wind rifling through the woods, making them rattle and bend. Just the wind, that's all.

That's all. Suddenly, I can't bear to be here another minute.

Leaping up, I head across the lawn and out to the street. Then I walk away from the house that doesn't feel like home.

I walk and walk, and finally, I start to run.

In a few minutes, I fly by The Killing Tree. Turning my head at the last minute to look, I stumble— but don't stop.

It's only after I've nearly exhausted myself and am almost all the way to Laurel's that I slow to a walk. Breathing hard, I pull out my phone and punch in her number to tell her I'm here.

But the phone only rings, then goes to voicemail. I text. Nothing. She's not home, either.

With a sigh I look up at the cloud-covered cobalt.

There's really only one other place I can go.

By the time I reach the Bennets', night's officially fallen, and it's only because of the hot orange ember of her cigarette that I see Bryn on the terrace that juts off the side of the house.

"He's not here," she says by way of greeting.

"Yeah, no, I'm not here to see—wait—do you mean David? Because I'm not—I came to ah, to . . . Kimmy . . . homework . . . just checking . . ." It's obvious I have no real excuse for dropping by, especially when I haven't returned any of the Bennets' phone calls lately.

Bryn stubs out her cigarette. "Want to get high?"

She pulls a mangled joint and matches from a pocket of her jeans.

I've never smoked anything—no gateway drug needed here, I'd gone straight to K, in fact I have an order in for more—so it's easy to say no. Plus I'm allergic. I'm not in the mood to be alone, though, so I make a few more stabs at excuses. "Kimmy . . . and Midnight . . . and—"

"Sure," Bryn says. And hands me the joint.

"I can't. I'm allergic to smoke."

"Isn't everybody?" She takes a giant hit off the joint and holds it in, so her voice is all squeaky when she says, "We had to get a new babysitter, you know."

"I know. I'll be back, I'm just—taking a break." *Just broken.*

She expels a huge cloud of smoke and it billows around us.

"I heard about that kid. Heard what happened. I'm sorry."

"Thanks." I stand up. I can't talk to Bryn about Cal.

Peering through the glass doors of the terrace into the lighted den, I catch a glimpse of Kimmy, sitting on the couch in front of the TV. On the screen, a ridiculously handsome boy sinks his teeth into a girl's neck. She seems to like it. He pulls away, blood dripping from his mouth. The girl falls to the ground.

I rub my temples, remembering suddenly what Bryn's room looked like last time I saw it: papers spilling from the desk, closet door gaping, clothes piled on top of shoes, empty hangers askew. Bryn's hand-painted universe had shimmered softly from the ceiling, a pulsing galaxy out of reach, as always, but something about the room, besides the fact that it was a wreck, had fundamentally changed. At least, that's what it felt like.

Bryn's changed, too, and I can't believe I didn't notice it before. Didn't notice the dark circles beneath her eyes, the hollows beneath her cheekbones. Like David this past summer, she's lost weight, lots of it. The blue TV light reflects off the glass doors, highlighting her pale face. And I see Bryn the bitch, Bryn the center of the universe—she's none of those things, not anymore. She's only . . . lost. Lost out here in the night.

I have a sudden urge to ask what she's thinking, but she gives me such a penetrating look now that I get a chill, along with the feeling that she's really *seeing* me, maybe for the first time.

"It's affecting you," she says quietly.

The words hang in the air between us, and I will them to dissolve. But then she says his name, and I know that they won't.

A small knife becomes lodged at the top of my rib cage. How much does she know? Laurel knew Rod was "bothering" me at Rafe's party, but that's all she knew. How does Bryn—

David. He must have told her. Now I think through what he said. How he'd told me Rod had given Bryn "some trouble." How he'd said, "She feels alone in this. I thought maybe if . . ."

A TV voice screams and I jump.

"He gave you a hard time, too, didn't he." Not a question. A statement. "At the Halls'."

"A hard time."

She laughs softly, looks down at her hands. "You're funny, Cate Reese."

"Oh, Bryn—" But I can't find any more words, and for once that makes sense—the horror of it is too much.

Rod Whitaker. And Bryn.

Bryn, in her own universe, with her untouchable beauty, her cold control.

My thoughts scatter like a flock of birds flying back through time. When, exactly, had she dyed her gorgeous blonde hair black?

As if she knows what I'm thinking, she takes a long lock of her inky hair in one hand, wraps it once, twice around her index finger— pulls.

"David blames himself. Thinks it was his fault, because he left. But he's my brother, not my bodyguard! I don't want him taking this on, not on top of what happened in Canada."

But I don't really know what happened in Canada.

So I say, "I guess David told you? About how Rod—"

"No."

"No?"

"Rod told me." Her lips twist. "Guess I was his second choice."

"I'm so sorry, Bryn."

"It wasn't your fault, either! Jeez. You needed a ride. That's all. You had no way of knowing—David had no way of knowing. That *fucking* asshole—". She chokes on the words, looks back down at her hands. A few long black pieces of hair hang from her fingertips now. She's ripped them out at the root.

"I never told David," she says quietly. "But he—he knew. There was another girl. She lives nearby. David told me how she was here, how he made her coffee and walked her home after—after Rod—*in our house!* And my dad—" She broke off, her upper lip dewy with sweat.

Her voice drops. "I have the clothes."

All at once she brushes her hands together. The strands of hair fall from her fingers. Then she just looks at me. Waiting. Waiting for me to say something.

This is the longest conversation I've ever had with David's sister. I'm desperate to say the right thing—amazed she thinks I might possibly know what it is.

"That party was the week before school started," I begin tentatively. "And now it's October."

"But you—kept your clothes, the clothes you were wearing when he—when he—"

"I never washed them." Her voice is so soft, I almost wonder if I imagined the words. I feel soft, too, now, like I might collapse in on myself. But also, I recognize that softness is not what Bryn needs.

"So you can do something," I say as firmly as I can. My voice quivers, but just a little.

Her eyes widen slightly.

A breeze tickles my neck— but there is no breeze. It's energy. I take it.

"Right?" My voice is solid, is rock.

"Right." She's watching me intently.

I nod. David's nod. And we've done it. We've made a pact. I'm going to help her. I'll talk to Sandy, to the police, whatever she needs.

But then she says, "Cate. I'm afraid—afraid if I don't do something, David will. He . . ."

"He, what?"

"He said he's going to kill him."

Instantly, I remember that day in the gym, how David wasn't at all sorry he'd broken Rod's nose.

Bryn says, "I know him. He means it. He says he doesn't care if he goes to jail forever."

My memory sparks. The way David lifted Kimmy in his arms, ran his fingers over her name on her duffel. The way he looks at me sometimes. In my mind I see him, watch the way *he* watches everything, the details of life, as if he's seeing them all for the first time—or the last.

I take a deep breath. "No. He wouldn't."

"He's in love with you," she says.

All the breath sticks inside of me for a long second— before it bursts out, along with a laugh.

"Your brother? Please. He's been with so many girls, he's not capable of falling in love."

Bryn's eyes are glassy. "You're an idiot, Cate Reese. He cares about you. He's not seeing anyone—he's trying to change his life! He *protected* you, and you just blew him off."

Then we're both crying, and the intimacy between us, instead of growing stronger, vanishes. Just like that, we are our own isolated islands of grief, and I know she's mad at herself—for letting me in, for sharing her shame, for asking for help, and finally, for betraying David, telling me how he feels. "You need to go."

I jump to my feet. In those few moments, she had made me her friend, but already she's pushing me away.

She buries her face in her hands, and for half a minute, I just stand there. I so want to put my hand on her back, stroke her bowed head. But she twists away before I can touch her, sliding out of her chair, rocketing to her feet, running into the backyard, into the night.

I don't want to go, don't want to leave. But I do *want*. I want so badly it hurts. I want—but I don't know what I want. I want everything, it seems. I want the summer back, and I want music. I want—my mom, and something else. Something more.

Now I feel a breeze—fingers through my hair, breath on my neck— but there is no breeze. *I want to know what could have been. I want time to rewind.*

About to go, I spot a blue hoodie hanging off a patio chair, the word "SWIM" spelled out in disintegrating white block letters across the back. The faded blue is so familiar—I've seen it on David a hundred times.

Tripping over to the chair, I snatch up the sweatshirt—

But I don't admit why I'm taking it, not even to myself.

HOME
CATE

Laurel's not in school the next day, so as soon as the bus drops me off, I do a little K—snorting it quickly, though it burns, so I can get going. Then I ride my bike—all slo-mo and dreamy now—through the drizzle to her house.

Before I have a chance to knock, the polished mahogany door of the sprawling Tudor swings open and Dee pushes past me. She's nothing but a scowling whirl of motion as she gets in her car and slams the driver's side door. She starts the car, revs it. The tires squeal in protest as she pulls away.

"Okay . . ." I waver on the doorstep, feeling not at all like myself yet completely like myself, pondering Dee's speedy departure.

"Not okay." I startle at the sound of Laurel's voice. She's standing in the doorway. Her eyes are glassy and very red. I can't tell if she's been crying or if she's high. Seems like, ever since she started hanging out with Dee, she's one or the other.

"Do you want to talk?" I ask.

"Not really, but you obviously do."

"You got my million messages?"

"And texts. Thought maybe skywriting was next. That's what Dee's going to have to spring for if she expects me to—" Laurel folds her lips. Then she says, "Sorry I didn't get back to you." She pulls me inside and into a hug, then she shuts the door.

I follow her through the grand foyer—*grand* is the only word for it, for the entire house really. "Late twentieth-century castle" would not be a pretentious way to describe the Ridgeways' palatial home with its surrounding gardens and acreage. Being here always makes me feel a little small, a little scruffy. At the same time I feel wonderfully welcome. My shoulders relax slightly.

We settle on the cushioned window seat in the kitchen, one of our favorite spots. Laurel looks out over the formal back garden, allowing her gaze to wander the paths that curve and cross, then disappear down past the massive central fountain as the property slopes toward the same woods that my house backs up against. I wish she'd talk to me about what happened with Dee, but her eyes have turned steely, and I know what that means, so I go ahead.

"Laurel. I have to talk to you. It's Cal, he's—"

"Aw, Cate."

I wave a hand. "It's not that; I'm okay, just listen—"

"You're obviously not okay, how could you be?" Mrs. Ridgeway says as she enters the kitchen.

Anne Ridgeway is the opposite of my mother. She's always around—and slightly round, where my mom is all sharp angles—and Laurel is the center of her world, in a good way. Mrs. Ridgeway isn't a helicopter parent; she just loves Laurel. Could be part of why Laurel is slightly spoiled, but why shouldn't she be? That's what her mom says to us all the time: "Why shouldn't I spoil my girls?"

Today when she sees me, she looks relieved. Laurel has joked more than once that her mother wishes Laurel was dating me instead of Dee.

I feel suddenly guilty that I'm high, but there's nothing I can do besides try to ignore the rubbery feeling in my limbs and act normal.

Mrs. Ridgeway sits down beside me and wraps me in a hug, kisses my hair. "How's my other daughter?" She doesn't release me, just pulls back enough to look into my face.

Sometimes I think it's when we have someone to lean on that we become unsteady. Lose our balance. Fall the hardest. Just like that, as soon as she asks how I am, my eyes fill with tears and I'm—flooded. That's the only way to describe it. I start crying, can't stop.

Laurel and her mom both coo reassuring words that I'm sure they know can't help the hurt, but what else can the two of them do?

The words they use now have an entirely different definition than any dictionary would assign them. They say, "It's okay," but they mean, "We love you." They say, "Everything happens for a reason," but they mean, "Your pain is going to pass." "Here's a cup of tea" means "We're here for you."

And they are. They pet my shoulders, pat my back. Laurel makes tea. Mrs. Ridgeway tells me to breathe, puts a pillow behind my back. Then she takes a fluffy mohair blanket from the back of a nearby couch and spreads it over me.

And it's that—the couch in the kitchen—that makes me hurt more but stops my tears. Because I realize this crying jag over Cal is like . . . a gateway. I miss him. I *want* his reflection in the mirror to be real, to believe that he's here somehow, but that *want* is part of so much more want—a desire for a home I don't have, with a mother who's always there, a sister, a couch in the kitchen that says "Sit down where I can see you." It's the same as all the want I felt last night, the same ache that music gives me, the one I'm so sure Cal Woods understood.

After finishing our tea, Laurel and I head up to her room. The pink cocoon, we call it.

"There's more," she says as soon as she shuts the door. "Isn't there?"

"Yeah." I tell her what happened, describing Cal's reflection in the mirror. My voice grows shaky as I come to the most nebulous part, the breeze I felt that wasn't a breeze but more like a touch. Then, although I hadn't planned to, I recap the conversation with Bryn.

"So that's what happened to her. I mean she was always kind of a bitch, but when she took it up a couple notches, I started to wonder. Then she dyed her hair, and I knew it was something epic, but I never— God, I feel sick."

"I told her I'd help her."

Laurel nods. "Good, but what about you? Who's going to help you?"

"What do you mean?"

"I mean, my mom's right. You're not okay. And this idea, of seeing Cal—"

"I *am* okay," I say, feeling a scowl crease my forehead. "I'm *fine*. The show's coming up; I've been practicing like mad." *I sound like shit, but still, as of yesterday, practicing like mad.*

"Yeah, well . . . Have you been sleeping? Eating? I mean, if you're hallucinating—"

"I wasn't hallucinating. I saw him!" I become more agitated as I realize she doesn't believe me. Oh, she wants to believe me, of course she does. But she's always been the more grounded of the two of us, the sharper one. I might do better in school, but that's because I put in the time. She's the alpha. I'm the sidekick. And that's okay. It's always been fine with me, to let her throw the party, carry the conversation. Find the right words. But she can't find them now, and a minute ticks by.

Finally, she asks slowly, "Cate, have you been to the cemetery?"

My stomach drops. "For the funeral. You were there."

She looks at me intently. "I think . . . it might be good for you to go again."

I start to object.

"I'll go with you," she says.

"What do you think, L? That seeing Cal's gravestone again is going to—"

A Killers' tune rips through the room. Laurel's cell jitters on the glass-topped dresser.

"Loud enough or what? Must've had it set to *deafen* for some reason—oh yeah, so I'd be able to hear it over Dee's bitching." She jumps up and grabs her cell, glances at the screen.

"Bryn Bennet," she says into the phone. "Hiya."

Laurel might have a wicked competitive streak, but she has her mother's heart. Now that she knows what Bryn's been through . . .

L's not a small-talk kind of person, but she's making it now, just to be nice, asking Bryn about school, about whatever.

Even though I don't want to admit it, I'm pissed at Laurel for not believing me, angry that she's suggested I go visit Cal's grave. I don't find it generous that she's offered to go with me and hold my hand—I find it patronizing.

But I don't wait around to say these things to her, because I know I won't. And even though Laurel is pointing at the phone, I don't wait to find out why Bryn of all people is calling. I just slip out the door, ignoring Laurel when she hollers after me—

"Cate! Bryn says don't tell anyone. She says you know what she means, *don't tell.*"

STATIC

CATE

Over the next few days and nights I practice so much that even my parents are worried.

Sometimes they knock on my door. I ask them, nicely, to go away.

I blow off my homework. Blow off my life. Still, my guitar sounds like a stranger.

Some nights I get high before bed. When I give in to sleep, I dream about Cal. I wake up with songs in my head.

Sometimes I don't know it's a dream, and I think Cal's in the room with me—*is he?* Those times, it's like a chess game—I can only plot so many moves ahead, can only see so far behind. So I don't ask Cal a million questions, like, "What happened after the crash?" "What happens when you die?" Instead, I cling to this moment. My move. I want to play music.

Except once, I ask him, "What's it like?"

It's like buzzing inside. Like static.

"L-like a TV screen, when the picture goes bad? Like the Internet dropping, is that it?"

He shakes his head. Tucks his hair behind his ears.

Nervous laughter bubbles up from somewhere inside me then—but it's from the wrong place. It's from the place that produces screams, I think. It's a strangled, choking sound.

The wind lifts my hair and I reach up to smooth it—

Waking myself up. I'm in a sitting position already. Sleep-sitting. Thoughts muddled. *Wind in my bedroom.*

I spin toward the windows— they're both closed. Cal, of course, is not here.

And—he is not at Carnegie Hall.

This time it's me who's onstage, at the Weill Recital Hall. (And straight as an arrow for the occasion.)

This isn't a dream—though it feels surreal—the date has finally arrived.

Weill Hall is an intimate place, not like Stern Auditorium where Cal played. It holds two hundred and fifty people or so, not two thousand, but still, I'm all tingly.

Tonight Weill Hall holds my dad and my mom, and Laurel and her mother. It holds the other participants' parents, and possibly the founders of Strings with Wings, and definitely the president and administrators of its child company, Pupils with Promise. Most important, Weill Recital Hall holds a handful of men and women from the audition panel of Juilliard, the Manhattan School of Music, and several other conservatories, including Eastman.

Laurel told me tonight that I look luminous, and I believe her. In the mirror I'd been black-and-white, all dark gown and pale shoulders, nude lips, hair in a low bun, wound tight.

And now, straight-backed, feet flat—jaw slack (lips together, teeth apart)—I begin.

My guitar is in my arms, as close as the lover I've never had. Fingers arched, hands hovering, really, I've already started. Before the first note slips from the sound hole, I'm playing the music.

See me now, a statue: dress draping, neck swanlike, left foot on a folding stool like every classical guitarist the world over. This is me, who I am.

Where I go, what I do—it may all depend on this single performance.

The first of Leo Brouwer's *Estudios Sencillos*—simple studies—spins out quickly from beneath my fingers, then ends abruptly after only a minute. I pause, as I should, then continue with the second.

Number two slows things down, raising goosebumps on my arms, hardening my nipples. No matter how many times I play it, it never ceases to captivate me.

I hope the audience feels the same—but then I'm on the third étude, *in* it. There's no time to hope—no time, period. A violently beautiful burst of sound, it's over before I can breathe.

Number four always throws me a little, maybe because the third étude is so short, or maybe because of the 5/4 time signature.

Cal, this is the one that gets me. You always made it sing.

And then I'm at five, meaningless to me except that it reminds me of an old song by R.E.M., and for the millionth time I swear I'm going to send an email to those guys. Six is about speed and steadiness and gorgeous harmonies. Étude seven is marked, *Lo más rápido posible* (as fast as possible). Eight is almost two studies, with a fast and a slow section, and nine is divided into three. Ten is very rhythmic with a slightly elusive downbeat—

Then it's over, but I barely notice the applause, certainly don't take the time to feel it, to pull in the praise. I simply move on to Bach's Chaconne. Segovia's transcription is unparalleled . . .

The finish of the Bach brings more applause, and cheers of "Bravo!" as well. But I couldn't care less. I'm finally here, the place I've been heading all evening: Quatre Pièces Brèves.

Frank Martin's harmonic dreamscape spreads out in time before me like a destination.

Written in 1933, this piece hits me in a way no other ever has. As soon as I begin the Prelude with its single sustained tone, I'm somewhere else. There are mountains in this movement, pastoral plains. Quatre Pièces Brèves has a mysterious prayer-like sensuality I'm afraid I may never fully understand, but I love it. I dive into it. Imagine it dives into me.

At some point while the music cascades over me, I realize I'm slightly out of control. There is an emotion building in me that has nothing to do with how I feel about this piece. But the music continues unwinding from my fingers, like magic, so I don't check myself.

Cal would, he'd reel it in. He'd never let the tempo get away from him like this.

Something at the back of the hall catches my eye. The flash of a camera or—

Focus. Cal would focus.

The music flies, almost plays itself now, but—

Cal. He would have played it better. Played it perfectly. He would have had total control.

Suddenly, in some unfair, twisted trick of time, the first few glorious movements of the piece are behind me, and I'm at the last movement of the Martin, *Comme une Gigue*, which is not a jig at all, but a deceptively disordered jitter. I don't have a second to spare now, for thinking, for worrying, for . . .

Remembering.

Thoughts jostle in my mind, but there's no time. *Don't think, just play.*

But again, at the back of the hall, something flashes, something white, too bright.

Still my fingers don't slip.

The audience isn't supposed to take pictures, but—the flare of white, it comes once more.

And I realize now it's not from the audience; they're unmoving, an ocean of eyes. The white slice like a sickle—

It's a smile.

It's a fierce thing, the sickle smile, as it cracks into the front of my consciousness. It sits below hooded eyes in a too-handsome face. It is framed with full lips that are gluttonous and cruel and coming down hard on mine—

My nails trip on the strings—

And then I hear it. *It's like buzzing inside. Like static.*

But not static—*words.*

Here, wrap your lips around this—

My eyes close for the briefest moment and I see Cal Woods, walking into a burst of light—not white light, but fiery *blueyellowred*—then I feel my skin crawl as Rod Whitaker's big, almost-man hand—but really a man's hand, yes, a man's hand—pulls hard on my hair.

My head snaps back—

The music—

Stops.

Because I stop. I just—stop playing.

But inside me, the sound doesn't stop. *It's like buzzing. Like static. Those words.*

Like a bolt I am up— gone from my seat, leaving the stage.

Minutes later, backstage, there are more words, and the echoes of words, as everyone—Marion, Mom, Dad—all say the same thing.

What happened?

It's as if there are only two words left in the universe.

What happened? What happened?

I, at least, have three.

Three words that break open a black abyss inside of me—

I don't know.

FRUIT

DAVID

Kimmy has a new babysitter. She is not happy.

I am not happy.

Sonya, however, the new sitter, seems very happy. And horny.

Sonya arrived at our house for the first time today, with a frowning Kimmy in tow. In the seven hours she's been here, she's brushed up against me like a wayward cat in search of milk at least twice, maybe more. I'm not sure of the number, because I didn't count the first time or two. Just chalked up the casual collision of Sonya's breast with my bicep to her being kind of—bouncy, or to me being in the way. Her hip bumping mine in the kitchen . . . had to be accidental.

But Kimmy's in bed now, so there can be no excuse, no coincidence that brings Sonya to my bedroom. I hear footsteps—one, two, three—someone ascending to my door.

She doesn't knock, just enters, her mouth forming a little O as if she's surprised. "Sorry! Didn't realize this was your room."

I don't ask her whose room she thought it was, I just wait for the rest.

"You don't remember me, do you?"

"Ah—" She's caught me off guard with this. All at once I'm acutely aware that I've just come from a shower and am wearing a towel like a skirt. She seems aware of it, too—her eyes are everywhere. Finally I say, "I don't."

"You don't, aw. You're so fun-ny." She draws out the last word in that way people do when they're saying something besides what they're saying. That in itself isn't worrying, but the "aw" is. She thinks I've done something cute, possibly on purpose, and I have no idea what that something is. I have absolutely no recollection of seeing this girl, ever, until three o'clock today.

"The Halls' end-of-summer blowout," she says.

Anger floods me.

"Must have been the beer talking. Look, I'm going to bed now." I nod toward the door.

"Oh, right, well, I just wanted to say good night. I mean, I don't think your parents are going to be home for another couple of hours, so—" She lifts her hands to her hair, pushing it back, the movement thrusting her already prominent breasts in my general direction.

For a moment, I just look at her.

Then I think about the guy I've been. The guy I could still be.

"I'll be right downstairs," she says. Paradoxically, she takes a step toward me. "Or . . . I could hang out up here for a while." I don't have a chance to respond before she goes on. "I won't tell Tammy, or Trish?" She giggles. "Can't remember which one you're going out with."

"Neither."

"Oh." Her eyes widen just a little. "Well, then . . ."

I notice her lips now, glistening, like the inside of a plum. She's standing close enough that I can smell their fruity scent. Can imagine them on me, sweet and sticky.

"It doesn't have to mean anything," she says, lowering her voice. "We could just . . ."

A sort of jolt travels through me. I say, "I want it to mean something."

"Even better." She reaches for the hem of her shirt.

"No—I mean, just go, okay? Please."

Because, yeah, I do want it to mean something, and with you, it wouldn't.

RIDE

CATE

Mrs. Bennet had all but begged, so even though I'd rather be home, high and hiding from the world, I'm sitting at the Bennets' kitchen table writing—something. Kimmy is in bed.

The thing that I'm writing might be a poem, but it's missing some crucial ingredient. I have no idea what that secret ingredient is, though I do know that, without it, the thing sucks.

The front door slams. Bryn. Time to call home. Actually, it was time two hours ago, but Bryn's late. Two hours late. Not that I care, except that I'm pretty sure Dad won't answer the line out in the barn at this hour. He's definitely in the zone by now. Mom might be up reading, but she'll be pissed if she has to come get me. I should just call a cab. I try Dad first.

Ring. Redial. Ring. I try Mom.

"This is Jan."

"Mom? It's me. Are you up? Can you give me a ride?"

"I thought your father was going to fetch you."

"He's not answering."

Bryn strides into the kitchen. Bitchy as she can be, I have to admire the way she wears fishnets with wellies and a miniskirt. Her face is wet with rain, and droplets cling to her raven hair. I give her a little wave.

She glares at me with bloodshot eyes and yanks open the fridge door.

Obviously, she's been making the most of the fact that her folks are out of town.

Static crackles in my ear. "What did you say, Mom?"

"I'm in the city. It's midnight—why are you still out? Don't you have school tomorrow?"

"I know, and I do. The Bennets are away."

"I don't remember you telling me that. Did you eat there? What about your father?"

"I told you, he's not answering. And yes, I ate here. With Kimmy."

"I'm sorry, honey." I hear her drop something. "You're breaking up."

No, you are. "I thought I'd be done around nine, and Dad said he'd pick me up, but I guess when I didn't call . . ." *He entered his netherworld.*

"So when Dad didn't hear from you by nine, what? He decided to disown you? Why doesn't that man pick up his phone?" More crackling. Then silence. Like Mom's waiting for an answer, like I have one.

"Mom." I lower my voice. "Bryn was late, so I'm late. Dad probably figured I had a plan. Look, I'll take a cab."

Bryn eyes me, then slaps mayo on a tortilla. She adds half a head of lettuce, rolls it up, and takes a huge bite. This strikes me as very un-Bryn-like.

"Is that your mom?" David comes in shaking water off his hair.

"You look," Bryn says, "like a dog."

Mom's voice cuts in and out. "Damn phone. What did you say?"

"A cab. I'm going to catch a cab."

"I'll take you home," David says.

"Oh. Okay. Thanks," I say to David. "Mom? I've got a ride."

"Great. I'll see you tomorrow, okay? Hate to stay over, but I just couldn't miss this. Hon, you should have seen the clothes." Then, as if it's the most important thing in the world, Mom starts describing what everyone was wearing at the opening she went to earlier. She goes on and on, and it hits me. All the words I can never find? She's got them.

Finally, she hangs up. David looks at me expectantly. Bryn does, too, for that matter.

"My dad says if she goes first, he's getting her a tombstone shaped like a phone."

"Our dad's would be a laptop," Bryn says around a mouthful of tortilla.

"The way he travels, this can't be the only place Dad thinks of as home," David says. "Where will we bury him?"

For a second we all just look at each other, realizing that talking about our parents' gravestones is just about the most maudlin thing on the planet. Then Bryn starts laughing madly.

"You're wasted," David says to her, but he starts laughing and then I do, too. Bryn pulls a pint of ice cream from the freezer, opens it, and plunges a tablespoon in.

David and I head for the door.

She waves the spoon. "Thanks, Davey."

"No problem, little sis."

"I hate when you call me that," she shouts after him.

"I know you do," he calls back.

We stand outside on the porch for a second, contemplating the best way to get to the car without getting wet. But it doesn't really matter, because although it's pouring harder than it has all night, it's, like, seventy-five degrees out. Finally, we take off our shoes and just step into the rain. Our bare feet slap wetly on the driveway.

"It's weird," I say, raising my voice above the sound of the rain. "To see Bryn coming home stoned on a school night and chowing down on a pint of Häagen-Dazs. Then again—I don't really know her."

"You know she loves ice cream. Ice cream for the Ice Queen."

"What about the getting-wasted part?" *Because that part interests me, very much.*

Water paints David's chestnut hair black. Courses down the straight line of his nose as he holds open the passenger door of his father's Porsche. I climb in.

"The getting-wasted part—is new. Watch your fingers."

But I'm not watching anything except him.

And he doesn't close the door, not right away. He just stands there in the rain, giving me plenty of time to see the little frown he tucks under a smile just before he asks, "What about me—do you know me?"

At least, I think that's what he says. But the rattling of the rain mixes with his words, so I don't quite catch them and can't be sure.

I'm not really sure about anything anymore.

ENAMEL

DAVID

Of course she doesn't know me. I'm not sure why I bothered asking.

Warm rain runs down my face.

I've been my brother. No, I tried to be him. Failed.

Jing. The keys hit the driveway with a wet smack. I scoop them up, tossing them easily from my left hand to my right—

Thinking of my father.

"Here, Son, catch this." Football. Baseball. Tennis. Golf.

"David, do that." Student council. Honor Roll. Mr. Popularity.

Be him.

I'd caught every ball he'd ever thrown me. And I'd caught his diseases. Lying. Ambition.

My father is a big-shot lawyer now, well known. But it wasn't always like that. He'd grown up on a farm in New York State. Beef-fed. Homeschooled. All-star athlete.

Scholarship recipient. Fraternity brother. National Leaguer. Husband. Lawyer. Father.

Father of one. Father of two. Father of three.

Father of two.

Then Kimmy came along and turned back the clock. Kimmy came along, and then there were three, like before.

Hell, I know more about my dad than I do about myself. Know more about my brother.

I get in the car. "Cate," I want to say.

I try to remember when her name began to sound like the answer to my questions.

Cate, I wish we could drive away.

I'm dropping all the balls now. Trying to loosen the carefully constructed Jack mask.

But I can't seem to drop the pretense.

So I give her The Smile—

It feels rusty.

RAIN

CATE

As he climbs into the car, David turns the full wattage of his smile on me. I'm not sure why he does this, but I don't mind. Then, I swear, he looks down at my legs.

When I was a few years older than Kimmy, I knew a bunch of girls in the city who were really into horses. Not like the people around here, who actually *ride* horses, who own them even, but in a different way. These girls *collected* horses. Their bedroom walls were covered with pictures of horses. Horse calendars hung on the backs of their bedroom doors. Books about horses lined their bookshelves. Those same girls prized small figurines of horses, made of hard plastic. I liked the feel of them. At one girl's house, I was especially drawn to a black figurine of a colt. Its knobby knees and skewed stance, its legs were somehow . . . familiar.

Now that I live in horse country, I know what the toy makers were going for when they designed that colt. The real colts out in the fields here in Middleburn have the same uncertain bearing. They're . . . wobbly.

For years, when we used to come out here on weekends, I rode, too—with Laurel—and loved it. We took lessons. Rode for hours. I relished the feeling of freedom, the wind in my face.

But one day, the English-style stable where we took lessons had a different groom. Laurel wasn't there, and there was a new instructor. She gave me a different horse, a bigger horse.

When I fell, I wasn't hurt. But the whole incident seemed like a manifestation of my own wobbliness. I lost confidence and stopped riding, but that wasn't the only change I made. I tried to be more still, to keep quiet, keep to myself. That way, no one would know I was wobbly inside. I've fooled a lot of people with my stillness. My parents, for example—although with the concert . . . the way I blew it. Surely now they know I wobble.

David must see it, he must. I'm way wobblier now than I ever was before.

As we drive along Chapel Hill Road there's nothing but the sound of heavy rain, the swish of the wipers. Hurricane season is over in New Jersey, but the tropical cyclone hitting the county tonight must not know that. Inside the car, it's uncomfortably warm. Or maybe it's me.

Then, all at once, it's as if we've driven out from under the deluge. The wipers clunk once, twice, giving a protesting squeak just before David turns them off. Our view of the glistening black road is suddenly clear.

Rolling down the window, David lets in the night. The air is weighted with humidity, the stars and moon hidden behind low clouds. The infrequent lights that mark a stable, or one of the long winding driveways leading off Chapel, glow grainy yellow in the dense darkness, and are ringed with misty halos. We pass field after field.

David nods toward the chlorine-scented bundle in my lap. My wet bathing suit, rolled up in a towel. As promised, the pool is still open and heated. "Been working on your cannonball?"

"Ha-ha. Not really. Making a big splash isn't my thing."

He laughs a little. "Yeah, I know that about you. You keep to your-self." He rubs the back of his neck. "You're so . . . calm. So many girls . . . I don't know. They always seem like they're . . . *wanting.* Wanting . . . something."

You. They want you. Since I can't possibly spit out this basic truth, I remain silent. The night is quiet as well, for now, except for the whisper-ing hiss of the tires on the rain-soaked road, an evocative sound.

"I don't get that from you. That wanting. You do your own thing." He glances over at me. "You're always writing. What do you write?"

"Bad poetry mostly. Sometimes I compose a little music."

"Compose a little music. You make it sound like it's nothing. You're a serious guitarist, right? Not that you've ever played for me—even though I asked you to." He shoots me a pointed look. "When I was laid up, remember?" Then his eyes are on the road again. "You want to make music your career?"

"Yeah, but you know . . ." My throat feels tight. *Yeah, but you know, I choked in front of the world, so now I don't know what I want.*

He gives me another quick glance.

"I think I want to be a writer," I manage to blurt. "Maybe a music critic." *Or maybe I'll just run away, live under a rock.*

"Really," he says, nodding a little. "So, you're good with words."

He didn't miss a beat—I'm so relieved. He doesn't know me, the musician. He hasn't heard about the concert.

"Mine just come out of my mouth," he continues. "I feel like I don't always choose them, feel like . . . I've been taught just what to say."

I shake my head. "I'm not good with words. I said I *want* to be a writer."

"But you are a writer. You write, so you're a writer."

"I don't think that's how it works."

"That's exactly how it works." More quietly he says, "That's how everything works. You do it. You make it happen. Also . . . the opposite: you are what you don't do. For example, if you don't show up, for a friend, let's say, then you're a bad friend. Only, everyone does stuff like that. But there are . . . bigger things." He speaks the next words so softly that I barely hear them. "You let someone drown, you're a murderer."

"What are you saying?"

But the only answer I get is the sound of car wheels on wet road, and the whoosh of night air rushing by David's window.

Maybe he didn't hear me, or maybe he decided not to respond.

Silently I count the white wooden horse fences. They remind me of Cal now.

SILK
CATE

The next day I'm back at the Bennets', saying to Kimmy, "We shouldn't be in here."

In all the years I've been babysitting at the Bennets', I've never actually been in Bryn's room. I look around at the blue-black walls.

Kimmy leaps onto the bed and reaches for the nightstand where Bryn's got an iPod connected to a set of speakers. She hits "Play" and a velvety voice fills the room along with an irresistibly rhythmic synth line.

"Everywhere, everywhere . . ." She's got it cranked to eleven.

"Check this out," she shouts, grabbing a heap of material off the back of Bryn's desk chair.

"Kimmy—" My voice gets lost under the music.

Silver discs dangle from the scrap of pink material Kimmy ties around her waist.

An orange flash comes toward my face as she tosses something similar to me.

"Put it on!" She starts moving her hips. Grinning, she lifts her arms, stretching them out at shoulder level. Pressing the ball of one foot into the ground, she pivots around it.

The voice coming out of the speakers is celebratory, but I don't feel like dancing at all.

"Try it," Kimmy commands. "Use one foot for an anchor, then just—" Again, she circles around the stationary foot, arms undulating. "Try it!" she insists.

Reluctantly, I tie the orange sash low on my hips. The material is thin, sheer over my jeans. I swish my hips a little, side to side. The silver discs shimmer.

"Try a figure eight," she calls over the music. She demonstrates, looking like a younger, happier version of Bryn, with David's hair and honey eyes. "Yeah!" she shouts as I swivel my hips. "Keep that foot nailed to the floor!"

"Where did you learn all this?" I yell over the music.

"Bryn taught me!"

For a second, I think I've misheard. It's hard for me to imagine Bryn taking the time to show Kimmy anything.

The coins on my belt start *jing-jinging* like Kimmy's.

"Now this," she shouts, lifting her arms. Slowly, I lift my arms.

"Tie your shirt up so your belly shows! It's *belly* dancing!" She yells the last few words like a war cry.

I undo a couple buttons and tie my shirttails together like Kimmy's.

"Right, but keep moving!"

I move . . .

"Here!" She tosses me another sash, midnight blue. "Take an end in each hand."

Imitating her, I lift the veil high overhead, stretching my arms out. Then, like Kimmy, I release one end, twirling the cloth so it creates a spinning spiral reaching to the floor.

"Gotta know, gotta know . . . You're beautiful inside . . ."

Following her lead, I grab up the end again, then lift the veil in front of my face, peering over the top edge. Kimmy laughs. I smile a little.

"The love that lives inside you . . ."

My babysitter mind hears the phone ring, but before I can come all the way back from where the music's taken me, Kimmy jingles out of the room at a run.

The song's set on loop. The synth is sinuous, atmospheric. Lifting the veil high, I follow it with my eyes, my head dropping back, my lips parting. Trying to let go of the heaviness that's always on me now, I allow my eyes to close. The music thrums. *I need this.*

Sensing something—movement?—I open my eyes just in time to see David jerk to a stop in front of Bryn's doorway. Childishly, I scrunch my eyes shut. If I can't see him . . .

But a few seconds later, when I peek through my lashes, I see that instead of continuing down the hall as I'd assumed he would, David is now standing directly in front of me.

The translucent scarf hangs between us, a swath of sheer-blue evening that does very little to hide me. Still, I don't lower it.

We stare at each other through the gauzy material as the music pulses against us.

David pulls his gaze from mine, looks down. "What—are you wearing?"

Inexplicably, the music stops.

Still holding the veil high, I follow his eyes down to my hips, and it suddenly seems like there's so much going on . . . I can't answer him. *Tongue-tied mental case.*

David's eyes flicker back and forth between my face and hips. The movement is hummingbird quick, but his hand, as he reaches out and touches the orange sash slung low on my hips, is moving incredibly slowly. Lightly, he grasps one of the discs between a thumb and index finger.

Finally I say, "It's a coin belt."

David looks amused and—something else. He doesn't let go of the coin; in fact, is he giving it just the tiniest tug?

"And you're wearing this because?"

"It's for belly dancing."

"I didn't know you were a belly dancer."

"I'm not."

His brows lift. "That is your belly showing, though, isn't it?" My arms burn from holding up the scarf, but ridiculously, it feels like my only defense against . . . against . . .

He's standing so close. Now he moves again in that slow-motion way, the tip of his finger brushing the skin just below the knot in my shirt. Goosebumps spring up along my arms and then rise everywhere as he continues to touch me, a little lower, just below my belly button.

He seems almost entranced as he watches his hand move slowly back down to the coin belt, and his thumb comes to rest lightly on my right hip bone, his fingers spreading out along the side of my hip. When I feel an increase in pressure, his fingers tightening just a little, my breath catches— but there it is, the difference between leaning his fingers against me and holding me.

"It's Bryn's," I say, as if this somehow explains everything. My voice is breathy, barely there.

"My *sister* Bryn?"

I laugh, and my laughter breaks some kind of spell we've both been under. I'm finally able to lower the scarf. David drops his hand. But he doesn't move away.

"She's taking belly dancing from Ms. Liu."

"Ms. Liu—the gym teacher?"

"Right. It's part of the junior curriculum. If you choose dance."

"And did you choose dance, too?" He looks perplexed, still amused, and very . . . beautiful. I like this new David, lost and laughing. He is . . . approachable. Finally, feeling as if I've waited half my life—and in truth, I realize, it's been a quarter—I step closer to him.

"I'm a sophomore," I say quietly. "I don't get to choose."

And just like that, he doesn't seem confused anymore. "That doesn't seem fair. You should be allowed to choose. If there's any opportunity for choice, they should give it to us. The school should. Our parents should."

Color has risen in his cheeks. This must be some kind of issue for him. But it's hard to think about that right now.

"You're right," I say. I'd intended to match his tone, but it seems that, again, I've lost control of my voice. The way it's wavering now, I might as well be shouting "Smitten!" And "Nervous!" Still, I'm determined. So I steady my traitorous voice, try again. "If I could have a choice about anything, it would be—"

You. I'd choose you.

But I don't even get to say the word *you*, because at that very moment Kimmy's voice layers itself over mine, getting louder as she comes down the hall, talking on the phone.

My face goes hot. Hastily, I untie the coin belt, toss it onto Bryn's bed.

"No encore?"

I shake my head.

David gives me an appraising look. "Seemed like you were pretty into it. Maybe dance is your thing."

Shrugging, I say, "You know I love music."

"I know—hey, you've got to hear this CD I picked up today, new indie release. Come on." He heads out of Bryn's room.

I follow, stomach swooping. Imaginary chorus, on loop.

Idiot, idiot, idiot.

IMAGINATION

DAVID

Kimmy cuts her call short when she sees us. "Where are you guys going?"

I nod toward the far end of the hall, to the short flight of steps that leads up to the door of my room.

"No fair! Cate's here to hang out with me!"

"Cate's here to babysit you and, I believe, you've been babysat—it's past your bedtime."

"Cate," Kimmy mewls.

"Actually—" Cate gives Kimmy her best sorry-I-know-it's-a-drag look. "Sorry."

"Aw . . ." Kimmy pouts but apparently puts on her pajamas, because when I stop by her room forty-five minutes later to see how close Cate is to getting her settled, Kimmy's nested among the covers and Cate's got a book in her hands. Now she closes it, and says, "Shampoo?"

Kimmy's eyes grow heavy-lidded as Cate massages her scalp. A "rinse" and a "blowout" are next. The sound effects are impressive. Laughing, I head to my room.

By the time Cate appears in the doorway, I'm lying on my back on the bed, scrolling through an iPod.

I hadn't given any thought to the state of the bed—the comforter's pulled down, sheets rumpled, pillows tossed—but now, as if Cate's presence makes it so, it seems suddenly intimate, and I notice the way the light of the bedside lamp casts everything in an amber glow.

For a moment, Cate just stands there, biting her lip a little, like she's undecided about something. But when I push up onto my elbows and smile—

She spills into the room.

"I thought you fell asleep in there," I say. She looks sexy, hair still ruffled from dancing, sleepy-eyed from Kimmy's bedtime routine. And suddenly I can't help it. Her hips are level with my eyes. I let my gaze wander over them— then immediately want to kick myself. *I'm not going to do this.*

"Almost," she says. "Must have been the dancing." She blushes.

She's one step behind me, but now she realizes how I've just looked at her.

"About that." I frown. "The dancing. We should talk. You were wearing Bryn's belt, using her scarf—what's the scarf for, anyway?"

"To add mystery to the dance, I guess."

She's flustered. It makes her look a lot less than sixteen. *I am* definitely *not doing this.*

I asked Cate to my room to listen to music, but during the hour I waited for her, while pretending not to wait, I thought about her. An hour is a long time to think about someone.

"Ah, what did you say the scarf was for?" I ask again.

"M y s t e r y." Cate drags the word out. I think next she may ask if I want her to spell it.

"Okay, well, there's no mystery about how the Ice Queen will react if she finds out Kimmy and the babysitter were in her room, listening to her music, wearing her clothes."

Cate's tone turns curt. "They're not her clothes; they're from school." She scowls at me, not sure what I'm up to. But she knows I'm right. If Bryn finds out they've been in her room, there'll be hell to pay.

"Look," she says. "Don't tell, okay? It's not like we were wearing her real clothes."

"I don't know; they looked pretty real to me."

The light from the lamp is shining in Cate's gray eyes, turning them silvery. Magical. But her tone is crisp. "What do you suggest?"

"Well, I might be able to forget what I saw here tonight." I pause dramatically. "No, actually, I don't think I can forget. But I might be able to *pretend* I've forgotten."

I let my eyes drift back down to her hips. She crosses her arms.

"Although that's going to be tough, too," I continue, heaving a sigh. *I can't seem to stop.* "But, maybe, as long as you're not actually dancing, I can be persuaded to look the other way."

"Ha-ha. Look the other way—as in not tell Bryn?"

"The crossing of the Bryn Boundaries." I shake my head. "She's killed for less. But possibly, for a price, I can keep this from her."

Cate bites her lower lip a little, like she'd been doing before. She's so cute—I just want to grab her.

"Okay. Fine. So what do you suggest?" she repeats. "Pricewise, I mean."

I run a hand through my hair, think of touching hers. It's so shiny. Real darkness, not like Bryn's night shade from a bottle. But other than her hair, there's nothing dark about Cate, and it's her light, I realize, that's what I like so much about her. She's got this thing going on, this hard-to-describe, ephemeral light. I must be an idiot, not to have noticed it before.

But I have noticed it.

Or maybe . . . I just want what I always want.

The thought makes me hate myself.

But I don't tell her to go.

216

SCAR TISSUE

CATE

"I might be able to keep your secret safe," David says. "In exchange for . . ."

He does that maddening pause thing again. It's infuriating. Also, I realize that as I wait for his next words, I'm holding my breath.

This is the old David, but the old David never talked to *me* like this, never flirted with me at all, and definitely never turned his golden eyes on me with this look of . . . of?

Frustrated, I let *my* eyes run over his body, look at him the way he just looked at me. I do it out of anger. But I also look at him that way *because I want to*. Want to look and want to stop trying *not* to look. So I stare and let him see me staring. Let him see all the things I can't say, won't say, shouldn't say. In a way, it's a relief. But it also makes me want to close my eyes and vanish. And the opposite: I want to lie down next to him.

He's looking at me intently. When he finally speaks, he says, "In exchange for my silence, you'll have to go to dinner with me."

Dinner?

Dinner. Talking. Words. And I won't be there as Kimmy's baby-sitter, I'll be there as Cate of the tied tongue. Still, *dinner* means that David Bennet has just asked me out on a date. But which David?

"Hey, if you don't want to . . ." His voice is soft.

"No, I mean, I want to, but—"

He looks at me quizzically. *Why aren't you saying yes?*

I look at him the same way. *Why do you want me to have dinner with you?*

Finally, I say, "Okay." Because I want to go out with David, and lately, I've said plenty to him. There's also a ton I haven't said, and twice as much that I want to, if I possibly can.

"Next Saturday?" he asks.

"Next Saturday."

"Unless my folks need a babysitter."

Ah. There it is. The out. I nod.

He smiles. "So, sit down." He gestures vaguely toward the foot of his bed.

Suddenly, I hate him. But I also . . . there's plenty of room for me on the bed. And there is a chair at the foot of the bed. It's sitting in front of his desk, which, I'm kind of surprised I hadn't noticed, is extremely organized and neat. I continue to stand.

He reaches across the bed to a low bookshelf beneath his window and grabs a white paper bag with orange stripes. Without even reading the black lettering on the bag, I know it's from Listen Up! Normally, the contents of *anyone's* Listen Up! bag would interest me, especially David Bennet's. But instead I'm totally distracted.

David's shirt rose up as he reached for the bag, and now a line of skin shows just above the waist of his jeans. Staring at the smooth strip of golden skin, all I can think is, *I want to touch it, touch him—*

Then I suck in a breath.

There's a scar near his hip—it's red, new. The scar disappears under his jeans.

Our eyes catch. He tugs his shirt down. And in that self-conscious moment, he transforms again, becomes the David Bennet who locked himself in his room for a month this summer, the David Bennet I checked on every day for nearly two weeks. The boy I played backgammon with, watched movies with. The sometimes shadow boy that I'm—that Laurel thinks I'm in love with.

"David, what happened?"

He simply ignores the question. "Are you going to sit? I want you to hear this band—"

"Please. Tell me." The words just come out. I don't think. Just ask. Then wish I hadn't.

He sits up, folds his arms. "What time's your dad coming to get you?"

As if on cue, a car honks down in the driveway.

"Now, I guess." Does he hear the dismay in my voice, or just my words?

Words tell everything. Words hide everything.

And now unspoken words crowd the room. *Why won't you tell me what happened to you? Have you told anyone? And what am I really doing in your room?*

"Here," he says, pushing the bag into my hands. "Take a listen. Tell me what you think."

Tell me what you think.

Dad's headlights hit the window. He's turning around. Now the light runs along the wall.

Light through the air, a line of light on the wall . . . and just like that, I get it: Words are three-dimensional. But we pretend they're flat. *Why? Why don't we say what lies beneath our words? Why is everything such a secret?*

Or maybe it's me. Maybe I'm just verbally challenged. Expressively . . . crippled.

The sound of the horn comes again.

"See you around, Babysitter." David's eyes are amber jewels in the light of the bedside lamp.

I'm already halfway down the stairs when he calls, "Good night!"

Great. I didn't even say *good night.* Two words. Two perfectly appropriate words.

If I were normal, they would have come out without a thought.

STONE

CATE

Inspired by the possibilities of last night, I finally decide Laurel's idea is a good one. Go to the cemetery. See the headstone. Try to let go.

I'm still upset that L doesn't believe me—I've turned that night over and over in my mind, and I know what I saw. *Cal was there.* Although the ketamine . . . I can't be sure what effect it's having. Sometimes when I wake up in the morning I feel high. *Maybe I'm losing it.*

As far as the concert, I told Laurel that I choked, that was all. Same thing I told everyone. I don't want anyone to know I was thinking about Cal. About his playing. About him—dying.

I don't want anyone to know that I was seeing Rod Whitaker's sickening smile.

And that I'm not sure how to live in a world where someone like Rod gets to live, while a boy like Cal . . .

I take Dad's Subaru, a step that's clearly not on the path to reestablishing my sanity, since I still don't have my license. But riding my bike in the dark through the icy rain doesn't seem so smart, either, and, contrary to what my parents think, I do know how to drive. Sort of. Laurel taught me right after she got her license. We hadn't left the Ridgeways', but their driveway is as long as some of the streets around here. As for the test . . . I decide it's a technicality at this point.

My parents are both in the city tonight, and I can't possibly get in an accident—I feel strangely invincible here. I've already been in *the* accident. Lightning doesn't strike twice.

But as I pull up to the stop sign at the foot of our street, the fact that one of the two roads I need to take is Chapel Hill momentarily paralyzes me. For a second, I even forget which cemetery I'm going to. Chapel has one at either end, something that, for the first time ever, strikes me as incredibly bizarre.

Driving like a little old lady down Chapel, I reach Olive Slope, the right cemetery, only to find the gate's closed. Of course it is. It's night. My headlights shine on the curling wrought iron. Parking in general was something I hadn't thought of. For a second, I forget how to back up.

Finally, I manage it, then drive to a nearby dead end to park. After walking back to the cemetery, I climb over a low wall, and I'm in. It makes me wonder why there's a gate at all.

I wish Laurel was with me, but she's got a makeup slash make-out session with Dee. She'd been so happy about it, so I'd tried to be happy, too. The same way I tried to convince myself that I hadn't hung up on her a little while ago. I'd just . . . hung up.

It takes me an hour to find the marker, and by the time I do, I'm soaked. It's unseasonably cold, and now the rain is changing over. A few big wet flakes of snow cling to my purple wool coat. The hood is already drenched, so I flip it down.

It's hard to look directly at the stone, so instead I close my eyes and lay a hand on it. When I do, I have the strangest sensation that the coldness of the granite, of the night, is somehow entering me. I welcome it, wishing the chill would turn my heart to ice, so I can't feel.

Stealing the car, thinking about Laurel, contemplating the cemetery gate—all these things were just distractions. Now that I'm here, the reason I've come hits me like a fist.

This is a *graveyard*. I've come to get it through my thick skull that Cal's body is here, *in the ground*. This means, of course, that I couldn't possibly have seen his reflection in my mirror.

But he'd seemed so real, looked so *alive*—

No. Cal is dead.

I try to imagine Laurel telling me that in the matter-of-fact voice she'd used earlier on the phone. She'd softened her tone a little, for me, but she'd been firm: "Cal's gone, Cate. He's gone." There'd been no room for questions. Still, I'd hung up on her.

But she hadn't believed me, because he wasn't there. He's here.

Cal Woods—You Live in Our Hearts.

All of a sudden I'm so tired, I just want to lie down. Instead I kneel, staring at the stone.

When I was little, I used to love to come here and see the "statues." Dad, artist that he is, used to bring me on the weekends. Silently, we'd walk the well-tended paths.

These outings infuriated my mother. "She'll have enough loss in her life, for god's sake—" She'd always cut herself off at that point, shake her head, leave the room. It was as if she didn't want to let the rest of the words out.

She still does that. Leaves the room, leaves the house, when she's angry. It's like she knows once your words escape, they go out into the world and wreak havoc. She stifles words nearly as well as I do. Maybe that's why she's such an advocate for visual artists, people who express themselves with something other than words.

I find a few choice words though, kneeling here in the dark, or maybe they find me.

"Fuck you," I whisper to the stone. But it's not nearly enough, and I turn my face toward the sky, attacking the true target. "Fuck you, God! Fuck you and all your—"

"Cate?"

My head whips around and I'm about to leap to my feet.

David Bennet kneels down next to me. "Hey. Sorry. Didn't mean to startle you."

I'm shaking so hard, all I can do is look at him.

It takes a moment for David to read the words on the marker. "Cate—"

"There's nothing to say," I mumble. "He's gone."

David nods slowly.

But he doesn't get up.

"He's . . . *really gone*," I repeat.

"You sound like you're trying to convince someone."

David is soaked. He must have been here for a while. Now he pushes his wet hair back from his face. More prepared than me, he holds a black umbrella in his hand. I'm about to ask him why he doesn't put it up when I notice it's all angles, metal rods skewering ripped cloth.

"What happened to your umbrella?" I ask. "And what are you doing here?" It's much easier to ask questions than to think about what he's just said. *If I'm trying to convince someone, it's probably me, which means I still don't believe Cal's gone. Which makes me certifiable.*

"My brother." He gestures vaguely with the busted umbrella, to a point someplace behind him.

I'd heard about David's brother. Heard the silences, was more like it. The conversations that snapped shut when I walked in the room.

"He died when I was Kimmy's age." David's expression hardens slightly. It's a look that dares me to pity him. I've never seen it on his face before, and I have certainly seen his face. I have *watched* that face—I can't deny it anymore—for years.

All the times I lay by the pool, sat on the couch with Kimmy watching movies . . . for years I hadn't really noticed David, *but I had*. I knew everything about him, knew he'd been a star athlete, knew he'd been someone's boyfriend—knew he'd been a jerk. I knew his smile. Knew he was changing. And, yes, along with all the other details I'd memorized over the years, I discover now, that I'd known he'd been *hurting*. Been missing something, though he had everything. Only it wasn't a something, it was a *someone*. How had I not known that?

For a minute I struggle to find the right words, to acknowledge the void in his life, maybe even compare it to mine.

But all I can think of to say is "I'm sorry," so I decide to say nothing at all.

If his brother died when David was nine, it's way too late to say sorry.

SNOW

DAVID

Snow doesn't produce a sound. Rather, it emits stillness.

Cate's stillness is not so different, and like the snow, that still aspect of her, I'm starting to understand, has to do with something frozen.

Now I speak carefully into the non-sound, the snow silence.

"Cate, it might help you to know, I chased the ghost of my brother for years."

It's snow quiet again.

The flakes have become slightly smaller, drier, the crystals more precisely shaped, icy stars beginning to stick as the temperature drops.

"Not at first. I was too young. But starting at about fourteen, I explored a lot of ideas. I was big on Buddhism. Thinking, you know, maybe in another life . . . I wanted to believe in something . . . *anything*. Anything other than the truth, which was that Jack was gone. That was it."

Cate's eyes say, *No*.

"That's too simple," she murmurs. "Do you really believe that? Believe that there's nothing? That we die and it's over?" Sounding slightly desperate she asks, "What did that look like? The chase, I mean. Chasing his . . . ghost."

"Besides my Buddhist phase?" I feel my lips twist. "I met with a priest. Contacted a—this sounds stupid—a medium. I'm pretty sure I tried yelling at God, too. Repeatedly."

"So you're saying it won't work? The yelling-at-God approach?" Cate says this lightly, as if she, too, is ready to give up. But her gray eyes are serious.

I shake my head. "Yelling at God, at the sky. Talking to these fucking stones—sorry. Don't listen to me. Everybody handles loss—"

"Differently, sure. But what about *finding*? Did you ever—have you ever heard his voice or, or . . ."

A sigh slips from my lips before I can stop it, though I think maybe she hasn't heard it, because in the same moment the wind picks up, sweeps away the snow quiet.

Then I tell her the truth, though it's not what she wants to hear, and push to my feet.

But the wind's kept my words from her as well. "What did you say?" she asks.

"I never heard anything," I repeat, raising my voice over the wind. "Never saw anything." I offer her a hand. Pull her to her feet. "I don't believe in ghosts, if that's what you're asking."

The wind kicks up a notch suddenly, tearing through the cemetery, sending wet snow into our faces, down the collar of my shirt. Cate shouts now so I can hear her over the gusting, says something like, "Then why are you here?"

"What?" I shout back.

Shivering hard, she pushes the words through chattering teeth. "Why do you come to see your brother *here* if you don't believe in ghosts, don't believe his spirit . . . resides somewhere?"

"I didn't say I didn't believe in his spirit. When he died—when anyone dies—I think they become a part of . . . everything. Everything in nature. A person's soul, essence—whatever you want to call it—I think it joins the energy that surrounds us. The sky. The . . . stars." I glance around at the trees bordering the cemetery, their black-shadow branches swaying wildly now in the wind. "The air, maybe."

It's ridiculous that we're trying to talk out here, in what's obviously becoming some kind of freakishly early winter storm, but it's like she can't let this go. It's as if, because my brother is dead, I must know something.

"You didn't really answer," she shouts. "If a person's soul, or whatever, becomes part of *everything*, why do you come *here*?"

Cate's lips are slightly parted as she continues to look up at me with what is, I see now, an imploring expression. This expression makes her look younger than she is. Like a kid, the kind of kid who comes to the cemetery on Halloween, not with a six-pack and a bunch of friends, but as a seeker: someone looking for a sign, a message, some words that can never be spoken because the speaker is dead.

I don't want to hurt this part of Cate, this hopeful kid. But I also know that the other Cate, the Cate who pulled me out of myself this summer, the grown-up part of her that's taken care of Kimmy for the last four years after my parents deemed Bryn and me too busy, or possibly too irresponsible—she can handle this, needs to handle it. She needs to get over this guy, Cal.

Then again, what the hell do I know? I've come here for years, I don't even know why. Not anymore. So that's what I tell her as the snow turns to sleet.

"I don't know, Cate, why I come here. But if there's a reason . . . it changes."

She nods and watches as the wind nearly tears the umbrella from my hands. For half a minute I wrestle with it, trying to get the spokes in order. Then I give up, putting an arm around her, pulling her against me as if, somehow, I can keep her dry. As if I can protect her.

SPLINTERS

CATE

David might not be keeping the weather off me, but he's keeping something off.

"Did you drive?" His lips brush my ear as he leans in to make himself heard, his breath warm on my cheek. I gesture toward the east side of the cemetery. He says, "I'll walk you."

As we angle into the wind, I glance down at the useless umbrella in his hand, suddenly understanding that he'd hit it against something. That's how it got broken. My intuition flares, and I picture David Bennet, smashing the umbrella against a headstone.

So he *is* still trying.

It's a visceral image: David, a granite marker, the broken black bat of an umbrella. All at once the gesture strikes me as utterly brilliant, necessary even. *I need to get home.*

Quickly, I say goodbye and get in the car, leaving David at the edge of the cemetery looking slightly stunned. Just before I shut the door, I think he calls my name, but I'm not sure.

Then I'm driving. Sleet splattering the windshield. As I pass The Killing Tree, my thoughts scatter like rain. *Cal's dead.*

Why can't I let him go?

Humming fills the garage, and the door closes with a clatter. But I don't move. I just sit there, in the car, in the garage, all the urgency I'd felt, the inspiration, drained away now.

The light snaps off, leaving me in darkness. Gradually, my eyes grow used to the lack of light. A row of trash cans, a couple of old bikes, and shadows . . . shadows . . .

My friend's brother did it in the garage, the night of her senior prom. Selfish bastard. Then again, they say that all suicides are selfish.

I let my head fall back against the seat. Suicide. There are probably plenty of people out there who want to die . . .

Cal's dad left when Cal was a kid, and his mom was never around. Cal hadn't had it easy, but he would never have taken his own life—why did it have to be him?

Suicide . . . it's a horrible thing.

It is also . . . a possibility.

Like many people, I have given this possibility a lot of thought, although not for myself. For me there is only one interesting aspect of suicide, and it is not the piece that leaves you dead.

Suicide is not contagious—it can't be spread, and that is what I find reassuring. While most people who consider suicide are comforted by the idea that they can always bow out, in the middle of the night, say, or the middle of life, I appreciate only the fact that it can't be passed to another person, like a germ.

That it isn't in your blood.

Suicide. I don't get how anyone can do it. Can't understand why anyone would *want* to do it. Why anyone would want to die in a garage, want to die at all. *I could never, ever kill myself.* I'd need a hit man. Need to hire someone to murder me.

I run my hands over my face. Cal. Why did it have to be him?

In my mind's eye I see the Sutton Prep girls circling The Killing Tree like birds or ballerinas, necks arching, faces dipping— looking, and *looking,* hoping to find something, some . . . remnant of Cal, that would somehow stop the loss of him from being so *total,* so complete.

Who would look for me if I disappeared in an instant the way Cal did?

Had my mother asked herself that question? Had she thought of me at all?

I remember going to visit her after . . . but I don't remember much. Just that big green lawn at the place she went to "recover," an endless lawn that stretched forever. A wide beautiful barrier I had to cross that day, to where she sat under a tree like some Buddha.

Beautiful gardens bordered the edges of that long lawn . . . gardens filled with tall purple irises, their petals sloping away from their wide-open centers . . . dark centers, that made me think of the color of the sky just before night falls.

I remember a stooped gardener, in a broad-brimmed hat . . .

Mothers . . . they're gardeners of a different sort. So what right do they have to walk away from their barely budding flowers?

I stayed with my gram for a while, then my cousins . . .

But it was my aunt who told me the truth. Told me the fighting between my parents had been so bad my dad temporarily lost sight in one eye. That made sense. He's a visual artist.

But my mom, she didn't wait for something to stop working. She decided she wanted to stop living. Pills. That's what my aunt said. A handful.

Not too long ago, I confronted my mother. Asked her to write it all down—probably because I didn't want to talk about it, but I wanted to know. Wanted the details from her, not from my aunt, not from my memory, which is thankfully *free* of the details. Because how can I know what really happened unless she tells me? She was alone when she took the pills.

God. I'd never want to die alone.

She never did write about it for me. Just a letter was all I wanted, so I could understand. So I could dissect her words. Try to find proof. A guarantee. Something that would tell me it was her, only her. That it wasn't my fault somehow, that I didn't drive her to it. And that I wouldn't, *couldn't* inherit what she had, that kind of crazy. Because she had to be crazy, right? When she tried it?

I wobble. *How close is that to crazy?*

On the upside: she did tell me she hadn't really wanted to die.

"I just wanted to *get out*," she said.

Um, *thanks?*

She'd waved a hand, as if my understanding of that part wasn't important. "It wasn't you; it was your father." But that still showed me that he had more effect on her than I did. Still meant, in essence, that I didn't matter. Whether she meant to kill herself or scare my dad, or both, or neither, she still left *me*. I was three.

She left for three weeks, or six weeks, or three months . . . I forget what she said. See? That's why I wanted her to write it down. How am I supposed to remember the story when I'm still trying to understand it? I wanted her to *write it down* so I could look at it, later. Study and memorize and analyze the literary DNA she'd leave in a letter. Compare her genes with mine.

I have memories of Mom dangling me over her knees as she crouched down on the kitchen floor, kissing my neck, the two of us laughing. Memories of her telling me she loved me.

But, at some point, maybe when I couldn't take the ups and downs any longer, her alternating presence and absence, I shut down. It must have seemed . . . safer. Even Laurel—who can be a cold bitch sometimes—used to tell me my soul was frozen. I told her she was just trying to get me to go with her.

Even as a musician I've excelled in technique, not expression. Most of my emotions have remained locked away, in a cage of music theory.

Then last summer . . . the emotions that slept in me the way fish sleep in winter water, began to wake . . .

But now, again, they're somnolent.

And, maybe, it's like this for everyone. Once you experience a loss or a betrayal. A death . . .

A trivial misunderstanding that simmers over the course of a day, then bursts into a fiery argument, like Laurel and Dee's.

A suicide.

An accident.

There are so many ways to lose love; is it even worth finding?

Love means ten thousand different things to ten thousand different people—there is no harder word to define.

My mother's love . . . is a ghost of what it was. My parents' love for each other, the same.

Maybe all loves die . . .

Turn to ghosts.

The thought propels me out of the car.

In the house, I trot upstairs and grab my guitar, then slip-slide out to the barn. I flash back to being onstage at Weill Hall.

This is one ghost I need to exorcise.

Once I'm inside the barn, I take the Martin out of its case.

It's killing me already, how it bounces off the old wood of the ladder as I climb, but this guitar is going to have a lot more than a ding or two in it before I'm done. I'm out for blood.

Up in the hayloft I pause, considering. But in the end there's nothing rock star about it.

There's not even the drama of David's umbrella.

I simply hold it over the edge—

And let it drop.

WEB

DAVID

The drop into the cyber abyss is effortless. I start out with a homework assignment but rabbit-hole quickly.

Man, where do they find these girls?

I am eyes.

The speed of sound—that was my question. What's the speed of sound?

Cartoon sex, that's pretty much what this is. Going to quit in a minute, just want to see . . .

I am fingers.

Wikipedia, NASA, Wired—any of these sites will tell me the speed of sound.

Some of these things—you can't unsee.

I am letters, numbers, shortcuts, codes.

Seven hundred and sixty mph, seven hundred seventy—it doesn't really seem that fast.

How fast did Cate Reese run away from me tonight? Cate . . . I'm going to stop. I just . . . want to check out this one site . . .

I am a keyboard, a credit card, an expiration date.

Wings at the Speed of Sound is an album by Paul McCartney. "Speed of Sound" is a Coldplay song.

I'm done now, as soon as I follow this last link . . .

I am . . . desire.

The speed of light is faster than the speed of sound.

So is the speed of a bullet.

Just need to click . . .

I am identifiable. But . . .

I am unknown.

PART III: WINTER

BLOOD

DAVID

"In a pool of his own blood."

"That's bullshit. You don't know that's how it went down."

"Listen to you, all badass, *'How it went down.'* I *do* know, though. My uncle's a cop."

You couldn't escape the conversations. Every class. The halls. The cafeteria.

"You going? Whitaker would've wanted his funeral to be a fucking party!"

"Would have wanted to be embalmed with beer."

"Buried between a girl's legs."

At lunch I sit next to my sister. My skin is gooseflesh. My head is stone. I never went to bed last night.

Laurel Ridgeway and her girlfriend—Dee, I think her name is—are at the other end of the table. They've been arguing. Now they're having makeup sex with their eyes.

Everyone else is talking about Rod. How he killed himself with his father's gun.

Sandy Clayton sits at a table not far from ours. Her eyes find Bryn's. Bryn looks away.

My sister was among the first to find out because, for some weird reason, the first call Mr. Whitaker made after he found his son's body was to our father. Not because our father had also lost a son, but because he's a lawyer. She'd overheard the call.

Bryn's already told all this to Laurel. Now Laurel, her eyebrows going ballistic, tells everyone else. "And," she says, "there's this: Rod Whitaker was far too fond of himself to take his own life, right?" She directs the last part of this comment to Cate, who, to my surprise, has just appeared at the table. Her gray eyes are ghostly oceans today, glassy, with dilated pupils.

Dee slithers onto Laurel's lap and slit-eye smiles at Cate.

"*I* heard," she says to the table in general, "there were signs of a *struggle*."

Signs of a struggle, possibly, signs of two people, definitely. That's the rumor.

Two chairs facing each other, two glasses on the table. One glass full, one glass empty. The rug mussed. A desk moved. Books and papers that had been piled up, scattered on the floor. The cops said it looked like a conversation had turned into an argument. *Two people, a friendly chat that went south.* Dee suggests this is why Mr. Whitaker called my father.

"*He* probably killed Rod and knew he'd need a *lawyer*." For some reason, Dee looks smug as she says this. Or maybe that's the expression she always wears. I don't like her.

Cate is silent, writing in a notebook. The rest of us eat lunch. Various people drop by the table with pieces of conflicting information.

Mr. Whitaker has been arrested. He's been released.

He'd been home at the time of Rod's death. He'd been away.

He'd caught Rod drinking. Stealing. Drugging. Dealing.

Screwing some girl in his parents' bed.

By dismissal, the most popular rumor was that a team of detectives had concluded Rod's struggle had been only with himself. Also, that Mr. Whitaker had been out of town at the time of Rod's death, and the only fresh fingerprints were those of his son.

That night, Rod's mom posted prayers on his Facebook page.

And she wrote that, although her son hadn't left a note:

"Rod recently confessed to having some sinful issues. Please pray for his soul."

LIE

CATE

With a start I sit up.

"Cate?"

Light leaks in through the crack under the bedroom door.

"Cate? Are you awake?" Mom's voice drifts up from downstairs. The front door bangs.

If I hadn't been awake, I certainly would be now.

"Can you come down, Cate?"

"Hang on," I call, pulling on a pair of jeans and grabbing a sweater—

A small square of paper falls to the floor and slides beneath the bed.

Bending down, I sweep my hand around and find the little packet up against a pile of notebooks.

Pulling it out, I finger the edges. I haven't seen my parents together in forever. Getting high right now is either a really good idea or a really bad one.

The utopia of feeling even a little "gone" is tempting. Especially because it's usually accompanied by feeling like everything will be okay when I'm pretty sure nothing will ever be okay again. I'd have no problem giving up K physically, but emotionally? I think how good it would feel right now to take just a little before facing my folks.

They went to some event in the city tonight, so I can't imagine why they're hollering for me at—I glance at the clock on the bedside table—just after eleven.

"Catherine?" *Catherine.* This must be serious.

I shove the K into my messenger bag between a bunch of ten- and twenty-dollar bills I've been meaning to deposit. By the time I get downstairs, my parents are sitting at the kitchen table.

It's such a rare thing that we're even all in the house at the same time, let alone together in the kitchen, that the hour seems by far the least off thing about this.

"Tea?" Mom asks.

I shoot a look at Dad. *Is this, or is this not, totally weird?*

A frown pulls at his lips.

Cal. They must have seen him—no. Impossible. This must have to do with Rod. The school counselor led the students in a minute of silence at an assembly today, then told us that, for parents, the death of a child in the community—

"Did we wake you?" Mom bites her lip, as if I'm going to reprimand her.

"Not really." My eyes are Ping-Pong balls—Mom, Dad, Mom, Dad. As much as I'd like to be in bed, stalling for time while I figure out what they want seems like a good idea. "How was New York? How was your, ah, your . . ."

Mom raises an eyebrow. "We went to Johann's opening."

"Oh. Right." It's surprising, even with everything that's happened, that I'd forgotten the show. The tall German artist who'd slept on our couch for an entire summer when I was nine has been a great friend to all of us. He'd been at our apartment constantly. "So was the exhibit a—"

As if he can't contain himself a moment later, Dad bursts out, "Cate, your guitar. Why was it lying on the floor out in the barn? What happened?"

"What happened?" Mom echoes.

What happened?

Once more I look back and forth between the two of them. Then I do what any self-respecting teenage girl would do.

.I lie.

"It's . . . an experiment for science—I mean an art project."

"What?"

"What?"

"Art. Project. For school."

"Catherine Reese. Do you have any idea how much that instrument cost?"

"Jesus Christ, Cate."

"Yes, and no—but close. The experience I mean. It was . . . a spiritual thing. I felt . . . called. To do it."

"But Catherine, the cost. I don't just mean the money—"

"But mostly the money. Holy Mother of God, Cate."

"Please." I hold up both hands and go still, like I'm a conductor about to cue an orchestra. "First of all, Dad. Your Catholicism is showing. I'm sure you don't want that. Second. You two. You should know better than anyone, except maybe Johann. Artists need to make sacrifices. Consider the guitar . . . to be a fatted calf. A tithe. To the art gods."

The kettle screams from the stove.

I swan out of the room.

LINOLEUM

DAVID

Tammy's waiting for me to look at her, at more than just her feet, but I don't look up. Only shove my hands deeper into my pockets, lean back against the wall of the cafeteria. Imagine that if I lean hard enough, the wall will give way. I'll fall through. Wind up in a different dimension or, at the very least, a different room.

"*What* is your problem, David? You don't return my calls, don't answer my texts."

Tammy's heels are so high she's standing at an angle. I'm thankful for gravity, or whatever it is that's keeping her from pitching into me.

She's going on now about "our relationship." Like she's forgotten we don't have one. I should never have given her a ride the other day. A couple of miles in the car, a hug hello, the chem-test answers—apparently it means that we're a couple. Trish did the same thing recently, went hot, then cold—and blamed me. She cried. Told me that I "send mixed signals."

Her voice is getting louder. I continue to study her feet. Cocking my head a little, I try for a different view. One that might possibly enlighten me to the "how" of her heels, maybe even the "why" of them. Her feet, balancing on the ridiculously steep slopes, are practically perpendicular to the floor. I can't look away.

"*What?* What are you staring at?" Her voice drops and she says something else—she's getting serious. But I'm not listening anymore.

For some reason, all I can think about now is the floor. The linoleum is a sickly yellow, while the walls of the cafeteria are gray. Wolverine Gray they call it. We're the Wolverines. Or rather—I *was* a Wolverine. Now I'm just me.

Apparently, like my father, Tammy isn't happy about this.

"All of those games I went to last year, and you just go and quit? The way you're acting like 'we' don't matter—does it mean you're quitting 'us' again now, too?"

How long did we go out last year? Seems like I should know this. But we've hooked up so many times . . .

She's going for the Oscar now, eyes filling up with tears.

"David," she whispers dramatically.

It's another chance. I can still jump in, say sorry, and pull her against me. Kiss her and tell her, *I want you.* Because isn't that all *she* wants?

High school guys get a bad rap for thinking about sex all the time, but we're not the only ones—

Suddenly Tammy *is* up against me—

Only all at once I've had enough. Hands pop out of pockets, reach for her shoulders—but then I think better of it, and sort of slide out from between her and the wall.

"Just not working out," I say softly, as if continuing a sentence I'd already started. I begin to walk away—only she grabs my arm, spins me around—and kisses me.

Through the edge of her blonde bob I see Cate.

Cate—sees me.

AIR
CATE

It's like their kiss is taking up all the air in the room.

Then Laurel has my hand and is tugging me out the back doors of the cafeteria, onto the flagstone patio.

I'm busy muttering "I'm an idiot" over and over again like it's the chorus of one of my favorite pop songs. Laurel objects.

"You're not." She settles next to me on the wall and searches my face. The wind lifts her long blonde hair. "You're just in love."

"In love? Please. How can I be in love with David Bennet?" *A crush. Maybe. For some sick reason, but what would that reason even be? I want to be used?* "He's gone out with a million girls. Plus, I babysit his sister. And he's a senior. He's like, in a different world."

"Hello? Last thing I knew? You, me, David—we were all inhabiting the same planet."

"Are you sure about that, L? Because I never, ever see you anymore."

Laurel frowns.

"I'm sorry," I say. "It's just . . . I miss you. Thanks for hauling me out of there, by the way."

"Yeah, sure. I kind of had to. That fish-out-of-water look? So last year."

"Ha-ha." But I don't know what my problem is. I *knew* he had a girlfriend. He always has a girlfriend. And a . . . whatever. A whoever. A few whoevers. "Dee's right: he's a slut. He's gone out with a million girls."

"You already said that."

"It's worth repeating."

"Is it? Is he going out with a million girls today? Besides, just because he's been with a lot of girls doesn't mean he's not a nice guy."

"Why are you defending him?"

"Because you're in love with him."

"I'm not! Besides, Tammy's beautiful. Magazine beautiful. Even after he went out with what's-her-name, he went back to Tammy. He's never going to break up with her, not for me."

Suddenly, the door across the patio flies open and slams against the side of the school. David Bennet strides out, swiftly crossing the flagstones, and stops right in front of me. One of his cheeks is red. The shape of the redness vaguely resembles a hand.

Inside the cafeteria, Tammy bangs on the window.

David purses his lips but keeps his eyes on mine.

"I think," Laurel says softly, "he just did."

The bell for fifth period rings.

"Where's your class, Cate?" David asks. "I'd—I'd like to walk with you, if that's okay."

We walk, but we don't talk. I try to figure out what he wants. His smile is lopsided. Mine probably is, too.

We reach my class and he turns to me. "Did you ever talk to my sister?"

"What—oh. You mean about—not really. Sort of. Well, yeah, I did. We did. Talk."

He nods a little but seems unsatisfied. I can't blame him, but what does he want me to say? "Is that why you wanted to walk with me?"

"No. Well, yes. And no. I'm worried. I think . . . Bryn might have been over there."

"Over where?"

"Rod Whitaker's."

CRACKS

CATE

Why haven't you been practicing?

Goosebumps spring up under my clothes. "Cal?" I'm high, but still. "Cal, is that you?"

I listen closely, but all I hear is the wind blowing in through the back of the barn, through a new crack up by the eaves that lets in too much weather and the occasional bird.

Miraculously, there are no cracks in my guitar. Just those few superficial dings from where it hit the ladder. The neck, however, is horribly out of alignment. The instrument is unplayable.

"Cate?"

I whirl around— Dad.

"You . . . are you talking to yourself? I've—hmm—done that before. Out here."

But he looks worried, and I'm not sure I believe he's ever talked to himself. He barely talks to me. Or Mom. Alone out here, maybe he utters a choice swear word now and again, but a conversation with himself? Not likely. I wonder how much he's heard.

Surreptitiously, I look around the barn, scanning the dark corners. "You okay, honey?"

"I'm fine." *And, yep, pretty high.* "Oh hey, Dad? Stop doing the dad thing. It isn't you."

"Hmm. Well, ah—your mom and I are going to the city."

"Gee, what a surprise." I set the Martin in its case. My fingers trip over the latches.

"Cate, are you . . . on anything?"

"Nope. You must be projecting." He looks stricken. "Dad. I was *joking.*"

But referring to his past addiction is a very bad joke, and we both know it. I know it, but I can't *feel* it. Can't feel that I've just stuck a knife in my father. Not with a bump of K in me.

"You'd better go. You guys are going to miss the boat."

"Right. I'd better. Have, ah—fun."

Fun. Painting is Dad's way of having fun now, but it wasn't always like that.

"Guess anyone can become an addict," Laurel had said to me one day after we'd talked about my dad, about how he'd slipped.

He'd used. I didn't know *what* he'd used, only knew that he'd disappeared for a few days and had sent my parents' marriage into a tailspin.

I'd tried to hang on—been yanked back and forth, back and forth—a reluctant rider on the most dangerous attraction at a theme park I was too young for.

The mental whiplash had sent me crying to Laurel.

She'd been a good listener, had even made me laugh. "The grace of Laurel," I'd said afterward.

"What?"

"Oh, you know. That expression: 'There, but for the grace of God, go I.' You're a close second, Lovecat." I'd grinned at her then. All better.

"I love you, too. But what does that mean, 'There but for the'—what was the rest of it?"

"Grace of God. It's something they say at meetings. AA meetings, NA meetings. It basically means without a line to God—without God's line to you—you're screwed."

"How do you know about those kinds of meetings?"

"Remember Johann? Artist slash gallery owner?"

"Family friend? Kind of whacked? I've met him a few times."

"Right." And then, even though twelve-step programs are supposed to be anonymous, I tell her Johann's story. How he used to show up at our apartment high on—well, I don't know what he was on, I was too little to know. But I knew what high looked like.

"They have this thing, in the program," I told Laurel. "A saying. Something like, 'Wherever three or more are gathered.'"

Laurel gives me a blank look.

"Basically, they started a meeting in our living room. I used to sit on the stairs and listen."

I love Johann, but at the time, I didn't know him well. He was funny and nice, though, so I wanted to help. But when I walked into the living room one night, Mom sent me back to bed. Which of course made me more curious about what they were doing.

"So I spied on them. It was only after another half-dozen people showed up over the next few weeks that I understood: My parents weren't just hosting a meeting. *They were active participants.* Once I started paying attention, I got it. Both my parents had problems with drugs and alcohol. There were other problems, too. Other people. Affairs."

"Wow."

"I know."

Now, in the barn, I imagine what Laurel would say if she were here: "I probably shouldn't have given that ketamine shit to you."

But it's my parents who have—had—problems with drugs, not me. Ketamine is the only drug I've ever done—I'm way too responsible. Then again, what I said to Dad tonight . . .

When he'd left the barn, he'd still worn that wounded look on his face. I'd used way too much ammunition. I'd only wanted to fire a warning shot, to get him to go. I hadn't meant to obliterate him.

I kick at the floor. If I forget about the fact that I just did something unforgivable, *I feel good*, and that's what I want: I just want to feel good. Throwing my arms out, I spin— and high overhead, the ceiling spins with me. I laugh, and for a second I think I hear Cal laughing, too.

But again, it's only the wind.

And just like that, my mood plummets. The barn suddenly seems dark and oppressive. Dreary despite Dad's vivid canvases. I wonder, if I got higher, could I get that good feeling back?

But another bump would probably put me in a K-hole. And despite my infatuation with the magical world of ketamine, I'm not in the mood to be immobile.

Sometimes that happens, when I take too much.

HOLE

DAVID

My locker is in the main hall. I hear everything.

"He was too smart."

"Too dumb."

"Too full of cum—he wouldn't have done it, it's bullshit."

"Yeah? Still think he was murdered?"

Rod Whitaker's death has been declared a suicide. For most, the results of the investigation are a relief. Not that anyone ever really believed he'd been murdered.

But. Suicide?

Shoulders slump. Brows furrow.

I see Cate coming down the hall. Watch as she stops Bryn.

A narrow strip of bright blonde runs down the center of my sister's scalp, a flaxen line bursting through inky black. But her eyes are shuttered, and she speaks before Cate can.

"He wasn't the type, do you think?"

I think of my brother. Watch Cate's face. But of course, Cate never knew Jack. And yet.

Her expression flickers, frames of a film: puzzlement, pain, and then—I think—something positive. But Cate Reese and suicide, what could she know?

"I don't think there's a type," she says. "You can't tell."

"You can't tell," Bryn repeats. Then heads down the hall.

But before she's gone more than ten feet, Sandy Clayton comes out of a classroom, beckons her. I wince. There's just one thing they have in common.

Bryn looks over her shoulder at Cate, tips her head, indicating Cate should follow. Then she glances in my direction. On impulse, I join them. Cate flushes, I give her a grim smile.

Down one hall, another, into the basement—we squeeze by a cabinet wedged under a stairwell. Supposedly, it's been here since the '90s. It's not a door with a lock, but it's what makes this corner a popular spot.

At the start of the year, when I'd needed some space, I came down here, stumbling on Blaise Mitchell, one of Rod's henchmen. I don't know who the girl kneeling in front of him was, didn't stick around to find out—though I'd frozen for a second, fixated on the snakelike movement of her head. I'm bummed now to discover that the image hasn't faded: his fingers splayed, laced tight in her hair, pushing her, like a machine. Dismayed, I'd spun on my heel and left, without finding out first if she was into it or not.

I guess it's because I'm thinking about Mitchell, his grin when he'd seen me, that I don't ask Bryn exactly why she's brought us down here. But as slow as I am to speak, Sandy's quick, her voice a darting thing, as if all of us crowded together in such a small space is a trigger for instant intimacy. "I'm glad he's dead," she blurts.

Cate gapes for a second, but I get it, because I was there.

"I know it's wrong," Sandy says. "I mean, it's messed up, to be glad someone's dead."

"Not if that someone was a total dickhead," Bryn answers drily and without hesitation, conferring forgiveness with a twist of her lips.

Sandy beams.

My sister nods, then says—

Nothing. Just opens her mouth, closes it.

"What is it?" Cate asks. But she's looking at me. Her pupils are dark, dark, dark.

"This place is skeevy; let's go," Bryn says suddenly.

And we go, but there's something unsaid. We all know it.

Cate glances at me, then at Bryn, then at me. But I'm as silent as my sister.

The four of us walk down the hall without speaking. But something's changed—we all feel it. The three girls have bonded—I've been their witness.

All three of them, victims of Rod's voracious abuse—a look, a leer, a shove, a violation. How long will it hurt them?

Rod would have graduated this spring, gone to college. Would he have been a rapist there, too?

The three girls are connected because of his cruelty. He was selfish in the worst sense of the word. He'd been brutal—done unspeakable things.

And yet, inexplicably, he'd been one of the most popular guys in the school.

DISSONANCE
CATE

In anticipation of telling Laurel that I heard Cal's voice, I've gotten high, maybe a little too high. I'm hoping L doesn't hold it against me. She's gotten pretty down on me taking K.

While I wait for her, I restlessly write random words on a pad. A dark melody hums through me. I think, maybe, it was inspired by Cal.

But then all at once, I picture the Deep Dark Love guy, picture his face, wearing that knowing smile, the one that twisted his lips, just before I ran for the cab.

I know now what that smile meant. He'd *known* that the music had floored me, known all along. He'd seen me from the stage—he'd said as much: "You sure were listening tonight."

Then he'd fanned me. He'd been all flirty, inviting me to another gig, asking for my number—which I'd stupidly given him, not that he ever called. It was all so much bullshit. He shouldn't have said anything— the music had already made me a fan. He should have seen that.

Just like I should have seen that Laurel wasn't going to believe me. Again.

When she arrives in my room, The Conversation gets under way immediately. But it doesn't matter what I say. Laurel continues to be extremely closed-minded in matters of the paranormal.

"I have enough trouble with normal," she says now.

"Laurel, I know you didn't really know Cal like I did—"

"Aw, Lovecat. I didn't." She pulls me into a hug, releases me slowly. "But I know you miss him. I'm sorry." Now Laurel shifts her weight. "Your mom told me about your guitar."

"What about it?"

"Come on, Cate. Art project? Did you really break your Martin? How are you going to play that date in Brooklyn?"

Something surges in my chest.

Did I really never call? Never cancel? I sink down on the desk chair. I don't believe it. I mean, I do believe it—having that date on the calendar connects me to Cal. But I never planned to actually play it. But I can't cancel, either. If I call to cancel, I'll have to tell them about Cal.

"It's soon, isn't it?" Laurel asks.

But I'm on my computer, scrolling through my calendar. When *is* it exactly? Where's the club? I need to at least look up the number. They must have a website . . .

"Okay," Laurel says. I glance up at her. Her blonde brows are drawn down. "Cate. Smashing your guitar—please tell me you didn't just do it to get your folks' attention."

"Fuck. You. L." I pronounce the words with quiet precision. "And I didn't *smash* it."

She rubs her forehead as though she can wipe away the scowl there. "Really? I'm glad. And I'm just saying. Your folks are never around, and I'm sorry I've been spending so much time with Dee lately, but—"

"I'm not looking for anyone's attention! But speaking of someone who wants *yours* 24-7, if you and Dee are so tight, why's she always hanging on Blaise Mitchell?"

As soon as the words have flown out of my mouth, I wish I could take them back. L's probably never seen Dee flirting with Blaise—Dee only does it when Laurel's not around. I shouldn't have dropped the news like a bomb.

But Laurel only examines her nails, saying calmly, "Blaise Mitchell? Are you sure?"

"Oh, what, so it's not just Cal? You think I'm imagining *everything* now?"

Her eyes snap to my face. "God, Cate, stop, okay? Just stop with—hey, are you *high?*"

"A little, so what? What about Dee? Why's she flirting with some guy if she's with you?"

Laurel scowls. "I'll ask her, but I have a hard time believing—"

I throw my hands up. "Obviously!"

"I'm going to go, okay? But maybe . . . maybe just talk to someone, you know?"

"I am talking to someone. I'm talking to you!"

"I mean . . . besides me." My lips part slightly in disbelief, but Laurel continues, saying hesitantly, "Cate, didn't your mom have some . . . some problems once? You told me she—"

My voice is a black hole. "We're done here."

LAUGH
DAVID

I stop midstride. Cate's laugh. I haven't heard it in a while, but I'd recognize it anywhere.

"School," she says now. "Where are you? Wow. Cool. Tell me more about that."

The one-sided conversation is coming from the corner behind the cabinet.

The school's got the furnace set to Tropical. Up in the classrooms, the girls are wearing next to nothing, turning the guys into walking erogenous zones. The teachers are slumped by the windows, mumbling about global warming. I've come down to walk the cool basement halls.

Cate continues, "I'm not sure when I'll be in. Soon." She laughs again.

My pulse picks up as if I'm running. Somehow, I know she's talking to a guy. I can also tell, because of the little curve in her voice, that she wants something. Girls' voices do that.

"You were great," she says. "How much? A *lot*. Yes, totally hot. Yes, *love*."

I lean against the wall. She's got a boyfriend. Of course she's got a boyfriend.

"Okay. Chinatown. Text me your address."

She doesn't know the guy's address? But she's telling him he's hot. Talking about love. Great. Suddenly she's in front of me, saying hi, flushing pink, passing by—

"Cate, hey, wait a sec. Have you, ah—" Does she know I was listening? When did I become this guy? I rack my brain for something to say. "Did you talk to Bryn again?"

She scowls. Shakes her head. Keeps walking, a book—*Lyric Writing*—clutched to her chest.

NAUSEA
CATE

Knocking on the Bennets' door, I become aware that I feel like complete crap. My head is groggy from the nap I apparently took a short while ago. I don't remember lying down. Maybe it's the K getting to me. But when I think about the drug, I only want more.

After ringing the bell, I'm lifting my hand to knock again—

When Bryn opens the door.

My thoughts blur. What had David said? That she'd been at Rod's? But—when?

Bryn cocks her head. "You look like you've seen a ghost."

I push past her, run into the powder room, and puke my brains out.

Later, swimming up through a dark sea, I bob unsteadily over curling waves—

And wash up on the shores of the Bennets' living room couch.

"What's with you, are you sick?" Bryn's sitting down by my feet.

"David—"

"Isn't here, so no, he didn't see you face-plant. But you really shouldn't show up all fucked up. Kimmy could have been here."

"Sorry, I just . . . wanted to see you." I push up onto my elbows. My head feels disconnected from the rest of me, but not as much as I'd like. "Look, is there something you want to talk about? Something you—I don't know—want to say?"

"Yeah, go check yourself into rehab or whatever. You need help."

"Shut up. I'm serious."

"So am I."

"Bryn, when we talked about Rod Whitaker—"

Bryn explodes off the couch. "Stop! Stop right there. You can't just come here and start spewing about him. Just because we talked that one time, you can't just bring him up like you're talking about the weather or, or—"

"I'm sorry, I—"

"Fine. Forget about it. About him. He's dead. It's over."

"It's not. There's more. There's something else, and you know it."

"I don't know it! Don't know what you're talking about." But she looks around— like she's searching for the way out of a burning building. There's something animal in her eyes, something horribly desperate.

I recognize it.

I just wanted to get out.

She must understand, finally, that I'm not going to leave till she tells me, because she begins to speak, her words coming slowly, making it obvious she doesn't want to talk about Rod, or whatever else this is about.

"He. Was. A monster."

Her voice is so soft. Like a flower petal hitting the ground.

But then it's not. "He made me want to *die*," she practically shouts. "I couldn't let it go. I told you, David was going to *do* something. I couldn't let him. I—I—"

I have a horrible sense of foreboding. The K is polluting my bloodstream, rotting some part of me, I know, but still I want it, especially now.

"He raped me."

Hearing her say it out loud, hearing her sum it up in three simple words that are about as simple as Hiroshima, just levels me.

And then she says it.

"He deserved to die."

And, I realize, Bryn's rotting, too.

But still it takes me a minute, to really get what she's said.

"Wait. He deserved to die, so you—you—"

"The cops said he killed himself, but come on! Anyone who knew Rod knows he was too in love with himself to take his own life. Not without help."

The struggle of it is twisting my features—I can feel it. The desire to believe that Bryn is innocent, that she had nothing to do with Rod's death, warring with the horror of what she's saying: *that she killed him.*

And yet.

"Here, wrap your lips around this—I'll give you something bigger in a minute, if you're a good girl. And if you're a really good girl, I'll straighten you out. Give you something Laurel Ridgeway can't. You're the one, aren't you? Who made her like that? No one who looks like Ridgeway could be queer. I'm going to try her next. Your girlfriend."

My ethics sit on an invisible scale.

Then, suddenly, something—his weapon words, the bitter taste of orange juice—sloshes heavily inside me. I bring my hands to my stomach. The scale tips with a jerk.

"Just the *thought* of him makes you sick, doesn't it?" She *is* shouting now, gesticulating, hatred making her ugly. "So imagine, Cate, imagine him—"

"No! Bryn—" I'm up off the couch, reaching out to her, as if I can pull her back from the Stygian place she's traveled to.

"He *ruined* me!"

"He didn't! No one can do that, do you understand? *No one.* No matter what they do, no one can touch that place inside of you, your— spark. That thing that connects you to something greater, to—to the—" A song title tumbles from my mouth. "Hotel Vast Horizon."

"What the fuck does that mean?"

For a second, I'm not sure myself. I only know how the sweeping sound of that song makes me feel. "It means you're bigger than that, Bryn, much bigger—you're connected to something *greater*, you *are* greater—than some physicality, some part of your anatomy. Our bodies don't define us. What Rod did to you? Doesn't have anything to do with *who you are.*"

But what you did to him . . .

"Did you really do it? Did you kill him, Bryn?"

"No. But—God." She laughs. It's a brittle sound. "*God.* It's like it's reflexive, you know, for me to say his name? Like it's a throwaway word, like it doesn't mean anything, like, 'Oh my god!' But there's no reason for me to invoke God in any serious way. No reason to send up some personal prayer. God's already failed me."

More quietly, she says, "I didn't shoot him. I admit, I went over with the idea of hurting him somehow. Went over there thinking, *Rod Whitaker doesn't deserve to live.* I was trying to justify it, whatever it was I was going to do to him. But what was I going to do? Tell his parents what he did to me? Scream at him and hope that they heard?"

Tears fill my eyes. "I told you I'd help."

She gives a dismissive wave. "My thoughts . . . just kept going darker. After that night, all I could think of was punishing him, hurting him, for what he'd done to me. I admit it. I was there. Early. Before school."

Her words are stones in my pockets. I sink down onto the couch. She sits beside me.

I have no idea how long we're quiet for, but finally, Bryn takes a big breath. When she releases it, the words rush out.

"I was afraid, like I told you, that David was going to do something. So I went to Rod's. When I got there, he was drinking. He did that sometimes, before school. I knew that from David. I told Rod to get another glass. For me.

"I let him slobber all over me, while I looked around, wanting to see where he lived, wanting to see if there was something in his life I could destroy, if there was anything I could *take*, that would leave him wrecked."

She brings a hand to her throat, stretches her neck, like her words are stuck, or like she still feels Rod Whitaker's hands on her.

I don't say anything. The silence works like a wick.

"I—I didn't think it through. I thought, that early, his parents would be there. But his mom was at work. His dad was out of town. I was an idiot to go there alone!"

"Bryn—"

"He told me he had a fantasy. He took me into his father's office. Leaned me over the desk. 'I'll be the boss,' he said. 'You work for me.'

"He obviously wasn't expecting me to fight. The desk rocked. When he slammed it back in place, a drawer slid open. There was a gun inside. I grabbed for it. He got it.

"Then he kind of laughed. He just—looked at the gun and gave this choked little laugh. Said, 'Funny thing about this gun. I already had it out once this morning. The sun wasn't up yet, though, so I—' Then he just stared at the gun, like he was . . . hypnotized. Like it fascinated him.

"I told him then. Said I still had the clothes. Told him I knew about Sandy Clayton. Everything seemed like it was moving in slow motion, and then I said—then I said—"

Tears roll down Bryn's cheeks. She's one of those people for whom tears are an ornament, like diamonds. Her fine features don't change. Her patrician nose—which I realize now is so much like David's—doesn't get red. Her blue eyes don't swell. They simply swim with tears. Swim beautifully. Shining, under a shallow layer of water.

David. Does he know about this? The idea holds less water than Bryn's shallow-end eyes. Now it evaporates. David knows Rod raped his sister. But he doesn't know this, or he wouldn't have asked me to talk to Bryn. No one—no one can ever know about this.

Bryn covers her face with her hands. It's hard to think straight, but I have to.

"Bryn. You're not a murderer. You didn't put the gun to his head. You only *said* something. People can't go around blowing their brains out over something someone says! Rod's suicide was his choice, end of story."

She drops her hands. Her expression is fierce.

"I would have used it, Cate, if I'd gotten it first. But in the end . . . in the end . . ." She looks away, into some invisible distance.

"It only took a couple of words, Cate. Venomous words. Then he put the tip of the barrel in his mouth . . . and pulled the trigger."

BREATH

CATE

I'm surprised when Bryn allows me to put an arm around her and guide her to the kitchen.

I brew a cup of chamomile tea and place it in front of her. *I'm here for you.* All the while I try to breathe normally, not wanting her to know how upset I am.

It's hard to unravel. She killed Rod. She didn't. It's huge. It's horrible. But in some back room of my brain, I'm secretly, silently, fist pumping the air. *Yes!* Bryn, warrior goddess! Take credit for helping humanity. For saving some other girl from what you went through. Rod Whitaker deserved to die, dammit. Your body is *yours*.

And my body is mine, you motherfucker, I hope you're in hell.

I take a deep breath. Try to reel in the mix of fury and self-righteous glee. But it's a big fish. A dirty happiness. Fatty street food that'll clog my arteries. Shameful as the brief fascination—and I confess arousal— I'd experienced when I'd looked at pornography online.

So, right, breathe. Hide the inappropriate feelings. Try . . . thinking of the facts.

Rod Whitaker was a rapist. He killed himself.

The rest . . . the idea that Bryn somehow assisted Rod in his suicide, the friggin' psyched feeling I have because the guy is dead . . . I need to make disappear.

And Bryn as a victim? I need to banish that, too. Because I can't bear to look at beautiful Bryn Bennet and think of her like that. I refuse to think of myself like that, as someone who's been abused. He shouldn't have the right, have the power, to stain us like that.

And I don't want to stain myself, either, by thinking he deserved to die. But I do. So I am. Stained by my belief in the death penalty. I can't damp this belief, like some ringing note from my guitar. Can only lower my inner voice to whisper—sans fist pump now—*yes.*

I take a bigger breath. Blow it out. My head is too full. I need a place to put all this.

Down on paper, in a notebook. Because where else? I can't set the streets on fire.

And if I can't find the right words? I'll write a screaming punk anthem. Dedicated to dicks everywhere. That seems about right. Somehow, I'll get this garbage out of my system.

Down on the paper, along with the facts, will go the idea that Rod deserved to die.

Down on the paper will go the idea that Rod is where he's supposed to be. *Hell.*

Inked on an eight-by-ten page—*yeah I might give you that much space*—will be his story, through my goddamn filter.

And Bryn. How long will it take her to put this away? Because she has to, right? Put it away so she can live with herself?

"Bryn," I want to say, "just don't put yourself away. Not anymore. Stay in the center of the room where you belong. Center stage, like the diva you are. Live."

Was Rod dead because of Bryn? She seems to think so.

But I think . . . Rod would have killed himself regardless. Because how could he live with himself? And maybe that's all she'd said to him. Something like, "How can you live with yourself, Rod?"

"Here, wrap your lips around this—I'll give you something bigger in a minute . . ."

My breath comes in shallow gasps. I get up. Go lean out the Bennets' back door.

A dark-green cover stretches taut over the pool.

I imagine Rod Whitaker beneath it, begging for breath.

"Begging for Breath." What a fucking great song title. I'll spin this shit into gold yet.

HEART

CATE

The next day, exhausted, I drive out West Front Street. Besides an abandoned industrial park and a few old farmhouses, there's nothing out this way but fields and nurseries.

Kimmy is sitting in the passenger seat, silent as a crash-test dummy—

I cringe. How can I even *think* the word *crash*?

"Kimmy, I'm sorry," I say, "that I haven't been around."

"It's okay. I know your friend died. Was he your boyfriend?"

"No."

"Do you have a boyfriend?"

"No."

"Why isn't David your boyfriend?"

I blow out a breath. "Kimmy," I begin.

"David does that."

"Does what?"

Kimmy makes a big exaggerated sigh, and I laugh. She does, too, and seems to forget all about her question. But I don't.

The pale early-winter sun balances precariously in a blue sky stretched thin and high over the frozen fields and into forever. Leafless trees stand alongside the road like some dark audience, their bare black branches—traceries sparkling with icy jewels.

I want to be clear, like the faceted ice. But my veins are filled with chemicals, and I feel sluggish. Bryn was still in bed when I picked Kimmy up. I envy her. I didn't sleep last night.

West Front comes to a T and I drop Kim at her old preschool. She's volunteering at the annual Winter Carnival. She won't be too long, and it's a haul to get here, so I head to the old red store a half mile down the road. I'll grab something to eat and read in the car till she's finished.

Pulling into the parking lot, I manage to squeeze between a battered pickup and a gray Honda without hitting either. I let out a breath. Having a license hasn't made me a better driver.

I've only been here once before. The place is far from appealing, with grungy linoleum and half-stocked shelves. The deli cases are full, though, so they must have a good turnover.

The door bangs closed behind me. It's freezing—no heat? With a shiver I walk over to the counter and order a roast-beef sandwich from an enormous man wearing an apron.

"Want that warmed up?"

"Um—" Hot roast beef. It never occurred to me. "Sure. That'd be good."

He nods. "Want some cheese on that?"

Mmm. Melted cheese. "Yes. Please." I smile at the man. He just nods. Sandwiches are, apparently, a serious business to him.

"Drink?" he asks, as I step toward the cash register.

"Coffee, please. Black."

He nods once more, pours the coffee from a pot that's sitting on the counter, and rings up my order. And then, to my surprise, he nods again, toward someone behind me. "See that guy?"

Peering over my shoulder, I see a man in a gray suit with silver-rimmed glasses and graying hair. A businessman is how I'd categorize him if pressed, a man with a long commute. Someone I can't imagine having anything in common with. I feel the same way about the huge man behind the cash register, actually.

But then the man in the suit smiles—

And the store *lights up*.

"Joe!"

The man behind the counter grins. His serious sandwich-making face is transformed. He says, "How are ya, Stu?"

"I'm great." The gray-suited man beams. "Just great. How're you doing, Joe?"

"Yeah, I'm good. Real good."

The two men smile at each other for another moment, then they exchange a nod, and the businessman turns away, heading down the narrow aisle to a cooler filled with veggies.

The guy behind the counter, Joe, leans forward. "That guy?"

"Uh, yes?" As the serious sandwich-making expression settles on his face, I realize I'm holding my breath. He leans a little closer.

"That guy was gonna die. Set to go. His heart was giving out. Some disease. The chances he'd find a donor, even though he was on a list? Not so good."

Joe and I lock eyes. Tears begin to well in mine.

"Now, he's got a brand-new one," Joe tells me. "Kid crashed his car on Chapel Hill Road over in Middleburn, back in September. Stu got his heart. It saved his life."

I fold my lips, but it's no use. Tears spill out of my eyes. I turn around, looking for Stu.

He's grabbing a paper, just an ordinary-looking man.

An ordinary-looking man—*with Cal's heart*.

Gulping air, I say, "Thank you. Thank you for telling me that story."

The man just looks at me and nods.

RUNDOWN
CATE

I want to drive until I lose the road, but it's time to pick up Kimmy.

Dropping her off at the Bennets', I'm about to race home—

When Bryn stumbles to the door, black eyeliner ringing her eyes. She looks like some morning-flagged club kid. As Kimmy heads inside, Bryn comes over to the car.

"Why are you in such a hurry?" she asks, as if yesterday never happened. "Heard your tires squeal when you pulled in." Her cool-blue eyes narrow slightly. "How come you look like you're about to fly out of your skin?"

I can't help it—I tell her what happened at the store. Then I tell her about Cal, about seeing him in the mirror, and in my dreams. About hearing him.

She shakes her head. "Wow, that's some heavy shit, Cate."

And then, she grins.

I don't know, maybe she feels like we're even, two tens on the one-to-ten psycho scale, but when she says, "You're fucking crazy, woman," there's a grudging admiration in her voice that makes the words sound like an affirmation.

But now I notice something else about her eyes, besides all the smudgy black liner.

They're luminous.

Bryn Bennet, I realize now, is always up for an adventure. Or maybe—

"Have you been hanging out with Dee Carson?" I ask.

"Like she has eyes for anyone but Laurel?"

"Not like tha—wait. Are you *gay*?"

"Why do you want to know?" she asks, sly-like.

I roll my eyes. "I didn't mean are you hanging out with her like *that*."

"Oh. Yeah, well, I wouldn't. Hang out with her like that. She's a bitch."

Huh.

"Okay, I'll bite," she says. "What *did* you mean?"

"I meant, are you getting drugs from her. Ketamine." Because although it had taken me a while, once I thought about it, it was easy to figure out where Laurel had gotten the Kit Kat.

"Please. That shit's fucked up. You can hurt yourself with—Jesus, Cate. That stuff's for animals; it's an *anesthetic*. The vet at Stone Stable uses it on the horses."

"Hey, it's not like I'm the only one doing weird shit." I eye her meaningfully.

"Yeah, you got me." She opens the passenger door and gets into the car, as if she needs to be physically closer to me to emphasize her next point. "I talked an asshole into blowing his brains out—I didn't try to kill *myself*."

"I'm not trying to kill myself," I say indignantly. "I'm just trying to . . ." *Get out.* "Have some fun."

"Paralysis and amnesia—that's fun for you?" But all of a sudden, Bryn's laughing and then I am, too. "No wonder you think you've seen your friend—you're taking that K shit! Maybe you're so dosed you forgot he was dead!"

"No—" But I can't talk, as another avalanche of laughter rolls over me, scree down a mountainside, unstoppable as the weather.

"So where are you going?" she finally says. "I want to do something."

Where I'm going is Google, to find out the full name of the guy who has Cal's heart. Then I'm going to look up his address, go to his house, and—well, I'm not sure what I'm going to do next, but that doesn't matter right now, I just . . . need to keep moving.

I say, "Well, first I need to stop home, and then—I don't know, but whatever. Do you want to come?"

"Yeah, why not," Bryn says. "You're full of crazy, and ketamine apparently, but I'm sure we can find some fun. I've got to at least wash my face before I go anywhere, though. Come."

We climb out of the car and go inside.

Upstairs, she jerks her chin toward her room. "Wait here, I'll be right back."

"Can I use your computer?" I call out.

"Sure," she answers from the bathroom.

I open her laptop. Type a few words into Google.

It's so easy to find him I almost start laughing all over again.

A Life Continued: Oakhurst Man Receives a New Heart

There are few details, probably to protect the privacy of the people involved, but there's a picture of the organ recipient, Stuart Wasserman. Another minute, and I have his address. A few more minutes, and Bryn and I are in the car and I'm punching it into the GPS.

Then jumping in my seat as David appears out of nowhere, knocking on my window.

I open it.

"Where are you off to? Can I come?"

FAMILY

DAVID

Before Cate can answer, I'm in the car, studying my sister, who's riding shotgun. She's wearing a long coat with a furred collar. Superdark sunglasses, even though the day's turned cloudy.

"What's with the glam?" I ask.

"Cate's taking me ghost hunting," she says. "I wanted to be properly dressed for the occasion."

"Ghost hunting?" I lean forward so I can see Cate's face.

She's glaring at Bryn.

"What? You didn't think I'd figure it out?" Bryn says waspishly.

Cate doesn't reply. I wonder if she's high, if Bryn is. I'm also still wondering who Cate was on the phone with, at school. If it's someone I can make her forget.

I can't quite figure out what's between us, and I need to. I've never felt like this before. But I have a bad feeling, like Cate doesn't want me now.

Of course that only makes me want her more.

I wonder how it would work, if I just told her how I felt. But as thunder rolls in the distance and we pull out of the driveway, the bad feeling persists. *When will I have the chance to tell her anything?*

She's wrangling the radio now, which inspires Bryn to complain of a violent headache.

By the time she's finished, Cate's pulling over, tires jumping the curb.

"So what are we really doing?" I ask. But my sister's talking, too.

"That's some fancy driving, Cate Reese." Bryn lifts her shades, looks around. "Hold up, are we really going to that guy's house? The guy with your friend's heart? What are we going to do, bodysnatch him? Leave a giant seedpod in his place? He has Cal's heart, Cate. He isn't Cal."

"I know," Cate says. "Just . . . give me a minute, will you?"

"You two going to tell me what's up?" But I already know. This is about the guy who died, my ghostly rival. I shouldn't have come—wait. Did Bryn just say what I think she said? "Back up. Are you saying—"

"Davey." My sister interrupts. "You're about to see your girl Cate in full-on crazy mode."

"Bryn." Cate turns the name into a single-word warning.

"Oh whatever. Cate, seriously, I figured maybe we'd wind up at Laurel's or in somebody's basement playing beer pong. Okay, not really. That would be too normal. But—"

Bryn falls silent as Cate points to a Colonial across the street. "That's his house."

A beat goes by. Then Bryn rolls her eyes. "Fine. I'll play along. When do we do The Ritual?"

"Ritual?" Cate asks. "Like sacrifice-a-virgin ritual?"

"Like on bad TV, yeah." She side-eyes Cate. "Looks like you're going down. Too bad, 'cause you were actually starting to grow on me. Now let's get the fuck out of here."

"Okay, but . . . just a second," Cate says.

"Fine. Since Davey and I can't walk home from here, we'll wait till you talk to the guy. Or maybe we should just knock him unconscious and rip out his heart? Davey, what do you think?"

Before I have time to think anything, Cate says, "Bryn, I never said . . ."

But Bryn's busy pulling a flask from her pocket.

Cate and I turn to statues.

"What?" Bryn looks at the silver flask in her hand, then at me, then at Cate. "Want some?"

"That's . . . Rod's," I say.

She shrugs. Swigs. "Come on. Let's go talk to this guy."

I'm sick with myself, for thinking Bryn could have had anything to do with Rod Whitaker's death, but—the flask.

"Talk to him how?" Cate's voice sounds far away.

Could she have taken it that night at the Halls'? But why? And if not then—

"Cate," Bryn says. "You dragged me here. What's the plan? Casually knock on the door, ask this guy to please hand over his heart so you can give it to the ghost of your old boyfriend?"

I run my hands over my face. Bryn takes another drink from the silver flask. When she looks at me, her eyes are bloodshot, bleary. She doesn't just need me watching out for her, she needs help. Professional help.

"Bryn," Cate says. "Cal wasn't my boyfriend. And I don't want his heart, I just want—"

He wasn't her boyfriend. Is that what she said? It's ridiculous that I care. The guy's dead. But—

All of sudden, it's like a show has started. Like we're all at a play, or in one. Our comments, thoughts, hang in midair, as a gray Honda pulls up in front of one of the two garage doors and parks. A man wearing a gray suit gets out. Goes inside.

The very air is still. But what just happened? Act I began. Ended. *What now?*

"Okay, Crazy Cate. Show's over." Bryn turns the flask upside down. "All gone."

"Fine. I'll—come back tomorrow."

"And do what?"

It sinks in now, really sinks in. This man is an organ recipient. Is Cate really thinking about knocking on his door? I blow out a breath.

"Maybe she's right, Cate. This can't be the greatest thing for you to be thinking about—"

"Look, you guys. I just—need some time. You don't have to be here."

"I want to be here," I say, leaning forward.

"I don't," my sister says.

"Okay, well, I'm just going to see if, I don't know, maybe there's a good time for me to talk to him."

"Cate. Your *timing* is not going to make ringing his doorbell and asking him to hang out any less insane," Bryn objects. "I mean, what exactly are you going to tell him? You know what? *I'll* tell him. Tell him you're certifiable, but he doesn't need to worry." Bryn opens her door, gets out, then comes around and leans in Cate's open window. "Because you're not a stalker or anything. Like me."

Bryn shoots Cate a terrible smile, then strides toward the house.

"Bryn!" Cate says, clambering out of the car. "Wait. Let's talk about this."

I follow.

"I don't want to talk anymore," Bryn says. "I want to show you that you need help. And the way I'm going to do that is to knock on this guy's door and tell him what's up. Then he'll call the men in the white coats, since your parents are too lame to do it and restraining people isn't my specialty."

"Bryn, wait," Cate begs.

"For what? For you to get it through your head that there's no way to stay connected to this guy Cal?"

"Cate," I begin, putting my arm around her.

She shrugs it off. "Bryn," she says in a low voice. "You're going to attract his attention."

"I *want* his attention. You do, too, obviously. You want *someone's* attention. The K, this crazy shit about Cal haunting you—you're screaming for help, Cate."

Bryn's almost at the front door.

"Bryn, stop," I insist.

But Cate's already grabbing her arm, dragging her into a row of bushes alongside the house, saying, "You can't just barge in there!"

Feeling ridiculous, I crouch down near the girls.

"I'm not. I'm going to say hello first. Then I'll barge in. And tell him that you want to go on a date with him so you can chat about his heart or whatever. Then *he's* going to tell *you* how crazy you are, and maybe you'll listen to him, since you won't listen to me, or Laurel."

"Laurel?" Cate stiffens. "You talked to Laurel? About me?"

"Jesus, Cate. You're best friends. Or are you so obsessed that you've forgotten that?"

Bryn rises up out of the bushes. At the same time, another car pulls into the driveway.

"Bryn," I warn, yanking her down as one of the garage doors clatters up.

We hear the car pull in. The door closes again with a rattle.

"Guess your friend doesn't live alone," Bryn says.

"You think?" Cate retorts.

Bryn mutters something. She's taller than Cate and closer to the windows. Now she gets up on her knees. From there she has a view that we don't: she can see inside.

"Oh man," she says softly.

"What?" Cate and I say together.

"Looks like your friend's heart went to a good cause."

Slowly I move over, kneel next to Bryn.

In what looks like a living room, the man in the gray suit is kissing a woman, probably his wife, because on either side of him, pulling on each of his hands, are two little girls, twins, about five years old, who resemble them both.

"Company," Bryn sings out softly, no longer looking through the window but toward the street. Yet another car is pulling up in front of the house. Now a beautiful Asian woman gets out.

Cate's breath catches.

"Who is it?" Bryn asks.

"Cal's mother. But I guess . . . that makes sense?"

"It does," I say. I understand everything now. Really understand. If I could talk to someone with Jack's heart . . .

Planting one foot on the ground, I motion for Cate to move in my direction. Then I kind of pull her up on my knee so she can see.

The man still has a daughter hanging on each arm, as his wife, frowning a little like she's confused, ushers Cate's friend's mother into the living room. The Asian woman makes a vague circle in the air with her hand, possibly indicating that she'd been in the neighborhood. She's saying something—an apology? Clearly, there's been a misunderstanding.

"I don't think they knew—" Cate starts.

"That your friend Cal's mother was coming," I finish.

I wonder about the little girls. Do they know their daddy has a new heart, one that belonged to someone closer to their age than their father's?

The man gestures to the couches. His wife sits down, saying something to the girls, who disentangle their fingers from their father's and go sit obediently next to her.

After a slight hesitation, Cal's mother approaches the man in the gray suit, whose smile holds steady.

Tears pool in his wife's eyes as she watches Cal's mother—who is not so steady, who is visibly trembling—embrace her husband.

The two stand with their arms around each other for what seems like a very long time.

And then, with one arm still around the man who has her son's heart, Cal's mother leans in a little so that the side of her face rests against his chest.

She closes her eyes and smiles.

Cate sags against me.

I rest my chin on her head. Gently kiss her hair. I don't know if she feels it or not. It is a stolen kiss.

A ghost kiss.

PROOF

CATE

"Hi, Cate."

"Hey, Cate."

These greetings come from Laurel and Bryn, who stand together at my front door on this frozen Saturday afternoon.

I've just woken up from a nightmare. In the nightmare, I never see Cal again.

And I haven't seen him. Not lately. Although I hear songs in my head all the time now, and I swear he's put them there. I'd prefer he put them directly into my notebook. I try to write them down but . . . most of them slither off the page like the snakes of fog that writhe over Ocean Avenue in the spring. I've only caught a couple.

"What time is it?" I ask quickly, suddenly scrambling for something normal to say.

Laurel and Bryn exchange a look. Too late, I realize I should have invited them in.

"We brought you something."

"We have something for you."

Their nearly identical words run across each other. My stomach lurches.

Laurel hands me a book. *Hallucinations* by somebody named Oliver Sacks. Its turquoise cover is illustrated with a detailed sketch of an eye. From the brow, yellow-and-blue lines radiate upward. The wide-open eye and the lines projecting like rays make the drawing look . . . mystical.

"Cate?" Laurel sounds like she's afraid I might break if she talks too loud.

Outside, Dee sits behind the wheel of her shiny Mercedes, looking like a getaway driver.

I blow out a breath. "You two join the Jehovah's Witnesses or something?"

Then I slam the door.

Then I realize: I'm out of K.

And the truth is, the door slam was only in my head, in the form of a brief wish.

"What's this?" I say too brightly, holding up the book.

"Just something, we, um . . ." Laurel mumbles. "Take a quick look."

"Take a *good* look," Bryn says.

It's a new book, the cover unmarred. But several pages have been dog-eared.

I glance at Laurel. Since we were tiny, we've been turning down corners, marking favorite pages in picture books, favorite places in stories. These days, we often dog-ear pages of novels before exchanging them, indicating that the page contains a beloved passage, or lines of dialogue uttered by a character we wish we'd come up with ourselves, words that perfectly mirror our thoughts. I'm particularly guilty of this, sometimes even underlining phrases with pencil, thrilled to have found the right words to match my feelings.

But now I wonder. If I were to go back and read them over, would the words I'd marked so carefully reveal additional information, maybe even entirely *different* information?

So much meaning swims beneath the surface of a word. I get that now. I get that some words are so deep, so wide—they're like glacial lakes, or oceans covering a landmass of implications. And I get that sometimes I'm down there, too, swimming in the depths of the word-water, muddying the clarity or filtering the mud.

For a second, my vision clouds—and I actually *see* water. See myself and Laurel, both of us down near the silty bottom of the cedar pond, red wordwater holding us under, instead of aloft.

But Laurel won't swim with me now. She won't even meet my eyes, which, with an involuntary flutter of lids and lashes, clear abruptly.

I skim the first dog-eared page—Chapter 13: "The Haunted Mind"—and let out a small sound of disbelief.

"*. . . the hallucinations we must now consider, which are, essentially, compulsive . . .*"

The sense of betrayal strikes as hard as a fist, making my face heat, but I read on.

"The emotions here can be of various kinds: grief or longing for a loved person . . . horror, anguish, or dread following deeply traumatic, ego-threatening or life-threatening events . . . the conscience cannot tolerate. Hallucinations of ghosts . . . are especially associated with violent death or guilt."

"I'm thinking about apologizing to you," Bryn says. "Thinking about it."

My eyes waver over the next few pages: *"Bereavement causes a sudden hole in one's life, a hole which—somehow—must be filled . . . Bereavement Hallucinations . . ."*

I shut my eyes, wishing that everything—Laurel, Bryn, the book—would just go away.

Laurel says, "Think this might fit?"

Like she's talking about a dress or something.

"It's . . . your brain's solution," she continues. "The hallucination can be hearing a voice, seeing an image, or both—" She breaks off as my eyes snap open.

Angrily, I turn to the back of the book, scanning the index: paranormal or supernatural . . . religious feeling. Then find myself flipping to another dog-eared page, this one talking about sensed presence.

Bryn and Laurel exchange another look. But suddenly, I don't care anymore, about the two of them conspiring.

I've found something that interests me.

Chapter 6: "Altered States."

"To live on a day-to-day basis is insufficient for human beings; we need to transcend, transport, escape; we need meaning, understanding, and—"

Outside, the sunlight bounces off Dee's windshield.

Escape will do nicely, thank you very much.

"Cate? Cate, are you here?"

Not really.

But my mother's timing is perfect for once.

"Hey, can you guys go say hi to my mom? She's been seriously on me lately."

"Sure," Laurel says. She heads toward the kitchen, looking relieved.

"Yeah, okay," Bryn says, about to follow. "But you owe me. By the way, David says hi. Now you owe me double."

DRAGON

CATE

Dee watches warily as I approach the car.

"Hey, Dee."

"Hey."

"So, you know that stuff you gave Laurel?"

Dee frowns. But I guess she figures there's no point pretending. "Yeah?"

"Think I can get a little more?"

"It's *gone*? Everything she *gave* you?"

"It wasn't that much," I say defensively.

"More than she *wanted* you to have. It was just to help you through—*you* know."

"Yeah, well, I'm through 'you know.' And I like the high it gives me."

"Fine with *me*. But I'm not holding. And—" She gives me her sugar-laced-with-strychnine smile. "You'll have to pay. You know Chinatown?"

"Enough."

She rifles through her purse, pulling out a scrap of paper and a pen. She jots something down and hands the paper to me. It's an address.

"How does *Laurel* feel about you wanting more?"

"How does Laurel feel about you dealing?"

"*Technically*, I'm not." She nods at the paper.

"Then I guess I don't have to say thanks."

She gives me a spiky look. I return it.

"How many?" I ask. "How many of Laurel's friends do you have coming to you?"

"They don't come to *me*."

"You know what I mean. First one's free, right? That's a little cliché, don't you think?"

"Worked with you."

"How many?" I ask again, eyeing the gleaming Mercedes.

"Enough," she says, mimicking me from earlier. "Enough that *I* don't have to drive my daddy's old station wagon."

That rubs, because although my family has money, Dad's cheap. When you make it on your own, you tend to watch your pennies. So I don't have as many shiny things as a lot of the other kids in Middleburn. Plus, the way Dad wears his sneakers till they have holes in them bugs me, and I *do* wish I had a car as nice as Dee's, so it infuriates me that she's even noticed our old car. Or maybe Laurel told her that my dad is tight. The thought makes me even angrier.

"You know, I don't need this shit." I toss the paper on the ground.

"But you *want* it, don't you?" she says as I start to turn away. "You feel strangely compelled to keep taking it. And you feel like that's *okay*, because you're not addicted. You're in control. That's the beauty of K. The when, the where . . . how much, who with. It's up to you, and you like that. You like having control over such a snaky substance, because you're *out of control* in so many other ways." She leans through the open window, fingers curled like claws, then she *snaps* her hands out at me. "*Boo!* Do I sound like your imaginary boyfriend?"

VINYL

DAVID

Restrained vocals, atmospheric keyboard pads. Drum loops drowned in reverb placed way back in the mix. The song cranking in Listen Up! has a hypnotic quality. The music fills every bit of empty space inside me. That's what a good band can do.

After flipping through half the vinyl collection, I check out the used CDs. Then I wander upstairs, grab a few songbooks. Dylan, Springsteen—their lyrics read like novels. In their stories, I find parts of myself I didn't know existed.

Taking a seat on a stool behind a glass case that holds collapsible music stands, ancient-looking sheet music, what appears to be a pile of clarinet parts, I read through the lyrics—not just Springsteen and Dylan, but Eddie Vedder, Eminem, Johnny Cash. Poets, all.

Stacks of CDs crowd the surface of the case. I'm supposed to be putting them away, but . . . it's like being surrounded by these tangible objects, something *intangible*, invisible, is opening inside me. Something I thought I'd let go, or thrown away when I'd been forced to make myself in my brother's image but that maybe I'd only *put* away.

It's like an unresolved chord vibrating inside me, a song with no final cadence. No finish. No end. It's like . . . this thing—this thing that's breaking open, or maybe it's waking, this thing that the music sheds light on, that lyrics illuminate—it's in my blood. It's me.

I've always loved music, always used it, almost the same way I've used girls. I can say that now, because nice as I've always been to the girls I dated, I finally get it. It was still using.

But maybe that's what people do. Maybe we all use each other. I don't know. Porn—that's using. But people? Yeah, I don't know.

I plunge back into the lyrics. Lose myself. Until someone says, "Hey."

Cate Reese stands in front of me, gray eyes scanning the shelves behind me, fingers tap, tap, tapping against her lips. She is lacking her characteristic stillness. This unsettles me. Or maybe it's just her. What she does to me.

Before I have a chance to say hi, she points suddenly at the air. "What is this?"

"'Low Roses.' How are you doing?"

"Fine. Are they from around here?"

I want to ask why she's here. Want to ask what she's thinking now, now that she's seen where her friend's heart is. I want to ask if the position of her own heart has changed.

I would have asked her all this after we left the bushes outside the gray-suited man's house, but the silence that fell over the three of us seemed like a weight too heavy to lift. Boyfriend or not, she obviously loved her friend Cal.

"Ah—no, the song is 'Low Roses,'" I reply. "The band is Sex Changes at Gunpoint."

She raises an eyebrow, and I nod in agreement with her speechless commentary. The band's name seems to be in direct opposition to the sound of their music.

A smile pulls at her lips.

She looks . . . different. Even from the other day. She's definitely not high. Her eyes are clear. Maybe it's something she's done with her hair. It looks good, but it's kind of hanging in her face. Like she wants to hide behind it.

And then there are those moving fingers, drumming on the glass now. They're a jarring juxtaposition to the stillness that's always emanated from Cate.

"Here—" I slide the CD in question across the glass countertop. "Check it out."

Again that smile, the halfway one.

I watch her as she pretends to examine the cover, read the lyrics. *What's up with her?*

"Good lyrics, right?"

"Definitely. I need a copy. Please."

Maybe it's just this: Me, being at work. Her being a customer, instead of my sister's babysitter, instead of a potential someone for me, instead of the almost desperate person she was the other day.

"Ah—sure."

She follows me slowly down the steps. She is, I think, wrapped up in the music. The song that's playing now shudders through the speakers with anxiety-inducing beauty.

Pulling a CD from a box near the front door, I say, "We've had the advance copy for a week, but the delivery just came in today. You're lucky."

"I'm not." Her tone is sharp.

Suddenly, I remember how at school everyone calls Cate *That Lucky Girl.*

"Sorry. I didn't mean it like that."

But she's talking over me, and I think, maybe, she *is* high.

"Not lucky. And not prepared. Luck meets preparedness, that's the definition of success, and I was neither. Not lucky. Not ready. All those people listening . . . *watching.* And I just sat there, immobile, the notes reverberating inside my skull. They weren't even the wrong notes! I didn't even make a *mistake*. I just—stopped playing."

"Hang on—"

"Did you hear about it? Because I'm sure Laurel told Dee, and Dee probably told the world. She hates me. So, did you? About my concert?"

"I didn't."

"And, now, I'm supposed to play again. A different kind of show maybe, but—I must be an idiot. *Why* would I want to get back onstage? Ever? I can't—I don't even have a guitar at this point. Still, I've got these bad-poem songlike things—" She sounds like she's about to cry.

"Hey—" I start to reach for her.

"And there's this guy, he's in a band in the city . . ."

I let my arm drop. She keeps talking. But all I can hear now is her telling that guy, "Text me your address."

"He said he'd help me, but he's the only songwriter I know. What if he can't? All the new stuff I've got—I've never played *songs* before, not songs with *words*, with *lyrics*. I can't—"

"Hold up. You told me you didn't play anymore."

"Because I didn't. I wasn't. Playing. Not when we had that conversation. I quit. And I still quit, classical. But I can't stop making music completely, that'd be like . . . dying or something."

"Cate. You do realize I've never heard you play."

"I know. It's weird, in a way, that you haven't. That Bryn hasn't. Kimmy has."

"Kimmy?"

"The few times your mom dropped her at my house, for whatever reason. Too much going on at your house, I guess. Kimmy always made me play for her."

"What about me, will you play for me? Because if you have songs, I want to hear them."

Cate looks up into my face, and there's something there in her eyes, some expression I've never seen. Like clouds clearing. She looks younger all of a sudden, looks . . . so hopeful.

But suddenly her eyes fill with tears. Almost frantically, she looks around—

"Hey. It's all right," I reassure her. "I mean obviously it's *not* all right, all the stuff that's going on with you, but—"

A sob bursts through her lips.

And this time, I do reach out to her. My hand firm on her elbow, I guide her back up the stairs, past the glass case, through a door that opens into a small office. I watch her take in the walls plastered with promo posters, the green-velvet couch with ornately carved armrests shoved into the far end of the room, which isn't far at all, because the space is tiny.

When I release her, she sinks down onto the couch cushions. I sit across from her on a swiveling chair. On the desk behind me, a laptop screen glows cyber yellow, the word "MELT" fading in and out, dissolving and re-forming in a sea of psychedelic swirls.

I pick up a box of tissues from the desk, hold it out to her. "Want a glass of water?"

She shakes her head, takes a tissue. I murmur something about crying, how it's natural.

"You know all about it, huh?" She sounds like a bitchy girl with a cold.

"I know what it's like to be sad, Cate."

"*Sad?* No, it isn't just—I'm not—I lost—" The last word lodges in her throat. At the same time, it seems to fill the room. Her chest hitches convulsively. I roll my chair closer.

Smoothing her hair back from her face, I say, "I know what it's like to lose someone you love. Things are going to be bad, for a while."

She swipes at her eyes. I offer the tissues.

Then I lean over, reaching into the corner where an old acoustic stands like it's waiting, and offer her that.

"Play me those 'bad-poem songlike things,' Cate. I'll listen. And I'll tell you the truth."

SEX

CATE

And he does tell me the truth. Somehow his mere presence, just him sitting there, listening, tells me the truth. David listens to song after song and, miraculously, as I play them for him, I know which songs work and which don't. It's uncanny.

"You must be my muse," I start to say, but then my heart plummets. *Cal. Cal was my muse.* "How can I thank you?" I ask instead.

He smiles his most beautiful David Bennet smile ever—is it possible to have more than one muse in a lifetime?—then offers to take me home.

At first we talk about the songs. "Cate, those songs are *good*, really good."

But when we're on Chapel, he reaches over and takes my hand, entwining our fingers.

I feel the pull all the way down in my pelvis.

"Don't you have a girlfriend?" I blurt. Then feel like an idiot. He's only holding my hand—I mean, that's not nothing, but . . .

"I don't." David watches the road. His other hand is relaxed on the wheel.

But I'd heard that there was someone, a senior named Trish. Heard she and David had this thing, some epic on-off endless fling. Everybody knows her. I've seen her in the halls.

I feel weird but ask him: "So you broke off with Trish?"

"Tammy. Although we weren't really—" He shakes his head, then kind of laughs. "I think you may have been there."

And I do remember Tammy, slapping her hand against the glass. But in my mind's eye I see the other girl, crouched in front of her locker last week, face crumpled and tear-streaked.

"But—weren't you going out with Trish?"

David shifts slightly in his seat. "Before Tammy. What about you?"

"What about me?"

"Do you have a boyfriend?"

Not for the first time, I wonder if David knows just how wobbly I am. Does he know I do drugs? Okay, one drug, but still, does he know?

I wobble now, thinking of the few boys I dated, back at my old school. Wishing I could say "No, but I *had* a boyfriend."

I think suddenly of Cal, wobble some more.

But the truth is, I've never had a *boyfriend*, not really. The boys from my old school? I was way too wobbly for them. And way too busy. I had my guitar.

"Cate, what are you thinking?"

I'm thinking, I wobble. I'm not like Trish, or Tammy. I'm thinking that I have trouble with words—finding the right ones—especially around you. Also, till not too long ago, I spent most of my waking hours with a guitar in my hands. Do you know what OCD is? Perfectionism?

I'm thinking that despite my songs and your praise, I'm still not ready to play out on my own. And that date that I can't seem to cancel is soon, so I'm screwed.

I'm thinking I might be done playing classical guitar.

I'm a songwriter now, because playing my songs in front of you made them real.

I'm a songwriter now. I am a writer.

"I—I'm thinking a lot of things." *I have songs. Someone's heard them. David's heard them—he works in a music store, he knows music—he says they're good!*

"Okay, well . . . tell me one thing. I want to get to know you better."

"Seems like you want to get to know a lot of girls. Or, I mean, it seems like you *do* know a lot of girls." Oh—I sound nasty, and petty, and jealous, not flirty at all, like I'd wanted to.

David runs a long-fingered hand through his hair, but as soon as he pulls his hand away, the hair flops right back down, falling into his eyes. I imagine that's what happens with girls. No sooner does he get tired of one than another fills her place.

"There's nothing wrong with getting to know people," he says, his brow creasing.

"But you sleep with them all!" The words spill out in sort of a wail. *Can I die now?*

The furrow along his brow vanishes. "You say that like it's a bad thing."

"Well, jeez, I mean, I'm not judging but—"

"I think you are. There's nothing wrong with having sex."

"Having sex," I say flatly.

"Making love, whatever you want to call it. I've heard the rumor that the two are different, but . . ." He glances at me. "Whatever you call it, there's nothing wrong with it."

God, I'm so embarrassed—and angry, too, although I'm not exactly sure why. But then I know why. It's because what David is saying is true. There isn't anything wrong with having sex, I really don't think so, but I haven't slept with anyone yet. Despite that, I'm very sure there's a difference between having sex and making love. Very sure that there are a lot of . . . *things* that are supposed to happen right along with sex, in the same way words can be flat but loaded.

My face feels hot and I know it's because I'm talking about sex like I've had it, and I haven't, but I *would* have, I think. If I hadn't moved, hadn't left my old school . . . if I had kept seeing one of those boys. I went to parties where couples slipped off, and I thought about one boy in particular. Not because what we had was so special, but because I was—I *am*—curious. He was nice, and nice-looking, and he made me laugh. So I guess that means that, eventually, I might have been happy to "have sex" with him—it definitely wouldn't have been making love—so I . . . am a hypocrite.

"Cate. We all make mistakes." It takes me a second to realize David's talking about himself. "Some mistakes are fun. They don't feel like mistakes at the time, you know? Others, well, maybe not so much. Not so fun. Sometimes, people get hurt. And, sometimes, people who are hurt, hurt you back. They lash out."

"As in, they gossip?"

"For one thing. Yeah. Maybe. Why, what have you heard?"

"Plenty," I say. And all of a sudden I'm laughing. "Lots and lots of stories."

"Stories? About me?"

Oh my god, does he really not know? Suddenly, I feel like the biggest jerk. "Well, um—"

"Kidding. I know the stories you're talking about, but believe it or not, most of them aren't true. I haven't 'dated every girl in the senior class.' I haven't slept with all of them, either. But, yes, I've dated a few people—okay, a lot of people—and, well, things went where they went. It was never a big deal."

Trish crying in the hallway that one day, crouching next to her locker like something had burst inside her—that was never a big deal?

Huh. And Tammy? The way she walks around looking like a thunder-cloud. Everyone knows that's about David. Was that also "never a big deal"?

But maybe he's not trying to convince me. Maybe he's trying to convince himself.

"I don't get it," I say. "You seem so . . . nice."

"I am." He shrugs. "I'm nice, but I'm not going to stay with someone if it doesn't feel right, if it doesn't feel good. Even if they cry." He scowls. "And especially not if they slap me."

In front of my house, he kills the engine, rubs a hand over the back of his neck.

"What is it?" I ask.

"I don't know. But it's . . . something. It's like . . . I'm wondering lately, where have I been? That's why I broke up with Tammy, and why . . ." His eyes rove over my face. "I think I've been an idiot."

"Does this have to do with what happened in Canada?"

I know it's not possible, but it feels like the air in the car has grown colder.

Now David squeezes the steering wheel so hard his knuckles turn white.

"I don't want to talk about Canada."

The tight tone, the hard expression on his face—it's as if a door has closed.

David looks different all of a sudden. Not the old David or the new one. For the first time, I see his resemblance to his father, a man who, for some reason, I've never liked.

I open the passenger door, but I don't get out.

Then David says *good night*—that's it, two words—and I do.

The driveway is slick with slushy snow. I half walk, half slide toward the house.

I'm nearly at the front door when David gets out of the Porsche. "Hey, Cate."

"You following me?" I call out. I'd intended my tone to be light, but my voice sounds as if I'm being strangled. My emotions have me in a chokehold. Still, I walk back to the car.

"I'm sorry, I didn't mean to, I don't know . . ." He glances at the maples that line the drive, no leaves to keep the slushy snow out, but big branches that hang over us and block the lion's share. "Didn't mean to freeze you out. I'm sorry. Are you okay?"

I'm not okay. But I wasn't okay before. Now I wonder . . . he took my hand earlier, would he take more, if I offered?

David obviously views sex as a form of entertainment, and I'm curious. Would it be more entertaining than the bump of ketamine I'd been planning to do once I got inside?

Maybe David can help me forget, just for a little while, the reasons I even do K.

A few fat flakes catch on David's eyelashes. They're my excuse. I reach up— and gently wipe them away.

"I'm okay," I lie, letting my fingers trail over his cheekbone, the line of his jaw.

He catches my hand, his expression unreadable.

I move closer. "Your skin's freezing."

"So is your hand." He releases it.

David's hair is wet from the snow and the sleet. Now I slip my fingers up the back of his neck, finding a layer of dry silkiness.

He closes his eyes—

Only to open them an instant later. "Cate," he says. And I'm reminded of that day, when he made my name sound like something special. Now it sounds like disappointment. His eyes say, "Anything you want." But his words say something different, even as he dips his head and I think he's going to kiss me.

"I'm just wondering if this is a good idea. You seem . . . I don't know."

The thing is, even as he's saying all this, one of his hands moves to the back of my neck. The other slips inside my coat. Now his fingers find my waist, the bottom edge of my sweater. He draws me against him, holding me tightly.

"Mmm . . ." My voice is muffled against his chest, and his arms around me feel so good. Couldn't I just tell him? *I want to turn this night over to my body, get the hell out of my head.* Couldn't I just ask him? *Can I do that with you?*

But people don't say those things—do they?

My mother . . . maybe she had the right idea. *"I just wanted to get out."*

Could I ever ask David if he's felt that way?

But in the end I just go for it. I loop my arms around his neck.

Then I tilt my face up— for a kiss.

DRUGS

DAVID

Cate lifts her lips— I step back.

She follows, rising up on tiptoe— leaning into me.

It's an awkward dance, and in another step or two, I'm up against the Porsche.

"Cate. You need to stop."

"Why?"

What she does next can't really be described as kissing me, more like devouring my mouth. Her lips are warm and soft, and the feeling I get as our tongues twine is liquid, goes all the way down to my toes. But this is not a first kiss, maybe not a kiss at all. Still my body responds, which might be the worst thing about this. I pull away.

"Cate, I know where you're at, but you're going to feel differently later. We can do this some other time, if it's right. I like you a lot, but—"

"But?" She slides her hands under my coat, my sweater, my shirt, lifts her own shirt a little so that I feel the smooth skin of her stomach as she presses against me.

I start to push her away—

But my hands catch somehow, my thumbs drilling her hip bones.

Her eyes darken, her cheeks pink. She laughs—a giddy high-pitched sound that isn't really a laugh but revved-up nerves or something. *Is she high?*

She tips her face up—

It's hard to put her off, when it's the exact opposite of what I want. But this isn't how I'd imagined things. Not with Cate.

I grab her shoulders, spinning her around so our positions are reversed, and it's her against the car. She smiles, and it's a smile I've never seen on Cate's sweet-sixteen face.

The air, which I'd magically become numb to, suddenly feels cold again.

"Don't you get it?" My voice comes out rough. I don't mean it to, but *damn*.

"Um—" She bites her lower lip a little. "Guess I don't."

But I see the realization cross her face. See the moment she becomes aware that I'd only been trying to give her a hug.

I blow out a breath. "Listen, I know something about what you're going through. I was a kid when my brother . . . killed himself. Later, like I told you, I chased his ghost. But when I stopped . . . I started chasing other things. Not at first. At first it was easy to get to that place, where it all went away. But then it got harder, became work, until I was chasing the dragon."

"What does *that* mean?"

"It means I got high. Tried a lot of different drugs, different . . . things. Always trying to find that first easy high again."

"*You* got high? But you're a jock."

"Ah—no. I mean, yes. I was. But that's got nothing to do with what I'm talking about. Who I was, who I am—it doesn't change the fact that back then, all I wanted was to forget.

"Like I said, it was easy at first. A few beers . . . I'd be somewhere else. Someone else. Someone who didn't feel so much. After a while, it took more. Vodka. Gin. Whatever my father wouldn't miss from the liquor cabinet. Prescription drugs—but they made me sick.

"Even when I found my drug of choice? Like I'm telling you, I always needed more. And until last summer, that was fine. It always worked. Maybe because, until last summer, I didn't get that it was a drug. I thought it was just something I enjoyed. Something I was good at."

"You mean sports?"

"Ah—no. But I don't want to talk about me anymore—I'm worried about you. What you're trying to do, using me, using drugs—"

Her eyes widen.

"Everyone knows, Cate. They see you at school. They see your eyes.

"It's not going to keep working. You're going to need more and more of whatever you're taking to stay in that state, where you don't have to think. No matter how you get to that place—even when that place is *no place*, just a place that isn't *this* one—you'll have to increase the dose of whatever the hell you're on to get you there, to keep you high."

"I'm not *on* anything, David."

"Maybe not tonight," I'm about to say. But she goes on.

"And I don't drink."

"Yeah, but you would've let me screw you up against the car, if—"

"*What?* That is *not* true."

But I'm looking at her face, and I see her asking herself, *"Is it?"*

"Not true, huh?" I fold my lips. Look away. Look back at her. She's wearing a fierce scowl, but I don't care. I want her to admit it, not for the strokes, for her own sake. So I nod and say, "Okay, maybe not against the car. Maybe you would have waited until we got inside."

"Fuck you, David." She spins away, heading for the house.

"Wait," I call after her. "Am I wrong? Hey, tell me I'm wrong, Cate. Come on! Were you even kissing *me*?"

"Fuck off!" she shouts over her shoulder.

Damn. "Cate!" I shout. "I'm sorry! Cate!"

But she's already at the top of the porch steps. Now she goes inside.

I yank open the driver's side door. *Damn, damn, damn. But hell, I don't want to be part of her downward spiral, don't want to be her escape hatch—I want to be more.*

Cate's changed since the accident, since losing her friend. She's hurting, and I get that. But she's running from the pain. Whatever she's taking, it won't work forever. She's going to crash, probably soon. I should know. I'm an expert when it comes to this kind of shit.

Did I really think I could help her by telling her all that? Was she even listening?

She's so deep in her stuff, still caught up in grief. *I can't compete with a dead guy.*

I start the car. Crank the heat. Pull out my cell.

I start to punch in Trish's number, then remember Whitaker's hand on her arm.

I call Tammy.

She practically purrs my name.

ROCK & ROLL
CATE

I hear David calling my name, but it's too late, I can't talk to him now. I never even kissed Cal, but I was about to drag David up to my bedroom—*to help me forget about Cal?*

To forget Cal, to satisfy my curiosity, for entertainment's sake—I'm sure if I keep thinking about it, I can come up with more sucky excuses for coming on to David Bennet.

What if he'd been someone else? What if drugs *had* been involved?

But maybe they had been. Maybe love isn't a ghost—maybe it's a drug. I'd been trying to use David like a drug. He basically said so.

That isn't love.

Sex then, sex is the drug.

Love. Sex. I know there's a difference, but that's all I know. *Why wouldn't he kiss me?*

Magazine girls, remember? That's what he likes. Girls who wear come-fuck-me shoes, like Tammy-Trish.

But Bryn said—

Bryn Bennet is messed up. Even more messed up than I am.

Definitely, I'm messed up, but apparently not messed up *enough* because when I get inside, I do a big bump of K.

And when I wake up in the morning, the edges of my life are all fuzzy, and I don't know what I want. David and I are so different. Thinking again now of his reaction when I asked him about Canada, a shiver runs through me.

By Friday evening when he hasn't called, I decide to call him and let him off the hook for the following night, let him off the hook for the dinner date we'd made so long ago. We already rescheduled once—it obviously isn't meant to be.

I call Bryn's line because I know it will be busy, and I leave a message for the Bennets in general, something about not being available tomorrow night, as if I've forgotten if they've asked me to babysit, like they usually do on Saturday nights, or not. As if I've forgotten that David and I have a date.

Then I text Dale Waters and tell him I'm going to be in the city.

I'm out of K so, right, that's the reason I'm going in, but it'd be kind of cool to see Dale, because even though I'm pretty sure he's fanning me—we had a long conversation on the phone, plus he'd texted—I *am* a fan. Also, I want to pick his brains about Deep Dark Love, ask him how the band got together and maybe, *maybe* play something for him. I'd told him I was looking for suggestions.

Of course at that, he'd said something, well, suggestive.

I'd glossed over it, just like I'd glossed over the rest of his flirtatious remarks . . .

I'd been at school—in that hidey-hole behind the cabinet down in the basement. He'd been in a recording studio.

"Wow. Cool," I'd said at that point in the conversation. "Tell me more about that."

"Show is always more fun than tell, why don't you come in? I'll show you the studio—and some Southern hospitality."

I'd laughed, mostly at the way he'd managed to pack two words with so much innuendo, then said, "I'm not sure when I'll be in. Soon."

"Soon. That's as far off as the moon, Angel. Gimme a date. A time. Let's jam. Or am I not a good enough player for you? You sure you liked my upright?"

"You were great."

"Yeah? So tell me how much you liked the band."

"How much? A *lot*."

"Would you say we were—what? Hot?"

Oh my god. This guy—his tone. I'd known he was joking, but it was boiling in school that day—the furnace set to Incinerate—and with his lazy smile coming at me even over the phone, it was too much, embarrassing. Still I'd said, "Yes, totally hot." Because they are.

"Would you say you love the music?"

"Yes, *love*." In the spirit of the "interview," I'd laid it on thick, but it was also true. I couldn't wait to hear him play again.

"So you'll come see us again." He was smirking—I could hear it. "And you'll come see me at my place in Chinatown."

"Okay. Chinatown. Text me your address."

Then I'd had to go, because how many classes could I cut? And I nearly ran into David Bennet. I mean, really, almost smack into him.

I'd wondered what he'd been doing down in the basement. I'd so wanted to stop and talk, but there was no time.

Now? After last night?

Who knows when he'll talk to me.

WAVES
CATE

White-capped waves slap against the sides of the ferry as it flies across the water toward the sparkling Manhattan skyline. I peer out windows covered with clinging droplets. The black night sky hangs over the black bay.

The 150-seat commuter ferry is the fastest way to get into the city, but at this time of day it's half-empty. In the artificially bright light of the boat's cabin, the scrap of paper I'd retrieved from the driveway is whiter than white, and Dee's loopy handwriting is a spiderweb. The address she'd written is followed by

Tues Thurs Sat, 6-8

I don't even want to think about the Saturday part of the equation because then I'll start thinking about David Bennet, about how this was supposed to be our night. I try not to care.

I stare down at Dee's writing, as if it will reveal what Laurel sees in her.

When I'd called Laurel just a little while ago, her tone had been matter-of-fact.

"No problem. You're here studying. Or sleeping over, depending on what time they call."

"But they won't call."

"I know." And she does know. She knows my parents. Knows they don't act like parents. "So what's so important in the city?"

I don't want to tell her I'm going in for K. I also don't want to tell her I'm going in to see Dale—because I don't necessarily want Dee to know. Also, I might not be seeing Dale.

I was supposed to meet him at his apartment, but our last stream of texts got interrupted. His drummer, Trevor, is playing a gig out of town and is apparently having some problems. Dale didn't go into detail, but he also didn't text back. I have a time but no address.

Laurel's voice is full of innuendo, so I go with that. "I—er—met a guy."

"What? You didn't tell me!"

"I'm telling you now."

She makes an exasperated sound.

"Hey, you're never around these days."

"Yes I am!"

"Yeah, if you count *wrapped around*, as in, you're wrapped around Dee's finger."

"Not for long," she growls. "But you don't want to hear that drama. Tell me about this guy."

But I can't, because there isn't one. So I just mumble something else about Dee.

"Once you know Dee better, you'll like her."

"Hmm." Why would I want to get to know someone I don't like *better*?

She gives a little Laurel-laugh, the vocal equivalent of rolling her eyes. "Lovecats?"

Offering up an exaggerated sigh, as if responding is an effort, I say, "Lovecats."

She smiles. I can hear it. She's reassured by the quick check-in, the use of our code word. But tonight, *Lovecats*, our way of connecting, of making sure everything's cool, only makes me feel worse. It reminds me that, lately, Laurel and I *haven't* been connecting. Not like we used to. It reminds me that I'm lying to her.

After I hang up, I think about Dee, remembering her serpent's smile. I think about Laurel, and that whole thorny visit. About Bryn, in the backseat of the Mercedes.

She'd been drinking from a bottle of something. She's definitely got a problem, but maybe I'm no better. Lying to L so she won't give me a hard time. Going into the city for drugs.

Now I picture Johann, his blue eyes and blond hair, his handsome face. I can almost hear his German accent, comic and charming. His paintings are violently beautiful.

Comparing Bryn and Johann is easy somehow, but me . . . do I fit the same mold?

Bryn's beautiful and angry, Johann's handsome and pissed off—well, he used to be, till he stopped drinking. Fair hair, ice eyes—they're not related, but they could be, although Johann has no family left. Bryn, of course, comes from a whole family of charmers. The old Bryn was just as golden as David.

But then came the night of the party and Rod.

Guess anyone can become an addict.

Again, I see Bryn, with a bottle to her lips. *You were right, Laurel.*

But Bryn has her part in Rod's suicide to contend with. Who could blame her for trying to wash that away?

With Johann . . . I don't know details about his past, but something made him leave Germany. When he came to the States, the art scene loved him, but he loved drinking, and it cost him. On his downward spiral, he met my folks.

But I'd seen Johann's transformation. I've seen my parents' struggle, too.

Maybe I can help Bryn after all.

(I imagine Laurel, wagging a finger at me, saying, "Pot calling the kettle black, Cate Cat.")

Or not.

The ferry sways over the bay, slowing as it gets close to Lower Manhattan.

In my mind I argue with Laurel, telling her K's different, that I'm not addicted, that I don't even like it, really.

That I just *want* it—to *get out.*

"It's not like I'm Johann," I picture myself telling her. "Or Bryn. Not at all."

CITY
CATE

Even with the hood of my purple coat up and my hands shoved deep in the pockets, I'm shivering as I search the fronts of the buildings on White Street for numbers.

I stop at the bottom of a flight of steps leading up to a black-brick apartment building.

The dark-haired singer from Deep Dark Love is at the top.

I do a double take. "Dale?" He's leaning in the doorway, a cell phone in his hand.

"Hey, Angel. An hour early, must be my lucky night."

"Wait—how are you here? And—you never texted me back. Do you live nearby?"

"Near as your nose. I live here. Check your phone, darlin'. Sent you my address an hour ago." He straightens and steps out of the shadowed recess of the doorway, then trots down the stairs.

In slow motion, I check, a knot forming in my stomach. There's his text. It probably came in while I was on the boat, no cell service there. I glance at the address he sent, then at the building. There's no number on it, but to my estimation, it's the address I'm seeking—the one that Dee gave me. My heart sinks a little. It's one thing to *do* drugs, but dealing?

"*You're* Dee's connection?"

"Is that what she calls me?" He gives a short laugh. "Girl's such a drama queen. I'm just about done doing her dirty work, thankfully." His lips make their way into that lazy smile. "Have to say, though, didn't expect to see you here for lychees."

His eyes narrow just a little, and he tilts his head slightly back. It's like there's something he can't quite see, but he thinks if he changes the angle, it might come into focus.

"I mean, I've helped Dee out a couple of times, but—" He's still got that looking-for-something-I-can't-find expression on his face, and now I recognize it. Disappointment.

"Lychees? No, I—"

His expression turns sharp. "I know what you're after. And I sure hate to put out a pretty girl like you, but I'm not gonna re-up, Angel."

This is a surprising combination of words, and I hesitate, trying to decide how to respond.

"But," he says, "gotta go anyway." He glances at his watch. "Come on with me. Won't take but a minute, then I'll explain why I can't hook you up."

"Ah—" Again, I hesitate, confused.

He lifts my left hand and runs his fingers over my calluses. "Come on—sooner we go, sooner I can wash my hands. You can celebrate with me. We'll jam."

He's speaking in low, smoky tones now, reminding me how much I loved the way he sang, loved the evening sound of his voice with the band.

"Sure."

We head over a bunch of blocks, then turn up Church Street. When we reach what's probably the last crumbling building in this gentrified

316

neighborhood—a skinny stack of red bricks slumped between two sleek, much newer buildings—he stops, and looks down the street.

"So your drummer. Is he okay?"

"He is. He just—hey, gimme a sec, will you?"

A long black car pulls up in front of us. The back window behind the driver glides down, and a man gestures for Dale to come closer.

They talk for a minute, then the guy passes a brown paper bag through the window. Dale doesn't take it, just says something. The guy yanks the bag back into the car. Next he rummages through it, uttering a string of vicious insults, and pulls a clear plastic baggie from its mouth.

After whisking the baggie into the car's dark interior, he shoves the brown bag back at Dale, who laughs and tucks it under his arm.

Then the man crooks a finger. Dale bends down.

He slides a hand behind Dale's neck—

And kisses him full on the lips.

Dale rears back. "The fuck!" He wipes his mouth. "That's just another reason I'm out, got it? I am *out*."

Then the guy says something I can't hear.

Dale shakes his head emphatically. "I don't owe you shit. Get rid of it someplace else." He bangs twice on the roof of the car.

The man inside the car shouts several choice words at Dale, then begins berating the driver. A second later the car roars away from the curb, the man's left arm hanging out the window, his hand raised high, middle finger extended.

Turning around, Dale offers me a crooked smile and then the bag. "Lychee?"

LYCHEE

CATE

When I don't take the bag, he pushes it into my hands. Then he gives me a little nudge, and we start walking back the way we came.

"What was that all about?"

"You don't need to know. You do need to try one of those, though." He nods at the bag.

Reaching inside, I pull out what looks like a bumpy strawberry with rough leather skin. It has a fairly long stem, and I've pulled it from a rubber-banded bundle of a dozen other long-stemmed, obliquely heart-shaped leathery berries. I'm confused.

"What? Don't want to mar your manicure?" He glances at my hands. "No nail polish. Nice. So what's the problem? Too messy for you?"

The problem is, I've just had an extremely intimate view into this guy's fucked-up life, and now, instead of walking away, I'm walking back with him to his place.

Also, I have never seen a lychee.

"I don't like lychees." I hand him the bag.

"What? How can you not like lychees?"

"I've tried lychee nuts. I don't like them."

"You tried lychee nuts—you never had fresh lychees? Chinese cherries?" He looks in the bag. "Although these fuckers gotta be from Mexico or something—Dee's asshole connection probably brought 'em in with a load—her real connection. Still, not a bad parting gift."

I cast a dubious look at the lychee. It is not something I want to put in my mouth.

"Here." He plucks the bumpy red fruit from my fingers and plunges his thumbnail into its rough skin. He pulls part of it—including the stem and what looks like a seed—away.

Then he stops, so I stop, too. Swiftly, he brings the rough fruit to my lips—which part slightly as I start to protest—and squeezes.

The slippery, tender wet flesh of the fruit slides out of the skin and into my mouth.

The texture is that of a peeled grape, the taste—perfume-like, delicate, and sweet.

He laughs, probably at the expression on my face, which must be a cross between furious and ecstatic.

"Another," I demand, like a child.

He tears the skin off another, tosses the stem and the pit, and before I can object—*I'll do this part myself, thanks*—my nostrils flare at the fragrant, floral smell.

He slides another of the luscious fruits with its pearly pulp into my mouth.

We're back to where we started now, and he waves me up the short flight of steps with a sweep of his hand. Standing behind me in the blue-black shadows, he pulls out a key.

"Excuse me," he says, reaching around me.

I get this sudden feeling in my gut—like I should leave.

But I step back instead, and when he opens the door, I follow him in.

SOLO

DAVID

"Why are you here?" Bryn asks from her perch on one of the kitchen stools.

"I live here." I eye the joint in her hand. "Or have you forgotten?"

"David." My sister takes a hit off the joint, holding it in so that her next words sound as if she's been pressurized, like a can of whipped cream. "It's Saturday night—" Coughing, she releases the smoke.

"So?" I wave away the cloud.

"So." Still coughing, she says, "I find it hard to believe that you've run out of willing volunteers." Finally, her hacking concluded, she takes a big breath, wipes her eyes.

When I still don't react, she cocks an eyebrow at me. "For your juggling act."

As if on cue, the phone rings. Our mother refuses to activate voicemail—she says she doesn't like the idea of "personal information being out there in space." We let the machine get it.

Bryn and I listen, her with interest, me without, as the voice of the caller fills the room.

"David? I called you on your cell, but you didn't answer, so I'm calling you at this . . ."

"Trish," Bryn says as the voice prattles on.

"Tammy," I correct.

"Same difference."

"Maybe."

"Why don't you pick up?"

I just shake my head.

"Does this have something to do with why you're home tonight? And remind me again, why *are* you home? I forget what you said."

"I didn't say."

"Yeah, okay, so tell me now. Why are you home on a Saturday night?"

"I believe," I say, taking an olive from the dregs of a martini that our mother has left on the counter—she likes a quick cocktail before a cocktail party, which is where they're starting out tonight—"that my date has blown me off."

Bryn laughs and lets out another cloud of smoke. I give her my best Disapproving Look, but since it's relatively new, it's not very potent and she only laughs again.

"Your date blew you off? Wow, that's different. Who's the girl?" Another fit of laughter overtakes her. It's disconcerting, because it's not really laughter but giggling. She's out of control. I know this not because of the joint in her hand but because of the melismatic sound she's emitting. Bryn is not, nor has she ever been, a giggler. Not until . . .

But I don't want to think about the reason she's always high these days, always slinking around, with her black-as-night hair. I miss my blonde, snotty-and-condescending-yet-somehow-always-popular sister, the one who wouldn't giggle if you paid her.

Tonight, Bryn is the babysitter. Wrangled into the position by me, because I'd thought that Cate and I were going to go out for dinner, and I knew my parents had plans.

As much as I'd still like to see Cate, Bryn has changed so much since that damn night that it may be a good thing I'm around. My sister is definitely not in babysitter mode. Not that she ever is, and neither am I, which is why my parents practically adopted Cate. But Cate—

"Cate stood him up," Kimmy calls from the other room.

I'd thought that, at least, Kimmy was upstairs.

"Give me that." Scowling, I pinch the joint from between Bryn's fingers and run the lit end underwater. Then I hand it back to her. "Smoke outside if you're going to smoke," I say quietly. "Kimmy doesn't need to see—"

"I can *heeear* you," Kimmy sings out.

I blow out a breath. "Great."

"Jesus. You going to play the good guy all night? It's horribly dull. What's with you?"

"I told you, Cate bailed on him," Kimmy says from the doorway.

"Is that what the weird message was about?" Bryn asks. "The sorry-but-I'm-unavailable-for-Saturday-night message? That was for you?"

"Apparently."

"Kind of a convoluted way to blow somebody off," Bryn says. "I'm giving her points for originality and for firsts. Why'd she do it? You guys get your wires crossed? Oh wait, she's always got her shit together. Well, almost always. But still. Let me rephrase that. What the fuck did you do to her?"

"Oh for god's sake—nothing. I must have misunderstood. It's no big deal."

But it is a big deal, and Bryn, even stoned as a '60s rock star, sees that it is. Sees right through me in that window-way of seeing that only siblings have.

"Sorry, but I still think it's totally weird—you making the moves on her. She's like—"

"Shut up, Bryn."

"Oh, how quickly we regress." She strikes a match, relights the joint. Kimmy's eyes widen as she watches Bryn inhale.

"Bryn, damn it—"

In the pressurized voice she says, "Maybe you scared her off. Did you do something Dad-like?"

Kimmy looks startled, then tries to cover it up, undoing one of her braids, then the other.

Looking down, I place my hands on the counter, tap my fingers, try to hold my temper.

In the quiet that fills the kitchen now, Kimmy rebraids her hair with the focused concentration of an Olympic athlete. It's never looked this perfect in her life. I'm tempted to grab a piece of paper from the pad on the counter, scrawl "9.7" on it, and hold it up.

"I don't know," I finally say. "She asked about Canada. And I just . . . I don't know."

Bryn looks at me like I've done something unforgivable, which is ridiculous.

"I was just a little short. It was nothing! She's—overreacting. Although . . . I may have said a few things." *Damn.*

But Bryn knows our father, and she knows me. She knows I don't want to be like him, and the fact that I am sometimes is a hot button for me. Bryn knows that, *hell,* just talking about him or being around him these days is enough to set me off.

What she doesn't know is that my anger now isn't really about him, or even about me fucking up with Cate—because, yeah, I *was* short with her, and I made those shitty comments. But that's nothing compared to Canada. The thing that's really eating me. Eating me alive.

Both my sisters know that something happened in Northern Ontario, but I'm the only one, besides my father, who knows the details. So I'm the only one who really knows *what* this is about. It's about guilt and the awful hollowness that comes from knowing another person lost his *life*, because of me.

Bryn continues to pollute the air, looking at me as if I've done something awful, and I have, but it has nothing to do with Cate Reese.

Kimmy's still busy playing with her hair, says, "Why didn't you want to tell Cate about Canada? I know you got hurt, but how about before that? Didn't you have fun? Canoes, campfires . . ." Kimmy trails off, probably because of the look on my face.

All at once Bryn says, "Dad told me."

"What?" The betrayal is sharp. Deep. The last thread in the complicated weave of the relationship I share with my father, cut. "He *told* you?"

"Told you what?" Kimmy asks Bryn.

"Nothing, Kimmy," Bryn says. Then she says to me, "Maybe you should tell Cate. She's got it together. Usually. She might have something decent to say. Might make you feel better."

"Yeah, because talking about our problems makes us feel so much better, right? That's why you talk about yours?"

Bryn's eyes shut like a door and, suddenly, I see our father—a younger female version of him. And that's when I get it. Bryn nailed it. I *had* been acting like our father: I'd shut down and shut Cate out. Dismissed her. I'd put on my Jack mask and added a couple of ice cubes. Clink.

But I wasn't the only one. Bryn, ever since that night, has been shutting out the world.

I don't know if I can help her. But, man, I need to fix this thing with Cate. Fix myself.

The phone rings. The machine picks up. "David?" A girl's voice begins tentatively.

"Tammy again," Bryn says over the voice.

"Trish," I correct.

"Same difference," she says.

"Yeah." I cross the room and turn the volume down on the answering machine.

This time, Bryn doesn't ask me why I don't pick up. Upstairs, Kimmy slams her bedroom door.

LOFT

CATE

Up three flights, another door, another key. I'm not sure how long I'll
stay.

But when Dale Waters drops the bag of lychees on a coffee table
between two low-slung sofas and says, "Sit down"—I do.

The loft is painted mostly white. One wall is a deep shade of gold.
The space is a shotgun, the area where I sit separated from a desk, bed,
and another sofa down near a row of windows by a swath of dark-blue
velvet hanging from a rod that runs across the ceiling. The blue curtain
has been pushed to one side. A large and very beautiful painting of an
angel hangs across from the foot of the bed. There are other paintings
as well—landscapes, portraits—and several floor lamps with beaded
shades. The nearest lamp casts a red glow.

"So what's with the drive-by produce guy? Seems like a weird way
to shop."

Dale laughs out loud, a full, head-flung-back laugh that catches me
off guard. "You are so right," he says. "So right, in fact, that I am never
gonna get my lychees from that guy again."

"No? You seemed kind of . . . intimate. Well, he did, anyway. At least it seemed like he wanted to be. Is he a good friend of yours?"

Dale's smile fades. "No. He . . . is a former acquaintance."

"Former? But you just saw him. You, um, took a bag of fruit from him? Remember?"

A smile plays at the corners of Dale's mouth. "That I did. But it was the last thing I'll ever take from him, including his shit."

"Okay . . ." I tear open a lychee. Dale passes me a bowl. A painted dragon circles the rim. For a second, I just blink at it. Then, holding the lychee pieces in one hand, I touch the dragon's scales with the index finger of the other. Trace the flames shooting out of its mouth.

"Chinese dragon," Dale says. "Supposed to be a symbol of power and good luck—for people who are worthy of it."

For people who are worthy of it. Like me? Like me, That Lucky Girl?

Dale looks at me quizzically. "For the pits," he says. "The skin."

"Oh. Right. Thanks."

"So let's celebrate," Dale says. "My dealing days, which were few in number to begin with—I was only helping out your buddy, Dee—are done. I'm back to being an honest man. Maybe even honest enough for a girl like you."

He leans over me and takes a lychee. He's so close I can smell his leather jacket, the clean scent of his skin. He slips the jacket off now. Hangs it on a hook by the door.

"Dee's not my buddy," I say, feeling the need to clarify that as well as shift my focus from the way Dale's T-shirt hugs his shoulders. "And wait." I'm totally confused. "So, you didn't get anything from that guy in the car? Any—drugs?"

Dale's brows lift. He shakes his head. His phone pings and he checks it.

"Ha. Like I said. Trevor's fine." He shows me the screen.

Portland rocks dude we have to play here lots of snow tho my dick is frozen ps thx for the straight talk.

"But—" But I don't care about his drummer. I press the nails of one hand into the palm of the other. It feels like the ferry, down below the Financial District, is far, far away.

The kitcheny part of the place is across from us. Dale goes to the fridge. Retrieves a beer.

"Want one?"

"I want what I came for," I say carefully, unbuttoning my coat.

"Ah, yeah. I was going to say. You look hot."

I glance sharply at him.

The lazy smile appears. "In your coat. You should take it off, stay a while. We're going to jam, right? And you wanted to talk, didn't you? Although, I don't know why we'd talk about music when, you know, we can play it."

"Yeah, well . . ." I don't take my coat off. Instead, I reach into the messenger bag slung across my body beneath the coat and pull out some money.

Dale presses his lips together for a few seconds. Then he says, "Sorry. Like I told you, I'm retired. But you're going to stay, yeah?"

But suddenly the idea of talking about music with Dale Waters seems ridiculous, and the idea of playing in front of him? Impossible. I mean, there were record companies at his gig. Industry people. I'm not in that league. I'd never get a record deal playing Bach, or Brouwer, and my songs? They have, like, three chords each.

"I—I don't think so. I mean, my song ideas aren't really, well, they're coming along, but they're nothing like your songs. For me to stay, and . . . bore you?" (I'm pretty sure he knows I'm more afraid of making an idiot out of myself than boring him, but still.) "Why should I? You—"

"Hmm. Thought the many reasons for that would be obvious by now."

He grins—it's a light among shadows—looking like the model he was, maybe still is. I've learned a lot about this boy in a short amount of time, but that smile . . . it's disconcerting. When I went to the show the other night—before I knew anything about Dale, before I'd seen him play, seen another guy kiss him—his smile had seemed less complicated.

Now he asks, "How long have you been playing around with K? You don't seem like the type. Who likes to lose control, I mean."

"You would know?"

"Maybe. What I know for sure is that except for a beer once in a while, I don't touch anything anymore. Except—" He side-eyes me.

"I should go," I say, "really." But I take my coat off.

"Kitchen." He points. "Bathroom." Points again. "Make yourself at home."

"Thanks." I head for the bathroom.

The room is white and very clean. The tongue-and-groove ceiling makes me think of a boat. A claw-foot tub sits in one corner. A wardrobe stands open against the far wall. I'm surprised to see a tux hanging there alongside a bunch of shirts.

I'm not sure why I'm in such a mood.

Pick a reason. Then leave.

Closing the door behind me, I fumble, dropping my messenger bag and the money I'd been trying to stuff into it. The bills fan out on the tiled floor. Two little packets stick out from between a pair of twenties, two tiny white envelopes.

Yes. Whatever the reason, there's your out.

Picking up the bag, I shove the money inside, then tug the top flap. It doesn't line up; I can't secure the clasp. It looks like a notebook that must have been lying lengthwise shifted when I dropped the bag, and now it's keeping the flap from folding over properly. I pull it out—

And see the orange-and-white-striped paper bag that's been squashed beneath it.

"Take a listen. Tell me what you think."

David's Listen Up! bag from forever ago. I open it and pull out a CD.

Deep Dark Love—*Dragon Fruit*.

What. The. Hell.

It's a conscious decision—to sit on the floor—and I consider the making of this decision to be a small feat, because my brain seems to have shut down.

I stare at the illustration of a red fruit with green spiked tendrils resembling a flame. Stare at the curved edges of the letters that spell out the band's name and the CD's title. Turning the CD over, I examine a picture of the same fruit, sliced open to reveal red flesh, black seeds. Then I read down the track list: "Dragon Fruit," "Easily," "Bluff," "Chinatown" . . .

I'm dying to hear the songs, but also I want to pretend the CD doesn't exist. Because I just. Can't. Deal. With the weirdness. I was supposed to go out with David tonight, and now . . .

Actually, I can't deal, period, and I kind of wish there was a door in the floor that I could just slip through. Maybe I'd wind up in the subway and take a train to . . . I don't know where.

But then I remember. I have a destination.

So I wash my hands with Dale Waters's grassy-smelling soap. Then I dump the powder from one of the packets into what I figure is his toothbrush glass, add water, and stir the mixture with my finger. Gagging slightly, I swallow it down.

Then I think, *Crap*.

I probably shouldn't have used the whole packet.

Inspired by a couple of the cheerleaders at school, I kneel in front of the toilet and stick a finger down my throat.

I throw up, and hope it does the trick.

But this is a new low for me, so I don't know if it will.

TOUCH

CATE

Dale Waters is sprawled on the couch, reading a book.

I hold up the CD.

"So you are a fan."

"Actually, a friend gave it to me. But, yes, I'm a fan. Can we listen?"

"Your friend has good taste, but you know, I've heard it so many times, in the studio and all; we did so many mixes. But listen to it on your own, will you? Tell me what you think."

I just stare at him. "Sure."

"Thanks."

I contemplate the two couches, then sit down next to him.

"So what's with the tux?"

"Work."

"Which is?"

"Besides gigs? Bartending. Your friend Dee used to work at the same place, waitressing."

"I told you, she's not my friend."

"Should I ask why not?"

"If you want to."

"I want to. Why aren't you friends? Besides the obvious differences between you two."

"You mean, like the fact that she's kind of a bitch?"

"Whereas you seem pretty cool? Yeah."

"She hates me, for one."

"No way. How can that be?" His tone is teasing, but Dale's eyes . . . they're just so pretty, and right now the expression in them closely resembles real concern. It's confusing.

I choose to respond to the teasing. "Ha-ha."

"Not trying to be funny." But he's grinning now, as he gets up for another beer. "Okay, maybe a little funny, but you seem like a sweetheart, Katydid. Why would Dee wanna bite you?"

"I really don't know. She's going out with my best friend, so—"

"So she's jealous."

He puts on some music. The long lines of "Retrograde" fill the sparsely furnished space.

"You like James Blake?" I ask.

"I like this song."

And that's all it takes to get us talking hard and fast about music—indie, alternative, dream pop, rock.

Our tastes are remarkably similar, and suddenly, I'm glad there's a late ferry.

It's music, so my words come easily, and in another few minutes, I'm yammering on about seeing Rabbit Daggers in Brooklyn with Laurel.

"Brooklyn, huh? You go for hipsters, yeah?"

The question cracks me up, as it's meant to, and when Dale comes over and takes my hand, I barely notice because I'm laughing so hard. He loops my arms around his neck, and in a minute we're both laughing and dancing. He knows how to move like . . . *mmm*.

"What'd you say?" he asks.

"Nothing." I laugh again. "Must be because you're a musician."

"What must be because I'm a musician?"

"You know." I gesture to where his hips glide against mine. He just smiles.

I say, "I want to go again, to hear your band play."

"You will. But right now . . . I want to play you, Katydid." He gently pinches one of my arms, his thumb sliding off—*on, off*—to the steady rhythm of the bass line. The low sound thuds softly in my ears, careful tonal footsteps, warm and shadowy, wending their way inside of me . . .

"So show me where you fit . . ."

Dale stops, brings his hands to my waist, and dances me down the length of the room.

Now that we're on the other side of the curtain, I can see back behind where it's bunched against the wall, by the head of the bed. Instead of a bedside table, there's a stack of amps, a couple of mic stands. Next to those are two bass guitars and the upright. Its deep honey-toned finish glows in the low light.

I say, "Can I touch it?"

"Touch anything you like."

I pluck one of the strings and a low note rolls out. I scratch another with a fingernail—*Zzz.* Like the bottom strings on the guitar, it's wound with metal.

"Will you play something for me?"

"I'd love to play something for you." He nods at a guitar leaning against the far side of the bed. "But only if you play, too."

Then he shuts off the music and takes the upright off its stand. He slides his fingers over the strings—that's what it looks like anyway, just a simple, effortless movement—and a series of warm tones I can almost feel on my skin surround us.

He lifts his chin in the direction of the guitar. "Come on, girl. Show me what you got."

And, in a minute, what I've got is his guitar in my arms.

Now I kneel on the bed, the guitar across my thighs.

He comes closer, bringing the bass.

With an instrument in my hands, I'm finally comfortable. This is how I'd imagined it: us swapping songs, me maybe asking, *Do you know any musicians who might be into my ideas?*

But instead, as he begins to play a slow ascending line, I just follow him. For each of his notes, I play a complementary chord. Only, while he goes up, I go down. And after a few minutes, it's not clear who's leading whom.

I'm not sure which one of us starts singing first—him I think, yeah—but I'm in right away. He throws out a line, and I toss something back, word upon word, till things start adding up. When we start stringing together phrases, I wobble back to where I'd left my bag, and get out my notebook.

He plays while I scribble. Says, "You're the boss of the song—you lay it out."

The part about love, I decide, is the chorus. "The way it repeats," I say now. "It's the chorus."

"The way it repeats—makes it the outro. The chorus has to be stronger than that."

"There's nothing stronger than love. It's the chorus."

"There's sex and death," Dale says. He laughs, but I don't.

I stand my ground. "You said I'm the boss of this song?"

"You're the boss, you know why? 'Cause you care, more than me."

Caring and bossing and everything now—it's all beginning to run together.

My Mia move had worked, only at some point after I'd hurled, but before I'd learned about being the boss of a song, I'd decided that getting high would assist the creative process—nope—and made another trip to Dale's white boat of a bathroom, where, in an "Oops! Meant to save half the packet, oh well, bottoms up!" moment, I did my entire last bump.

Now I set the guitar aside and stretch, my words stretching with me.

"I reeeally like the way you play, Dale Waters. I *like* your voice."

"I like you."

"I—like you, too."

"Maybe we should take a break."

"Maybe we should. Take a break."

Then we're both sitting on the bed. Or rather, I'm sitting. Dale's lying down, hands behind his head, lanky frame sprawled across the white coverlet like city streets on a map.

He unclasps his hands and reaches up to touch my hair.

As if in protest, the wind blows a fierce gust against the row of windows.

My mood swings fast, the arc of an ax, blade edge burying with a thunk in some crepuscular part of my psyche. I shiver and cross my arms.

"How old are you, Katydid?"

My birthday isn't till spring. I'll be seventeen. "Old enough." I lift my chin slightly.

Dale's eyes glitter, darkening a shade as his gaze roves my face.

"Got a boyfriend?"

I look away from Dale's curling black hair. His pretty sky eyes.

A bouquet of red roses dominates the desk. The wind rattles the windows. A petal drops from one of the roses. I study the abstract painting of the angel. The white and gold. The suggestion of wings.

Dale gets up, crosses to the windows. Opens one. Closes it. The sound of the wind quiets.

"You're taking an awfully long time to answer me," he says, climbing back onto the bed.

"You have a girlfriend." I nod at the roses. Their edges are swirling prettily.

"Had."

I arch an eyebrow. Look back to the flowers.

"Let me clarify. I ended it six months ago. Can't help it if it's not over for her."

"Not over for her."

The words seem to reverberate in my chest.

Outside, a heavy rain begins to fall. At the same time, I start to fall harder into the high.

Because that's what K does. It doesn't lift me. It lowers me. Lowers me down, into a dark, dreamy hole . . .

Dale Waters slides off the bed and kneels on the floor in front of me. He places his palms on the tops of my thighs and looks into my eyes.

My lower lip finds its way between my teeth.

With an index finger, he traces shapes on my legs. Circles. Squares. Triangles.

I close my eyes. Wish . . . he was David.

I need to leave.

But the thought is mist, sea spray from the water I crossed to get here, and the shapes are repeating, insistently. They're letters. Words.

Kate. Katydid, he traces. His fingers press into my jeans.

"Katy, do you?" he asks. "Want to?"

My eyes flutter open. I do want to.

He draws an *X*. Draws an *O*. "I like you, Katydid." The area his fingers traverse grows larger, expanding down, along my inner thighs.

We watch each other.

I, he traces, then he traces it again. *I*.

Now *L*, and again, *L*.

My breath quickens as he writes the whole thing, fast, on the top of my right thigh.

I like you.

He says, "Katy did. Katy does? Has Katy done it? I think . . . maybe not."

I like you, he writes again. Then more slowly, he writes,

I

Want

You

He wipes it away, his palms rubbing the tops of my legs, down along the inside of them, up the outside. The pressure increases. His hands move to my hips, and I lean back, put my hands behind me for support, and lift them.

He stands, grabbing me behind my knees, yanking me toward him—

I hit his body hard. My legs wrap themselves around his waist. It's not me; it's my body.

I'm dissolving, like the powder did earlier, and I *want* to dissolve, into the netherworld of the drug, leave my body behind, with this boy.

Standing now, he leans over me, slides his hands beneath me, lifting me up.

I tilt my face, offering my lips.

His low laugh resonates in his chest as he climbs onto the bed with me in his arms. He hovers over me as he lays me down on my back. My legs are still wrapped around him, but now I release him and straighten them. He sinks down onto me, using one arm to bear his weight. His free hand comes up toward my neck, his fingers exploring my collarbone.

Then it's one button, two . . . three buttons, four . . .

He grazes my lips with his, and another laugh hums in his throat as a soft moan escapes me, but finally—his mouth comes down on mine.

A sudden sharp thought pierces me, a momentary flare of light in a darkened room: *this is wrong for so many reasons*. But it *feels* right, so I don't stop, even though I'm unsteady—here and not here. If I'd thought earlier that the ferry dock seemed far away, now it's in another world. And home—home seems like a *vanished* world.

I tug at the waist of his jeans, and he pulls his mouth from mine, laughs out loud. Again, I moan—the sound just comes. He looks down at me. I swim up, into the blue pools of his eyes.

As I swim, I whisper. I whisper, *"David."*

A breeze blows across the pools, rippling the surface.

"What did you say?"

I hesitate—bring my teeth to his jawline.

He gives me a gentle nudge. I drop back.

His brows draw down. But he's not angry . . . I don't think. "What did you say, Angel?"

But I'm slipping away into a dark whirlpool . . .

Then the boy, the boy above me—.

Something's not right.

"Huh," he says.

I start to cry.

"Don't cry. I've got you."

I slide my hands up under the boy's shirt—under David-but-not-David's shirt—push it up, trace his ribs. When I duck down, bringing my mouth to one of his nipples, we turn into a tangle of limbs and clothes and jagged breaths. His mouth crushes mine.

We tumble over each other—

Till he pins me.

Says, "No."

I say, *"Yes."* The word is half moan, half cry. All want.

Then I feel his hips press hard against my pelvis, feel my own hips pressing back—

And I gasp in surprise as he bites me, gently, on the neck.

OBLIVION

CATE

Just before rolling off me and onto his side.

"Who's David?" he inquires softly.

Then I feel the boy's fingers on my face, wiping the wetness away. Wiping my tears.

"Cate?"

But I'm too far down. I don't even know this guy's name. Not anymore.

Something's wrong.

The room has grown dark, too dark to see. The room—*where am I?*

The pleasurable, ecstatic feeling has given way to something else, some kind of panic. It buzzes through me. I want to get up. Want to go home. Only—

I can't move. I try to say it. But my voice has disappeared into the darkness.

A face appears above mine. I blink up at it, at him. Do I know him? No. No, I don't know this boy with empyrean eyes, tumbling night hair.

Especially now, as the black curls begin to move, become spiraling snakes.

The boy's expression darkens, his pretty lips twisting. His laugh is a blade.

"This—this is why I never touch that Special K crap. Thought you were out." His face is close to mine, his breath hot on my skin. "Come here." His voice is deep as the ocean.

Then I feel his fingers fumbling with my shirt. I try to lift my hand to stop him—

But I'm immobile. Buried, in a blacked-out oblivion.

SHADOWS

DAVID

The bluish light on the closed laptop glows, then dims—glows, then dims—with silent, pulsing machine breath, indicating the computer is asleep. I lie on my bed, watching it.

Outside, the sky hangs over the land like a threat, the clouds dark-gray monstrosities shot through with a sickly yellowish color, like the light before a tornado. Snowdrifts lie in waves across the backyard, turning it to a silent white sea, stunned somehow into stillness.

Tammy comes in from the bathroom, and desire snakes through me, slithers on my skin.

I pull a small square packet from my bedside table drawer but don't open it.

Playfully, she knocks the pillows over my face, nips the packet from my fingers with her teeth— climbs on top of me.

I let the pillows lie. Hear a crinkling tear. Feel her fingers on me.

A moment later she pushes the pillows aside.

I turn my head, avoiding her eyes. Watch our shadows on the wall.

She makes all the effort, and I let her. She's so attentive, I feel a little sick.

When the ocher light fades, she whispers in my ear, "Where've you been? Why haven't you called? This weekend, do you want to go to—"

Shh . . . the central heating kicks on, and I kiss her. I can't talk to her. I hate liars.

Then, because I feel so bad, I make her feel good. So good she says, *"I love you."*

I stroke her hair, can't say the same. So instead I say, "You want me to do that again?"

CONCRETE

CATE

"What's your emergency?" a woman's voice asks calmly.

"Drugs. Drug overdose. No, wait. Car accident. I—I've been in a car accident."

"Please give me your location."

I look around the narrow alley with its crumbling walls. One side is a skinny redbrick building that leans sharply toward me, about to fall. The air smells of urine and vomit, of fear.

"Some kind of urban hell," I want to say. I name the nearest cross streets.

"We're sending medical assistance. Please state your name."

"Katydid."

Laughter sounds behind me. I spin around.

The handsome snake-haired boy stands at the mouth of the alley. He holds up my phone.

"Hey! I was just using that, you can't—"

"What you're using is shit. Horseshit. Dumb shit. Animal drugs."

"What's it to you?"

"Don't know yet." He walks toward me.

I whirl as an ambulance screeches to a halt at the other end of the alley. Two white-jacketed men jump out. One goes around to the rear of the vehicle. The other hurries over to me, a small case in his hands.

The next few minutes are a blur of activity as the man checks my breathing, my pulse. He shouts something, and the other man comes running. The two EMTs are eerily familiar.

My stomach twists sickeningly. *What's wrong with me?*

But then I know what's wrong. I'm not supposed to be here.

"I have to go!" I shout to the boy.

At the same time, one of the techs hollers "Clear" and spins toward the boy— presses two pads to his chest. The snake boy jerks— falls to the ground.

Suddenly I know his name. Dale Waters.

"No!" I throw myself down on the ground next to him. "Why did you do that?"

The EMT kneels next to me. He's holding an oxygen mask over the boy's face.

When he pulls it away, I see that it's Cal.

I freeze for a second.

When I unfreeze, there's a guitar in my hands, a gorgeous classical guitar. Rosewood. Mahogany. I balance it on one knee. Play through some chords. My fingers love the buttery strings. Only instead of music—

A horrible banshee wail rips through the air.

With a cry, I raise the instrument over my head—

Bring it down hard on the concrete. The world is splinters and snapping strings.

And then it's David who's on the ground.

I lean over him and whisper, "Hang on."

HORSES
CATE

"Welcome back to the land of the living."

Dale Waters sits to one side of the bed, on the couch near the windows. A book sits beside him.

My hand flies to my chest—

But my shirt's neatly buttoned.

My heart gallops—not so neatly—beneath it. I try to slow its wild stride.

I'm sitting up, in Dale Waters's bed. A blanket lies across my lap. I look around. The room is awash with lavender light. It's early morning. My boots are off. But that's all.

His lips twist. "Don't worry. I was a gentleman. Still am, in fact. You, however, Katydid, are a wild child, a wanton woman. I had to struggle to protect my virtue. And you're lucky I'm a fool for love. I let you stay. Should probably have my head examined. I mean you never know. You could be an ax murderer or something."

Or something. I finally take a breath.

Now I notice he holds a phone in one hand. My phone.

When he sees me looking at it, he says, "It's for you." And hands it to me.

"What the hell, Cate? Where are you? Why didn't you answer your phone last night?"

I cringe at the sound of Laurel's voice. Her volume level's set to Stun. And I am. Stunned. I can't think. Can't figure out—

Dale mouths *"Coffee"* and rises from the couch, heading toward the kitchen.

Laurel's soundscape continues, populated with craggy peaks and canyons.

"Are you with that guy you told me about? You know, the one you *didn't* tell me about? He sounds really hot, by the way, all like—" She lowers her voice. "'*Yes, Cate's here. She's fine.*' Except he said 'fine' like *fiiine*, in this hot I'm-in-my-bedroom voice. What have you been up to, Miss Cate Cat? I thought you just met him?"

"Laurel," I say, in an unsuccessful attempt to interrupt her.

"Didn't think I'd actually have to cover for you, but when your mom called this morning—"

"Wait. My mom called?"

"Yes, she said you didn't leave a note or anything. No email. No text. She and your dad wanted to know where you were, so I—"

"My dad? What did you tell them?"

"So I *told them*, you went to a yoga class. Something sunrisey. In the city. Have you checked your messages? They want you to meet them at Johann's studio. Also? Your mom must be taking lessons from my mom. She got all touchy-feely-talky with me."

"You're kidding."

"I'm not. She said she misses you. I told her I miss you, too."

I blink at the phone. "And I miss you, L, but Dee—"

"Dee and I are done. We broke up."

"When?"

"Last night. She told me what she said to you."

Dale sets a creamy-looking bowl of coffee on the low table near the couch. Points at it. Points at me.

Laurel sighs. "The *boo* thing. That is just messed up. You were right. She's a bitch. Not to mention the fact that she was trying to turn my best friend into a druggie. Hey, I've got to go. Bryn and Kimmy are here."

"Bryn *and* Kimmy?"

"I know, right? Kind of cool, though. Of Bryn."

"Very cool. What are you guys going to do?"

"We're going horseback riding—the Bennets bought Bryn *a horse.*"

"Wow. That's . . . amazing."

"Bryn says she's gorgeous, a chestnut. Sixteen hands. Her name is Alina. Bryn's calling her Al."

"Sounds like Bryn."

"It does. Which is a good thing. So we're going to the inside arena. At Sunnyside. If you get your butt back here in time, you might just be able to go with us. Lovecats?"

GHOSTS
CATE

Dale walks with me to Johann's gallery on Twenty-Third Street, where my mother pounces on him, then pulls him around the spacious rooms, extolling the virtues of each painting.

Dad and Johann try to talk to me about paintings, too, but my head is splitting—no way could I have gotten on a horse today, although I am kind of excited to meet Alina, and I think it's time for me to start riding again—so when my parents ask if I want to go for Sunday dinner at Johann's, I say no thanks.

The disappointment on my mother's face surprises me.

Then again, when was the last time I really *looked* at her face?

Before I go, Johann pulls me aside. "How bad is it, Cate?"

And now I get it, why my parents wanted me to meet them here.

I study Johann for a minute, thinking of all he's been through, all Dad's been through. "Well," I say, hesitating. "I might have a couple of questions for you."

"Shoot," he says.

So I do.

Then it's time to go, and Dale and I step outside.

The wind whips down the city sidewalks, smelling of sugared street nuts from the vendor on the corner, and the hard-edged tang of winter. While we were inside, it started to snow.

Dale catches a few snowflakes on his hand, where they melt in an instant. He smirks.

"Oh, come on," I say, and catch a few of my own.

But they stick around a little longer on my skin than they did on his, and he laughs.

Then he says, "I'll get you those players, okay?"

"Yeah? That'd be great."

"Trevor will do it, if we throw him some cash, and Ruby can sit in, unless you play lead. What do you say, meet in a week? We can use my place, if you want."

I look at him intently, but his sky eyes are guileless. "That would be easiest. Thank you."

"Sure thing. But like you may have gathered, I've been where you've been. Trevor's still in it, but he's a good friend. Me, Ruby—we're clean, just so you know." He checks his watch. "Angels and demons. That's what I used to see." His voice holds a question.

But I can't answer it. Not in its entirety. Not now, anyway. Maybe not ever. I look away.

He doesn't.

And I find, as I gaze down the sparkling street, that I want to answer him, and although I don't have all the words to do that, I have at least one.

"Ghosts," I say softly. Then I say goodbye and head uptown before walking over to the East River to catch the boat home.

SKY
CATE

Even though it's cold enough to see my breath, after I get on the ferry, I head up to the top deck. The boat speeds away from the city, white wake cutting dark water.

Along the receding skyline, tall buildings glint with final flashes of silver and gold. A fuse of fiery sunset separates the sea and sky, reminding me that winter days are short.

Searching for gloves in my coat pockets, the fingers of one hand come across a sharp edge—no, a corner, the corner of a tiny envelope.

God, this stuff. It's permeating my life, permeating me.

Blinking hard, I stare down at the packets.

One is already open, the powder gone, disappeared into a drink maybe, or the folds of material inside the pocket, the white grains as irretrievable now as the sand from the beach that most likely lines the pockets of my summer Windbreaker.

Summer . . .

When I fell in love with David Bennet.

I was never in love with Cal, not even for a minute, and I know that now. But I loved him because he was my friend, and I was *in love* with the way he played. I was in love with the music.

"You can't keep it, you know."

I start at the sound of his voice, at his dim, wavering reflection in the deck's silver rail.

I don't have to ask what he means—I get it. Cal lost his life. And he's right. It all goes.

But it's all here, too, in every infinite second. *Life.*

I'd be a fool to throw it away on a bunch of shitty powder.

I look up, up, up. High above me, a single gull hangs— hovering on some invisible air current like a still kite, its wings two stenciled white arcs against a darkening cobalt wild.

And when I look back down to the rail, Cal's reflection is gone.

But that's because . . . it was never there.

Like his voice, that was me. All me, and my wanting. With a little help from the K.

Still, I say softly, "It's you I can't keep." *It's you. And the music we loved.*

Now the last light of day plays tricks on my eyes. The last spark on the skyline—

Is fire.

Then it all rushes through me—that night that I'd buried—in a terrible wave of remembering.

Like a kick in my gut, a knife in my side—I start shaking and crying. Hands to my ears, eyes squeezed shut tight—but I can't keep it out any longer.

The wind and the stars, the car going so fast—

Like a film, it plays now, scene after scene, sound after sound, and then—

Silence.

The rail is slick with snow and my hands slide as I sag against it—

But I'm still clutching the envelopes. *Still clutching Cal.*

I couldn't save him. I couldn't.

Eyes back to the sky. *Forgive me. Please. And please know . . . it wasn't my fault.*

Snow falls thick and fast as I look down at the packets. Yes, one is empty. But the other is full. My pulse tick, tick, ticks as I take a deep breath—

And hurl the contents over the side.

The wind whistles across the top deck. Still, I swear, as I lean over the rail, I can see the tiny white specks of K among the swirl of snowflakes, falling straight down to the water, as if even the wind knows how worthless the powder is and doesn't want to touch it.

Crumpling the paper, I stick it back in my pocket and look out, vision blurred, to the Sunday sea beyond the bay. Look out at the great expanse of the Atlantic with its infinite colors, too myriad to name.

And then *pain*—like the night of the accident—rips through my chest. So sharp it scares me, and I feel like I'll fall.

Still, I find strength, as the wind whips my hair, to throw my head back—

And shout to the sky:

"I love you, Cal Woods! I love you. Goodbye."

HEARTBREAK

CATE

Then my heart

        S h a t t e r s
Into a thousand pieces—
Breaking—
free.

PART IV: SPRING

COFFEE
DAVID

I stop typing midsentence when I see Cate come through the door of Listen Up!

She's carrying a guitar case but doesn't head to the back, where the shop is. She walks through the lower level and up the stairs to where I'm sitting behind the glass case, my temporary desk.

"Cate Reese. You didn't even glance at the vinyl."

"Or the CDs, I know."

"You must be extremely preoccupied." I shut my laptop.

"I am." She sets down her guitar and a cardboard tray holding two takeout cups.

"Milk, no sugar," she says, handing a cup to me.

She remembers. Even though we haven't had coffee together since last summer, when, without even realizing it, she pulled me out of myself and back into the world. She remembers.

"Thanks." I nod at the cup in her hand. "Black?"

"Yes."

Now she knows I remember, too.

"How are you?"

"What are you writing?" she says in reply.

"Paper for English. About the similarities between an athlete running a marathon and a musician who's touring."

One of her dark eyebrows lifts. "Guess we have a lot in common, David Bennet."

"Do we?" The two words disappear into the dark corner of a song that's playing through the store speakers.

"David, I'm sorry about that night, that Saturday night we were supposed to go out."

Her gray gaze is steady on me, but her voice . . . sounds different. My imagination kicks in and I see Cate's eyes as twin bodies of water and Cate herself as a sea of changes, her voice coming now from some great depth, instead of from just below the surface, as it always has before.

"And I'm sorry I didn't give you what you wanted. But it wouldn't have been cool. You were upset. As far as what happened on that canoe trip . . . I should have been happy you asked. Unfortunately"—I step out from behind the case, "my rudeness seems to have cost me a date."

She puts up a hand, like she wants me to stay back. "Maybe, but I could have handled things differently. There was just so much going on in my life . . . I got confused."

"I'm sorry if I had anything to do with that confusion."

She smiles. "You might have."

I think about asking if she's looking for something in particular, but I don't want to find out she's come in for music, not for me.

"So, David Bennet," she says. "Have a girlfriend these days?"

"These days, I do not. Why?"

"Well . . . maybe we should resurrect that dinner date."

"Oh really?" I move to close the space between us—

But again she holds up a hand. "Do you think we can make an actual date?"

"Ah . . . sure. Absolutely. For when? Tonight? Tomorrow?"

"Um." She worries her lower lip between her teeth for a second. Then she says, "How about three months from yesterday?"

STRINGS

DAVID

After Cate tells me that she'll explain the time warp later, that is, the reason our date has to wait, she asks if I want to go downstairs with her.

"Sure. What do you need?"

"A new guitar."

"Wow."

"Yeah. My guitar . . . needs some repairs. But more than that, it's not the right instrument for me anymore. Classical guitar . . . just isn't my thing. I mean, I love it—I love all music. But just because you love something doesn't mean it's right for you."

Downstairs, we walk through the door near the back of the store that leads to Ye Olde Guitar Shoppe, the part of Listen Up! that sells instruments, mostly guitars and what players need for the care and feeding of guitars: amps, cables, pedals, strings.

Cate gets out her guitar, which, I can tell by the way she handles it, is precious. Precious to her or in value, I don't know. But when Bird sucks in a breath and says, *"What the hell happened?"* Cate's eyes tear up, so I assume it's both. As Bird turns the instrument this way and that,

I understand his alarm. But he assures Cate he can set up and sell the guitar, no problem.

He disappears, off to check numbers. Cate continues the conversation she started upstairs.

"It's like with people. You meet someone, maybe you really like him—or her—maybe you even get that feeling, like, you *know*. But just because you *know* doesn't mean that person's the person for you."

"But if you *know*—"

Bird comes back, and I drop it. But I'm not so sure I agree with Cate.

She, however, is very sure that she wants to trade in her nylon string guitar for a steel string. She strolls around, checking out the guitars lining the walls. Every once in a while she calls to Bird to pull one down. Then she sits and plays.

"Compared to my classical, these almost chime. There's something . . . magical about their sound. This one . . . sounds like sunlight. This—is The One."

"That was fast," Bird says. "You got lucky. Be right back."

Cate murmurs, *"That Lucky Girl."* But then she smiles, plays a few chords on the black Takamine. "Definitely, this is it. Sometimes you just know."

"Hold on," I object. "You just said—"

"I did. But, see, you have to go with it, that feeling, the 'you *know*' feeling. Because usually you're right, you *do* know. It's just *what* you know—that's where you can get confused."

"Was I actually supposed to follow that?"

She doesn't look up from the guitar in her arms, just says, "Mm-hmm." And I imagine the hum of her lips on my skin.

Bird reappears. They talk about the Takamine. It's an acoustic electric, so Cate can play it through an amp, if she wants. She wants. Bird shows her a few models.

"These are great," she says, "but I need to be able to lift it."

"I'll carry it for you." I wince. I sound like a Boy Scout.

Bird laughs. "Bet you will."

"My own roadie," Cate says. "Could be cool. But you might be too busy writing articles about athletes and musicians. About all the things they have in common." She grins.

Bird finally shows her the smallest tube amp they carry, possibly the smallest tube amp in existence. Then he hands Cate a cable. She plugs in the Tak.

The fingertips of her right hand race over the strings, her left hand forming chord after chord.

But after a while, she plays the same three chords, over and over, humming a little.

"Three chords is enough," she says.

"Enough for a song, yep," Bird agrees. To me he says, "Gonna be a riot girl, with wicked chops."

I simply stare at Cate. It's like something's been stripped away. I can see her more clearly now than before.

Cate and Bird toss around some prices. In a few more minutes, she's ready to go.

She kisses—yeah, kisses—her old guitar goodbye. Puts the new one in a fake-fur-lined case. She says she'll take the amp, two sets of strings, and half a dozen picks—because you never know. A new tuner, two cables—she's done. She pays Bird the balance due.

I hold the door for her, since she insists on carrying both the guitar and the amp.

But just as she's about to cross the threshold back into the store, she stops. "Hey, Bird, can you show me some microphones?"

STEPS

DAVID

Coffee. School. Homework. Practice. Horseback riding with Laurel and Bryn.

Coffee. Meetings. Coffee. Practice. Sleep. Rinse. Repeat. Again.

This is Cate's life now. There's no room for me.

Not yet.

Once in a while, we talk on the phone.

Her sponsor suggests she go to a meeting every day, and Cate tells me that sometimes she protests. "It's a proven fact. Ketamine isn't addictive."

But then her sponsor asks if she knows the name of the longest river in Egypt and reminds Cate that lots of things are addictive.

I tell Cate her sponsor is right.

It's this same sponsor, the girlfriend of an old family friend, apparently, who warns Cate away from me. Who keeps reminding her she shouldn't date for ninety days.

Damn.

Luckily, no one counts a band rehearsal as a date.

MUSIC

CATE

Ruby, the thin guitarist from Deep Dark Love, steps on a pedal—

Her electric guitar spins out a line of dark satin . . . filling the rehearsal space.

I've got the black Tak strapped across my body. Now I begin to play.

Ruby weaves in and out of my chord sequence. I start to get that feeling, of lift.

Behind me, Trevor lays down a primal groove on his new toy, a cocktail drum. I turn to look at him, standing behind his strange kit, and when our eyes meet, he switches up the rhythm until it settles somewhere in my pelvis.

Goosebumps rise on my skin. I am in a big car, being driven. Yet I am the driver.

Dale Waters is standing to my right, a step or two behind me, his white sword of a smile sheathed, his hands not moving yet, just a premonition on the upright.

When he sees me looking at him, he flashes me that ravening grin, and then, holding back till the *last* possible part of the beat—he *slides* into the groove just in time to catch me as I swoon into the song. At this musical moment, we are made for each other.

Then his evening voice leans into mine. Our chemistry sizzles. No wonder I'd been confused.

The volume grows. The chorus comes—

Dale's voice is the resistance I press against. And just like that night, he won't let me go too far, this time holding me down with the midnight sound of his gleaming bass. Grounding me as I push into the dark places, although he's there, too.

I've written these songs, but it doesn't seem like it now. Deep Dark Love—minus the horns and keyboards—are as much a part of this as I am. Yes, they're following my map, but they're following so closely we're like lovers spooning.

Then we're making out, and it's love or lust or whatever you want to call it. I may not have had sex yet, but I have this. May not have made love, but I make music.

Finally I find David, sitting still and stunned in the back of the room. He smiles and I almost get lost in the spill of honey.

So I swim away, back into the music pooling around me, before I lose my place.

My place . . . this is it. Not just in the music, but in the words, too. As I sing, they expand— sometimes literally. Multiple notes for a single syllable—I've always known words are huge, are more than meets the eye, but now, they're like skyscrapers. Mountains. Volcanoes.

But when the band begins to improvise—

My fingers stumble.

"Give it up, Angel," Dale says, his lips close to my ear. I shut my eyes, but it's hard. I'm just so used to all those little black notes strung out across the page like a bridge.

Now I have no page, no bridge. Just a set list taped to the side of my guitar—twelve tunes born over a handful of weeks, over my entire life— and these strangers who are not strangers because they know everything about me. They must, or they wouldn't be able to talk, talk, talk to me like this without words.

But that's not enough, not yet. Not to let go completely. It took this long to get here, but I can't go any further.

"It's down south," Dale says. "Come on, Katydid."

"What the hell?" David mouths at me. He's wearing a terrific scowl.

Dale flashes a lightning grin at him, and David flips him off. He laughs and turns his back to David, making a gliding motion nobody but me can see. "In the hips."

My breath catches, but I get it. I let go, still not with my guitar, but with my voice.

And this time, when I stop playing, the band fills in the blanks. Their sound swells around me. Waves carrying me atop a sea, their instruments making up for the fact that mine is missing.

After a while, I slowly make my way back into the groove with my guitar. Now I see the whole picture. Next time I'll be ready.

Playing with a band is like having a parachute of gossamer and steel. It's having people who have your back, who know your secrets, who know you.

Singing with a band is trampolining with your breath. A sound you make, that makes you, too.

Being in a band is instant trust, because you have to. You're using everybody's blood. And if there's someone who doesn't feel that, it doesn't matter. Musicians have huge egos—or fragile egos—and everybody wants to be a big cat. No one wants to blow it.

At the end of the rehearsal, Dale and I talk about this very thing. I tell him my worst fear. I tell him about Weill Hall.

He just looks at me with those sky eyes, with that unchanging blue. He's unimpressed that I've played such an amazing venue and unconcerned that I screwed up.

"No biggie, Angel. It doesn't mean shit."

I fold my arms. "Easy for you to say—you weren't the one up there blowing it."

"I've blown it before. Everybody sucks sometimes."

"Yeah, well, I don't want to suck."

"Want to be perfect, yeah? Fuck that. Perfect wrecks it, the whole creativity thing. I'll tell you what," he continues, "we'll play that gig of yours, and we'll kill it. But do us all a favor, leave *perfect* out of this."

Now David calls out something about the last song, about the tempo. Dale glances at him, then nods in agreement. David says something else. Dale nods again.

He waves David over, says approvingly, "What you said was dead-on. So what do you play?"

"Sports," David says. Then he looks straight at me. "But I'm a really good listener."

CANADA

DAVID

Friday night I call Cate to confirm our date for the following evening—our First Date, Cate calls it—and then, we just keep talking. And when we stop, the silence stretches between us, becoming a place of its own. A room where we're together just hanging out, like we did last summer.

When I tell Cate about the room idea, I can hear her smile, then the silence isn't so silent anymore.

"I can hear you thinking," I tell her.

"That's . . . pretty cool."

"So what *are* you thinking?"

"I'm thinking . . ." She hums a little under her breath, probably jotting down a song idea. She does that a lot lately. We may not be dating, but she's at my house a lot, almost as much as she used to be, taking care of Kimmy.

"I'm thinking," she repeats, "I don't want to wait."

"Ah. And what is it you don't want to wait for?"

"Our First Date. Can you come over?"

"You mean, like now?" It's nearly midnight.

"Like now."

When I arrive at Cate's, I'm suddenly struck by the fact that I've never been inside her home. But apparently, that's not going to change tonight. She meets me on the porch and we go behind the house to a big old barn.

Inside, it's color. Enormous, breathtaking canvases are everywhere.

I want to know everything about this place. The studio, Cate calls it. I want to know about her father and what drives him to create such wild beauty. I want to know—

"Come on." She gestures to a ladder that doesn't look like it can hold either of us. "There's someone I want you to meet."

I must look confused, because Cate laughs and gives me a little push.

We climb up to a hayloft. It's filled with paintings and, also, hay. Piles of old, dusty hay, bales of new hay. Moonlight slices in through a crack in the wall and spills over the new hay, turning it to gold.

"The old hayloft door," Cate explains, watching me follow the line of light with my eyes. She crouches down, so I do, too.

In a nest of hay is a litter of kittens. She picks one up.

"This is the one I'm giving to Kimmy. What do you think?"

The ink-black ball of fur is the size of my fist. "I think it's great, but my mother . . . isn't around right now so . . ."

"Exactly," Cate says. Her eyes are full of sympathy. I try to smile but can't.

Cate's smile, though, is another slim line of light in the dark loft as she returns the kitten to its mother's side. Now she moves away from the fluffy huddle and sits back against one of the hay bales. I sit next to her.

"Bryn told me your mom left," she says. "Do you want to talk about it?"

"Not yet," I say.

She nods. Then she looks around the loft. "My dad wants to get animals, turn the studio into a real barn."

"What about his paintings?"

"He'll sell them and start a new series. He says the new paintings will be small. Microcosms—that's how he envisions them."

"And what do you envision?" I ask, walking fingers down her arm, entwining them with hers. "Why did you want to see me tonight?"

"Because tomorrow night is our First Date, and because we've waited so long, there are a lot of first-date things I want to do."

"Three months *is* a long time to wait for a date."

"I was thinking more like three years."

"Are you saying . . ."

"I'm *saying*, since we—or at least *I*—have waited for this date for years, there may be, besides the first-date things I want to do—that *we* want to do, I hope—some second-date things."

"Ah."

"Ah. Yes."

"You're afraid that we're going to run out of time."

"I'm not afraid of anything." Chin lifted, Cate's eyes dare me to say differently.

"I'm sure you're not. So then, what is it you'd like to do tonight, on this predate of ours?"

"I'd like to get some of the talking out of the way."

"Oh really."

"Stop looking at me that way!"

But she keeps looking at me the exact same way—until she doesn't.

"David, I want to know about Canada."

The sliver of light coming in at the edge of the hay door vanishes as the moon moves on and we're left in nearly total darkness.

"I know you almost died," Cate says quietly. "I want to know what happened. You said you understood why I asked. Well, nothing's changed."

She takes my other hand, entwining her fingers with mine the same way I did with hers. My palms are pulsing. I want to touch more than just her hands. It would make this so much easier. I imagine kissing her neck, like I nearly did in the pool last summer. That day was a lifetime ago, but it's still vivid in my mind.

Canada is vivid, too, the memories sharp as shards of glass.

And I know if I don't tell her, if I don't share the thing that changed everything, then everything won't really be changed. *I* won't be changed. And the glass will continue to cut me.

"It was my fault."

I say this first, because it's the worst thing about me, and if she can get past it, maybe we have a chance.

"I hadn't looked at the trip guide, not that day. I knew some waterfalls were coming up—we all knew—but I didn't know how big they'd be. Not that we were supposed to have anything to do with them—we'd finished the portage and were supposed to cross the lake *above* the falls. But one of the canoes—someone hadn't tied it tightly enough. When I came off the trail, it was in the center of the lake.

"I went into the water. Dan, one of the trip leaders, went in after me. The current was strong. It took us both."

"David." Cate's squeezing my hands tightly, or maybe it's me gripping her.

"The falls at the top fed into a pool. It was rough. There were rapids. I was knocked unconscious. But somehow . . . I survived. The other counselor found me, on the shore.

"Dan wasn't so lucky. He . . . went over the second set of falls. The drop from there . . . He didn't make it."

"I'm so sorry," Cate whispers.

I shake my head. "I still can't believe it."

"I understand."

I know she does.

KISSES

DAVID

Before she has time to say anything else, I ask, "Cate, did you ever really look at me—really *see* me—before I came back from Canada?"

"I think . . . I've always looked at you. Just didn't let myself admit it. Then, right before you left, there was that day, with the dresses. You told me I was pretty."

I'm dumbfounded. And so, so disappointed.

I laugh an ugly bark of a laugh, so loud in the quiet night that Cate cringes.

"Wow," I practically shout. "*You're* easy! That's it, huh? That's all this is?" Anger burns through me. *How could I have been so wrong about her?* "Here I was, thinking that something was happening between us, something *real*—"

Cate leans in and kisses me. Just gently presses her lips to mine.

I go completely still.

And in that stillness, I no longer see the ugly things about myself I saw last summer. I'm not *that guy* anymore, who uses girls like a drug.

The self-blame for Dan's death remains, but Cate's kissed me after all. So maybe even that can be forgiven.

When I finally open my eyes, Cate's wide-eyed, like she's afraid of what she's just done, that I might freak over it.

But then she's the one who's freaking, words spilling out of her, fast and breathy.

"It *is* something real," she says. "And I think, maybe it's *always* been here, between us. Waiting to be . . . discovered. I just, I thought you could never want *me*, you were so . . . everything.

"When you called me pretty, I heard something else. I heard *possible*. And when I saw you, that night in your room toward the end of the summer, you were still everything, but you were also . . . you. And that was so much better. And it made me want you even more."

I can't help it now. I wrap my arms around her. Bury my face in her neck. She shivers and hugs me to her.

"I don't want to waste any more time," I whisper against her skin. "Don't want to waste one more second." I lift my face and kiss her mouth, but lightly. "Not this one . . ." I bring my lips to her cheek. "Or this one." I kiss her other cheek, repeat the words, punctuating each phrase with a kiss: on her forehead, her eyelids, her collarbone. Then I pull back. "Why didn't we know?" My voice is a cross between a sob and a laugh. Something is shifting in me.

"We did," she says. "We do. We *know*."

We can't stop smiling now. We just stare into each other's eyes and grin.

Soon, in silent agreement, we climb down the ladder, and even though the spring air is cool and damp, we walk back behind the barn, into the woods. No words, just her hand in mine. Relief floods me— along with adrenaline—as I step into the invisible field of electricity that's been living between us for so long.

Deep in the woods, everything is black-and-white and moonlight. We crouch, picking pebbles out of the still-winter-cold creek. When we stand, I reach for her hips, slip a pebble into her pocket. She slips one in mine. The fronts of our bodies are nearly touching, the inch of air between us wildly alive. I laugh softly.

Then I turn back to the stream, choose a larger stone. It's round and white as the moon. Smooth as her lips. I place it in the palm of her hand, where it fits perfectly.

Then I tell her all the reasons I love her—going back to last summer.

"You sound like a poet," she says with a smile.

"I'm not anything," I say. "Not anybody, just—me. And compared to all this?" I spread my arms wide, not sure if I mean the woods or the world or the entire universe—or maybe what's between us. "Compared to this, I'm nothing. Or maybe, I'm part of it all. Maybe we are. Cate, do you think there's a plan?"

But even as I ask the question, she radiates the Yes of it.

She inclines her head then, the simple movement appearing almost formal, like an abbreviated bow, and makes a sweeping gesture with one arm, as if inviting me to go before her on the overgrown path.

I do, and soon I've led her so far into the woods that we come out the other side, where the trees give way to moonlit fields spreading out before us like a silvery sea.

Cate sweeps her arm out once more now, her open palm upturned.

"Welcome, to the Hotel Vast Horizon," she says.

"I like that."

"It's a song. Come back with me to my house. Come inside. I'll play it for you."

SPLIT

DAVID

My father chooses the night of Cate's show to corner me.

"You received a letter today from South State. I thought, at first, it was a plea for funds."

Opening shots: *The college of your choice has no money.* And *I read your mail.*

Of course, I know the letter had nothing to do with fundraising. The application to South State was the only one I sent. I assume I was accepted, but . . .

Strategy: *Move into defensive position. Door? Ten steps away. Keys? Check.*

"Oh yeah?" I say. "What did the letter say?"

"*'Yeah.'* Is that how they talk at South?"

It's a ridiculous comment. Everyone says "yeah." But I want to get out the door, so I don't reply.

"I imagine many of the students at South hail from the Pine Barrens. I suppose there *may* be a more backward place on the East Coast, but if there is, I don't know it."

Apparently, I got in.

"Dad, I'd love to celebrate with you, but I've got to go." In my happiness, I'm careless.

"Dad? *Dad?* You sound like a Southie already! I'll thank you to continue addressing me as Father, as you always have. If you want to go to some downwardly mobile college, that's up to you—for now." He mutters something about my mother being behind my low-level choice, and I wonder how he can blame her for anything, now that she's left him. "But you will continue to adhere to the high standards we keep in this house."

In this house. Right. If my parents pooled their frequent-flier miles, they could spend a year in the air. But ironic as this may be, my mouth has gone dry.

"I have to go."

"Do you. And where are you off to tonight?"

"To hear some music."

"Ah. Some lowlife from that record store, I'll bet—don't look so surprised. Did you really think I wouldn't find out?"

"Ah—I don't know." I try to move on, not wanting to discuss the fact that I've been working at Listen Up! all year. "But actually, it's Cate Reese, she—"

"Cate Reese, our babysitter?"

"Yes."

"And how old is Miss Reese now?"

"Bye, Dad." I open the door.

He shoves it closed with his foot. "Don't you walk out on me!"

"I'm not!"

"You are, in more ways than one, and you know it. Choosing a Podunk college like South, hanging around with a bunch of tattooed losers—"

"That's enough." My voice is shaking, but just a little.

"Is it? Is it going to be enough for *Cate Reese* when you're sweeping out the back alley of a record shop for the rest of your life?"

"First of all, I don't sweep anything, I help—"

"Is it going to be *enough* when all your friends are graduating from colleges people have actually *heard* of? Is it going to be enough when you're *no one*, and your friends are pulling down six figures? What the *hell* can you possibly learn at South? It's in the middle of the woods for Christ's sake. We live forty-five minutes from Manhattan. If you didn't want to go to a school you could play for, why not the city? Why not finance? Your Cate Reese would spread her legs if—"

I don't think—just swing.

But this is his game, and he grabs my arm, effectively blocking me.

I don't want this, ever, but especially not tonight. I need to get to Cate. I don't need his fist in my face—

I get it anyway.

Staggering back, I bring my hand to my cheek where the punch connected—

But he's already on me. As though we're in a slow dance, he's close, nearly against me. I'm also focused on my partner. On him, on his body. This time I see his fist coming up.

Enough, yes. I dodge the punch.

He throws another—

And this time, *I block him*—for the first time in my life—and now I *do* think.

Think how wrong it was, to actually swing at him in the first place. Time s l o w s . . .

And I vow not to swing again. Even though, at this moment, he's planning his next shot. But to take a swing at my father is to *be* my father, and that is what he wants.

It's like the spring evening air has gotten inside the house now, gotten inside my head. Not only will I *not* be my father, I will be more than *not my father*. I will be myself. Yes, I went for that first swing, but that's all it took. I wish I'd done it years ago, because now I know more than ever who I don't want to be, and that sets in sharp relief just who I am.

Time recovers from its momentary lapse. My father's fist catches me beneath the jaw.

I spin sideways.

Then he's in my face, laughing. "Go ahead. Try again. I'll give you one free shot. Maybe a few pointers, too, so you can actually—"

"I've had enough pointers from you, thanks." I stumble to the door, swing it wide. He doesn't try to stop me this time. He just stands there, breathing hard.

"Go then, but please, enlighten me first. What the *hell* are you going to study down in South Jersey with those rednecks?"

"Teaching. I'm going to be a teacher."

My father's eyebrows lift so high it looks as if they're imploring the heavens, but the odds are good there'll be no redemption for this man in the $800 disguise. The things he's done are unforgivable.

"Teaching. My, won't that be lucrative."

"It'll be fine," I say, my hand on the edge of the door. But I can't seem to go, not while he's talking.

"Fine," he echoes. "The boy says it will be fine." He starts to nod, and I feel the beginnings of relief, until he says, "You didn't play for the teams. You dropped student council. It took me all year, but I finally get it. *You couldn't cut it.* So you quit. So, 'yeah,' as you say, everything will be fine. After all, those who can't *do*, teach."

"South is one of the best teaching colleges in the country," I counter. "Plus, I'm lucky." I step outside. "I *can* do. And I've had a lot of good coaches over the years, so I'll have a jump on teaching all the things I *can* do. And you know what else? I think I'll be a pretty good teacher. Because, unlike you? I care about kids."

CONVERTIBLE

DAVID

I'm about to slam the door but catch myself, and shut it softly instead. Then I walk down the driveway to the old Miata that's parked near the street. I bought the used car a few days ago, though I won't be driving off into the sunset anytime soon. That'll be at the end of summer.

Until then, I'll live under my father's roof. But I will not be his whipping boy.

It was like, as long as I played Jack, my father could forget that he was gone. Could forget the hole that he'd left in our family. But whenever I took off the Jack mask, Jack disappeared yet again. Then my father blamed me for his absence, as if he'd forgotten—

Jack took his own life, nine long years ago. He really is gone.

Suicide is a solo act, but my father turned it into a twisted trio. He hated me when I played Jack, because he hated Jack for what he did. He hated me more when I played myself, because then Jack was gone again. But I doubt my father ever hated either of us as much as he hates himself. Each time my Jack mask slipped, Jack vanished anew, and my father blamed me. But I'm *not* to blame for my brother's death, just like I'm not to blame for Dan's.

I'm done bearing the burden of Jack's death now—or his life, as the case may be. Done carrying the weight of Dan's death as well. It was an accident, and I'm sorry that Dan's dead, but he made the choice to come after me. We all deserve the right to make choices. I'm putting it down.

This leaves me free to pick up Cate—in the convertible I bought with money from my job. Which means, possibly, my father is right about some things. I'll have to figure out which ones.

STAGE

CATE

We can't make it.

Four words that change everything.

I'm still in the car when I get the text. I'm still in the car, because David's new old Miata had some trouble, and we had to stop at a gas station, but the gas station was really busy, so we had to wait until someone was free, but that someone wasn't a mechanic, and *oh my god, I can't believe this.*

"David, I can't do this."

"What's the matter?"

But I don't elaborate—too busy texting like a madwoman.

Wtf do you mean you can't make it?

Pure panic races through me as I wait for an answer.

Little gray bubbles. Dale's writing. He's going to say he was kidding, that he's inside the club. After all, I'm the one who's late.

Trevor's fucked up he's ok but can't leave him sorry.

My stomach goes into a spin.

"Cate, what's wrong? What can I do?"

"Nothing. They're not coming. I have no band. Trevor is wasted, or—I don't know. I hope he's okay. Maybe he just decided my gig wasn't hip enough," I say bitterly.

David remains motionless as I rave on, except for his eyes, which look back and forth between my face and my phone. Finally, when my diatribe shows no signs of slowing, he reaches over and gently disentangles my fingers. He looks down at the screen. Scrolls.

Now he lifts the phone, so the screen's facing me.

`Angel break everything. Fly. Xxx`

"Hate to say it, but I agree with Southern Man. Come on." David gets out of the car. Comes round my side. Helps me out. I'm barely registering all this, though, because my mind is whirling.

Now I whirl on him.

"You don't get it! I'm not playing."

"Cate—"

"I'm not ready, not to play these songs on my own! I can't do this!"

"This," David says, opening the door to the club—and it's bigger than I imagined . . . a *lot* bigger . . . there must be eight hundred people here—"is exactly what you need to do."

"David, no. They don't even want me! Look! Look at that girl!" A girl wearing a T-shirt with a fiery dragon fruit emblazoned on the front is busy plastering the place with posters showing Dale Waters and the rest of the band gazing out stonily from a dark background.

David purses his lips. "Guess I shouldn't even suggest that you fall back on your classical—"

"*Lovecats!*" Laurel's waving wildly, like a kid, as she hurtles toward me. Bryn saunters up behind her, blonde hair shining like a beacon. "Holy shit, Cate!" Laurel shouts over the din. "Look at this crowd! You're famous!"

"They're not here to see me."

"They are so—look!" Triumphantly, Laurel unfurls a flyer. "I managed to grab one."

I immediately recognize Ruby's artwork. Her graphic designs are . . . unique.

At the center of the flyer there's a black-and-white photo—me, with the Tak in my hand, head thrown back, laughing. It's from one of our practices. I'm wearing a black T-shirt Kimmy made for me at art camp last summer. On the front, a white silk-screened tree reaches its bare branches heavenward. Underneath the tree there's one word: "Naked." A row of silver coins dangle off the hem. I have the shirt with me, was going to wear it tonight, but now there's no time to change, no time to even look at the rest of the flyer, which says something about me sharing the bill with Deep Dark Love.

"Sorry to get you guys out for nothing," I begin.

"No sorries," Bryn says. "Time to step up. If you can't do it for yourself or your BFF here, or"—she knocks her shoulder against David's, "this guy, then do it for your friend."

I get a rush of feeling—not a change in temperature exactly, but something physical like that—surging up from my belly into my chest, raising goosebumps all over my body.

She's right. David's right. That twisted Southern charmer Dale Waters is right.

Leaving David and Laurel and Bryn behind, I head across the club to a knot of people surrounding the soundboard. An insouciant hipster checks his watch as I approach. Another guy squints at the stage. I introduce myself, and a girl with a cell phone glued to her ear shakes her head but then shrugs.

"There's time," she says, "but not much. We'll check you on your first tune."

"Thanks. Sorry I'm late. Here's my mic." Squinty guy takes it, trots toward the stage.

I'm about to head up there myself when the girl says, "Hey, aren't you supposed to have a full band? Or, at least, one other person?"

A beat goes by. Then I tell her the truth. "No. I'm a solo act."

Then I'm crossing the room, walking onstage—

And starting my set, with my voice.

HOTEL VAST HORIZON

DAVID

Cate's guitar case sits somewhere between her lap and her legs. Now she repositions it— slips onto *my* lap.

I'm still dazzled by her performance tonight, by her voice, her lyrics. By seeing facets of the gem that is her I hadn't seen before. I push my seat back as far as it will go.

Having Cate on my lap is unexpected, to my mind at least. My body seems unsurprised, though, responding greedily, hands grabbing before I can think to do anything different.

But Cate's different from any girl I've ever known, and I want to be different, too.

Still, when she wriggles a little, I give in to sensation, grasping her hips. She must feel what she's doing to me.

I imagine dropping the seat back, sliding her pants down, and it's hard, hard, hard to stop kissing her, but finally, I do, because I don't want her first time—*our* first time—to be like this.

She whispers something I don't catch and slips back into her seat. I'm relieved, but also sorry. She sees this, gives a breathy little laugh. We both want the same thing right now.

Leaning back, I run my hands over my face. Turn to her. Grin.

She grins back. "Um, yeah," she says.

"Okay," I say. Then blow out a breath.

Then we're both laughing, smoothing our clothes. I start driving—driving and thinking about what Cate said a little while ago when she was talking about lyrics, about how there's something behind every word.

Now I say, "Sometimes, there's nothing. Words just mean what they mean."

"Sometimes there's nothing," she concedes.

"Kisses are the same. There's something behind a kiss, or there's nothing."

"I think," she says, "those were something kisses."

The top is down—an apparently permanent feature the former owners didn't disclose—and it's probably a cool night, but I don't feel it. I'm looking back and forth between Cate and the road. Watching the way her dark hair mingles with the night sky. Like she's part of everything.

I consider telling her that I think there's a whole world behind the kisses we just shared. An entire Hotel Vast Horizon.

When I finally do, she says, "I agree. Now tell me. Where's the backseat in this thing?"

ACKNOWLEDGMENTS

Thank you.

To my mother, for teaching me to love words and books.

To my father, for teaching me discipline and how to tell—um . . . stories.

To Danielle Burby and everyone at HSG. Danielle, you're my Ideal Reader, and so much more! Josh Getzler, thank you for believing in me. (And for Sex Changes at Gunpoint, heh.)

Carrie Hannigan, thank you for helping me get to know Bryn a bit better.

To Miriam Juskowicz, Lisa L. Owens, Carrie Wicks, Karen Upson, and everyone at Skyscape and Amazon for bringing *Before Goodbye* out into the world. Faith Black Ross, you've got eagle eyes. Thank you.

To Kathy Temean, Natalie Zaman, Suzy Ismail, Susan Heyboer O'Keefe, Annie Silvestro, David Harrison, Tara Kelly, and all the other wonderful writers I've met through SCBWI and Twitter. You are my tribe. Joëlle Anthony and Charlotte Agell, you're in there, too, as are the agents and editors who encouraged me along the way, especially Holly McGhee and Steve Meltzer.

To Emma Dryden. Emma, there aren't enough words to—oh wait, there are too many! Thank you for your guidance and your friendship. Let's meet again soon for lobster rolls!

To River Road Books and the awesome women who run it, especially Kim Robinson, who knew before I did that Body of Writing was ready, and who always treated me like a rock star.

To Kevin Salem, for "Deep Dark Love." To Brian Kelly, for the loft.

To Oliver Sacks, I'm a longtime fan. I hope I got it right.

To Emily Winslow Stark and Heather Lennon for being on board from the beginning.

To Rosanne Cash, for the years of friendship and inspiration. You and the Redroomers have been my bridge back for so very long. Jennifer and Barbara, thank you. RBW—we did it. Xoxo, Dust.

To Stacy Dahling Smith, for the calm. To Jason Rich, for Rabbit Daggers.

To my Kickstarter supporters, especially Everet Milner who reminded me that sometimes it's okay to trust a stranger. P.S. This isn't the book I promised, but I swear that one's coming.

To Ally Condie, Cameron McClure, Merrilee Heifetz, Molly O'Neil, Ginger Clark. You may have forgotten the comments you made about my writing, but I never will. Thank you.

To Charles, for inspiration. You're better than the best, and my favorite person. I love you.

To Dan Whitley, for your generosity. And to Chris Whitley, who is missed.

Chris, I hope to see you one day at the Hotel Vast Horizon. I'm sure you're hanging with the luminaries and the stars.

Middleburn is a cross between the town I grew up in, a town I live near now, and a town in my imagination; any actual streets, parks, et cetera, have been fictionalized by me; however, the music of Chris Whitley, Leo

Brouwer, Frank Martin, the Killers, James Blake, Coldplay, Suzanne Vega, and Kevin Salem is very real, and inspired many of the scenes in this book. The song "The Medicine Down" is available on Kevin Salem's gorgeous record, *Ecstatic*. The song "Hotel Vast Horizon" is on Chris Whitley's record of the same name. Information about the classical guitarist David Russell can be found at www.davidrussellguitar.com.

This book depicts issues surrounding sexual assault, drug use, and domestic violence. If you would like more information or are a victim of sexual violence and need support, the Rape, Abuse & Incest National Network (RAINN) is an excellent resource: www.rainn.org. For information dealing with alcohol or drug addiction: www.na.org. For information about domestic violence: www.ncadv.org.

ABOUT THE AUTHOR

Photo © 2015 Danny Sanchez

Mimi Cross was born in Toronto, Canada. She received a master's degree from New York University and a bachelor's degree in music from Ithaca College. She has been a performer, a music educator, and a yoga instructor. During the course of her musical career, she's shared the bill with artists such as Bruce Springsteen, Jon Bon Jovi, and Sting. She resides in New Jersey.